THE CURES

John Doriot

Dedication

To Hope

Chapter 1
A long, long way to run

I remember the exact date and time when the doctors said they had cured cancer. It was 1:39 p.m., Friday, April 26, 2023. I was at school in my history class. Everyone was saying what a great achievement it was. One of the teachers, a Mr. James Edward Cannon, declared it "one of the greatest days in the history of man." Since he was a history teacher, I would have expected him to say something like that. He liked to quote people. I guess if you are a history teacher it comes with the territory. I remember him telling us on the very first day of class that an Edmund Burke once said, "Those that don't know history are doomed to repeat it." I bet Mr. Cannon didn't consider Mr. Burke when he said this was one of the greatest days in the history of man, but I did.

I enjoyed reading about history and I also liked my English class, especially when the teacher talked about famous authors and poets. Mr. Cannon's latest comment prompted a memorable quote from one of my favorite authors, C.S. Lewis. He said, "I have learned now that while those who speak about one's miseries usually hurt, those who keep silence hurt more." He was a very famous author who didn't believe in God but, over time, realized he was wrong and came to believe that there was indeed a God.

I liked the idea that there were other people who struggled with the idea of a God. People who were a lot smarter than me. I thought C.S. Lewis was a very smart man when he said that about pain and silence. I think he would understand why I struggled with a belief in God as he did when he was younger. I often imagined talking to him, both when he didn't believe and when he did. Those were always interesting discussions regardless of what stage in life Mr. Lewis occupied or how old I had become.

Perhaps for all those who believed in God, curing cancer was another sign that He existed. I could understand why they may have thought so, but I wasn't sure it was absolute proof. All the teachers and students were screaming and high-fiving or fist-bumping each other when they heard the news and Mr. Cannon's comment. I didn't ask any of them if they believed in God or not or whether this was some sort of divine revelation for them. I just stood there watching them and tried to think of the right word to describe their reaction. I only had to think for a moment about God, church, and the hymnal. "Rejoice" was the word for what I was witnessing.

My initial reaction was much more subdued and uncertain. I tried to think of the right word for what I felt and I found it fairly quickly too. But not in the church or in a hymn. No, my word was a lot more common. On the farm, it would just be another word they used as they went about their work. Used in another environment, it would be considered coarse and perhaps even swearing. But I liked the word and I used it a lot. It wasn't a surprise to me that it jumped into my mind at that moment. "Bullshit" was the right word to describe many things, and I thought it was very appropriate at this particular time.

Why, out of the millions of words I could have thought of, did I choose bullshit to describe my reaction? Probably because I knew doctors. I had known a lot of them as I had grown up. I remembered what each one looked like and all their names too. I could even remember the doctor who brought me into this world. Her name was Dr. Cox. I saw her blue eyes behind her glasses as she cut me right out of my mother's stomach. She was wearing a mask and head covering when she yanked me out. I wish I could have told her she was a little rough with me that day but I never saw her after we left the hospital.

Don't ask me how I remember that because I couldn't tell you. There are just some things that I don't ever forget. The faces of doctors and their names happen to be two of them. The school referred me to a lot of doctors and I saw at least a dozen others during the times my mother took me to the ER. She didn't like doing that and only did so when she thought I was hurt really bad. Regardless, I never have trusted any of them. What they said or what they did. None of them ever fixed a goddamn thing that was wrong with me. None of them even understood what was wrong with me or could see that my body would have healed itself over time. If they had truly looked, they would have seen the evidence of that. None of them ever knew what was wrong with my mother or sister or father either. None of them.

As I thought more about everything, I decided that should I ever see Dr. Cox, I would thank her for framing my opinion of the world from that very first day. Like I said, she was pretty rough in the way she handled me. She handed me over to the nurses like I was just another object for them to deal with at work. Nothing special. Just another day at the office. I now see that Dr. Cox was simply showing me that life was rough and I needed to be tough in order to survive. That was a good lesson, Dr. Cox. If I ever see you again, I will indeed walk up and introduce myself and thank you. After all, you were just laying the groundwork.

So, when they said the doctors cured cancer that day, I think you could see now why I was suspicious of this great achievement. Hell, if I hadn't been there in school and heard Mr. James Edward Cannon mention it, and seen the reactions of the students and teachers, I doubt I would have even known about it. At least not for some time. I'm sure the subject would have never come up at our house. As far as I know, no one in our family had ever had cancer. If they did, no one had ever talked about it to me or my sister. And I would have remembered if they had as I would have asked a lot of questions.

I did that a lot. If there was something that interested me, I asked a lot of questions and did my own research at the library. Knowing that something like cancer killed some relative of ours, I would have wanted to know how it did that. And if you could catch it like the flu. Or why some people got it and others didn't, like sickle cell anemia. I had a good friend named Billy who had sickle cell anemia, and he explained to me that mostly black people got it. "Well, mostly black people," he said, but he added, "there are some other types of sickle cell disease that some Mediterranean people get."

When he told me that, I studied the origin and specifics of the disease at the library. I didn't tell him, but white people could get sickle cell too even though it was a lot rarer for that to occur. It was more common in blacks, those from Central and South America, and people of Middle Eastern, Asian, Indian, and Mediterranean descent. That sickle cell disease he was referring to in Mediterranean people was actually called thalassemia and the severe form of it could lead to death. I didn't tell my friend what I had discovered with my research, because I knew it would have been useless information for him. It wouldn't have helped him get better. And if I didn't know better, I would've sworn that he was yanked out of his mother by Dr. Cox too. He had learned to be tough from a very early age just like me. He always reminded me of that C.S. Lewis quote I mentioned earlier. I saw him wince in pain but he never complained. Never.

So, there you have it. When they said they had cured cancer, I said, "Bullshit." Then I asked, "What's the big deal?" I knew it wouldn't be that big of a deal for my father. And I was right. He never mentioned it that day or any day in the future. Not one time. Ever. And I saw no reason to bring it up. As soon as I did, I knew exactly what my father would say. "Bullshit." He had a way with words. I think I learned that from him.

I remember seeing a lot of interviews with doctors on TV after this cure mania started to take hold of everyone. Man, there was a steady flow of bullshit coming out of their mouths every time they got in front of a camera. They talked about how wonderful life would be now. How a bunch of other diseases besides cancer would be eradicated too. I kept hoping that I would hear one of the many scientific experts say they would soon have a cure for sickle cell disease but I never did. I know Billy was listening for someone to say it too. I felt sorry for him that he didn't hear those words.

But that didn't stop the doctors from going on about how no one would ever have to die from this terrible disease again. I wish I could have been there when they were conducting some of those interviews. I would've gone over to the stupid prick in the white coat and told him people died of other things besides cancer. Things more terrible than cancer. I know they would have "ushered me away," but I would have made sure they heard me before they took me off, screaming and hollering. And maybe someone would've heard what I was saying and thought, "You know, he's right." But it never happened.

"Usher them away." A polite way of saying, "Get them the hell out of here." I heard a doctor say, "usher them away" to a nurse once when we were in the ER. He was talking about me and my mother. I told my mother about it, but she said that they wouldn't have said anything like that. My mother thought the best of those people but she was naïve in that regard. She didn't realize that's what they were doing to us every time we went into the ER. And if the doctors happened to be wearing white coats over their scrubs, they were inclined to say it even faster. Not sure why it was that way, but I could tell each time as soon as the doctor in the white coat saw us, we would be out of there within thirty minutes. I was never wrong.

On the way home, I told my mother that we should stop going to the ER because they weren't fixing the real problem. I told her that they didn't want to know what the real problem was. I told her that they were no different than the people we saw on the road patching the holes. The patch of tar they put down would last a little while and then they would have to do it all over again. Why? Because they never addressed the real problem that created the hole. She just looked at me and said I was a very smart boy and then reached over and brushed my hair back from my face. And though I wanted to tell her more, I couldn't. I never could say anything else after I saw the tears in her eyes. Like Billy learning about thalassemia; what good would it have done for me to keep talking? So, I just looked out the window of the car at the holes in the road.

Just as soon as we got home from the ER, each and every time, we heard the same words of criticism from my father. Only it wasn't stated as a conceptual abstract, as my English teacher would have said. He was a lot more direct, my father. He just said whatever it was they did was a waste of time. And he was right. My father was right about a lot of things. He was a major influence in my life and shaped the way I looked at things from an early age. He was very insightful and observant. I am certain I learned how to be similarly aware from him just as I had learned how to be such an effective wordsmith.

Soon after I was born, I remember my father looking down at me in my crib and telling my mother that I was different. I didn't know what he meant by that word and am still trying to figure that out, but I do remember it. You may not believe this, but I can remember the day he said it. It was February 27, 2005. I was only four days old. Like I said earlier, I remember a lot of things. Not many people remember being born, but I even remember things before that. I know. I can hear what you are saying. Bullshit. But it's the truth.

I remember my mother reading to me when I was in her womb. "One Fish, Two Fish, Red Fish, Blue Fish" by Dr. Seuss. I heard her read that book to me a lot. I started reading it on my own when I was two years old. I read every one of the Dr. Seuss books. He was the only doctor that I ever knew of that never tried to "usher me away." I always felt he wanted me to stay there in the world he created inside the pages of his books. I have to admit, there were many days when I thought about doing just that.

My mother took my sister and me to the library a lot when we were young. We loved going there. It was always clean and warm in the winter and cool in the summer. My mother read to us or let us pick out our own books to read. I almost always chose Dr. Seuss when I was very little. But as I got older, I started reading Edgar Allan Poe and Arthur Conan Doyle's "Sherlock Holmes" stories. I loved Rudyard Kipling's "Jungle Book" and his short story about Rikki-Tikki-Tavi. I must have read that short story thirty times. I even read that one to my sister over and over. She loved for me to read to her.

But she didn't care for the Poe or Sherlock Holmes stories. She preferred "Nancy Drew" and the "Hardy Boys" books and she and my mother loved looking at travel books or magazines. They always talked about what it would be like to go there, wherever "there" happened to be on that particular day. I didn't really enjoy reading those types of books. I thought it was just a waste of time as I doubted we would ever be able to go to those places. My father agreed. He said it was a waste of time to be looking at those kinds of books and even reading so much. He said life wasn't a mystery and that the only book we needed to read was the Book of Life. Of course, then he would say in a sarcastic manner, "You can't read the Book of Life, you just experience it." As I said, he was very insightful and direct.

And somewhere in every conversation I overheard between him and my mother, he would find a way to tell her that I was different. And though he may have been the first to say it, he just became the first of many. And looking back, I realize the son of a bitch was right about that too.

I always felt different than everyone else around me. Once your own father calls you that less than a week after being born, it makes an impression on you that you never forget. I remember as Dr. Cox jerked me out of my mother's womb, I felt some sort of electrical sensation in my body. As if the umbilical cord was plugged into an electric socket of some kind. Maybe that's why she handled me so roughly. Perhaps I shocked the shit out of her.

When I started going to school, I heard the word "different" even more. As if I had the word stamped across my forehead. I learned when people called you different what they really meant was that you were strange. Over time, I learned there were other people, other famous people, who did strange things and I hoped I shared some of their genius because it was apparent to everyone that I shared some of their strange behavioral traits.

When I went to school in the first grade, I liked going around and shocking the other kids in my class as I rubbed my feet across the floor during the winter. That was the first time I heard a teacher tell my mother and father that I was different. My father just looked at my mother and shook his head and muttered, "I told you so," under his breath. My mother never responded when she heard the teachers or my father use that word. She just took me by the hand and led me away, often to the library. She's the one that prompted my interest in Benjamin Franklin and Edison and those other people who were considered different. The people at school taught me that the word different meant something was wrong with me. She taught me that the word different meant something uncommon.

Being labeled as strange made me research "strange" in the library. I found out that Benjamin Franklin started his day with an air bath; half an hour each day in front of an open window, stark naked. He said it got his mental juices flowing. Many people who read Poe's stories thought they were too gory and morbid and unreadable. He also called his cat "Catterina" and thought that she was his literary guardian. Einstein was so aloof as a child that everyone thought he had a learning disability.

Edison insisted that people who applied to work with him eat a bowl of soup. If they added salt to the soup without trying it, he didn't hire them. They made too many assumptions, he reasoned. He didn't go to sleep either. Well, you know, like normal people. He just took naps. Francis Crick (you know - the guy that helped discover DNA?) believed in "directed panspermia." What the hell is that you ask? Good question. It meant that he believed that aliens "seeded" life on earth. Or another way of putting it: we were all sons and daughters of alien life forms. I kind of liked that idea.

Ever heard of Paracelsus? Well, he was a scientist around the 15th or 16th century. Considered the father of modern toxicology and he linked chemistry to medicine. Some of what he did led to the chemotherapy practices that they used to treat cancer. Granted, he will become just a footnote now, considering that they supposedly cured cancer, but he was still a genius for his time. He also believed that you could create a tiny human being by keeping semen in a warm place and feeding it human blood. If I said shit like these famous people, I would have been locked up and sedated. Hell, everything I did pales in comparison to those guys. So, if you wanted to call me different or strange, go ahead. Bring it on. I was good with it. I liked the idea of being on the same short bus as those students.

When I was in the first grade, I got bored very easily. That was one of the reasons I went around shocking everyone. There was nothing else very interesting going on. I was reading books at a sixth-grade level by then. But it didn't matter, because the teacher, a Mrs. Evangeline Sanders, said I needed to be evaluated by a doctor. She said I was different. She said she could see that there was something wrong within my eyes. Too bad she never bothered to look at my back. Or my legs. Or my arms. I heard her tell another teacher that I was full of demons. If she had bothered to look elsewhere, she could have seen more evidence of demons besides those she thought were staring back at her.

I didn't like that teacher. Mrs. Evangeline Sanders. She was short and fat. I wasn't sure where her breasts ended and her stomach started. She liked jerking people around by their ears when, as she said, "They acted up." She did that to me one time and I bit her hand. She screamed a lot that day but she never jerked my ear again. After that incident, the principal said I had to see a doctor or I would not be able to come back to school. So, my mother took me to see a doctor. In case you are wondering, the doctor we went to see was wearing a white coat; though not over scrubs, but over a light blue shirt and striped blue and orange tie with navy blue pants.

The doctor was a child psychologist. His name was Dr. Robert Milhouse Banks, Ph.D. He had a big fish tank full of tropical fish in his waiting room. I knew the names of every fish because I had seen them in a book I read at the library. I told my mother what the names of each of them were and she smiled and said that was amazing. When Dr. Robert Milhouse Banks asked me what I wanted to talk about that day, I told him, "Fish."

I proceeded to tell Dr. Robert Milhouse Banks about each of the fish in his fish tank. He then asked me one of the stupidest questions I have ever been asked: "Would you like to be a fish?" I told him that seeing how I couldn't breathe underwater I didn't think that would be a very good idea. He smiled and asked me a few more questions and then asked me to draw a crayon picture for him, which he looked at one way and then the other before he sent me and my mother on our way. I learned later that he told Mrs. Evangeline Sanders and my mother and father that I had an overactive imagination and was probably just overly influenced by cartoons or something I saw at the fair. My father just said it confirmed that I was different.

Mrs. Evangeline Sanders was very happy to send me on to the second grade but things didn't get any better there. In fact, it seemed like I was always in some sort of trouble. Whether it was shocking the other children, eating chalk on a dare, or standing in front of the window naked; it didn't matter. Every teacher that I had told my mother and father that I was different. The teacher in the sixth grade, a Mr. Brian Lancaster, was the first to suggest to my mother that I had anger issues that needed to be addressed.

That's when I started seeing a lot of social workers and more doctors with a Ph.D. at the end of their names. Some of them referred to themselves as "life coaches." What a bunch of douchebags. Though I have to admit, if I am being honest, some of them did seem to care. If I had bothered to listen to everything that they said, maybe they could have helped. But I didn't care. They just stamped me with the same label which was impossible to wash off. So, I said "fuck it" because I knew that there was really nothing I could do to fix the real problem.

One day, I managed to get and read one of the reports they had given my mother. It said that I exhibited "a wide range of anger management issues that need to be addressed. Seems angry with everything and everyone in the world around him. Appears unwilling or unable to resolve anger issues in a constructive manner. Exhibits anti-social behavior. Does not display any interest in changing. Resents authority. Very intelligent." Signed, Dr. Frank Littleton, Ph.D.

Dr. Frank Littleton, Ph.D., was very good at describing me. But he missed several things. He didn't mention that I had good hygiene or that I hated people who had bad breath or body odor. I wasn't afraid to tell anyone about it either. I mean, how hard is it to brush your teeth every morning or at least eat a Tic-Tac or something? And take a shower every once in a while, for God's sake.

Sometimes it isn't easy to do it, I get it. When you are poor or living on the streets, it's a challenge but it's still doable. I know because I've been there for short periods of time. I ran away many times as I got older, but my mother always came and found me. I think if it had been up to my father, I would've been left out there on the streets. But I learned a lot being out there on my own. In fact, I felt more at home on the streets than at home. On the street, being different kept you alive. At home or at school, being different just got you sneers and whispered finger-pointing and slapped around.

As I was saying, though it isn't easy, there is always a place you can find that will let you take a shower. Provided you haven't already said "screw it" and started carrying around lice or have some open sores on your face and skin like something out of a horror movie. Then, yeah, I understand why it's a little harder to get people to let you in to clean up. Who wants a fucking stinking zombie in their shower? I sure as hell don't. But all I've got to say is why did you let yourself get like that? Perhaps you will call me insensitive for pointing fingers at the crazy and the addicted that begin to look like extras from a horror movie. I don't give a shit. Call me what you want. You may sleep where rats live, but you don't have to become one.

Talking to people that aren't there or seeing things that aren't there is no damn excuse for not staying clean. Take the fucking hallucinations into the shower with you. Believe me, that six-foot rabbit that you're talking to all the time will appreciate the fact you brushed your teeth and showered. Be a lot better world out there if all the crazy-ass people walking around the streets didn't smell like they were carrying around a dead animal in their pocket. Why don't the damn politicians or doctors in the white coats focus on something as simple as that? Everybody gets a meal and a shower. Doesn't sound that hard to me. But I see things they don't. Remember? I'm different.

I remember an ER doctor telling my mother that I was different for the first time when I was seven years old. She had taken me to the ER to get some stitches in my head. That was also the first time I had gotten stitches. The doctor said it was going to hurt but it didn't hurt. I think that's why he thought I was different; because I never winced or cried. In fact, the procedure didn't bother me at all. I guess in his case, being called different at that time was a compliment.

For some reason, cuts and bruises and even broken bones never really bothered me too much. And I became very familiar with all of those types of injuries while I was growing up. Some of them, my mother never saw. I knew it would have bothered her more than me so I just took care of them myself. Like I mentioned earlier, I was a fast healer. Broken bone one day; several weeks later, as good as new.

"Overcoming adversity makes you stronger," my father used to say. "Everyone gets knocked down. How you get back up is what matters." He was very good at demonstrating those philosophies to me. The son of a bitch was right though. My bones got stronger each time they encountered an adverse break of some kind. Funny how the doctors who patched me up never saw that.

Some of the social workers suggested to my mother that perhaps I was a product of my environment; an environment which they failed to define and one in which she didn't ask questions about, knowing there was little she could do to change it. Other doctors, like the neurologist Dr. Littleton referred me to, told her that I had something wrong with my head. They told her the EEG suggested the electrical impulses in my head were very irregular and I was probably having seizures, which were not evident to either her or me.

They didn't know what caused them but they told her they knew it probably made me want to do things that so-called "normal" little boys didn't do. They prescribed a bunch of pills for me to take, but I didn't like taking them so I stopped. They made me feel tired and slow. Made me move around like I was a zombie and I didn't like that feeling. I had to put up with a lot of shit but I wasn't going to feel tired all the time or not have the ability to run away. That would have been dangerous in the house where I lived.

My mother tried to protect my sister and me from the other person that lived in our house but she could only do so much. She did the best she could. She fed and clothed us. She was always looking for things we could enjoy doing together and didn't cost much money. She made us smile. Laugh. Even forget the bad; at least for a moment. Yeah, she did the best she could and made sure that we stayed alive during the years we were growing up, but I don't think my sister thought that being alive was all that good most of the time. I know I didn't.

My sister and I wore a lot of long-sleeved shirts. Even in the summer. We did that to hide the bruises and cigarette burns on our arms. They never lasted long because my sister was a fast healer like me. Unfortunately, when one injury went away, there was always another one to take its place.

I never understood until I was much older why my mother didn't take us away from that world. I realized that when you're scared, you don't think in a rational way. You can even convince yourself that a world of abuse is better than a world of loneliness and poverty. You can convince yourself of that but in the end, you will always realize that you were wrong.

I asked one of those people with a Ph.D. at the end of their names how a parent could harm a child and he said it was because they were battling their own demons. When I first heard that, I thought it was a lot of bullshit but as I got to thinking about it, I realized it was true. I knew the doctor was referring to demons in a metaphorical way, but he was still right. I didn't feel it was necessary to tell him the demons he was referring to were real. He would have just said something like I was different or strange for suggesting demons were real and would have told my mother to stop letting me read Edgar Allen Poe. And yep, he was one of those doctors in a white coat.

That aforementioned same doctor in the white coat, a Dr. Patrick Macturf, told me that he could tell I was strong and that eventually, I would be a much stronger and better person as a result of these "growing up pains," as he called them. I almost pulled the lips off of his mouth when I heard him say that bullshit. But instead of standing up and making him a ton of money as a real-life phantom of the opera, I just laughed and was quickly "ushered away." My mother understood laughing was a coping mechanism for me. She taught me how to do that. Laugh. She introduced me to "The Three Stooges" and they were able to make me laugh each and every time I saw them.

Those doctors with the Ph.D. at the end of their names, or the doctors in the emergency room, would never understand why people who lived in a world of abuse would find humor in what "The Three Stooges" did to one another. But it did. I think it was because we could watch Moe hit Larry in the head with a shovel and not see blood squirt out onto the floor. Larry would just yell and then hit Moe in the face with a two-by-four. And instead of Moe falling to the floor with a broken nose and jaw, he would just say some wisecrack, and it would start all over again. No matter how many times they hit each other, they never hurt one another. They lived in a world of abuse but it didn't hurt them. Their world of abuse was funny. It may be a twisted way of looking at things but it sure helped me manage the world in which I lived. That's why my mother and I enjoyed "The Three Stooges." It was sort of like reading Dr. Seuss in the sense that we could both escape into another world and not be hurt anymore. We could go there, wherever "there" was, and just laugh.

My sister didn't like watching "The Three Stooges." She would watch them with us, but I could tell she never really enjoyed it. She watched because she could be with me and my mother, but she usually had her head in a book while she was sitting there with us. Looking at pictures of someplace in Alaska or Hawaii, or maybe all the way around the world in Australia or New Zealand.

What my sister really loved to watch was Julie Andrews in "The Sound of Music." As such, I have seen "The Sound of Music" forty-seven times.

My sister even told the teachers at school that her last name was Von Trapp until my mother asked her to stop. I could always predict when we would be watching "The Sound of Music" instead of "The Three Stooges." Whenever I saw my father take my sister down into the basement, I knew the next day, we would watch "The Sound of Music."

My father was smart. He did things to me and my sister that could be explained away as just accidents. Kids are always having accidents as they grow up and they often have broken bones as a result of those accidents. And when you are on summer vacation or not in school over the holidays, those broken bones or smaller accidents have time to heal. Almost everything could be explained away. Almost everything.

But, if I'm being honest, I have to say my father's sadistic nature was helped by the fact that we never saw the same doctor. The ER clinics we went to always had different doctors and they were usually residents just learning how to be a doctor. Plus, the people working there always looked stressed, especially the nursing staff. On more than one occasion I heard the nurse or technician complain about poor record-keeping or problems with the computer and how everyone was being overworked.

I guess we could debate if that was a good enough reason to miss so much prolonged abuse, but since I could understand their frustration, I never brought up the fact that I had similar injuries a year ago, or the same broken arm four times. And my mother and sister weren't going to say anything either because they were afraid, though the fear arose from different origins. My mother feared my father and my sister feared being taken away from my mother. Yeah, I know. A pathetic circle of life without a cinematic theme song, right?

Regardless, since no one said anything, they couldn't tell there were similar injuries when they looked at our bodies, because my sister and I healed fast. They couldn't see with their technology that the real problem with our bodies was the foundation. The home. Just like those people that worked on the road. The ground was shifting but they couldn't see it. All they saw was a hole that they needed to fix, so they fixed it.

It's also our fault for not telling them about the cigarette burns. But we were never in the ER with a fresh burn. My father was smart that way. Insightful. He knew not to cause an injury that would take us to the ER when we had fresh cigarette burns. He knew that would create suspicion because children didn't have those types of accidents on their own.

I was certain if I had said anything about the burns, my mother would have suffered and my sister would have been taunted like I was at school. And I couldn't allow either of those things to happen. So, I kept silent. In fact, eventually, I didn't even feel any pain. And being taunted at school never bothered me. I think it was because there was something in my genetic makeup that allowed me to ignore the pain and the verbal abuse from my classmates. I had a good teacher at home and had studied his "Book of Life" very well. And like he had said more than one time, I was different. Plus, I didn't suffer at home to the extent my sister did.

I never spoke to my sister about the sexual abuse she endured and she never spoke to me about it. I hope she knows I would have stopped the pain for her many years earlier if I could have. When I turned 18, I believe I stopped some of the pain for her. I know I stopped a lot of the pain for me. It happened soon after my sister and I watched my father strangle our mother to death on the kitchen floor.

He had grabbed my sister by her hair and thrown her out on the porch. While I was trying to help her, we heard the backdoor lock. We ran to the kitchen window and though we both screamed and tried to get into the kitchen before he killed her, we couldn't. I was only able to get into the house as I heard the last breath of air escape through her mouth. I will never forget that last breath. It wasn't an anguished gasp of a dying woman. It sounded more like a sigh of relief, and when I looked down at her face, I saw her smile. I was sure she was telling me with that smile that she prompted that last argument with my father because she knew we were old enough now. Old enough and strong enough. Not old or strong enough to save her, but old and strong enough to save ourselves.

My father saw me out of the corner of his eye and turned around and yelled, "Asshole!" at me before I took away his ability to say anything abusive like that ever again. Unlike the shovel that Moe used to hit Larry in the head, the shovel that I swung at my father took the top of his head off. As he fell to the floor, his scalp dropped onto the tile. Blood didn't gush from his head as I thought it would. It just trickled out like a spilled cup of grape juice that only had a little left in the glass. I sat there and watched as the trickle turned into a small reddish-brown pool around his head, thinking about what Dr. Littleton said about my inability to resolve anger issues constructively. Missed that one, didn't you, Dr. Littleton?

I thought the blow to his head had killed my father but it didn't. He was still alive thirty minutes later when my sister came into the kitchen and dropped the white charcoals onto his closed eyes. When he started to scream, she dropped several more hot coals into his mouth. We held him down as we watched them fall like lava down his throat and open up several holes in his neck. We stared as the charcoals burned through his eyelids and dissolved into his skull until the glow of the fiery green and blue embers revealed the demon that we knew existed there beneath his skin. That's when we knew he was dead. We let loose of his body and watched as the demon hovered for a moment in the air above us before it disappeared.

My sister pulled our mother up into her arms and began to sing.

"Do - a deer, a female deer; re - a drop of golden sun; mi - a name I call myself; fa - a long, long way to run."

I looked at my sister when she stopped singing. I saw her smile as soon as she looked back at me and I knew why. I heard that C.S. Lewis quote in my head and I whispered it to myself as I looked at her. She didn't need to finish the song. She had stopped running that day. In fact, we had all stopped running that day.

Chapter 2
Mrs. Cunningham

I sat across from my sister as she held our mother in her arms. I watched her stroke her hair and talk to her for over an hour. She told her how much she loved her and that she forgave her. She said that over and over and I wasn't sure if my mother could hear her or not. Though I didn't consider myself very religious, I had read the Bible and gone to church with my mother and sister on those occasions my mother thought we should go. I never really knew what prompted my mother to decide when those occasions should occur and I never asked. But now that I was sitting here and thinking about it, I believed I understood. She went there when she wasn't sure if she could carry on in the world in which we all lived. She went there seeking strength and forgiveness. Forgiveness because she couldn't find the strength to get to the exit door that she knew existed but could never find and open.

And even though I thought about the same thing as I got older, I could not fault her as I looked at her in my sister's arms. Like I said, I didn't consider myself very religious but for some reason, I believed my mother could hear my sister as she talked to her that evening. I hope she did because she would have liked what she heard. My sister talked about how much she loved going to the library and listening to her read to her, looking at all the travel books and magazines and dreaming about going there one day together, eating the cherry cake she made for her every year on her birthday, going to the dollar movies and to all the county fairs, and how much she treasured the dress she made her for her thirteenth birthday. Everything that they had enjoyed together in the past seventeen years, she talked about with her in that one hour.

The way my sister talked made me realize she had a memory like mine, and I had never seen any evidence of that until now. She recalled specific days with my mother going all the way back to when she was just a baby. That was a blessing and a curse, I thought, as I listened to her recite day after day, event after event, moment after moment. It was wonderful that she had all those memories of special times with our mother. But I knew that meant she would also have memories of places that were much darker. Places she went with our father. Places where monsters were real.

And then something hit me like the back of my father's hand. In all that time that she was talking to my mother, my sister never mentioned watching "The Sound of Music" with her; the one movie she truly loved. And I knew why. It was because of that dead asshole laying over there on the kitchen floor. The one thing that helped her get through whatever hell she encountered in that basement with that fucking piece of shit, was something that she would never bring up again. She wouldn't forget the movie. She couldn't forget it, but she also wouldn't relive it by watching or talking about it ever again. I realized something very important at that moment. I discovered that my sister was probably stronger than anyone I had ever met before.

I then looked over at that thing that lay dead on the tile floor and I started to snicker. At least now I thought, we had made the outer appearance of the man reflect his true self. The monster was no longer hidden behind a friendly smile that everyone saw outside of the house. The guy who delivered the mail each and every day to people he really hated would never do it again.

And though the smell of burnt flesh filled up the room, I could still distinguish the asshole's body odor that emanated from his body. I don't know how the son of a bitch ever kept his job because he always stunk. And then I started to laugh. Not out loud, but I was laughing. Laughing my head off. Of course, he stunk. He was an asshole.

I always wondered how someone so smart could not understand how bad he smelled. Then the light bulb went off. God damnit. He knew, he just didn't care. He knew in the end it wouldn't matter. Like I said, he was very perceptive. How else could someone know I was going to be so different when I was only a week old?

And nothing against the postal service, but I often wondered, why would anyone so smart want to be a postman? I am not kidding. My father was probably a genius. How else could he know every god damn answer on "Jeopardy?"

Answer: Invaded Spain in 711 A.D. Question: "Who were the Moors?"

Answer: The most poisonous animal in the world. Question: "What is the Poison Dart Frog?"

Answer: The third wife of Henry VIII. Question: "Who was Jane Seymour?"

Answer: The first explorer to discover Jamaica. Question: "Who was Christopher Columbus on May 5, 1494."

Answer: A fundamental constituent of matter that combines to form hadrons. Answer: "What is a quark?"

Who in the fuck knows all that shit? My father did. I never heard him miss a question. I had finally realized why being a postman was the perfect job for him. He chose to be a postman because he could hide in that job. It was a convenient costume with good pay and benefits. He wouldn't have to reveal himself to anyone because it only required the most basic of skills and interactions. Smiling and saying, "Hello," and, "Have a nice day," were the only things he needed to remember. Be on time. Deliver the mail. Never miss a day of work. Perfect. Insightful.

God, I hated that son of a bitch. And he knew it. He was very intuitive; almost as if he had a sixth sense. For seventeen years he never got caught. He knew people saw the postman as just some "thing" on the street or country road, like a large tree or a red brick house with a black door, or a red barn with "See Rock City" painted on the roof that they walked or drove by for years without ever really seeing it. He was an "it" that people didn't really notice. They didn't care about "it." And he knew that. People didn't want to get involved with the postman and ask questions about the family that he lived with who was scared every day when he walked through the door.

When you are scared, many things can be hidden. Crimes are not revealed. Even when the evidence was there, being stared at and treated, or talked about by the doctors; he knew nothing was going to be done. Somehow, he knew. Shrewd. Perceptive. Call it anything you want except lucky. He wasn't lucky. He was devious and smart and didn't leave things to chance. He could tell you about someone just by looking at them. He knew their habits. Their secrets. Their fears. He was good at understanding fear.

He knew that everyone liked scary movies. Everyone could relate to them because everyone had been scared at some time in their life, even If for only a moment. But at that moment, everyone shared a common bond - the thrill of being scared. It was enjoyable because it was temporary. A sense of elation from the adrenaline that rushed through their body as if a switch had been turned on and off, all in one motion. But when people know that thrill wasn't temporary, when the unknown and scary were behind every door they encountered, they would be less inclined to open it. In fact, they would shy away from it. It wasn't thrilling anymore. The thrill had transformed into something else: fear.

He knew that's what stopped me from ending the abuse years earlier. I even told one of those doctors with a Ph.D. in a round-about way, that I didn't want to go home ever again. You know what that dumbass said? He said that what I was really trying to say was that I needed to hear him tell me that I should go home because I had unresolved issues there. Probably with my father. "No shit," I replied as I stood up and pulled all the plaques off his wall and then pulled out my dick and pissed all over them. He prescribed some other pills for me after that incident and told my mother that I was "different" and "unable to resolve anger issues in a constructive manner." No, it wasn't Dr. Littleton. It was some other dumbass with the Phony Degree letters they liked having attached to their last name.

Fucking different. "God damn you," I said as I looked at my father and the pool of blood that had widened around his open skull and was no longer bright red. I couldn't tell if the blood looked more maroon or brown as I stared at it on the tile. "Were you perceptive enough to know that I would take the top of your head off with a shovel when you looked down at me and said I was different when I was just a week old? Maybe. Maybe not. But we'll never find out now," I said as I asked and answered the question within my head. I didn't say it out loud as I didn't want to disturb my sister who was still talking to my mother, but as I looked over at her, I realized it wasn't her voice that I heard. And the voice I now heard wasn't talking.

I'm not sure how long our neighbor, Mrs. Cunningham, had been screaming at the back door of the kitchen but when I turned around and looked at her, she stopped. I could see in her eyes that same feeling I had felt for so many years. She was scared. Scared to the point she could do nothing but stand there and stare at the horror that lay sprawled across the kitchen floor.

I stood up and walked toward her and her body began to shake as if the wooden porch beneath her was the epicenter of a fault line tremor. I glanced at my sister but she hadn't even noticed that I had gotten up. She was still focused on my mother. As I turned back around, I smiled at Mrs. Cunningham and I heard something inside of her body change. I now heard the anguished gasps for breath.

Looking back on things now, I realize that smiling at Mrs. Cunningham as I was walking toward her with a shovel in my hand and blood and brain specks all over my clothes, was probably not the best way to handle things. I suppose, to Mrs. Cunningham, I looked like a crazed psychopath. Knowing that she believed I was different, as I had heard her tell my mother many times, I had now become the picture she had painted in bright colors in her head. So, in a very calm voice, I started talking to her as I neared the back door where she still stood as if her trembling body had her feet nailed to the wood planks.

"Mrs. Cunningham, it doesn't look like what you think. Well, maybe it does. What do you think it looks like? I'm not an ax murderer. As you can see, this is just a shovel. Never mind. That's not relevant, is it? No need to answer that. But you don't have anything to fear from me or my sister. You just need to go back to your house and call 911. Just slow your breathing down and turn around and walk away. There's nothing you need to worry about. We, my sister and I, will be here waiting on the police and the ambulances. Though I don't think the ambulances really need to come. My father killed our mother and I killed him. He was on top of her strangling her and I hit him over the head with this shovel to make him stop."

Again, reflecting back, holding up the shovel and showing it to her close-up with the blood and bits of bone and hair on it, probably wasn't a very good idea. As soon as I did that, the gasps increased. Louder and more rapid. I tried again to talk to Mrs. Cunningham as I put the shovel down on the floor.

"Please, Mrs. Cunningham. It's okay. Really. Just calm down, turn around and go call 911. I need to stay here with my sister. We will be here in the kitchen. Just go back to your house. I promise you. You will be okay if you just leave."

My sister was still unaware that I was talking to anyone and when I turned back around toward the door, I saw that Mrs. Cunningham had finally found the strength to move and was gone. I let out a sigh of relief and nodded my head and looked back one more time at my sister as I told her that I would be out on the porch, waiting for the police to arrive. I wanted to catch them before they went into the kitchen. I wanted to tell them that I had done everything to my father after I saw him strangle our mother. I would tell them that I hit him over the head with the shovel and then put the charcoals in his eyes and mouth. I would protect my sister. I owed her that.

As I pushed on the back door, I felt it catch, like it often did. The house was so old that the back door had wood rot and often got stuck. So, I pushed on the door with both hands and as I did, I felt that there was something other than the bloated surfaces of wood keeping it from opening. I pushed even harder and it was then that I realized I was shoving something back from the door. When I looked down, I saw that I was pushing Mrs. Cunningham's body.

I got the door opened far enough so that I could get out and bent down to see if Mrs. Cunningham was still alive. She was, but her breathing was very erratic and strained. I mumbled, "Shit," and I realized right then, that Mrs. Cunningham had come to one of those doors that we all encounter in our lives, and she had looked in when she should have walked away. The scary thing that she saw wasn't a temporary jolt of adrenaline that gave her a thrill. It was an electric shock created by intense fear that pulsed through her body and blew the breaker box.

When I went back into the kitchen my sister finally looked up at me. I told her that everything was going to be okay and that she should just stay there and keep holding onto our mother. I reached into my father's pocket and pulled out his cell phone. I told my sister that I would be out on the back porch, waiting for the police and ambulances to get there.

She nodded her head as if that made perfect sense, so I walked outside and called the police.

I gave them the address and said that there were three people dead and that I had killed them all. I told them my name and that I would be waiting for them on the back porch. I said that because of Mrs. Cunningham. I was sure that when they revived her, she would tell them she saw me hit my father in the head with a shovel and saw my sister dump those coals in my father's eyes and mouth. And I had no idea what she thought about my mother or how she died. Just like my father, I knew what needed to be done, so I simplified the story.

The shovel went through Mrs. Cunningham's neck without too much trouble and her head rolled off the back porch and onto the ground. I placed the shovel next to her head and sat down on the top porch step and waited. I was sure that once the police read all the teacher and doctor reports and files they had on me they would not have to look any further for a killer. They would know they had him. I was the poster child for what a crazed killer looked like. I was the one that everyone would always refer to as "different" and "ready to snap at any minute."

As I sat and waited for the blue and red flashing lights to come down the street, I began to wonder if anybody would ever say I found a constructive outlet for my anger issues. I smiled because I knew that none of the people with the Ph.D.'s at the end of their name would believe that, but they would be wrong. If they bothered to interview me some more, I knew what I would do. I would pull all of their plaques off the wall again and piss on them. And if they interviewed me in my cell, I would just piss on their computer or notebook or their leg. Or maybe, take a shit and throw the turds at them like a monkey in the zoo. Yeah, that should stop the interviews.

I hated that son of a bitch who was our father and the abusive world he created for my mother and sister. I hated myself for not doing anything about it until now. But I realized, on this evening, that I had now found a constructive and helpful outlet for my anger. I had now done something that was meaningful. I was sorry about what happened to Mrs. Cunningham but it had to be done.

Knowing that I would be in jail for the rest of my life didn't bother me. I was familiar with prison. I had lived in one my entire life. Being in a 6 x

8 room with iron bars didn't scare me. I realized I would never be scared of anything again. My father had taught me how to read people. I had learned to be perceptive and intuitive and I knew that the other people in the jail would leave me alone. They would know what I had done and about all of my anger issues and every once in a while, I would remind them they were still unresolved. Yeah, they would leave me alone.

I smiled again as I thought about my sister, knowing she would be free from her prison for the very first time. I smiled because I knew she would never be afraid again. I smiled because she would know and understand. She would be the only one that knew and I was okay with that. That was all that mattered. Doctors with Ph.D.'s after their names would say that four people died that night and I was okay with that brainless analysis. At least they wouldn't be able to say that five died that night. Nope. One of them would live. Free and fearless.

Chapter 3
Carnival Ride

I heard the sirens long before I saw the flickering blue and red lights in the distance. The cool breeze that blew against my face and the dark night and flashing lights reminded me of the county fair my mother took my sister and me to in our small rural East Tennessee community. For a moment, the smell of popcorn and cotton candy swirled around my nose and those memories put me at ease. The fair didn't come every year, but when it did, we never missed it. It always arrived in the fall, so the fact we were wearing long-sleeved shirts never seemed inappropriate or brought unwelcome attention to the other bruises or cuts that could not be hidden.

Though we liked the Scrambler, the Ferris wheel, and the bumper cars, our favorite ride was always the Haunted House ride. The large metal chair with a football-shaped back and weathered cracks in the leather seats, that took you through the haunted house building, was just big enough for my mother to sit in the middle with me and my sister on either side. The lights flashed red and blue just before the creaky metal chain jerked the chair forward and pushed against the wooden doors. The letters that spelled "Haunted House" were painted in red on the doors to look as if they were dripping blood. When they were opened, we found ourselves in complete darkness.

As the chair rattled along the tracks, we first felt the cool air blowing against our faces and the sinister sound of someone laughing next to us. We pulled each other closer as if we were frightened by what we felt and heard, but we were never really scared. We screamed as the detached hands reached out in a flash of red light and tried to grab us from both sides of the chair, but we weren't screaming out of fear.

Werewolves, vampires, and the Abominable Snowman lit up and growled at us as we went by them and lunged toward us awkwardly when they weren't broken. We screamed and laughed when they were able to carry out their threats. We screamed and laughed even more when they couldn't. We rode that ride again and again because we realized the scary things in it were not real, and even though we knew when they were coming, we played our part. We always jumped and screamed and laughed because that is what you were supposed to do. It was supposed to be scary and fun and it was. But things that jumped out at us from the dark never really scared us. It was what walked straight up to us in the light of day that we feared.

As I remembered the ticket taker at the ride who always said the same thing, "Keep your hands and arms inside the ride at all times," I began to think about the police that were on their way to our house. Regardless of their training and experience, I knew the call that went out alerting them about a house with multiple murders would alter the way they thought and acted. They would know that the person who called and claimed he was the killer told them he would be waiting for them on the back porch. The dispatcher would warn the officers, "Be advised, the killer said he was waiting on the back porch."

"Keep your hands and arms inside the ride at all times" were the words they needed to hear, but I knew that advice would not be followed now, any more than it was years ago by me or my sister. The police opened scary doors every day, but this time as they approached the unknown, they would be on edge. Alert. Reactive. Maybe even angry. I knew that I would be perceived as a threat to their lives as soon as they saw me and I would have only seconds for them to realize I wasn't. Seconds for them to hear me. Seconds for them to hear my confession.

I looked down at Mrs. Cunningham's head and the shovel, and I knew what I needed to do. I turned around and looked back at the door to see if I could see my sister but thankfully, I couldn't. "Please, a little while longer," I whispered. "Stay there on the floor with mom just a little while longer as I try and make the unpredictable less threatening to those that are coming." Like the Haunted House ride, I thought, as I stood and picked up the shovel and walked over to stand next to Mrs. Cunningham's head.

I saw the police cars come down the alley and I heard the gravel flying up from their tires and slamming into the wooden fences that aligned the alleyway. I heard the cars slide to a halt and the multiple doors opening and the sound of snaps and Velcro as guns were being removed from their holsters. I heard the loud clicking sound of several shotguns being pumped and though I couldn't see them, I knew there were many guns pointed in my direction. Ready to be fired at the slightest provocation. Now was not the time for a severed hand to jump out at them from the dark. Not now. As soon as the spotlights found me, everyone would be waiting to see what I did next and ready to eliminate anything that frightened them.

The white spotlights blinded me for a moment as they lit up the backyard and moved around until they found me. I closed my eyes and heard one of the officers yell, "Shit!" and I knew he was the first to spot Mrs. Cunningham's head on the ground next to my feet. I knew that the only thing that kept him from shooting me was the weapon I held in my hands. I gripped the shovel handle that I had planted into the ground and blood trickled down my neck as the sharp tip of the metal spade pressed against it. I knew this image would stop them from shooting, at least for a moment. They wouldn't be threatened by someone that rested his head against the top of a shovel. No. This crude, broken totem would make them pause.

"I'm the one who called you. The one that you're looking for. I know you are scared and anxious. I know you don't want to be here. But you are here. And I am here. And I need to tell you what happened. Before you come any closer, you need to know that the shovel rests against my jugular and I will jam it into my neck if you don't let me tell you what happened. It will only take a minute and then it will be over. If you don't let me talk, you will never know what happened."

No one said anything. They were listening and watching the broken monster that was not threatening them.

"I killed my mother and father. It was an abusive childhood and I had all that I could stand. My sister is inside the house. In the kitchen. Right behind me. With my mother in her arms. She had nothing to do with any of this. She is a victim. She has been one her entire life. The head you see next to my feet is our neighbor. Mrs. Cunningham. She just happened to be at the wrong place at the wrong time. I didn't want to kill her but I had no choice. My sister is inside; please be gentle with her. She has suffered enough. I am the one you want. I killed them all. She is just a victim. An innocent victim. Been one her entire life," I repeated as my voice began to waver and I stopped talking.

I knew I couldn't let them hear the uncertainty in my voice. I couldn't let them see the monster lunge at them now. Not now. And as I waited, I heard nothing. They listened to me. They heard the confession. And then I heard one of them speaking to me and I told myself to listen to every word they said. I heard them tell me to get on the ground and to throw the shovel off to the side. And I did just what they said as I heard the voice in my head say, *"One more time. You need to tell them. Matter-of-factly, tell them. One more time. Tell them."*

"I'm doing what you're saying. Look," I said as I pointed to the shovel on the ground and knelt there with my hands in the air. "It's me that you want. I did it all. I killed everyone. My sister is innocent," I said again as I lay down on the ground and extended my arms out from my body.

Within seconds, several policemen surrounded me, pulling my arms back and tightening the plastic handcuffs across my wrists. One of them said, "Fucking crazy son of a bitch," as two others picked me up and held me. Several more ran past me toward the porch. I looked into the eyes of the two men that held me and I could tell which one had called me a "crazy son of a bitch." The fear of the unknown had been replaced by the fear of what he had now seen and his pupils reflected his anxiety by doubling in size. I knew I needed to calm him down through my actions and my words. Continuing to make sure that he heard what I needed him to hear.

I lowered my head and just started saying over and over again, "I did it," like a crazy man who had realized the end had come. I knew when he made his report, he would write down what I was saying and how I acted and that all of that would help frame the story. We stood there, not moving, and I heard the officers yell from the porch that they had my sister. I turned my head and saw several of them escorting her down the steps. I smiled at her as the officers started walking me toward one of the cars parked in the alley.

"Why?" my sister cried out to me. "Why did you tell them that you killed our mother?"

Everyone stopped. The ride had stopped. We were sitting there in the chair. In the dark. Waiting for them to fix the chain.

"Because I did. I allowed it to go on too long. I killed her. But you will be safe now. You had nothing to do with any of this. Remember that. Do what the officers tell you and you will be safe. Do what they say," I said as I turned to one of the officers and told them to take me away.

We restarted our walk to the cars waiting in the alley, when I heard a female officer behind me yell out, "Stop her!"

Immediately, I knew my sister was running toward me and I knew the police officers didn't understand what she was doing. The ride was still broken but my sister hadn't kept her hands and arms in the chair while we waited.

I turned my head and hollered back at my sister to stay away. That I would be okay. To let me go. To follow their orders, but she wouldn't listen. A bright white light flashed across her face and I saw her eyes and realized something bad was about to happen. She wasn't running over to me to say goodbye or receive any comfort from me. She was running toward me to help me get away. I started shaking my head and yelling, "No!" but the ride wouldn't re-engage.

One of the officers tackled her and threw her to the ground and I tried to get away. I needed to get out of the chair now too. I heard the officer yell at my sister as he and a female officer jumped on her back.

"Goddammit, lady! Stay the fuck down. Now. On the ground. I don't know what you are thinking but I need you to stay away from your brother and just calm your ass down!"

"Leave her the fuck alone!" I yelled, struggling to get away. The officer who was holding my arms pulled out a Taser and jabbed it into the right side of my neck. I heard the Taser arc and felt the strong current travel through my body, trying to overload my nervous system. The electricity that coursed through me made my knees buckle for a moment, but only for a moment. And then, I felt the chair moving again as the electricity moved along my nervous system. I wasn't incapacitated by the Taser. No, I actually felt stronger and more focused and had an overwhelming sense of calm and purpose.

The officer asked, "What the hell?" and he zapped me several more times. The more he zapped me, the stronger I felt. I flexed my arms and broke the plastic handcuffs and pushed both the officers away from me as I ran back to my sister.

"Goddammit!" I yelled out. "She's innocent. Didn't you hear me? She's innocent! Leave her alone!" But they weren't listening to me. They weren't listening because she was fighting them.

"Keep your hands and arms inside the ride at all times!" I yelled out as I leaned down and picked up the male officer that was on her back and threw him to the ground as if he was some dirty laundry that I was tossing into the washer. When he was off of her, my sister rose up and knocked the female officer away and then stepped on her face with her foot. I heard something crack and I knew that we were about to be thrown off the ride and told to leave for breaking something we shouldn't have.

Then the gun went off. I wasn't sure what was happening but somehow I could see the bullet in the lights that were shining on us. I saw the flash as it left the gun and I saw the bullet heading toward my sister. "Fuck!" I yelled as I pushed my sister away and felt the bullet enter and exit my bicep. We had ignored the warnings. We were out of the chair and the ride had been shut down and we were all now in the dark.

The officer that I had thrown off my sister had gotten back up and was running toward me. He was not alone. Three of them hit me and knocked me down while another tackled my sister. He moaned as he fell over; his hands trying to hold his broken jaw from moving anymore.

I threw one of the officers off of me in time to see the female police officer who was lying next to my sister, reach over and grab my sister's ankle. My sister bent down and wrenched the officer's hand away and bit it. The police officer screamed as the fingers she bit off fell next to her face. I heard the overhead warning as the speaker cracked and buzzed in my ears:

"The ride has been shut down. Do not move. We will come to remove you from the cars."

I heard the loud clicking noises from behind my sister. I saw the shotguns flash and watched as the pellets went through her body. I yelled out "No, Fucking, no!" as I watched my sister fall to the ground. I shoved the other two officers off of me and got up and tried to get to her. The bullets hit my legs and arms and I slumped to my knees in front of my sister. She wasn't moving and then the bullet entered my head before I fell on top of her.

The ride started back up sometime later. I wasn't sure when. But there we were. My mother, sister, and me. In the chair. In front of the blue and red flashing lights. The ticket taker had taken our tickets and told us to "keep our hands and arms inside the ride at all times" and the chain engaged and the chair pushed open the doors. We rode that Haunted House ride over and over for the longest of times. Each time the monsters lunged out at us, I felt small surges of energy pulse through my body. And each time we exited the ride, I laughed and waited for the doors that were dripping blood to open once again.

Chapter 4
Heavy Metal

I can't tell you when the images of the ride started to fade away, but they did. The monsters always seemed to be broken and one day when I went through the doors, I looked over and my sister and mother were gone. There was nothing but darkness and I felt sick when the chair came to a halt. The air was stale and hot and I knew I was going to throw up. I leaned over the chair and though I gagged several times, nothing would come up. I felt something at the back of my throat and I knew if I didn't get it out, I would not be able to breathe. I heaved one more time and caught hold of something with my hand and started pulling it out.

I wasn't sure how a snake could crawl down into my throat, but that's what it felt like. But that was odd. I had never read about snakes doing that. It must be some fucking tapeworm. I had read about those foul things in books and knew that they could get big, but I couldn't understand how one could be inside of me. It didn't matter. It was coming out. I pulled it and felt its mouth tug against my throat and I yanked even harder before it came flying out of my mouth. Once it was removed, I threw it to my side and started to cough and began to taste blood.

I turned my head and gagged several more times until I threw something up and the blood taste in my mouth disappeared, replaced by the taste of sour milk and sweet potatoes. *I'd rather taste blood* I said to myself as I continued to gag but nothing else came up. I thought I heard voices yelling at me but I didn't recognize any of them. I tried talking to them but I couldn't as I felt something being applied to my face. *What are you trying to do now, smother me? What the fuck are you doing?* I wanted to scream but no sound came out and I then felt a cool breeze coming through my mouth. Against my nose and mouth. The stale air was gone and I wondered if the ride was starting back up. I waited for the diabolical laughter, but it never came. Something warm entered my arm and began to flow through my body. I wasn't sure where I was but I didn't care. There was cool air blowing on my face and it made me relax as I felt my head drop onto a soft pillow and I fell asleep.

I'm not sure how long I was asleep but when I opened my eyes, I could see a dim light in a corner of the darkness. As I tried to focus, the light became clearer and I could see the outline of someone walking toward me. *The ride must be broken and they're coming to get us with a flashlight* I thought. But as the flashlight got closer and brighter, I realized I was alone and it wasn't a flashlight at all. The light came from overhead, like one of the lamps the doctors blinded you with, except this one radiated within the red hair of a young woman and I didn't want to turn away. Before I could speak, she started telling me not to say anything.

"You pulled your ventilator tube out, but luckily, you didn't cause much damage. Most of the injury is to your throat, but even that is minimal, which is amazing. It would be better though if you didn't try to talk for several days. There is bruising and some swelling but we'll watch that. Your lungs are stronger than we thought and you don't need the ventilator, so we just have you on some oxygen. That's why those little prongs are in your nose. They are providing you some oxygen as you continue to wake up," the red-haired female said as she looked down at me and smiled.

You thought it was a tapeworm, you dumbass and I started to laugh. *It was a ventilator tube. Nothing but a damn ventilator tube. Why the hell did you think it was a tapeworm? The girl with the red hair is very pretty. I don't remember ever seeing her here at the fair. She's a lot better looking ticket taker than that creepy old man who smelled like paint thinner and cigarettes, that's for sure.*

Wait a minute. She said ventilator tube, didn't she? Hell, I'm not at the fucking fair. "Where the hell am I?" and "Who the hell are you?" are what I wanted to say but all that came out of my mouth was a coarse rasp that hurt my throat. I tried to move my hands but I couldn't and as I looked over at them, I saw they were in leather restraints tied to the side of a bed. I looked back up at the woman and it was as if she could tell what I was asking without saying anything.

"You have been asleep a long time, Mr. Deaux. A very, very long time. We're surprised you woke up as you did, but I don't know why. Nothing about you has been what we would consider normal. Your body has been fighting to recover ever since they brought you here. You are in a special unit at the University of Tennessee Medical Center in Knoxville, Tennessee. You are still under arrest though for some crimes you committed. That's the reason you're restrained. That and the fact that we don't want you pulling out any more tubes. Knowing what I do about your injuries, I'm amazed you don't have any brain damage but your EEG is normal. Well, not normal, but it doesn't indicate you have any brain damage. I know I am rattling on a bit, aren't I?" the pretty woman asked.

The words "nothing about you has been what we would call normal" bounced around in my brain but all I heard were the words "he's different" again. I closed my eyes and knew the red-haired woman must be some type of doctor to utter that mantra I had heard so many times before. But this time the person who said it was a pretty young woman. *At least that's an improvement.* I tried to clear my throat and even though it felt like there was a hot coal in it, I managed to get out three words: "Name? How long?"

"I'm sorry, the very first part of our value statement and I messed it all up," the young woman answered. "I just didn't expect to be talking to you so soon. Anyway, my name is Samantha but everyone calls me Sam. I am your nurse. Well, one of your nurses. I guess there are about a half dozen or so that have taken care of you since you've been here. But I've been with you the longest. The entire two years."

Two years. I closed my eyes and felt as if I was going back into the Haunted House ride. Spinning around and going backward, I could see the monsters lunging out at me and my sister sitting next to me. She was holding my mother. She and my mother were smiling at me but neither of them had any eyes. And then I saw all the holes in my sister's body. "Holey Moley," she said as she stuck her fingers in each hole. "Pretty cool, huh?" I wanted to scream as my body began to shake.

"No!" I shouted as loud as I could, but it was not loud. It was an angry whisper at best, and I heard Sam say she was going to give me something to help me and I knew what that meant. I opened my eyes and shook my head no, but I she was coming toward me with the syringe. "No!" I growled again and this time she paused as she looked down at me. "Please, no," I heard my gravelly voice plead.

I could tell she was listening to me but she still had that syringe in her hand. *Get her to talk to you,* I kept telling myself. *Ask some more questions. Let her know you aren't dangerous. That's what she needs to see.*

"Today?" I asked.

"It's June 23, 2025."

I couldn't understand how that was possible. I watched her put the syringe down on the table next to my bed and pour a glass of water for me. She put a straw in the cup and pressed the button on the arm rails that raised the head of my bed. She put the straw in my mouth and I drank. It was the best-tasting water I had ever had and I finished that cup as quickly as she would allow me to drink it. Then she filled it up again and let me drink some more.

I could have kept drinking but she said that was enough for now and I just nodded and smiled. The water made my sore throat and my entire body feel better.

"Thank you."

"You are very welcome, Mr. Deaux."

Why is she calling me by that name? That's not my name. I don't think that's my name but I can't remember now. What the fuck is my name? I asked myself and then forgot about it as soon as Sam continued talking. *She's doing it,* I thought. She's talking to you and I smiled. Or perhaps I didn't smile. I wasn't even sure I could smile.

"Your level of recovery is nothing short of amazing. You have had multiple surgeries and been on a ventilator for two years, but no one would ever know it by looking at you. You haven't lost any muscle mass at all laying in that bed, which is just unheard of. Never seen anything like it. In fact, you look like you've been working out for years. I know the therapists have been coming in here every day and working with you, but you still shouldn't look like an Olympic gymnast. Mr. Deaux, you are quite different than any other patient I have ever seen."

There it was again - the word "different." When I heard it, I pulled the leather restraint loose and grabbed Sam's hand. She screamed and immediately a police officer and several people wearing blue scrubs ran into my room. A voice came from the lights saying something about a code purple and I wondered what that meant. I heard the word "Goodness!" coming from Sam's voice and then nothing else as my eyes closed and I was in the dark again.

I tried to resist the drug-induced restraint but although I couldn't free myself from its restrictive properties on my body, I could stop it from completely dissolving my ability to think. Though they were cloudy, images of the past began to form like silhouettes made by the sun filtered through a window blind. I saw myself standing in the kitchen looking down at my mother. This time she had eyes and she was smiling up at me but she still didn't look right. Something was wrong and then I realized what it was. It was her face. It was purple.

And that's when I saw him looking back at me and smiling too. The twisted smile of a large reptile basking in the sun. It was arrogant and offensive and I heard the word "asshole" before I saw myself swing the shovel and take the top of his head off.

I saw my sister walk over to my father as I was on my knees next to him, holding his hands and arms. From that point forward, I watched everything that occurred that night repeat itself. Sometimes the images were grainy shadows but other times, they were colorful images projected onto a large white screen. In a slow and sequential fashion, I saw the charcoals drop onto my father's face, Mrs. Cunningham's head, the police spotlights, and the fights. I saw the bullet go through my arm and the pellets from the shotgun go through my sister's body. And then, for the first time, I felt it. I felt the bullet enter the back of my head and this time, I saw it come out of my forehead and watched as my body fell on top of my sister.

And then I think I fell asleep for a moment before I woke up and found myself sitting on the back porch of our house watching an electrical storm. The lightning bolts lit up the sky and the storm never stopped. I began to wonder if I was in Hell. It was always dark and all I could see was the lightning. Nothing else. No thunder. No rain. No voices. No one was there but me, just sitting on the back porch. I wondered if this was my punishment for killing my father and Mrs. Cunningham. Was this what eternity looked like for me? Sitting there on the porch looking into the dark and occasionally seeing flashes of light that looked like lightning bolts, only there was no thunder?

It was then that one of the lightning bolts hit me and I fell backward. *Shit, that should have killed me* I thought as I sat back up. But it didn't. And then it happened again. And I was knocked backward but just as the time before, I sat back up. I looked around and then began to walk. No matter if I took a left or right, there was nothing there. Just darkness and lightning. And though there was lightning all above me, I didn't get hit by it anymore. At least not a direct hit to my body. Now it just hit the ground all around me and I felt waves of electrical charges roll across my body as if I was wading in some sort of electrified ocean.

I thought I would spend the rest of my life in a 6 x 8 cell, not walking around in a strange world, if it was indeed a world. But then I remembered. *This world isn't real. Remember Sam? She's real, isn't she? Yes, she's real. You felt her wrist and you felt the drugs enter your body and knock you into this obscure realm.*

She said she has been my nurse for two years. Two damn years? How is that possible? And why keep me alive for two years just to kill me later or send me to prison for the rest of my life? Why not just let me die? And why didn't I die? I was shot in the head. I saw the damn bullet come out of my head. I remember it. I remember everything now, but why?

Why am I in a hospital? I don't want to be kept alive by doctors or pretty nurses named Sam because there is nothing in this world anymore. My mother and sister are dead. I am chained to a bed. Nothing about any of this makes any sense.

Wait a minute. Yes, it does. Think. This makes perfect sense. You know Hell isn't some dark place of fire and brimstone. Hell is what you lived in on earth. You lived in it for eighteen years. Now, I guess if Sam is correct you are beginning to awaken in a new world. Somehow, you're alive but you're still in prison. This is just a different kind of prison. You have prepared for this situation, so don't fight it.

A life in jail without my mother and sister. It's not Hell, it's just the door opening to my new home. At least now I know they are both at peace and are both free from the chains of this world. That will help me get through each day. Knowing that they are at peace and free. I can make it knowing that.

I opened my eyes to see Sam looking down at me. She smiled when she saw my eyes. I looked at my hands and found the restraints were gone. I looked up and Sam saw the confusion in my eyes.

"Yep, they're gone. I had to sign some sort of form to keep being your nurse. The form releases the doctor from any damages should I get injured taking care of you. But I don't think you'll hurt me. You won't hurt me, will you?"

I shook my head no.

"You have been moved to a more secure room. People can only get in and out via a retina scan. The glass doors and windows are stronger than steel one hundred times their width. I don't know how that's possible but that's what I was told. I have never seen a hospital room like it. Well, any other room like it to be honest. You would have to take one of my eyes to get out of here."

I saw her try to elicit a smile as if she wasn't sure whether she should smile or not after mentioning me taking out one of her eyes.

"Sometimes, I don't know why I say stupid stuff like that. Don't get any ideas in your head about taking my eyes. I need them you know. To do my job and take care of you," and this time when she spoke, she did more than feign a smile. She laughed a real laugh.

Her laughter reminded me of my sister and I loved hearing it. *Maybe she can be my nurse for a long time. That would help ease the thought of living in this empty world. Yes, that would help a lot.* That laughter gave me strength and I spoke with a much stronger voice this time.

"You have nothing to fear from me, Sam."

"That's good to hear, Mr. Deaux," she answered as she smiled again. I hoped I was smiling back at her as she continued to talk.

"I'm not sure you heard me say this earlier, but you have remarkable healing powers. Just four days ago I was talking to you about the ventilator tube you yanked out of your throat and your voice was only a gruff whisper. Now it's almost normal. Amazing. Like I said before, you are unlike any patient I have ever cared for."

Unlike. Different. Same word. I heard it. But this time when she said it, it sounded as if my mother was explaining to me that the word meant "uncommon," not weird or strange.

"I need to get some blood from your port. That's the tubing right there just below your shoulder. We used to do blood tests on you every two hours when you first got here, but now it's only daily. It won't hurt. I just need to clean off the port access and pull the blood from your veins. You okay with that?"

"Yes."

I watched her collect six tubes of blood and label them.

"I know it looks like a lot, but it's not really that much," Sam said as she looked over at me. "Especially for you. Your body seems to have very active bone marrow. Much more so than others. Very, uh…"

I could tell what she was going to say and I knew why she paused. For some reason, she seemed to think that I would take one of those eyes out of her head when she said what she was about to say. But I wasn't going to do that. At least not with her, but she didn't know that. I knew I needed to finish the sentence for her and let her know everything was okay.

"Different?" I asked.

"Yes, different," she said and sighed. "I really can't explain it. You have absolutely no organ damage. No anemia. No brain damage. No kidney failure. No liver disease. No shortness of breath and your lungs are clear. Getting stronger every day. No cardiomyopathy. No hair loss. No diarrhea and no overall weakness that I can see. I have never seen anyone snap those leather restraints. I've seen many people wriggle out of them, but you snapped them. Like they were a piece of string. Do you have any nausea or abdominal pain?"

I shook my head no.

"That's amazing," she murmured as she labeled the tubes and then pulled a computer screen around so that I could see the monitor. "Look at these blood levels," she said as she moved my bed to a sitting position.

"Cadmium – 2000 ng/ml. 2000? That's unbelievable. Toxic is greater than 50.

Copper – 1500 mcg/ml. I've never seen anything over 150, unless there was liver failure.

Zinc - 10 mg/L. Upper limit should be about 1.

Aluminum – 60 ng/ml. Upper limit should be no more than 6.

Selenium – 15,000 ng/ml. 15,000! Should be in heart failure at 150.

Manganese – 1500 mcg/ml. Upper limit should be 15.

Iron – 2000 mcg/dl. Upper limit should be about 170. And these levels of lead, mercury, arsenic, and thallium. They are all poisonous at high levels and you exceed the upper limit tenfold on each one. How are you not dead, I keep asking myself?"

"Because I'm different?"

"Yes, John Deaux. You are very different!" She swung the monitor back around and started out of the room. "Do you need anything before I leave?"

"Yes. Several things. What do those letters mean after those blood levels? When do I get real food and why do you call me John Doe?"

Sam smiled again and I realized I could look at that smile for the rest of my life here in prison and be just fine.

"The ng denotes nanograms, ml is milliliter, mcg is micrograms, dl is deciliter, and the L means liter. It's just a way the lab denotes the upper and lower limits of the analytes in your blood. I can ask the doctor about real food. I'll have to send him a text because I have never actually seen or met him. I am not aware of any nurse that has. Somehow, he comes and goes during the night and no one ever sees him. But the orders are there the next day, like clockwork. Every morning on the computer. And the other thing, regarding your name. I'm not sure. That's what we have called you since the beginning. It's never been changed. I think someone wants to make sure you maintain your anonymity."

"You're the one that suggested the removal of the restraints, aren't you?"

"I thought it might be helpful for your long-term recovery and well-being," she replied as she picked up the blood and everything else from the table and then turned and put her eye up against the scanner.

"Thank you, Sam," I said as she left. I watched the almost invisible door slide open and then close silently.

I closed my eyes and put my hands behind my head. It felt good to put my arms up behind my head as I thought about those blood levels she showed me. I thought about how great it would have been to show those test results to those doctors with the Ph.D. at the end of their names. When they said I was different, I would have said, "Hell yes, I'm different, and here is the proof. Check this out, you dumbass!" That would have shut them up and I laughed as I thought about how the conversation would have taken place.

Selenium 15,000 nanograms per milliliter. Oh yeah. What is your selenium level doc? 50? Maybe 60 tops. Or your iron level? About 100? Never seen anything like it, have you? Well then, I think this little chat is over, don't you? I would have said that and thrown down the paper and walked out of the office. Of course, as I walked out of the office, I would have made sure that I acted like I knew what those values meant, even though I didn't have any idea. At least not yet, but I was determined I would find out what everything meant. But for now, all I knew is what Sam had told me. I was unlike any other patient she had ever encountered. And she seemed to like that. I kind of liked that too. At least she called me a patient and not a prisoner. And that smile. Yes, that smile was something that I could get used to seeing every day.

I heard a whirring sound and noticed the four IV bags hanging around me. Hooked to three tubes that went into my arms. Something warm was going into my arm and it made me relax. I felt myself drifting off and though I was in the dark again, it wasn't scary. It was like the ride-at-the-carnival dark. It was there but it didn't bother me. I didn't see anything. No monsters. No lightning bolts. Nothing. It was just dark.

For a long time, I rested. I don't know when, but at some point, I seemed to be floating through the darkness. I saw a small colored light and as I tried to focus on it, I thought I saw the outline of a little puppet sitting beside me in a chair. The light was coming from its eyes that glowed red in the dark. I could see the puppet moving its mouth and eventually I could hear it talking to me.

"Amazing," the puppet said. "Amazing."

I wasn't sure what drugs were circulating through my body that made me believe that I saw and heard a puppet, but it didn't bother me. I liked puppets. Ever since I saw "Sesame Street" as a child. I loved the Swedish chef. This puppet didn't look at all like the Swedish Chef, but it didn't scare me. Even if it did have red eyes. It was dwarfed by the chair it sat in; its tiny legs just reaching the end of the seat. It couldn't have been more than two feet from its tiny little feet to its head, which as I looked at it, seemed pretty big for a puppet. And then it hit me. He looks like Beaker from "Sesame Street." Beaker had come to visit me. I didn't know what these drugs were but I liked what they were helping me to see right now.

"Hey, Beaker. Glad you could come to visit with me. I heard you say 'amazing.' What do you think is amazing?"

"The blood levels that you possess. Did you know that iron is the most abundant transition metal in biology? It is a cofactor for many enzymes. That may not mean anything to you now but let me just say, it helps your body do many things much more efficiently and effectively."

"You were always real smart, Beaker. I learned a lot from you. And you're right, I'm not sure what that means. All I know is that it makes me different. Sam, the nurse, told me that."

"Oh yes. Very different. The heavy metals in your blood enable your body to do things that no one has ever seen before. It's amazing. Truly amazing."

Why does he keep saying amazing? Maybe I'm missing something.

"Yeah, I heard you say that Beaker. Are you referring to iron and selenium?"

"Yes, those and all the other heavy metals and the fact that you are not the only one who has them," Beaker replied.

Chapter 5
The Ventriloquist's voice

"Yeah, that's nice to hear, Beaker," I replied. "You know, I learned a lot from you when I was little."

"The selenium levels in your blood that are, quite frankly, almost alien-like, suppress cancer cells from growing. In fact, I don't think cancer cells have a chance of growing within you. Maybe we can test that hypothesis later. Your selenium levels seem to seek out any free radicals and destroy them, almost as they are being created. And your manganese levels. They help your body heal. Wounds that would take months to heal, take days for you, and they never get infected. The bugs and viruses cannot get a foot up, so to speak, in your bloodstream. It is toxic to them. It is just simply amazing," Beaker continued.

"Do these heavy metals in my blood make me crave certain foods? I'm really hungry, Beaker. I would love a couple of cheeseburgers and some French fries with chili and cheese on them and a strawberry milkshake. Could you ask the Swedish chef to make that for me?"

"I will take care of your food requirements, Mr. Deaux, as you so request."

"Thanks, Beaker."

"Of course, everything that I just told you is subject to change because of the mutations. You always have to consider the mutations, because the mutations always occur. But I would think that would take many years to happen with you, provided we do not overreact to them, unlike my colleagues have done so many times in the past. Idiots. Prescribing antibiotics for a virus. Idiots. I told them over and over but they would not listen. Even when I helped them develop the new chemotherapy drugs, they did not listen."

"I agree with you there, Beaker. Doctors are idiots. And yeah, I thought that selenium level was pretty damn special. I was going to show that to some of the doctors with the Ph.D.'s at the end of their name and laugh in their face."

Wait a fucking minute. What did he say? What did Beaker say about me not being the only one that has these kinds of blood levels? He did say that, didn't he? Or was that something I heard over the loudspeaker?

"Though that manganese level is not going to help you with your high level of aggressiveness. We will have to watch that. As well as those arsenic and lead and thallium levels. And be aware of any hallucinations or further degradation of your social integration skills. I am sure that these blood levels will only make things more difficult for you in that regard."

"Wait a fucking minute. Just wait a fucking min…" I started to say before Beaker interrupted me.

"See. A fine example right there. You assume I am someone named Beaker. Someone that you had fond memories of in your childhood. Yet, you use that kind of language with him. It's not even Beaker you are talking to. It is me, but you do not know who 'me' is yet. Interesting. It is as if you cannot control it. Not sure it will work, but we will see. We have a lot of work to do. A lot of work."

"God damnit, Beaker," I said as I started to move but before I could lift my shoulders from the bed, I heard the whirring sound again and the warm fluids reentered my arm. "Shit," I mumbled and immediately fell back into the darkness. But this time, I could see mom and my sister at the fair again and I was ordering two cheeseburgers and some chili cheese fries, and a strawberry milkshake. I could taste the food and it was the best thing I had ever eaten. I sat there at the table and savored each bite. I turned to tell my mother and sister how good it was before I realized they weren't there but I wasn't worried. I knew they were around somewhere. *Probably went off to get some cotton candy* I told myself and I lay down on the table bench and closed my eyes, waiting for them to return.

It only seemed like a thirty-minute nap when I opened my eyes and found myself in the hospital bed again with Beaker sitting in the chair looking at me. And then I remembered. He said he wasn't Beaker but he knew a lot about me. This guy that looked like Beaker was talking to me about what all the different blood levels meant like he was a doctor. *Is this the doctor Sam told me about that she had never seen?*

Even if he wasn't, he understood what everything meant and he knew there was someone else like me that had similar blood. I needed to know more about all of that and in order to get that information I knew he couldn't feel threatened by me. Otherwise, he would just put me to sleep. I thought about pulling the IVs out but then I realized that the little puppet man might have the ability to kill me if I pulled out the wrong one.

So, I decided to just sit there. Be calm and relaxed and talk to the man in charge of the ride.

"How did you like the food you requested?"

Damn. That's right. When I was asleep, I could taste the food. But there's not any evidence of any food around. How did that happen? Before I could answer my own question, the little puppet man began to talk as if he was reading my mind.

"It's easy enough, Mr. Deaux, to fool the body with regard to taste. I did a lot of work with food in attempts to ease the suffering of my chemotherapy patients. It's really quite simple once you understand how taste occurs. During chemotherapy, patients' sense of smell and taste are diminished, therefore, nothing tastes good. But if one analyzes the molecular composition and true characteristics of food and then develops a way to stimulate the trigeminal nerve in a way that tells the body it is eating what it desires, you can ensure that your patients do not have to suffer that indignity.

"I was able to do that. I developed the science of Molecular Transition Dynamics and I developed the Symbion molecule that was able to stimulate that nerve. The nutrients were all there in their IV but they felt like they were eating their favorite pizza, or fish, or cheeseburger."

I wasn't sure what the little man was talking about but I knew what he said was true. I did taste that cheeseburger and shake just a moment ago. This little man had the answers. I just needed to understand what it was he was telling me because right now nothing made much sense.

"The food idea or that science thing you were talking about is damn cool. And please understand, I don't mean to appear aggressive when I swear sometimes, but you need to give me a break, don't you think? I just learned yesterday that I have been in a coma for two fuck…, I mean, two whole years, and I am waking up in a world that tells me I have a selenium blood level of 15,000 nanograms per milliliter and an iron level of 2000 micrograms per deciliter, whatever the hell that means. And now you tell me you developed some Kumbaya molecule that makes me think I just ate a cheeseburger. I just want to understand what the hell…uh, heck is going on."

"Your ability to process information in a drug-induced state is amazing. Simply amazing. And even though you have a very high IQ, at least over 176 I would surmise, I didn't expect this level of lucidity so soon. Amazing."

"Would you quit saying amazing in every other fucking sentence and start to answer some damn questions for me?"

"Anger, Mr. Deaux. Impatience and anger. I suspect it's more the manganese than the other elements and I think we should test that theory as we move along."

Shit. I almost fucked that up. But he held off. He didn't send me back into the darkness. He wants to talk to me. He wants to explain to me why the ride isn't working.

"But as you say, you wish answers. I can provide those for you. First of all, the molecule is called Symbion, spelled s-y-m-b-i-o-n. Next question."

"Well, who the hell are you?"

"My name is Dr. Po, capital P, little o. I am the doctor who has been taking care of you for the past two years. Two years and 58 days to be exact. "

So, he is the doctor that Sam was talking about. Well, at least he doesn't look like the ones in all the white coats.

"What do all those blood levels mean?"

"Depends. For now, all you need to know is that it allows your body to heal quickly, keeps it immune to infection, and has an almost unmatched ability to survive traumatic injuries to the body."

"What was that science you said you invented?"

"Molecular Transition Dynamics."

"I suppose I have helped you write a gazillion papers for the Molecular Transition Dynamics Gazette, by now, haven't I?"

"Ah yes, sarcasm. I read that in your file. I can imagine that did not go over very well with anyone in authority that treated you."

"No, not really and you can tell me what an asshole I am as we go along, as you say, but before we do that, you just said an *almost* unmatched ability to survive a traumatic injury to the body. So that means someone else has this ability, correct?"

"Excellent, Mr. Deaux. Excellent. Your level of comprehension is amazing, considering the drugs in your body and your limited time of awareness." Dr. Po started. "Yes, there is another person who possesses the same type of chemical composition within their blood and the same healing and immune properties. Did you know that everyone's body is a good conductor of electricity? Think of a normal person's ability to conduct electricity as the number one. Using that as a reference, then your body's ability to conduct electricity is the number 266,235.9999 if my math is correct. And my math is almost always correct. As I calculate it, at least 11.5 sigmas."

"Doc. Don't take offense, but you are talking like a robot to another robot and I'm not a robot."

"No, you are not, Mr. Deaux. What I was saying was that my calculations regarding science are seldom if ever wrong. In fact, I seldom make a mathematical error."

Damn, this little puppet doctor is sure the hell full of himself. Son of a bitch likes to talk. But even so, he doesn't seem like an arrogant prick like all the other doctors I've ever met. No. He seems different. Maybe it's because he reminds me of Beaker. Funny. But it's true. You can't get mad at Beaker. Just let him talk. Let him know you're interested in everything he says. He'll give me all the answers I want if I just let him talk. He will eventually tell me about the other person. Just wait for it.

"Dr. Po. Just what kind of doctor are you?"

"I am unlike any other doctor you have ever met, John. I have Ph.D.s in Biodiversity and Conservation, Chemistry, Biochemistry, Physics, Microbiology, Molecular Biology, Electrical Engineering, Nuclear Engineering, and Structural Engineering. I also have medical degrees in Internal Medicine, Pathology, Radiation Oncology, Medical Oncology, and General, Orthopedic, and Neuro Surgery."

Shit.

"As I was beginning to explain earlier," Dr. Po continued, "our body is mostly water. Salty water. And that salty water in our body, along with our skin, is very conducive to electrical charges and moving them along throughout the body. Sweat helps that process. It spreads the electricity over a larger area, allowing more electrical current to enter the body."

"That's very interesting, Dr. Po, but what does this have to do with that question about the other person?"

"You know, John, because of the elements in your body, your sweat is unlike that of a normal human being. It is a very advanced mechanism that allows your body to regulate the environment you are in, as opposed to other humans where the environment prompts the body to react. That may seem like a trivial and irrational statement but it is not. And with the right structural enhancements, it could help you to survive. Actually, it has already helped you survive."

I can't keep this shit up. Regardless of how many Ph.D.s and medical degrees you have, Dr. capital P, little o, all this talk without answering the question, is really pissing me off.

"Why in the hell won't you answer my fucking question?"

"Do you not wonder why everyone calls you John Deaux?"

"Yeah, I did. I even asked Sam about it. She said she wasn't sure but she thought it was because I needed to maintain my anonymity."

"She was right. Let me read you something," the little doctor said as he drew an outline of a square in the air and pinched his right forefinger and thumb together. When he did, writing appeared in front of him.

"What the fuck?"

"It's my computer, John. It's with me wherever I am. It's a part of my body. But we can discuss that later. Like I said, let me read you this police report.

"April 26th, 2023. Called to home at 412 Tennessee Avenue, Erwin Tennessee. Received notification that a Jules Duggan called and stated that he had killed three people. Upon arriving at home, found the caller, a Mr. Jules Duggan, in the backyard. The head of his neighbor, a Mrs. Nancy Cunningham, was at his feet. Mr. Duggan rested his head on the shovel stating he would kill himself if we did not listen to his confession. He stated he killed his mother, father, and Mrs. Cunningham. Stated he and his sister were abused by parents. Officers subdued Mr. Duggan without incident upon hearing confession and retrieved sister,

Emily, from the kitchen. Sister tried to free Mr. Duggan from officer's custody and a fight ensued. Mr. Duggan broke the arm of one officer and the shoulder of the other officer that was holding him as he snapped the plastic handcuffs and tried to stop the officers from subduing his sister. Sister broke nose of one officer and the jaw of another officer. Sister bit off two fingers of the left hand of a third officer. Three officers took Mr. Duggan to the ground and his sister was shot with multiple shotguns, receiving lethal wounds to her abdomen and neck. In an attempt to reach his sister, Mr. Duggan broke free of the officers that had him on the ground. In doing so, the back of one officer was broken, the neck of another officer was broken, and a collapsed lung was incurred by the other officer. As Mr. Duggan ran to his sister, the threat was removed by several shots to his head; one of them fatal."

"Lethal wounds to her abdomen and neck and a fatal shot to my head?"

"Yes, that is correct, John. You received two shots to the head. One of them came through your neck and exited through your left jaw, shattering your mandible and removing your wisdom teeth, premolars, and molars. The other shot severed your brain stem, moved through a segment of your frontal lobe, and then exited from your parietal lobe. Though the officer was not aware of all the medical issues that resulted with the bullets that entered your head, he was correct in his assessment that one of them would be considered fatal."

"I don't understand what you are saying."

"The brain stem controls your breathing and heart rate. The frontal lobe is responsible for your cognitive function. The parietal lobe is responsible for movement and your sensory perception and ability. You should have been dead."

"Should have?"

"Yes, should have. But when they shocked you, trying to revive you, it triggered your body to do enough repair on its own that the brain stem was reconnected in a primitive manner. It was still functioning. At a very low level and with need of assistance, but still functioning."

"How is that possible?"

"How indeed," Dr. Po replied. "Perhaps if I continue?"

I nodded my head.

"Upon removing the threat of Jules and Emily Duggan, the murder scene revealed three victims. The parents, Buford and Mary Duggan and the neighbor, Mrs. Nancy Cunningham. Mrs. Duggan, the mother, appeared to have been killed due to strangulation. Mr. Duggan, the father, was killed by a decapitating blow to the head and Mrs. Cunningham died due to decapitation."

They got it wrong, but it doesn't matter. That asshole that they defined as a father wasn't ever a father and he wasn't killed by a decapitating blow to the head. His head was still intact when my sister put those coals in his eyes and mouth.

"Yes, I know, John. They didn't get everything correct in the report."

"How the hell do you know what I was just thinking?"

"I can read the EEG monitor that I developed. It's an enhanced version of the one that they use in hospitals and neurology offices. The undulating waves indicate your frustration with the description I just read, but let me continue.

"The murder weapon was determined to be a shovel used by Jules Duggan. The mother, Mary Duggan, died of strangulation but the fingerprints on the victim's neck do not coincide with Jules Duggan's assertion that he killed her. The fingerprints from the other victim, Mr. Buford Duggan, indicate that he killed his wife. Mr. Buford Duggan was found with the top of his head removed, from the same shovel that decapitated Mrs. Cunningham. In addition to the top of his head missing, once dead, his eyes and mouth were disfigured by burning charcoals that were placed into them."

"I find it very interesting that these reports show an equal level of sophistication and ignorance."

"What do you mean?" The letters hanging in the air disappeared as I watched Dr. Po tap his left-hand forefinger and thumb together.

"First of all, they were wrong about your neighbor, Mrs. Cunningham. She did not die of decapitation. She died of a pulmonary embolus. She was dead when you decided to remove her head from her body with that shovel. Second, they were correct in determining that your father strangled your mother but they failed to realize he was still alive when those charcoals were placed into his eyes and mouth. Also, if they had looked a little further, they would have seen that your father was in the end stage of pancreatic cancer. I'm not sure if the pain from the charcoals in his eyes and mouth would have been as painful as the last several days of his life would have been, but I am unable to test that theory. I doubt that he even knew he had weeks to live but that is also open to discussion."

"How do you know all this?"

"I examined Mrs. Cunningham and your father and mother and I saved you from the police, John."

"What the hell are you saying? Is that why my name is John Doe? I have to be hidden from the police? They can't know I am still alive?"

"Yes."

"Why"

"Because I knew one day you and I would be sitting here having this conversation. You have an option now, John. You can return to your life as Jules Duggan and probably spend twenty years of your life in jail for manslaughter, provided you get a good enough lawyer and I provide them access to my medical observations. Or you can accept the new life that I have given you as John Deaux."

"You didn't do all of this just because you got all those damn little letters after your name. What the fuck did you care all this time whether I lived or died?"

"Though full of anger, your observation is astute. I need you, John. I need the special body you possess and the abilities it provides you. You can help me correct some miscalculations that have occurred with the cures that took place several years ago. That, in fact, continue to occur even today. Regardless, your body's immunity, ability to heal, and especially its ability to demonstrate the highest level of Molecular Transition Dynamics, would enable me to execute those corrections."

Before I could answer, Dr. Po continued talking.

"You know, John, you and I share some similarities. Like you, I was unwanted by a parent. I did not suffer the abuse that you did though, as I never even knew my father. My mother discarded me just as she had done with other brothers and sisters that I will never know. She was a prostitute and I was an aborted fetus that somehow survived. I was found in a toilet and taken to Tulane University and there placed in the neonatal intensive care unit where I lived for a year before I became strong enough to survive without the aid of a respirator and twenty-four-hour nursing care.

"I was later adopted by a woman who was a doctor. A Professor of Molecular Biology. She saw something in me and I saw my future within her. Though physically restricted, she recognized that my brain was highly evolved and helped it progress. I owe everything to that woman. She saved my life and gave it purpose. I can do the same thing for you, John."

"I'm guessing it doesn't just involve me sitting here allowing you to study my body and its amazing analytes."

"Again, sarcastic in nature, but a perspicacious response. I need you to agree to help me with those medical miscalculations that have occurred."

"I thought you said I could go a lifetime without seeing you make a mathematical error."

"I did. And I didn't. But others did. Others discounted their arrogance and inability to resist financial pressures and ultimately ignored their sacred oath. They did not truly understand the science that I had developed or the medical cures that resulted from them. They failed to realize that human perfection doesn't exist. They failed to understand that within 10,000 cures there would be at least one that would not conform to the new science, even though I showed them time and time again that would occur. So, I left. As far as the ones that misused the science are concerned, just like you, John, I don't exist."

"Did you change your name too? Is Po just a variation of Doe?"

"You are a very interesting man, Mr. Deaux. I was always looking forward to the day you would awake. She said I would enjoy the first conversation we had. And she was right."

"Who the fuck are you talking about? And this time, don't go somewhere else in that cosmic universe you call your mind, in which we discuss my sweat or the side effects of my selenium or manganese levels."

"I am referring to the other witness at the incident on Tennessee Avenue."

"What other witness? What's her damn name?"

"Jane Deaux."

"John and Jane Doe. Fucking hilarious."

"Actually, it's not meant to be funny at all, John. Brothers and sisters should share the last name, don't you think?"

Chapter 6
In the same science class for the first time

Before I could move or say a word, I felt the liquid grip on my body. It wasn't like the other drug that sent me into the darkness but I was paralyzed. I yelled at my arms and legs to move but they would not listen to the words I could not speak nor the thoughts that echoed in my mind and bounced silently off a wall of neurons. I could still see and hear but I could not move any other muscle in my body.

"You are feeling the effects of the curare compound I developed, John. It is a paralytic agent that blocks the nicotinic acetylcholine receptor at the neuromuscular junction. Too much and you die from paralysis of your lungs. But if used in the proper amount, you have a compliant person in a hospital bed willing to listen. And in approximately 67 seconds, that person will have the ability to speak once again."

I watched the second hand of the clock on the wall at the end of my bed and after a minute, I tried to speak. It was just barely a whisper but as the time elapsed, I could form a sentence that Dr. Po could hear.

"My sister? You said she received lethal shots to her body. I saw them; all the holes in her body from the shotguns. How?"

"She is like you, John, and for both of you, lethal does not mean fatal. Her recovery was an easier task because the majority of her trauma was in her abdomen. Her intestinal tract and liver were injured but with the surgery I performed and her healing abilities, it didn't take long before she returned to normal. Though using the word 'normal' is truly irrelevant for the two of you.

"Plus, unlike you, she did not have a severed brainstem. Nevertheless, she has developed into quite an amazing woman. Though anyone would be limited somewhat in understanding how extraordinary that statement is by just observing her from a physical perspective."

"Can I see her?"

"I believe she has been waiting for you to ask that."

As soon as Dr. Po finished his sentence, the doors opened and a woman walked in wearing a brown and green form-fitting suit. What I saw was almost as paralyzing as the drug that circulated in my body. My sister was no longer just my little sister. She was a beautiful young woman who smiled at the sight of me. My vision blurred from the tears in my eyes and I watched her grab a tissue and felt her tenderly wiping them away. I looked into her face and I did not see any tears in her eyes. She looked at me with care, but there was something different in those eyes that looked down at me. I saw no fear; only strength and confidence in eyes the color of a cedar chest.

Her hair was short and brown. *Damn, just like Julie Andrews* I thought. She had the round nose and lips of our mother and was just as pretty as she had been before life and our father wore her down. She was taller than our mother though, at least six feet tall and her body was muscular and lean. Her entire body exuded a resolute self-assurance and I felt somewhat shocked by the transformation.

"Hello, John."

"Emily. My God! I can't believe I'm seeing you, talking with you. Oh, my God, you look amazing!"

Yeah. I said amazing, Dr. Po. I can't help it. She truly looks amazing.

"It's Jane, John. Emily died several years ago. Just as Jules did. See, look at your wristband," she said as she held up my hand.

I saw the name on the wristband. It read John Deaux with a barcode under it.

"And all this time, I thought it was just plain old John Doe."

My sister smiled.

Man, I've missed that smile. What's my EEG doing now, Dr. Po? The squiggly lines are spelling happy, aren't they?

"Tell me how you've been, Emily. I never thought this day would happen. I still feel like I'm dreaming. Am I dreaming, Emily? I still feel like we're on the Haunted House ride at the fair. You and me and Mom."

"Please don't call me Emily, John. I know you're trying to process everything and there is so much to understand, but don't ever call me Emily again. Emily doesn't exist. Our life together starts now. Jane and John Deaux. Sister and brother. Listen to Dr. Po. He'll tell you what has happened since we've been apart and how we can both help him now. I've been waiting for two years to be here with you and have my brother with me again. I have missed him so much."

I nodded and realized I was beginning to regain the ability to move my muscles, but I also understood I needed to just lay there and listen to my sister and Dr. Po. She wanted me to listen and I would do that for her. At least for now.

"Thank you, Jane. Let me try and explain everything to you, John. Some time ago, I developed a cure for cancer. The Symbion molecule that I created enabled the science that I advanced to achieve those and other types of cures. But the Symbion molecule was just one component of that science. I was, and am still, also the only scientist who can grow a bacterium that permits the tubeworm to exist in volcanoes on the floor of the ocean. Without this bacterium, the tubeworm cannot digest nutrients. It was unnamed until I grew it in my laboratory. I named it after the woman who gave birth to me. It is called Dahliarium."

Shit. What does this have to do with curing cancer? Just listen. Look at your sister. It's like she is watching "The Sound of Music." You can do this for her now. You did it for her for so many years.

"Cancer cells secrete cytokines which develop blood vessels, a process called angiogenesis. It's what allows the tumor to proliferate. It is like a parasite. That analogy is what allowed me to see cancer in a completely different manner. Like a parasite, cancer is always hungry. Instead of a symbiotic relationship with its host, it is willing to kill the host in order for it to survive. Unaware that by killing the host it will also die. It is that blind awareness that enables us to bring about their early demise. But I am getting ahead of myself.

"In the past, we used chemotherapy and radiation therapy, along with surgery in some cases, to eliminate the tumor but it was not always successful. And with leukemias, there are not any large tumors, just cancer cells circulating in the body. But I saw them as the same. In my mind, they were just single-cell parasites.

"Were you aware of the level of radiation found in the bodies at ground zero in Hiroshima, John?"

"No, but I have a feeling you're going to tell me about it."

"9.46 Gray whole-body radiation. Four to five Gray will kill you and it was double that. I am glad their bodies disintegrated because the agony they would have endured from that level of radiation would have been akin to the medieval-like torture of those acting under the pretext of holiness when it was as sadistic and demonic as hell itself."

"Familiar with hell and demons are you, Doc?"

"There are many kinds of hell, John, and many kinds of demons. You of all people should understand that."

I glanced at my sister who was now sitting there staring at me. The woman I saw didn't react at all to the word demon though I knew she had been tortured by one almost her entire life.

She seems like she's immune to the word or to those thoughts now. How is that possible? Hell, you need to focus. He's still talking.

"But radiation science took giant strides over time. Before I altered the protocols, doctors were delivering as much as 55 Gray in a thread-size beam to millimeter-sized tumors in the lungs or brain, killing the tumor and minimizing the death of the tissue around that tumor. Even so, depending on the type of lung or brain cancer, and the extent of the tumor, some of that radiation was only done to improve the quality of life for a short period as opposed to realizing a cure.

"This is where my science of Molecular Transition Dynamics becomes relevant. Once I was able to grow the Dahliarium in my laboratory and alter its composition with the Symbion molecule, I was able to create a heat-loving bacteria that had the genetic properties of macrophages and granulocytes within the human body. Those are the white cells or immune cells that attack the 'microbial invaders' in our body. As such, the Dahliarium moved throughout the patient's bloodstream without concern from the body's guardians, because its cellular composition reflected the guardian's structure."

My sister looks interested in all this stuff he is saying. How in the hell did that happen? I haven't heard him mention Tahiti or London or...

"You look puzzled, John? Do you understand what I'm saying?"

"Yeah. I got it. The Dalai llama bacteria looked like a white blood cell to the body so the body didn't attack it."

"Dahliarium, but excellent, John. Your comprehension is concise and correct. So, let me continue. Knowing that solid-state tumors lured our immune cells to their ever-expanding vascular network for nutrients, I knew that they would attract these altered cells but I also wanted to get the Dahliarium to seek out and digest the tumor in a similar fashion as they did in order for the tubeworms in the ocean to survive. Therefore, I needed to make the tumor site or area of genesis, 'hot.' With the radiation protocols I developed, we widened the beam of radiation and increased the amount of radiation to 75 Gray within the body and lymph nodes, and up to 100 Gray for total marrow radiation for some leukemias.

"When I did that, it was like a magnet had been created between the cancer and the Symbion enhanced Dahliarium. The tumor attracted what they recognized as immune cells, and the modified Dahliarium was attracted to the 'hot zone' in their new environment. This new Dahliarium attacked the radiated tumor and cancer cells in the body or bone marrow with vigor and destroyed them. But there was an issue.

"Once the tumor was destroyed, I knew that the enriched Dahliarium would continue to digest the body's cells unless I could find a way to destroy them. Depending on the cancer, its location, and its metastatic nature, I developed protocols for the strength and duration of the radiation and the amount of Symbion-Dahliarium injected into the body.

"And then perhaps the most important phase of the cure and the key to survival: I created the protocol and equipment for exposing the body to profound hypothermia through central venous catheters with saline cooled to 23.5 degrees Celsius, or 74.3 degrees Fahrenheit. By doing this, the Symbion-Dahliarium is destroyed after it has eradicated the cancer. Then, all those dead cellular components are removed from the body with an enhanced dialysis system that I also designed, so that the body's own removal mechanisms would not be overtaxed.

"But, and this is critical, all of these protocols could not be altered in any way because if you did, the mutations — the defects would occur at an even higher rate than expected. Because they always occur. As I stated earlier, 1 in 10,000. But with any alteration in protocols that number would increase sometimes ten to twentyfold. Even though I warned them repeatedly, they didn't listen. They altered the protocols. They shortened them in order to treat more patients under the guise of therapeutic and life-saving medicine when corporate or individual financial outcomes were what actually drove their decision-making process."

"Them being other doctors, right? So, in other words, the doctors fucked things up. Shit, I thought you said things have changed for the better," I said.

"Things have changed, John," my sister answered in an angry tone that got my attention real fast. She scowled at me and I don't think I had ever seen her scowl at me. "Just listen a little more to Dr. Po. Please, just listen."

I nodded my head and Dr. Po continued.

"Things have changed for the better, John. We did actually cure cancer, and you cannot ignore that fact. Life for millions was improved. Children no longer had to die from cancer. But there were problems."

"The defects that you mentioned?"

"Yes. They are quite troublesome."

"When you say they, do you mean, the defects are humans of some kind?"

"They were once human but they are no longer. They have a hunger and lust that at times makes them blind to their environment. Though some are quite good at the art of camouflage.

"They are all violent and insatiable carnivores and very dangerous. So, I needed to create a being that could track and stalk these misguided creatures. I did that with your sister and I am certain I can also do that with you."

"What the hell are you talking about? You want me to become some sort of zombie killer?"

"These creatures are not zombies, John. They are not created from the dead. They are created from the living due to scientific misjudgments."

"Scientific misjudgments? Bullshit. That's a nice way of saying doctors fucking things up and not understanding what different means."

"I understand your cynicism, John, but with the science I have developed and the unique characteristics of your body, I can make you a very efficient hunter. The Symbion molecule I developed has other unique characteristics besides enabling me to cure cancers. It has the ability to create bonds that were never thought possible and has reshaped the understanding of cellular science.

"If exposed to a high energy electromagnetic field, within a very metallic environment, the double helix DNA molecule can be transformed into supercharged cylinders ready to transport and accept the new energy that the Symbion molecule provides to it. That molecule affixes itself to the energy units - the mitochondria, Golgi, and endoplasmic reticulum, found in all types of animal, plant, or fungi cells. And thus, once activated, these supercharged cylinders provide energy and healing properties to a being that already possesses superior energy and healing properties."

What the hell? I looked at my sister again but her eyes were transfixed on the doctor. *Shit. Just keep listening.*

"Do you remember what happened when you were being tased by the police officers?"

I didn't reply but I could remember the energy surges going through my body. *Oh shit. Is he about to say what I think he's about to say?*

"You felt the energy pulsing through your body because of the composition of your plasma. It was like plugging your body into an electrical socket and turning it on. You snapped the plastic handcuffs and threw the policemen off of you like they were weightless beings. Do you remember the electrical pulses going through your body while you slept?

"How do you know that?"

"Remember, John, I can see what your brain waves are doing. I can imagine you were in darkness seeing lightning all around you, at times shocking your body. That was your body feeling the effect of the defibrillator at first and then the electrical pulses I sent through you in a more consistent and less harsh manner, to help your body heal."

This isn't possible.

"Your eyes and brain are saying it is not possible, but it is. And with a surgical device that I can implant in you, I can enable you to access that energy anytime you need it. That device is a Symbion umbilical cord. Think of it as a universal energy plug. The Symbion molecules will appear to melt into whatever it is affixed to and once fused, break apart the cells in rapid fashion so that all that energy is provided to you."

"Shit. This isn't some damn hospital. It's a fucking insane asylum. And I'm just some nut-job that woke up by mistake. I'm dreaming. So just turn on the juice, Beaker, and send me back into the darkness."

"You don't trust people, John, because you have only seen the worst that life has to offer. But humans have redeeming qualities. Think about your mother. She wasn't perfect but she tried. She tried to protect you and your sister to the best of her ability but it wasn't enough. I think in time, I can make you trust people again. I can give you back a life with your sister. It will be a much different life, but you will be making a difference."

Upon saying that, the puppet doctor that I had been talking to lowered his chair and was lifted forward until his feet touched the ground. I watched him push a button on the arm of the chair and saw it start to move and disassemble itself until it was small enough for him to carry like a book.

"I am the only one who can activate that chair. Even if they could fit in it, I don't like people sitting in my chair and I abhor sitting in other chairs. I don't like sitting in the microbial stew that is created by their anus, dirt, and sweat."

He started to leave but turned to me and smiled. At least, I thought it was some sort of smile.

"The Symbion molecule has many unique properties. It has the capacity to act like all the cellular components within a eukaryotic cell and transition them into another host body. On an atomic level, depending on the environment, it can create bonds that were never thought capable of being formed. It changed the foundation of biological, biochemical, and molecular science but they, and they being some but not all of the other doctors, were unable to see that. Because I lost my trust in medicine as it was being practiced in some very large and prestigious facilities, I removed myself from that environment and started to keep all my scientific knowledge and creations to myself. It saddens me to see that my apprehensions were reflective of the truth. It was a justifiable distrust, John, not unlike your own.

"The medical community referred to me as a mutant, which was a convenient way to dismiss my achievements and accomplishments. It allowed them to preserve their ego when confronted with my list of degrees. They could say it wasn't possible for any human to do that rather than to admit that a man of very small stature did. To say that such learned individuals are devoid of ignorance would be a misstatement. But enough is enough. I know I have bombarded you with a lot of scientific data, but if I am correct, I believe you have the ability to understand all of the monumental changes that have occurred. Nevertheless, you need time with your sister.

"Enjoy the time with her. She will let me know how to proceed from here. It was a pleasure talking to you, John. I know science classes can be quite dull sometimes but I hope this particular one wasn't that way for you. And please know, I am so very sorry, I wasn't able to save Billy."

As the little man left the room, I wanted to stop him but he was gone before I could.

"What did he mean he couldn't save Billy?"

"Dr. Po created many cures, John. He created one for sickle cell anemia but not in time to help your friend. It bothers him still today."

As I processed those words, I leaned over and asked my sister for a drink of water. I drank the entire glass and then asked, "So, can you help me get out of here? I don't think having some umbilical cord attached to me is something I want to do. And I sure wasn't put here on this planet to fix the mistakes of doctors. Hell, I tried to fix them a long time ago but no one listened. Damn. Doctor Po is a talker, isn't he? Granted he seems to know a lot, but hell; I did this, I made this, I created that. Okay, I get it. You're very smart."

"John, you're being overly dismissive of probably the most significant change within medicine."

There's that scowl again. I have never heard her so forceful in her words. She certainly believes in this little man. Shit. He cured cancer and sickle cell anemia for Christ's sake! You are a dumbass and allowing all your prejudices about doctors to make you blind. Wake the fuck up. Hell, he has his own collapsible chair because he doesn't like sitting in other people's germs. You gotta admit, you wish you had one of those.

"I'm sorry, sis. I am thankful he tried to help Billy. No one else really did. Though everything he said could have just been a pile of bullshit. I would never know."

"It's not bullshit, John," my sister said as she lifted up her top to show me the implant on her abdomen.

"Is that one of those Symbion umbilical cords?"

"Yes."

"And it does what he says it will do?"

"Yes."

"Shit. It all seems too impossible to believe, Emily, I mean, Jane. Not real. More fiction than science. I was dead. You were dead. And now, this?"

"If you don't do what Dr. Po asks, I'm not sure when I will see you again. It may be two years. It may be ten years. And I'll be coming to visit you in a prison. I would hate to see my brother in prison. And a lot can happen in that amount of time. Science and technology change so much every day. Dr. Po ensures it changes. He says if it remains static, we will all die."

As I looked at my sister, I saw a shadowy image of our father standing beside her. I heard him calling her names. Telling me that I was a bigger fool than he thought if I listened to her. That I would truly become the crazy child that he had told my mother I had always been. And that's when I laughed. In my mind, I was laughing so hard my sides hurt. I laughed as I listened to his raspy voice created by the hole in his throat and looked at the black holes in his head that were once his eyes.

"I bet that hurt like a son of a bitch," I said as I smiled.

"I didn't even feel it," my sister replied.

I turned to my sister when she said that and realized that she thought I was talking to her.

I looked back at the ghostly image of our father and smiled again as I spoke the words "I'll help you, Jane" and heard the raspy voice of our father say, *Fucking dumbass.*

"I've waited a long time to see my brother's smile again," my sister said as she hugged me. She sat and held my hand and told me about all the changes in the world and how strong she had become and how much she had learned from Dr. Po. As she talked, I realized that she never mentioned any of those mutations that Dr. Po had discussed, but I suppose that the good doctor had cautioned her not to at this point in our relationship.

I enjoyed listening to her. Sometimes, I'm not even sure I heard the words but it didn't matter. I heard her voice and as far as I was concerned, we were back at the fair with our mother. And this time, I wasn't afraid about going home.

I enjoyed the idea of pissing off the ghost of our father that was no longer there, but I knew he would be back. As I continued to listen, I came to realize that by helping her, I would be doing something my mother wanted. I would be there for my sister. I liked knowing I would have the chance to do that.

"So, what kind of music do you listen to these days?"

"Glad you asked," she said as she pressed a device in her ear. As soon as she did, Black Sabbath's "Children of the Grave" blared over the speakers in my room.

The music vibrated my whole body and I laughed. Though Dr. Po said that Emily and Jules would no longer exist, I knew he was wrong. You don't ever forget your past. It shapes the way you are, one way or another. What Dr. Po was asking me to do was to go into the Haunted House ride with my sister again. Over and over. Everyday. That in itself would have been enough, but considering he had found a cure for sickle cell anemia and was actually sorry about not being able to save my friend Billy, it was like getting to ride for free. For the first time in a very long time, I looked forward to tomorrow.

Chapter 7
Jack

My sister left a little after midnight. We talked for almost five hours and I can't think of one moment that I didn't enjoy listening to her. She had a real cheeseburger and cheddar cheese chili fries and a milkshake with me. She still preferred chocolate milkshakes and it was good to see that hadn't changed. After dinner, we talked about candied apples, cotton candy, funnel cakes, caramel popcorn, and everything else we enjoyed when we had gone to the fair. I didn't want her to leave but she said she needed to and that she would see me tomorrow. Just before she walked out the door, I told her I was sorry.

She looked at me and said that I didn't have to be sorry. Ever. That world was gone and I didn't need to dwell on it. I nodded my head and told her I loved her and she said she loved me and was so excited to have me back in her life. I'm not sure what other things Dr. Po did for my sister, but I was amazed by the self-confidence that he had produced in her. Shit. Po was right. It was very difficult to get away from using the word amazing and then I laughed out loud. About ten minutes later, I closed my eyes as a warm feeling spread through my body and was soon asleep.

I dreamed about Billy and remembered how much fun we had just tossing the football back and forth on days he felt well enough to play. I then heard Dr. Po's apology again and even heard him telling Billy he was sorry, though he wasn't there anywhere on the field. It didn't matter. Billy told him that everything was good and that he was glad I was now back with my sister. Billy looked at me and said he hoped we would enjoy a much better life now and then he disappeared.

I called out to him but I knew he wasn't coming back and I found myself sitting on the bleachers thinking about everything Dr. Po had said.

I realized I had never heard a doctor apologize before or say he distrusted physicians and I was thinking about that when I heard someone ask me a question. I turned around to see a man standing behind me.

"Hello. Mind if sit with you for a while?"

I didn't know who the man was but he seemed nice. He looked to be in his fifties and his hair was beginning to thin. But he had a wonderful smile and tone of voice and an accent that I had not heard before.

"No. I don't mind. Free country."

"Thank you and you are right. It is free indeed. My name is Jack, Jack Lewis. I haven't seen you at this field before."

"I came here as a young boy, but I'm not a young boy anymore."

"No, you're not a young boy anymore. But I am not sure you ever were. You know, I lost my mother to cancer when I was only nine years old. I never got over it, completely. It probably had something to do with my doubting God existed. He never seemed to be listening to me."

"Do we know each other?"

"We do. Your name is Jules Duggan, correct?"

I nodded my head.

"Why don't I remember you?"

"It wouldn't be unexpected for you to not remember, considering the trauma you encountered. I have learned now that while those who speak about one's miseries usually hurt, those who keep silence hurt more."

Damn. I know those words.

"C.S. Lewis. You are C.S. Lewis."

"My friends call me Jack."

"I always dreamed about talking to you."

"This is a dream, isn't it?"

"Yes. At least I think so."

"Then I suppose your dreams have been answered."

"Perhaps, but I never expected them to be answered now. But as I think about what I just said, I realize, I don't know when I expected those conversations to ever happen. I think it was just something I said, knowing it would never really happen. I suppose I sort of had those conversations without you, with me being you and me being me, if that makes any sense."

"It makes perfect sense. It's just a way in which your brain works out problems. It works differently for other people but what you just said is logical."

"But now here you are. I am staring at you. Well, I'm not staring, or at least I hope I'm not staring. Really, Mr. Lewis, I don't know what to say. You have me at a loss for words, which many folks would say was quite an accomplishment. Do you visit other people in their dreams?"

"Yes, on occasion. The manifestation occurs because of the person, not me. I was blessed to have been given a voice that resonated with many people."

"Have you ever met Dr. Po?"

"No, I have never met him."

"He's a doctor and a scientist who has kept me alive for over two years. Saved my sister too, after our mother died."

"Yes, it must have been horrible to witness that. My father wasn't a bad man. But we weren't extremely close as a father and son should be. There was always some distance between us. I think it was because he wasn't sure how to raise two young boys on his own."

"I wish there had been more distance between my father and us. My mother and sister didn't deserve his abuse."

"You are correct. No child should ever be abused, be it by a parent or any other person. The cowardly acts that one sees and feels occurring to them make them question their religious tenets. In fact, many use pain as a way to remove God from their life. I know because I did. Thankfully, he returned to my life, but it was still not a life without pain.

"Also, do you realize there was something very interesting in what you just said? You said your mother and sister didn't deserve the abuse. Yet you were abused too. Do you believe the pain you received was justified?"

"No, not at all. I'm actually surprised I didn't kill my father much earlier in life or hurt other people."

"Yet you didn't. Though you certainly did put a scare once or twice into a few teachers and doctors," the kind man said as he winked at me before he continued to talk.

"You were a good son and brother during that entire time. You were also a good friend to those that were able to break through the defensive barriers you put up. You did lash out at your father but considering that you just saw him kill your mother and with all of the years of abuse you endured, your actions were understandable. Mind you though, I am not justifying those actions or condoning or condemning them. I am merely stating it would not be an unexpected reaction by a young boy of your age considering the circumstances.

"Even after your father's death, you tried to protect your sister from suffering anymore and that was indeed a very noble act. I would suggest to you, at that point in time, you were closer to God than you knew."

"Are you saying that believing in God means you must believe in pain and torture?"

"Pain is inescapable within life. It creates doubt and sometimes undermines the believer's faith. It gives atheism a crutch to lean upon. It supplies fuel for the fire of those that subscribe to evil. But without evil or pain, there is no God or goodness. Life is indeed a difficult road to navigate and the knowledge that wisdom provides us is at times nothing more than a reason for us to lash out at the heavens. For some, they yell and don't wait for an answer. For others, they hear a voice that comforts them."

"I haven't heard a voice that comforts me."

"I would argue that point. The voice of your mother comforted you many times. The love from your sister propped you up when you were falling. Your friend Billy made you happy and you suffered because he suffered. You understood his pain. As God understands our pain. In many ways, you were filled with the Holy Spirit, only to deny its existence. I was the same way for a long time.

"Just a moment ago, I told you I lost my mother to cancer. I also lost my wife to cancer. Her absence left a void in my life that remained until I died. That void caused pain at times, but also made it possible for me to come even closer to God. You see, I never sought out God to get a reward. I only wanted to know the goodness and the truth. He provided that to me. It was one of the greatest mercies he bestowed upon me."

"I believe Dr. Po wants to turn me into some killer. To hunt down some ungodly mutations. You think that is God's will?"

"If we find ourselves with a desire that nothing in this world can satisfy, the most probable explanation is that we were made for another world."

"You speak in riddles sometimes."

"I don't ever mean to, but I think at times, people hear what they want to hear. Sometimes the truth. Sometimes confusion. Either way, your free will dictates what you hear."

"You talk about free will a lot. It doesn't seem like I had any choice in things at all. I didn't want to live in an abusive home. I didn't want doctors to examine me and tell my father he was right, that I was just different and had unresolved anger issues. I didn't want to see my mother and sister abused. I didn't want to see my friend suffer. And now it looks like I am in some sort of chemistry and biology experiment just because I have very high selenium and manganese levels in my blood. How is that free will?"

"You had choices all along the way, John. You could have run away but you didn't. You could have harmed yourself, but you didn't. You could have harmed others, but you didn't. You can get out of this bed tomorrow and go to jail for the next twenty years, but you have decided to stay. Is that not free will?

"I saw nothing in my life that demonstrated to me that anything we do will eradicate suffering. If a thing is free to be good, it is also free to be bad. And free will is what has made evil possible. Why then did God give us free will? Because free will, though it makes evil possible, is also the only thing that makes possible any love or goodness or joy worth having.

"Here, I brought you something, John. They are two books that no matter how many times I read them I always find that I learn something new. They will help you as you navigate through this very difficult but, oh so wondrous, world."

I took the books and looked at them. One of them was the Bible and the other was a journal on Molecular Transition Dynamics.

"I thought you said you didn't know Dr. Po."

"I said I never met him. But I have read this journal seven times. I need help understanding what he's saying, but there are numerous scientists around that I can ask for assistance in interpreting what is written. They all say he is a genius who comes along on this earth only once every hundred years or so. They tell me the science he has developed has and will continue to change the world."

"He purposefully left some information out, you know."

"Interesting. I will need to let some of my friends know that. I am certain that will lead to a very interesting and spirited discussion. Oh, how I so enjoy those."

"I'm not sure I want to be a killer. I want to protect my sister and I'm not sure I'll ever be able to forgive myself for allowing what occurred to her and my mother."

"There are two kinds of people in the end: those who say to God, 'Thy will be done,' and those to whom God says, 'Thy will be done.' All that are in Hell, choose it. Without that self-choice, there could be no Hell. No soul that seriously and constantly desires joy will ever miss it. Those who seek find. For those who knock, it is opened. If you ask for forgiveness, John, it will be provided to you."

"I'll still be haunted by my past, won't I?"

"Your past is part of the present and part of the future. You are never without it."

"You should consider being a writer. You have a way with words."

"Yes, I will give your suggestion a great deal of consideration," Jack said as he smiled and winked again just before he stood up.

"Good luck, John. Remember eukaryotic organisms have cells with a cellular membrane and a nucleus and organelles. Prokaryotic organisms have cells with a cellular membrane but are devoid of a nucleus and any organelles. If you don't understand that basic premise, you will be lost."

"What?"

"Chapter one in Dr. Po's book. Start reading it. I think you will understand more than I ever will and I even suspect that you will find it fascinating. And refer to the other book too. It will help you. Though you will think it speaks in riddles sometimes, it doesn't. The truth is within the words. Sometimes it just takes some effort to find it. It is well worth the effort. Believe a former non-believer. They often speak with greater understanding because they have cursed the pain and rather than avoid it, they have embraced its existence, with the knowledge that there is more good than evil within the world. And within man."

I watched Jack walk off the bleachers and as soon as he stepped onto the ground he disappeared. I opened Dr. Po's book and began reading about the endoplasmic reticulum, Golgi bodies, and mitochondria. As Jack said, the science was indeed fascinating. I could only think about one word as I thought about my conversation with Jack and with what I was now reading. Amazing.

Chapter 8
A different perspective

"Good morning, Mr. Deaux," a female voice called out when I opened my eyes.

I could see that I was no longer in the hospital room and was now lying on a large king-size bed made from some dark wood. I felt like I was floating on air and as I became more awake, I sensed that my body was settling down into the mattress.

I looked around the room and noticed the walls looked like a blue sky with a few clouds floating against it. The dresser and bedside tables were all made of the same wood as the bed. There were no lamps on the bedside tables but there was so much light coming from the walls no other lights were needed.

"You had eight REMs during your rest period. That is excellent. Your pulse is 60, blood pressure is 110 over 70 and your O-2 saturation is 100%. All excellent. Are you ready to shower and dress?" the voice asked. "Dr. Po and your sister have already awakened and are waiting for you down in the main room of this resting quadrant."

Resting quadrant. What the hell does that mean?

"Who is talking to me? And where the hell am I?"

"I am one of the monitors within Dr. Po's residence. Just think of me as a computer that is integrated into the matrix of the environment in which you now find yourself. I have been given the name Emily. I am told it is a name familiar to you."

"Yeah, I'm familiar with it."

"Very good then. The shower has been turned on and it is a perfect 33.3 degrees Celsius. The antimicrobial soap is embedded within the water so you have no need to look for a cleansing solution. There is a disposable washcloth on the counter next to the shower. Once used, please place it in the bin marked waste. The oral hygiene materials are sealed and can be found in the cabinet behind the mirror over the sink."

"I don't like sitting in the microbial stew that is created by their anus, dirt, and sweat." I remember the little man saying those words. I think I'm going to like this part of my 'new environment.' He really understands what good hygiene means. I like the way this is going although it is weird talking to someone who isn't here. Says, the man that just spent an evening talking to C. S. Lewis. Okay, okay. Talking to a computer. That's weird, but at least she has a good name.

"Just place the sleeping wear in the disinfectant cabinet in the bathroom. They will be cleaned and ready for you this evening. Is there anything you need before you begin to shower?"

"How do you clean the pj's or as you call them the 'sleeping wear?' And how long have I been sleeping?"

"With ultraviolet rays. You arrived here at 3 a.m. and it is now 11:01 a.m."

Damn. They must have zapped me with some good sedatives. It was cool talking with Jack though. And I'm really looking forward to talking to Dr. Po about Molecular Transition Dynamics. But wait a minute. You didn't read that book. It was just a dream. You were just going over everything he discussed with you. But Jack was right. I do want to read it. Probably wouldn't be a bad idea to open up the other book that Jack suggested too. You need to read it at least once.

"Cool, Emily."

"To what temperature would you like the room cooled?"

"No, the room temperature is fine. Just never mind that last comment. I am assuming the clothes for me are in the dresser?"

"Yes, please note I have activated the cabinet display so that the wood grain is now clear. You can see the articles of clothing that are in each level of the cabinet."

"Damn. That's cool. I mean, never mind. The temperature is fine. Thank you, Emily. I'll take a shower and then get dressed. By the way, are there monitors in the bathroom too?"

"Yes. I am required to watch at all times to ensure that no harm comes to you and that everything is operational."

"How old are you, Emily?"

"I do not understand the question. I have no age. I simply am."

"Yeah, it probably doesn't matter. Compared to showering with a bunch of men, I'm sure I can handle this."

"Dr. Po does not allow more than one person within the cleaning area."

Of course, he doesn't. Makes perfect sense from a good hygiene perspective.

"Do you require any other information, Mr. Deaux?"

"No. Thank you."

"I am here when you need me."

The bathroom tile floor lit up and lights glowed from the tile shower walls as I entered. The disinfectant cabinet on the wall across from the shower looked like a large microwave and I placed my pajamas in it. A locking mechanism engaged and the cabinet began to glow purple.

The shower felt wonderful. *It should have* I thought. "You haven't had one in over two years," I said out loud and chortled. As I washed, I noticed my body had indeed grown muscle mass as Sam had mentioned. I also could find no scars anywhere on my body.

How in the hell is that possible? Is Po that good? Maybe there is something to all this stuff he's been telling me. We'll see.

The shower felt so refreshing that I didn't want to leave but then I suddenly realized I had not seen my face and my curiosity regarding that feature of my body brought the shower to an end.

The water turned off when I stepped out of the shower and I was exposed to warm radiant heat that covered me in soft waves from every part of the room. Within a minute I was completely dry and I walked over to the sink and looked in the mirror. The lighting over the mirror turned on automatically and lit up the image that I had not seen for a long time.

I didn't even recognize the person looking back at me. His hair was cut so short that it looked just like brown stubble. The person in the mirror was a man and not a teenager anymore. I don't remember my eyes being that brown either, and my nose and mouth looked different too.

How could that be I asked and then I remembered Dr. Po saying that I had been shot twice in the head and one of the bullets shattered my jaw and removed some of my teeth. "Reconstructive surgery," I whispered as I felt my face for scars but I could neither see nor feel any. There was no evidence of a hole in my head either and nothing that I could see in my arm though I remembered the bullet going through my arm.

That night that I died. How is all of this possible? I know what Dr. Po said but it just seems like I have woken up in another world. Maybe I have.

When I returned to the bedroom, I could see the various items of clothing through the cabinet door and selected what I wanted. After dressing, I watched as the clear drawers regained their dark wood appearance and I just shook my head and grinned. When I walked toward the walls, the sky disappeared and dissolved into nothing so that it was as if I was looking through a large store display window.

What the hell?

I found myself now looking down into a maze of shrubs and plants that resembled hands with large fingers of thick hedges, and trees with streams that formed the creases between the green appendages. I could even hear the streams flowing and see small caps of white water, but no matter how hard I looked I could not find the source of the water. The streams flowed back and forth under dense growth only to emerge next to the dark green "palm of the hand" before the water became a small waterfall that seemed to fall into a moat beside the house and had no beginning nor end.

"I don't recognize those plants," I whispered and immediately received a response from Emily.

"They are Dr. Po's creation. He refers to the science of their propagation and development as Botanimy. It is recommended that you do not aggravate or brush up against them."

"Botanimy? Damn. Is anything around here just called normal shit?"

"Yes. Normal fecal matter can be referred to as normal shit. I have heard Jane say that on numerous occasions as she flushed the toilet."

"I'm guessing Dr. Po analyzes the shit, or fecal matter, doesn't he?"

"All fecal matter is assessed for biological and chemical content."

Of course, it is. "Don't aggravate the plants, huh?"

"Yes, that is the recommendation from Dr. Po. Some of the thorns on them can cause serious infections, even death."

"Good to know, Emily. Thank You. Now, where do I go from here?"

"To join your sister and Dr. Po, exit the room and turn to your right. Go down the hallway until you come to the stairs. As you are walking down the hall, you will be able to see the area in which they are seated. This section of the house is much like a square with sleeping quarters on the upper level, surrounding the central seating area."

"Thank you, Emily. I look forward to knowing how my pee looks."

"It is amber, with a PH of 7.5. Specific gravity 1.015. Protein and glucose normal. No ketones. Negative leukocyte esterase. No microscopic abnormality detected."

"Shit."

"No sample obtained."

"Don't worry. I'm sure I won't disappoint you later."

The hallway was constructed of wood and stone and as I walked, lights engaged at certain points from the stone, emanating a soft glow onto the dark oak floors. I soon saw the center room below and the square shape of the area Emily had referenced. Dr. Po and my sister were sitting there in leather chairs and I heard my sister call out.

"Sleeping awfully late, John. But I understand that you had a good rest. Dr. Po was just telling me about it."

"Did he tell you about my pee too?" I asked as I walked down the steps and over to her.

She looked even more muscular than she had in the hospital room as I gave her a hug. I couldn't get over the look in her eyes. What were once vacant parts of her face that suggested a suicidal tendency, were now a beautiful cedar chest color that indicated someone who was much more confident. She almost seemed defiant in the way she looked at me. I sat down next to her and looked at Dr. Po.

Though his eyes were still red, I could now see that was due to the glasses he was wearing. His hair was thick and shiny black and even with those glasses covering his eyes, his face appeared to be oriental in origin. His body looked frail but there was nothing to imply that any of his limbs were impaired.

It's just the smallness of his body. That's what suggests the frail nature.

"I did not discuss the characteristics of your urine with your sister and though I understand you asked the question sarcastically we can discuss it if you so desire."

"No, Doc. I have too many other questions. Your science class the other evening has really got me intrigued. I haven't had much to talk about for the past two years so I would like to get caught up on some things."

"Certainly. I knew you would be very inquisitive this morning. I would think you are hungry too. Would you like something to eat?"

"Sure. what do you have?"

"Anything you would like."

"How about a cheeseburger and a strawberry milkshake?"

"You certainly like that type of food, don't you? But yes, that is doable. Marie, can you initiate Mr. Deaux's request?"

I looked around to see who Dr. Po was talking to but didn't see anyone.

"Marie is my personal assistant, John. She is the main computer system for this facility. I named her after my mother. The kitchen is actually more reflective of an automobile assembly line but it is quite efficient and effective. She tells me your meal will be ready in twenty minutes. Would you like anything, Jane? I am sorry I didn't ask."

"Just one of your protein concoctions, Doctor Po."

"So, Doc, are you some kind of half-human, half-robot thing like a cyborg?"

"Heavens, no! I am very human, though I understand how my appearance and conversation with Marie might make it seem otherwise. But Marie is just a computer, one that enables me to be here even though I am not here."

"What the hell does that mean?"

"It means that right now I'm just a computer image. I'm not in the room with you and your sister. I'm afraid it would be too dangerous for me."

I got up and tried to touch him. My hands and arm went right through his body as if I was pushing them through an image made of smoke.

"Damn! That's pretty cool. But wait a minute. You just said it was too dangerous for you to be here. Why in the hell would you say that?"

"Because you and your sister are being watched."

Chapter 9
An unfair encounter

I looked nervously around the room as I heard the Casper version of Dr. Po explain. "You won't see them, John. You won't see them until they want you to. They have adapted to their condition quite well and have become almost invisible as they seek out relief from the hunger their deficiencies create. "

"I suppose this is one of those mutations you were talking about the other evening. One of those mistakes the other doctors made, but you didn't."

"That is correct. This is a cancer patient who has become something that has created a reality out of a Bram Stoker myth."

"Bram Stoker. He wrote Dracula. Are you telling me there is some sort of vampire up there looking down on us? If so, give me a stake and let me and Xena the warrior princess here take care of it."

"It's not like that, John. A wooden stake will not kill this vampire, as you say, though we prefer to refer to them as Vahemics. They will only die after their body consumes all the oxygen in their depleted quantity of red blood cells. That's why they want your blood. They need your oxygen-rich arterial blood primarily, but even your venous blood has more oxygen in it than their own diminished volume."

"Vampire. Vahemic. Crap. Shit. Same damn thing."

"Regardless, I suspect you have about thirty seconds before it makes its presence known. Jane, would you begin the training?"

"John. This is a plasma knife. It's made from argon gas and an ionization process that heats it up to three thousand degrees. Keep your finger on this button to keep it activated. And don't point it toward your body. You will lose whatever the blue arc comes into contact with. Got it?"

"Yeah, I got..."

Before I could finish the sentence, my sister hit me with a taser several times which knocked me back into the chair. I watched as she jumped over the furniture toward Dr. Po and then I saw why she jumped. Another thing was now on the sofa where she had just been, looking down at me. The taser did nothing but piss me off and I felt enraged as I picked up the knife and activated it.

The chalk-like being looked over at my sister and then stared at me. Every blood vessel in its body was visible and it looked like some fucked up road map. Its neck and face were pulsating because of two large blood vessels that went up the side of its face. The creature let out a noise from its mouth that reminded me of the monkeys we saw at the fair. The ones that looked like they hated being inside those tiny cages and showed their dislike by throwing turds at you.

Then it showed me its teeth like those angry monkeys, only this wasn't a monkey mouth. This looked like more of a mouth that you would see during Shark Week on TV, with several rows of jagged and pointed teeth. I knew what was coming next and as it lunged toward me, I brought the knife across its neck and watched its head fall off onto the floor. The hands of the being were still moving though as if they were trying to dig a hole into my abdomen. But the clothes I was wearing stopped their claws from tearing into my skin long enough for me to use the plasma knife to cut both of them off and then kick them and the body to the floor.

"Well, that was fun. Kick-ass knife."

I got up and walked over to the head of the creature to get a better look. The eyes were completely white, devoid of any pupil or iris. Just white empty spaces. There were no eyelids or eyebrows either. In fact, there was no hair on the head at all. The only color at all on that chalk-like face was the lips, which were blue. I wanted to see the teeth so I reached over to move its lips back and the mouth began moving up and down like Pac-Man except you could hear the teeth snapping as the jaw moved.

"Careful, brother. The Vahemic is not dead yet and its body will continue to function as if it's alive. Its head is like that of a venomous snake. Still very deadly even though you remove it from its body. If you want to see the teeth, let me help you."

Jane put one hand on its forehead and the tip of a very large hunter's knife against its lips and as if on cue, the mouth opened. In one swift motion, she jammed the blade into the roof of the mouth and wedged the steel handle against the lower teeth. Though the jaw wanted to close, it couldn't, and after I watched it try a few times, I said, "I'll be damned," and then looked up at my sister. "Who the hell are you?"

"Jane. Jane Deaux," she answered with a grin.

"Yeah. Ok, I get the James Bond lingo there," I said as I examined the teeth. They appeared razor-sharp and just like sharks, there were indeed two rows of them. I couldn't help but think about Shark Week and the crazy sons of bitches who would chum the water and then jump in there with the sharks. Over and over, they would say how docile and non-aggressive the animal really was as it tried to pry open the bars of the shark cage with its teeth. Stupid fucks. If they weren't dangerous why did the news shows report every fucking shark attack? Docile animals my ass.

I noticed that there was very little blood on the floor. Just the severed head, arms, and the rest of the body. I sat down on the sofa and handed the plasma knife back to my sister.

"Where is all the blood and aren't these things supposed to burn up or turn to ashes?"

"We aren't filming episodes of 'Buffy the Vampire Slayer.' Even though they are mutations, these are still carbon-based humans. When they die, they just die. The lack of blood is because the plasma knife cauterizes the wound as it cuts through the body. That and the fact that the being has very little viable blood left in it. That's what causes it to hunt."

"First of all, impressed that you remember Buffy, sis, because I thought you were never paying attention to it. But, hell," I said as I looked toward Dr. Po. "Can't you come up with something that makes them disintegrate? You made a fucking plasma knife, for God's sake! Seems like there is something we could zap them with that would make them vaporize or something."

"I need to study them, John. Only by studying them can we be prepared when they evolve."

"Evolve? You're fucking kidding me. Next thing you'll be telling me is that they are protected under the endangered species act."

"As of this time, they are not."

"I was just kidding."

"Yes, I know. I am becoming most familiar with your sarcasm, but you are right in asking that question. There have been a few political representatives in the house and senate that have suggested something similar so that the beings are allowed to pass on in a more controlled, humane environment."

"Humane environment for something that is not human?"

"They were human at one time, John, remember that. But also, you don't have to be human to be treated humanely."

He's right. Zoos. Animal shelters. I get what he's saying. But I wonder why he can't kill them? He made the devices to kill them. He knows where they are and all about their anatomy, brain, and shit. Think a minute. Look at him. He's the size of a puppet. Probably about as strong as that hologram image too. He needed Jane. And he needs me to kill them. He told you that.

"Okay, now that the entrance exam has been taken, I have another question. I thought Emily was the computer in charge of this quadrant. At least that's what she told me earlier."

"Emily does oversee this area, but Emily is a part of Marie and Marie is a part of me. We are all integrated. Just different computers set up for different processes. But the main computer, Marie, enables me to oversee everything inside the house."

"Speaking of the house," I said as I turned to my sister. "Don't you think this place looks like one of those homes you were always looking at and dreaming about at the magazine rack in the grocery store?"

"It is everything I dreamed about and much more. You'll see."

"Well, what I'm dreaming about right now is that cheeseburger and that strawberry milkshake I ordered right before the 'rassling match.' There isn't something else lurking in the shadows that I need to get ready for by putting my hand in some water and then sticking my fingers in some wall socket, is there?"

"Nothing else, John. By the way, you dispatched that Vahemic in less than 20 seconds," the Dr. Po hologram said. "That is excellent work. You handled the plasma knife like you had used it many times before. Again, excellent. Are the clothes comfortable?"

"Yes. And they seem to be rather impervious to sharp claws."

"Not completely, but they are very durable. Made from Lignum vitae. The trees are indigenous to the Caribbean and the northern coast of South America. I have found it to be very conducive to developing clothing materials with other synthetic polymers I have made in the lab. It's almost like Kevlar but much more flexible."

Dr. Po looked at John and Jane and contemplated the two siblings that sat across from him. *The brother sitting beside his sister seems even more capable than her. His brain did not appear to be cluttered with any moral conflicts about killing the Vahemic. He dispatched it as if he had been doing it for years. He did not even ask about the Taser or why we did it. He just accepted it as his body received the energy from it and used it to protect himself. He did not give it a second thought.*

They will become a powerful team. Provided the hallucinations do not overwhelm him. I will have to make sure his blood levels are monitored very closely. Hallucinations with a lack of regard for authority and with a high propensity for anger could lead to a situation where I might have to activate the kill switch. But first things first.

"Jane, why not take your brother out to the veranda that overlooks the waterfall in the back of the house? I will have Marie deliver the food there. I will get this area cleaned up and then I would like for you to bring John down into the dissection area of the laboratory. Just hold your hands out as you walk through the corridor, John. The disinfection of your body will occur as you walk toward your destination."

"I have to admit, Doc. I do like the way you think regarding hygiene and keeping things clean around here. God only knows what was on that chalk outline on the floor."

"Chalk outline?"

"My brother is referring to the pale nature of the Vahemic's body and referencing a crime scene," my sister said as she started to laugh.

Oh, how I have longed to hear that laugh. I really hope this isn't a dream. If it is, then just don't wake up. The effect is the same. I am here with my sister and she is laughing.

"We aren't going to be cutting up frogs and shit are we, doc? You know down in the lab?"

"No, I wish to show you what kind of being you killed today."

"Yeah, let me eat first before you show me something which I am sure is smelly and disgusting. Then I might be able to get Emily that vomit she didn't say anything about but I know she is wanting."

"Yes. Perhaps," the Dr. Po hologram said before it hummed for a second and then disappeared.

"Come on, John." Jane took me by the arm and touched the wall with her finger. The wall panel seemed to dissolve and we were in a circular metal corridor that lit up as the door engaged. "Follow me."

We entered the metal tunnel and I turned around to watch the wall re-form. I held out my hands and watched as the purple and violet lights bathed them and thought about what had just occurred. Though there were similarities, I knew the ride I was now on with my sister was going to be different than the Haunted House attraction. Yes, she would be there with me, but the darkness which we rode into now would be unlike the stale lack of light I remembered. The monsters we would face on this ride would be different too. Very unlike those that just stood there and waited for a repairman. No, if given a chance, I now knew, these would kill the repairman.

Chapter 10
Cheeseburger in Paradise

"Interesting corridor. Reminds me of a bunker. Or a sewer, without all the floating turds and rats."

"They go all through the house – the corridors, that is. I'm not even aware of them all. They can be sealed off if need be and set up to deter invaders."

"Like giant cockroaches?"

Jane laughed. "If you only knew."

She's making jokes and laughing. I can get used to this.

"I'm afraid to ask. First Emily mentions Botanimy to me and now there's something called a Vahemic. Am I going to need some sort of Po dictionary?"

She laughed even more and shook her head no. We came to another stone wall and when my sister touched it, the stone disappeared once again, and a small porch surrounded by large trees and flowering vines became visible. There was a stone table shaped like a herniated extension of the stone wall that formed a semicircle around the porch. Our food was on the table. We stepped outside and I turned around to watch the clear opening reform into a solid wall.

"Damn. Do all the walls just melt away when you touch them?"

"No, not all of them. But you'll learn which ones. Some, only Marie or Dr. Po can open."

I bet it's his own toilet. Yeah, knowing how he is, he doesn't want anyone shitting in his bathroom. Hats off to you, Dr. Po. I would be the same way.

"And you won't need a dictionary. Either Dr. Po or I will teach you everything you need to know. The wall there is something Dr. Po calls a plasma door, similar to the plasma knife. He has done something to the material that reacts with our chemical nature and the Symbion molecule to create a veil-like mist. You aren't even aware it's there as you step through it and then it reforms into what looks like a stone wall once we are several feet away. It's not really stone but it is just as strong, perhaps stronger since it has the ability to repel unwanted trespassers."

Unwanted trespassers? Kind of creepy there, sis, but as long as you're safe, I can accept it.

"I did feel something as I stepped through it. How did that happen?"

"You have some of the Symbion molecules in your body. They were needed to repair your injuries."

"Got it."

"I just love coming out here to eat," Jane sighed as she sat down at the table.

"You're going to be drinking some sort of protein concoction that Dr. Po made for you. I'm not sure I call that eating."

"You should try it."

"Maybe later. This cheeseburger looks pretty damn good. I got a lot of catching up to do, you know."

I had eaten half the burger before I tried to talk with my mouth still full. "Is...good...this...time"

"Yes, everything is this good all the time. You do know, we're being watched and recorded, don't you? So, all that food on your face and shirt is there for me to watch over and over if I want."

"Laugh all you want. Don't matter to me. I'm with you now until Po gets sick of my ass and runs me off."

"That won't happen. He knows how powerful we can be as a team. Just so you know, he would have never done that to me. Letting a Vahemic loose like he did with you. Without any knowledge or training and only a few seconds to prepare. But he just knew what you were capable of. I knew it too. In fact, I was the one that encouraged him to test you. He didn't think it was a good idea, but he's always listened to me."

I could see how at ease my sister was. It was then that I understood that Dr. Po had become the father she never had. A man that helped her become strong and encouraged her and listened to her. But is she more like a daughter or just a trained attack dog to him? That remained to be seen and I needed to remain cautious.

"Is that why he had you hit me with a Taser? To energize my body? To show me what he meant when he was talking with me the other evening? To show me I wasn't hallucinating everything even though I thought he was Beaker at first?"

"The taser was my idea too. Dr. Po liked the synergy of the demonstration though. You felt the energy from it, didn't you?"

Synergy of the demonstration? My younger sister never talked like that. She has certainly changed.

"I think I felt more pissed than energized but perhaps feeling pissed and ready to react, is actually becoming energized as you suggest. I'll be interested in finding out how that really works. I know I've sat through the first lecture more or less, but I'm pretty sure I didn't have complete control of my mind. Have you read that journal of his on Molecular Transition Dynamics?"

"I have read it. But I don't understand it as well as I know you will. And just so you know, you have me to thank for some of the names of the beings and plants. Dr. Po lets me name the new beings we encounter or the new plants he's able to cultivate."

New beings we encounter? She says it so casually, as if we were looking at a new hummingbird species. But I'm guessing these new hummingbirds can peck out your skull.

"Botanimy? Vahemic? That was your creative mind at work?"

"Yes, it was. Botanimy is the science of plants and animals co-mingled in such a way that the plants take on animal characteristics in some form. There were already plants in the wild that ate insects, like the Venus flytrap and Pitcher plants. Some plants protected themselves like an animal would if attacked by the presence of thorns or poison in their bodies. He just extended that natural ability with the Symbion molecule. And Vahemic is an anemic cancer cell mutation in need of blood. Sort of named itself, don't you think?"

"Yes, I suppose it did. I get the Bram Stoker reference now. But where is this waterfall Dr. Po was talking about? I don't hear it or see it."

"You can only hear it if you drown out the noise in your mind. You have to imagine it first in order to see it."

Shit. She sounds like a fortune cookie. Okay, that's not fair. Actually, it sort of sounds like something Jack would say. Just take a sip of your milkshake and close your eyes and listen. Well, I'll be damned.

"I hear it but I can't see it. I hear it from over in that direction. It's over there, isn't it?"

"It's there and here and over there."

"Shit. No, it isn't! There is nothing there but plants."

"The plants are able to reflect the image of the water. It's like one of those pictures, John. The ones you stare into for a few minutes and can finally see the true image hidden within the various colors and shapes."

"Well, I got an A in staring in high school, so I should be pretty good at this."

I stared out into the distance toward the sound but despite how long I looked, I saw nothing. I could hear the waterfall but I felt like no matter how long I stood there, I wasn't going to see it today. I glanced at my sister and saw how content she seemed. Sure of herself. Unafraid, even happy. I had only seen glimpses of that in the past. And now it seemed like it was her everyday demeanor.

"Do you have any memories of that night?"

"No, not now. Years ago, when Dr. Po was working with me, my head felt like someone was hitting it with a hammer over and over, but my skull wouldn't break. It just hurt. But that feeling is gone. He made it go away. I never have that feeling anymore. I can see a grainy image of a man with vacant eyes but that is all. I remember only the times with our mother and with you; especially at the fair. That's what I remember."

"'I saw nothing in my life that demonstrated to me that anything we do will eradicate suffering. If a thing is free to be good it is also free to be bad. And free will is what has made evil possible. Why, then, did God give them free will? Because free will, though it makes evil possible, is also the only thing that makes possible any love or goodness or joy worth having.'"

"That is very true, John. You were always a poet at heart. I knew that."

"Well, those aren't my words, Jane. I'm quoting one of my favorite authors, C.S. Lewis. He understood suffering and pain. He's even helped me understand why I'm here today standing next to you trying to find a waterfall I can hear but can't see."

"Have you ever heard of the box jellyfish?"

"Yes. They are over in Australia, I think."

"They are there but also throughout the Indo-Pacific waters. The box jellyfish, which is also known as the sea wasp, is one of the most lethal natural-occurring creatures on earth. Its sting can kill a man with a dose that weighs about as much as a grain of salt. I swam with them, John. I was stung hundreds of times and though each sting initially was very painful, the more I was stung, the less pain I felt. In fact, I swam for ten miles that day in the ocean. I know this sounds like science fiction but it's true. The pain, the energy from those beings, was transferred to me. I'm no longer afraid of the pain. It does not define me nor consume me as it once did. I am strong enough now to define who I will be."

"When do I get to see the interview on the Discovery channel? I'm sure they did one, didn't they? Right after they said sharks weren't interested in harming you."

My sister laughed. "You always made me laugh or feel better about myself. You saved my life on more than one occasion even if you weren't aware that you did. Since I had seen Hell, I wanted to see if there was such a thing as Paradise and I thought Dr. Po would enable me to do so. But Paradise isn't easy to find, John. We have all been trying to find our way back there ever since we were thrown out of it. And I knew it would be impossible to find without you and now all my patience has been rewarded."

Jane hugged me and my eyes clouded due to the tears. I wondered how she had become so wise. I felt like I was now swimming with an army of box jellyfish and my whole body was on fire. The pain was unbearable but I knew it would go away. I had to make it go away.

Though this world had names as strange as those you'd find among the pages of a Dr. Seuss book, I wasn't sure if my presence in it would help my sister to find the garden she wished for. I hoped that her utopian dream didn't end up killing us with fangryloufangs or curlysueclawthings and I pulled my sister closer to me and whispered words to her that I was certain she had not heard in a very long time. Words that I had wanted to say just before I was shot. And as my eyes blurred even more, I began to see the waterfall over her shoulder, and *all of the wonderful plants that grew; some of them green and some of them blue.*

Chapter 11
The second day of science class

"I could sit out here all day," Jane said as she finished her drink.

"What's stopping us? I'm ready for my next cheeseburger and milkshake. Why can't we just stay out here as long as we want? You can blame everything on me if we're late to Po's Anatomy class."

"You need to see what he wants you to see, John. It's important. It will help you learn."

"Learn what?"

"About us. About them. About our purpose. About the universal energy plug device and what it can do for us."

And with those words, he showed up. Standing there right next to her. Hell, I knew he would be back.

There she goes again with that stupid damn universal energy plug thing. Hell, it's not possible. Po is a quack. Your sister is an idiot and you are a damn fool for listening to all of them. At least when I was alive, I taught you that you couldn't trust doctors. They all told you the same shit, didn't they, boy? That you were different. I said that from the first day you were born.

"It never gets old listening to you try to talk. All you do is make me want to do more with Dr. Po," I answered.

"Thank you, brother."

Shit. I'm going to have to stop doing that. She thinks I'm talking to her instead of that image of our dead father. Wait a minute. You aren't real, you piece of shit. You are just a figure in my head. So, since you're in my head, then I'll just talk to you via my head. Ghost telepathy, yeah, that will work. Can you hear me, old man? How's the throat and eyes? Oh, sorry. You don't have eyes, do you? Just black holes. But you know what, they look good on you. You know, more reflective of your dark nature.

And with that gaping hole in your throat, it's the total package. I have to admit, I don't think you've ever looked better.

Asshole! I always said you were different. I never said you were stupid. You finally figured out you don't have to speak out loud to communicate with me. Hooray! You do realize you got your intelligence from me? You certainly didn't get it from your mother.

Don't talk about my mother, you shithead! You have no right to speak about her. Though I hope she can see how nice you've turned out. That would make me really happy.

What are you going to do if I don't listen to you? Kill me? You already helped your sister do that.

I'll find out where you were buried and dig up your bones and make a birdcage out of them so birds can shit on them. Over and over. And for the bones left over, I'll grind them up and put them into pig slop. Though I doubt you are having much fun in the afterlife, and now that I think about doing all that to your body, I realize it probably wouldn't be much worse than what you are already experiencing. But maybe it would put you on a lower rung on the shit hierarchy in Hell. I can only hope. An abomination in life with a desecrated body; that can't look good on the resume, even in Hell.

Fuck you.

Back at you, Jacob Fartley.

Pathetic Dickens reference. Not funny at all.

You wouldn't know funny if it was a hot coal dropped in your eye. Ooops...maybe you would.

The grainy image of my father lunged at me when I said that and as he tried to grab me, he just disappeared. I smiled.

"Are you ready to go?" I heard Jane asking.

"Yes, Ms. Deaux. Lead on to the lab."

Each wall we came to disappeared with a single touch of my sister's hand, only to reform after we went through it. We stopped at one and I asked her to let me touch it before she did and it felt exactly like stone. Unmovable. Hard. Dense. "I like these plasma doors."

We got on an elevator that appeared behind one of the walls of stone. I wasn't sure how far down we went because my sister simply said, "Dissection Lab," and the doors closed and the elevator moved. When it stopped, we entered a corridor that looked like one of those plastic tube walkways for hamsters, only made for humans. With each step, different lights came on and I felt a fine mist several times that was gone within seconds.

He's sterilizing us. Well, not sterilizing us, but disinfecting us because we are headed into his lab. I get it, Dr. Po. Got to have a clean lab.

We soon saw the face of Dr. Po, standing over a metal table and the chalk-white being lying atop it. "Come in Jane, John. Stand behind that clear shield next to the table. I want to show you something about this being."

Dr. Po's face was embedded inside a robotic device that had metallic arms, legs, and hands. It was just like looking at something from one of those "Star Wars" movies only this thing was real.

I'll be damned. A Po-bot. That would be a good name for a sandwich. I should say that out loud. Maybe later.

I watched as the robot split open the being with an object that resembled a plasma knife and placed a device inside the incision that spread the torso and kept it open.

"Do you know anything about human anatomy, John?"

"I know that thing on that table is far from human. If it wasn't as white as chalk, I would think you had just unzipped a garment bag."

"Garment bag. Understandable, sarcastic remark and not unexpected. But, note the normal human anatomy image I just projected onto the protective barrier in front of you. See the differences now between it and a garment bag?"

"I'll be danged. Old Casper there seems to be missing a few organs."

"Actually, that is a very good observation except that it is wrong. They aren't missing, they are just reduced to the size of a pea and basically inactive. Note the spleen here and the liver. They are so small because the being doesn't want the removal of red blood cells to occur. For us, our body makes about two million red blood cells per second. Within the Vahemic mutation, the hematocytoblast produced within the bone marrow is defective, so it must seek out another way to obtain red blood cells. Thus, its desire to get them from another human being."

"The hematocytoblast is a stem cell that makes the red blood cells, correct?"

"It is, John. I am impressed."

"He was always reading when he wasn't watching 'The Three Stooges,'" my sister said as she nudged me with her elbow.

"I want to show you something else. Note the pancreas here. Again, though smaller than a human's, I wanted you to see its location. Your pancreatic cells are a unique set of four cell types different from the rest of your body. That is where I found the converter gene that you and your sister possess. It's this gene that controls the chemical process that enables the Symbion molecule to remove energy from eukaryotic cells in animals, plants, insects, and fungi: provided the proper electromagnetic environment is created for your blood. This along with the chemical composition of your blood enables all of the molecular transformation and regeneration to occur. You are the only two humans that I am aware of who possess that gene. Remarkable, no?"

Well, at least he didn't say amazing.

"The umbilical cord device, this universal energy plug as you called it. Is that what you are referring to when you say the proper electromagnetic environment is created?"

"You are correct, John. The umbilical cord creates that environment."

"And the gene, it makes us different," my sister said as she smiled at me.

"Not only different, John, but it provides unique genetic anomalies that allow superhuman activities to occur."

With that statement, my father's image manifested, fading in and out as he stood next to the examination table.

If you believe all that shit, boy, you are not only different, you are a fucking retarded alien.

That is a politically incorrect term and wrong on so many levels, you fucked up piece of spectral shit. But I learned from a good friend not so long ago, that if man has free will to do good, then the opposite is true; he has free will to do evil. And you were one evil son of a bitch. My only regret is that I let you live for so many years. Now I know what I'm going to do with your remains. And I promise you today, I will find what they did with your disgusting pile of bones that resembled a human in life. I'm going to find them and grind them into dust and sprinkle a little bit of it into the toilet each time I am getting ready to take a shit. Call that different. Call it fucked up. Call it whatever you want. But every time I hear that plop, I am going to smile for more than one fucking reason.

"Dr. Po?"

"Excuse me for a minute, you two. Marie wishes to speak with me."

Yes, Marie, I see it. John is hallucinating. In fact, it appears as if he is carrying on a conversation with the hallucination. I will have to do something to reduce the thallium, lead, and arsenic levels. Perhaps even the manganese. I will do it with dietary restrictions first, but if that doesn't work, we will filter them out via heavy metal dialysis.

"Yes, John. What questions, do you have?"

"Can you explain that to me one more time? I want to make sure I have a good basic understanding of everything."

"All eukaryotic cells possess organelles. Basically, organelles are structures within their cells that allow them to synthesize chemicals needed for the body to function. There is the endoplasmic reticulum, a network of membranes connected to the nucleus, which in the pancreas and liver are large structures that enable the body to store lipids. The sarcoplasmic reticulum in the muscle cells, stores ions that the cells need later; for example, if you are running and need calcium ions. The Golgi bodies in the cells help to moderate those processes. The ribosomes are the site of protein synthesis, where the amino acids are assembled and the mitochondria release the energy stored from food molecules. Plants have an additional organelle called a chloroplast that helps them conduct photosynthesis."

"So, we can access that energy with the Symbion molecule and this converter gene?"

"Yes, but only if the proper electromagnetic condition is created so that your DNA helix form is reshaped into a cylinder that is more conducive to assimilating the new energy released from the cells that the Symbion molecule sought out and the converter gene managed."

"Is all this going to be on the test? Kidding. I get it. And the cord...when we use it, we take that energy from other cells. But in doing so, doesn't that destroy the cells from whatever it is that is providing us the energy we need?"

"Yes, that is correct."

Shit. What the hell does that make us? Giant parasites?

"Doc, didn't you say at one time that the selenium level in my blood, and I'm assuming in my sister's, was almost alien-like? And that microbes, viruses, or similar infectious bugs can't grow in our blood? That our bloodstream is a toxic environment for them?"

"Yes, I did say that."

He has an amazing capacity to recall everything he has been told, considering I said all of that when he was just coming out of a two and one-half-year coma and still heavily sedated. And I can tell he is bothered by the knowledge of the power he possesses. He needs to see why it is so important that he and his sister possess that ability.

"Considering we are the only two you know of with this type of blood and considering we are the only two with this converter gene, doesn't there exist a possibility that we are not human?"

"There does exist that possibility. But considering your mother and father were both human, it is very unlikely, but not impossible."

"Wait a minute," Jane said as she looked over at me and then at Po-bot. "John is suggesting that we may be aliens? Why didn't you ever tell me that?"

"I didn't think it was necessary. And I am not saying you are. I am only agreeing with your brother's statement that the possibility does exist that might be true. And if it was true, would that really matter?"

My sister was not prepared to answer that question. The shock of considering herself a being from outer space stopped her from responding. All she could remember as a child growing up were images of extraterrestrial beings on TV or in magazines that looked like monsters and giant insects. I knew she was thinking she couldn't be one of those. I then saw the figurative light bulb go off over her head and she realized that if she was an alien, it truly didn't matter. She knew she was more human than a lot of things that now existed.

"No, Dr. Po. It doesn't matter."

"Ok, Doc, say I go along with everything you've told me. How do you know when these mutations occur?"

"I have some very sophisticated computers that do that for us. SAM keeps up with all the Symbion activity within the world. I have labeled the material in such a manner that only I can identify it. No one that uses Symbion knows anything about that label. And because I own the patent and sole distribution rights, I know when, where, and who uses it at all times."

"Sam?"

"Oh, sorry. Symbion Activity Monitoring. SAM is just the acronym for the computer system."

Of course, it is. I know for a fact it's not as good-looking as your nurse though.

"And ADAM is a computer that monitors the news for aberrant incidents and descriptions of what we would call abnormal. ADAM is an acronym for Abusive Destructive Attacks and Mutations. Marie monitors those alerts and feeds that information to me, as appropriate and as needed. Like I implied earlier, Marie and I are always connected. I guess you could say we are essentially one being."

"Marie is your main computer named after your mother, right?"

"Yes, that is correct."

Yeah, I get that. I would have named it after my mother too. And you named that special bacterium after the woman who discarded you like a piece of trash. I bet all the psychs in the white coats would have some fun with what that little honorarium would reveal about you. I kind of wonder what it means myself.

"Before I agree to this surgery Dr. Po, I would like a few things from you, if you don't mind."

"Of course. Name them."

"First, I want to read the journal you wrote on Molecular Transition Dynamics. Second, I would like to read and see how the surgical procedure is done."

Dr. Po nodded his head.

"And lastly, I would like information on the Symbion molecule and I would like to read the medical record that you kept on me."

I could tell Jane wanted to say something to me but Dr. Po replied to my requests before she could utter a word.

"Certainly. It will be on the computer in your bedroom. You can read it anytime today or this evening. I don't think we have anything else to do today. Jane, why don't you take your brother out into the gardens? He needs to see the new world. He's been asleep for a very long time. He also needs to understand what is safe and not safe around here."

"What the hell do you mean what is safe and not safe around here?"

"Jane will show you," Dr. Po said as his face disappeared from the robot, though the mechanical being continued to work dissecting the body and putting the pieces it cut up into metal containers.

"Come on, John. You'll love the gardens. They are quite special."

"Yeah, I'm sure they are."

"You know that converter gene that Dr. Po discussed? He didn't find it until much later. He didn't even know it existed until he started working to heal us."

"He didn't know it existed?"

"No, that's what he told me. That was also very interesting what you said about us being aliens. It would explain a lot, wouldn't it?"

"Yeah, maybe."

If he didn't know the converter gene existed, how the hell does he know there are just two of us that have it? There's something he isn't telling us. In fact, I think there is something that Jane isn't telling me. But, just go along for now. Watch and listen and learn.

"Maybe we aren't the only ones out there like us, John. Wouldn't that be something?"

Shit. How did you... It doesn't matter. At least for now, it doesn't matter.

"Yeah, that would be something all right. Going to need more fried chicken and 'tater salad' though for the converter gene reunion, if that's the case."

"John. You are a funny smart ass and I love you." My sister laughed out loud and hit me again with her elbow as we left the lab.

Chapter 12
Botanimy is something crazy to say in the neighborhood

We left the laboratory and got back on the elevator, I sensed we were going down, but that didn't seem right to me.

"Wait a minute. Are we going down to go outside? We aren't already on the bottom of this castle or compound or whatever it is you call it?"

"It will all make sense. We have to go down in order to go up."

"Jane. You aren't Alice and this is not Wonderland. So don't start saying shit like that."

Jane laughed. "The entrance to the facility we are in is underneath it, John. You just thought you were at the bottom of the building. I can understand. We've been more or less going through a maze. Easy to be disoriented when all you see are stone corridors and then the lab. But the entrance below us is the only way in. And before you ask, because I know you are, Dr. Po has told me there are other ways out but I haven't bothered to ask him where they are. I trust him to show me when it's necessary and it hasn't been necessary. And you will just love the gardens. You might rethink what you just said about Wonderland."

Once the elevator doors opened, we walked down several stone hallways until Jane came to another stone wall and touched it. Again, it disappeared and several slivers of sunlight shone through the dense growth of plants that surrounded the portal. Jane took my hand.

"Stay directly behind me. Don't vary your path and do not let go of my hand. Those plants are called the death bush. They are firethorns that have been genetically modified by Dr. Po. They have two-inch thorns and are highly venomous. The thorns possess a version of the faint-banded sea snake venom; one hundred times more lethal than any other snake in the world."

The bushes moved away from Jane as she walked into them. It almost looked as if they were not real, but mechanical devices, only highly sophisticated ones, a NASA length away from anything we ever saw at the fair.

"They move because of the Symbion molecules in me. Because you are holding my hand, their molecular composition and functional ability are transported into your body through our sweat. If you tried to walk in here without me or without those cells, you would probably die, though you do have some Symbion in you, so we might be able to save you." My sister giggled when she said that.

Death bush. Not very Seuss-like but still very effective with its description.

"Hence the name death bush. Yeah, I get it. Good description. I get the point."

Jane rolled her eyes at my pun.

"Plants that move. That's some pretty weird shit. Do they talk too?"

"They all talk, John, but I don't think you have the ability to hear them yet."

Oh, hell. My sister, the Buddhist. Stop thinking like that. You sound like your asshole father. Look at all of the self-confidence she possesses. Just look and listen.

"By the way, what do you call this place. Po-ville?"

"Funny, John. Like Who-ville and Horton. You loved that book. I liked it too, now that I remember. No, nothing like that. Pretty simple really. I call it home."

Damn. What a mature answer. Everything about her exudes a confidence and peace that I have never seen before. Yeah, sis, this might truly be Wonderland.

"I love coming out here in the gardens, especially when I get back from a mission. I love this place. I truly do and I know you will too one day."

"Mission?"

"Yes. When we go out to destroy the mutations. If we don't, more people will die than necessary."

What the hell am I getting into? He kept me alive all this time because he needed another assassin. One just like my sister. I know that now. Dr. Po more or less said as much and the spook attack was the first clue and now this little comment has confirmed it all. He sends her out on missions. Damn. But killing something you knew was a monster is different than killing what you know is now defined as a monster. These new monsters were human beings who got sick. Someone's family member. Maybe someone they really loved. Not necessarily someone like our father that I wouldn't have cared if he died with pancreatic cancer, as the doc said he had. Though it was nice to hear him say it would have been painful.

Can I really do this? Kill what was once human and turned into a monster because a cure made them that way? I don't know them, but I do know that they will kill me if given a chance. That thing standing over me earlier would have killed me and my sister, though I have a feeling she's now pretty adept at handling these things. She sure didn't seem too worried about shoving that knife in his mouth.

Wait a minute, didn't the Doc say that what made them that way was because a doctor treating them altered the protocol? Hell, the doctor that did that should be held accountable, shouldn't he? Shouldn't he go to jail or something? Shouldn't we do something to those guys? Or is Po lying? Is he covering up his own mistakes? I'll have to find out the truth but regardless, I have been given another chance to protect my sister. How I do that remains to be seen.

It seemed like we walked the length of a football field before we came out from within the death bush wall. Now I could see different types of gardens all around us and in front of us, a forest. My sister let go of my hand and started walking toward the forest. I recognized some of the trees but I had no idea what others were. The sun felt warm as it rained down on my body and I tilted my head upward and soaked up every bit of it.

"You will go with me on these missions, won't you, John?"

I brought my head down and looked at my sister as we headed into the forest.

Don't answer that yet. Talk about something else. "Do I need to be worried about anything in here?"

"I'll let you know. I won't let anything harm you. The forest is beautiful, don't you think?"

"Yes. It really is."

"You know it's God's work we are doing. On these missions."

There it is. I hear you again, Jack, in my sister's words. Discussing free will with me as I try to understand her comments. You said, "If we find ourselves with a desire that nothing in this world can satisfy, the most probable explanation is that we were made for another world." She and I were made for another world. Is that what she's saying?

But how can she say such a thing about doing God's work when she lived in a world that was devoid of God? No, I hear you, Jack. It wasn't devoid of God. You reminded me of his presence. Even in a world surrounded by evil every day, there is the presence of good. It should be intuitive but it isn't. It requires a passion and desire to see it when there is nothing around you that suggests there is anything but pain and sorrow. Has my sister been transformed? Is that what you're telling me?

"So, you believe in God? You see him? Talk with him?"

"I see God all around me now, John. It's impossible not to see him in the world where we now live. I see God in the brother standing next to me. I talk with him because I can talk with you and Dr. Po and with the waterfalls or animals."

Are her eyes open to the truth, Jack? Her eyes are no longer consumed with pain and sorrow? Though there are still monsters, she sees the good, the beautiful? Not just in movies but all around her. Free will at work here, huh, Jack?

"Don't you think it's odd that our father would have been killed by pancreatic cancer and we have a genetic mutation in our pancreatic cells? And with this gene that Dr. Po calls the 'converter gene' and the atomic Lego he created, the whole world of science changed? And that he can change us too?"

"Atomic Lego. I like that. You always had a way of simplifying things. That's a gift you know."

"Most people usually refer to it as sarcasm."

And you avoided answering the question.

"Yes, and at times it is. But you were never harsh toward me. For the longest time, I didn't know if you would ever come back to me. Dr. Po showed me your body lying there in the hospital room, but he always told me that you had a chance. That was all. Dr. Po helped me so much. He's a great man. In fact, I even told him one day that I wished he had been our father."

There it is. You saw that in her eyes before when she looked at him. She does see him as a father, not as a trainer. Still, something isn't right here. I can sense it.

"Really?"

"Yes. And he said that would have been a mistake. That we were born to the right parents even though we suffered. Without them, we wouldn't be who we are today. It took me a long time to understand that, but I see that now. He told me that I was like a missionary and when I read about them, I understood. I finally understood."

Well, that's a very honest response from him regarding that father issue. That makes me feel better. But missions? Missionaries? Oh, shit. That makes me a bit worried. He saved me and my sister, but missionaries? We are not that, sister. Far from it. Again, it makes me wonder. Who is he really helping - us or him?

Can you hear yourself rationalizing all this shit? You two - missionaries? What a joke! Better you kill your sister and yourself now before the doctor does and you know he will. You are intuitive – like me. You always had that ability. You were different in that way from everyone else and I knew it long before you did.

'By the pricking of my thumbs, something wicked this way comes.' That's from 'Macbeth,' if you want to know, asshole. Can we not put a bell around your neck so I can know when you're popping up? Oh, we can't, can we? You don't have that much of a neck anymore. Damn, what a shame. Well, never mind.

Big deal. You can quote Shakespeare. So what?

"Jane. Do you know where our father is buried?"

Don't you dare go there, you little shit. I will haunt you for the rest of your life.

Like that's a threat. As a matter of fact, seeing you as a ghost is actually an improvement. But, still....

"No, but I'm sure that Dr. Po knows. Why?"

"I want to visit it and our mother's gravesite."

"Sure, when we get back, I'll..." My sister stopped talking in mid-sentence and picked me up and carried me about ten yards away from where we were standing. She told me to look back and I saw what looked like a little brown cloud floating down toward the ground.

"Those flowerball spores are quite dangerous. I didn't know any of those types of flowerballs were out here in this part of the woods. There is a whole field of them about two hundred yards down that path. But sometimes nature does what it does. Dr. Po has told me that many times. You always have to be wary."

"Flowerballs?"

"Yes, it's another hybrid he created from the flower urchin and the puffball mushroom. The flower urchin's spines are toxic and will make you very ill. The puffball mushroom releases its spores once it's agitated. Now, the hybrid releases very toxic spores when it's agitated. I saw it there on the ground, but you stepped on it just as I moved you out of the way. I don't think it would have killed you but it would have made you very sick if you inhaled those spores. I know if you went through an entire field of them and they released all their spores, they would kill you.

"When we come back this way, I'll take you to that field so you'll know where it is and also so that you'll recognize them the next time you're out here. But I want you to see the waterfall first. The one that you couldn't see from where we had lunch. It's just about another half mile through this forest."

I looked back at the diminishing brown cloud and shook my head.

She just picked me up like I was nothing and carried me ten yards. Shit. She IS some sort of superhuman as Dr. Po was implying. And she doesn't know I saw that waterfall, but that's okay. I would like to see it up close.

As we walked on, I bent down to pick up a rock from the ground. It was pointed on one end and I closed my fingers around it and gripped it as tight as I could to see if I could feel the pointed edge enter my skin. I felt the pain, and when I opened my hand there was blood in the palm of my hand from the cut. I just wanted to make sure I wasn't dreaming.

Pain and evidence of blood. Good. I think.

We could hear the waterfalls long before we saw them but I was taken aback when they came into view. The main waterfall was at least three hundred feet high and rushed over the edge of the cliff down into three other pools which became smaller waterfalls. The origin of the water could not be seen from where we stood because of all the dense brush and plants. The plants were varied shades of green and what I thought was blue, but were really an albino-type plant that somehow mirrored the color of the water.

"Those white plants you see are highly poisonous if you should eat them and can cause a lot of skin irritation if you just brush against them. But aren't they beautiful around the water? They are like little leaves of glass."

Little leaves of glass. How poetic. Walt Whitman would have been proud. And of course, they're poisonous.

"Yes," I replied to my sister. We stood there enjoying the waterfalls, but all I could think of was Botanimy and my sister's reference to the land here as Wonderland.

It is very apparent that Dr. Po doesn't want people coming around. But why not?

And then I heard myself saying out loud, "Wonder you are still alive land," and I heard my sister laugh.

Chapter 13
A grave response

I will never tire of hearing that laugh. I couldn't remember if I had ever seen my sister's face light up like that. Maybe she does consider this paradise. There is certainly enough beauty around here to suggest it is. It's a different world from where we once lived, that's for sure. And even though there are things that can harm you in this world as in the old one, she's not scared. She can protect herself. She is not afraid of anything in this world it seems.

Perhaps that in itself is indeed paradise, huh, Jack?

"I could stay here all day."

"You said that when we were out on the porch eating lunch. Do you say that wherever you go around here?"

She laughed again and nudged my shoulder with hers. "Not everywhere. I wouldn't want to stand in that field of flowerballs that I'm going to show you on the way back. And I sure as heck don't like being in the presence of a Narcoleptan."

Oh shit. This doesn't sound good. "Narcoleptan?"

"Yeah. They are much more dangerous than the Vahemic. They're like chameleons in the sense that they can blend into the environment. If not for the chemical composition of our sweat and the Symbion molecule, we would have a heck of a time dealing with them. But our sweat will alert us to their presence. It tingles and when it does, you need to be ready. They are ten times stronger and much more vicious than the Vahemic."

"What, why, who, when, where...you know all the w's."

"Accidentally, when Dr. Po began curing brain cancer, he found he could cure other brain disorders, like epilepsy and even sleep disorders, like narcolepsy. But they didn't follow his protocols and bingo, the Narcoleptan was his name-o. Seriously they are much bigger than the Vahemic and their faces are wolf-like in appearance with 12 long fangs that protrude from their long snout. Their eyes look like round pieces of peppermint candy with red swirls, only these red swirls are blood that drips from their eyes. Dr. Po says the blood dripping from their eyes makes them even angrier as it burns their face. Their entire body is covered with hair and their hands and feet have long sharp talons, and really, if you just looked at them separately from the body, you wouldn't know what was a foot and what was a hand. And they are fast. Really fast. Plus, like I said, you can't see them, that is until you kill them."

Are you shitting me? Another monster in paradise. But she isn't afraid at all. She is just talking in a matter-of-fact manner. Describing what exists.

"So, our sweat tingles. Got it. I'm glad my little introductory quiz didn't involve one of those beings."

"Dr. Po knew better than to do that. It would have probably killed you. Their claws and fangs are very poisonous too. The fangs and talons are covered with deadly bacteria and viruses. Very nasty."

"Good to know. Sounds like an important piece of information."

"Oh, John! I would have killed it before it did anything to harm you, even if there had been a test with it. But there wasn't because we both knew you weren't ready to face one. Like I said brother, you watched over me for a very long time; now it's my turn to repay the favor."

"Why the name – Narcoleptan?"

"I thought about narcolepsy and how the being reminded me of the Wolfman, ergo, Narcoleptan."

Fangryloufangs and curlysueclawthings with a very sick man called a Narcoleptan. Yeah. I hear you, Dr. Seuss. This sure the hell isn't Whoville, is it? More like Booville but this time you really need to get the hell out of the way when you hear "boo," don't you?

Jane put her arm through mine and led me away from the waterfall and back toward the forest. On our way, we went down the trail to see the field of flowerballs. While we were there several of them burst open, shooting off a cloud of spores into the air.

"Why are they doing that? I thought they only exploded when something brushed up against them?"

"There are mice hiding in these fields around here that are immune to the spores. Probably a copperbrown looking for them. And before you ask, Dr. Po took the poisonous eastern brown snake found in Australia and made a hybrid with the copperhead found here in America. It's a much more deadly snake but it's not really that aggressive. And because snakes only have small nostrils, they aren't really affected by the spores. Checks and balances."

"But what about us? You know the humans?"

"I thought you suggested to Dr. Po we were aliens?"

"Ok, what about us - the aliens?"

Jane laughed as we moved away from the field. "If one of the copperbrowns bit you, it would make you sick but not kill you. It would kill others though, without a body filled with Symbion. I don't even worry about them anymore. My Symbion cord almost makes me immune. Yeah, I can feel the bite and I feel a little burn but that's all. More like a bee sting like we got when we were playing outside on those days Mom took us to the park. Next to all that clover. That's funny. I hadn't even thought of that until now. See what you do for me? You bring back memories I had long forgotten."

I smiled. She was talking as if I was just like her, but I wasn't. So, I knew I needed to watch my step for the time being. I was happy I had triggered that memory for her but she didn't even realize I had done that earlier with Horton and Whoville. Now, I began to wonder if I could trigger those memories, could my presence also bring forward the others that she said she didn't have anymore? Make her remember all the bad ones she said she had forgotten? I needed to ask Dr. Po about that. I didn't want to cause my sister any more pain. Surely he must have some way of preventing that from occurring.

"Does our body tingle when the snakes are around?"

"No, and thank goodness it doesn't."

"Why do you say thank goodness it doesn't?"

"Because it would be tingling all the time."

Shit. Look down. Look around. Look for that copperbrown. Not now, Dr. Seuss. Not now.

As we reached the entrance of the forest, I noticed some flowers that I had not seen before. "Were those flowers there earlier?"

"Yes, they were probably closed so you didn't notice them. Watch."

Jane walked over to them and they closed up and became almost hidden within the greenery that surrounded them.

"Is that because of the Symbion molecule again?"

"Some. But mainly because they are sensitive to light. In shadows, they close up. They open toward the sunlight."

"The yellow and orange colors are beautiful. What are they?"

"They are various types of poppies."

"Well of course you'd have a poppy field. Is the Tin Man down the field a way?"

Jane laughed again. "Damn how do you do that? I never even thought about 'The Wizard of Oz' until you said that. I'm so glad you're back here with me. I had always looked at them from the perspective of Dr. Po until you said that. But if you recall in the movie, the poppies made them all go to sleep. These will too, except you may not wake up. These are quite poisonous. They have Stonefish venom in their pollen and petals."

Yep. Gonna need the Po Wildlife Survival Guide with the 1-5 skull and crossbones rating scale beside the pictures.

"Stonefish venom? Shit. Does everything around here kill you?"

"Not everything."

"What about that thing coming toward us? A thing I believe to be a Komodo Dragon."

"Get behind me, John. That thing coming toward us is indeed a very large Komodo Dragon. There are about fifty or so on an island Dr. Po built. That is a large male and they usually don't wander over here this close to the home, but occasionally they do swim off the island and come this way, usually looking for a deer. Their mouth is full of bacteria. Even more than usual thanks to Dr. Po. If they bite you, you will die in less than four hours. The Symbion device in me will prevent me from dying but I still don't like being around them."

Before I could ask what we were going to do, my sister pulled out a pen-like device from her back pocket and pressed something on it that shot a small stream of light toward the creature. The light entered its eye and it immediately turned its head and ran away in another direction.

"What the hell is that?"

"Nothing fancy. Just a small laser light. You could pick one up at Staples. This one has a little more power though. It burns their eye. It would blind them if they kept looking at it and they always run away from it. They just know it hurts, so they get away from it as quickly as possible."

"What if they are old and blind?"

"You don't have to worry about that. If that happened, the others would end up eating it."

"Well, this has been a delightful tour. I can't wait to see the other things around here that can kill me. Do we get cotton candy now?"

My sister laughed. "Maybe if you're good and after you have the operation for the Symbion implant device."

A hint of sarcasm from my little sister. That's good.

I nodded my head and smiled but I still wasn't sure I wanted to have that device implanted in me. But I also wasn't sure how I could live here with my sister without it. I needed answers to some questions. I knew I needed to read the journal about the Symbion molecule and watch the operation on the computer that the doc had set up for me. I'd like to see my medical record too.

Jane led us back to the elevator at the house and this time I could tell we were going up. We emerged from the elevator into a large odd-shaped solarium. Dr. Po was trimming one of many bonsai trees in the room and waved as he saw us. He was sitting on a metal chair that resembled an adjustable aluminum ladder with a seat.

"Did you enjoy your walk?" he asked my sister.

"Very much. You know I always do. The waterfall was so beautiful today. I never get tired of seeing that. John now knows of the death bush, the white mirrors, flowerballs, the poppies, and the copperbrowns. Oh, and we saw a Komodo too."

I hear at least six things that can kill me and all she can think of is how beautiful the waterfall was. Could all that really be due to the Symbion device that is now a part of her and makes her feel so invincible?

"Strange for the Komodo to be over here. We may need to check on that. Jane, will you go down to the armory and get several plasma knives? SAM and ADAM have alerted me to something that you need to investigate in Tennessee. And I imagine your brother wants to ask me some questions."

"Sure," she answered. Jane left the room and I looked suspiciously at Dr. Po. "How did you know I have all these questions in my head? I don't really like you being able to read my mind. I don't like that at all."

"I wasn't reading your mind. I was reading your face. I could see the first question you had as if it was tattooed on your forehead. It's in regard to the confidence that you see in your sister. Well, first of all, as I am sure you suspect, the Symbion implant has certainly made a difference but there are many other things that have helped create the person you see today."

"Like what?"

"Many things, John. She gained confidence when she realized she had survived a world that she believed could not be worse than the Hell she had been taught existed from her early religious encounters. I am certain she would have killed herself if you had not taken the action that you did that night."

"She was going to kill herself?"

"Yes. I believe she would have probably killed your father and then killed herself; provided you didn't do everything that you did that night. But you changed her life in more ways than one. She eventually realized that she could not only survive those gunshots but she could also thrive in this new world, and she began to understand how her body empowered her to do that. With each day, her self-assurance and confidence grew. Seeing you getting better each day also helped.

"She learned how to live in this new world. A world that was very dangerous but she came to understand she could survive it because I taught her about her body chemistry and how the Symbion implant would allow her to overcome the obstacles that she encountered. Plus, I had the most skillful assassins in the world teach her how to defend herself and she fears nothing now. She knows that she can be injured and survive and heal because of what she is. All of that together has made that person you see today. And now having you back with her, well, I don't think she has ever been happier."

"Is that why she calls this God's work? She talks about missions and being a missionary. That seems a little far-fetched to me. How did that happen?" I asked.

"I didn't tell her that but she had mentioned it to me after she was reading about Operation Auca. Evangelical Christian missionaries were trying to bring Christianity to the Huaorani tribe in Ecuador in 1956. The Huaorani were savage people who ended up killing all of the missionaries. But a widow and a sister of two of the missionaries went back several years later and were able to convert them. That story made a connection with her and what she was doing and I saw no reason to alter that line of thinking. I believe it has helped give her even more purpose, and considering what she has to do, she needs as much focus as possible."

Freedom to be good means freedom to be evil. Yeah, I hear it, Jack. I wonder how she happened to be reading that story.

"Yeah, about that. This Vahemic and something she called a Narcoleptan. Why did you let the doctors alter the protocols? Why aren't they being called to answer for what they did? They are the ones that created the monsters."

"As soon as I discovered what had been done, I stopped the distribution of the Symbion technology. But that was after a year and a half of it being out there in the world. Most of the doctors were doing the right thing. A very few allowed their desire for money to influence their decision-making and altered the protocol due to corporate influence on the doctors.

"But let me add, John, even if they hadn't altered the protocols, the mutations would have occurred. They always occur. It pains me to tell you, but the thinking of the medical community was that the mutations were an acceptable side effect. I couldn't reconcile that and, as a result, lost my faith somewhat and retreated here. Here, where I can work to correct the problem and not allow any more statistical tolerance for monsters to become just a side effect of the cures."

"But didn't you say you cured cancer? And Jane said you cured sickle cell anemia and neurological disorders."

"Yes. That's true."

"But if you cut off the ability for those cures to happen, doesn't that make…. Wait a minute. Shit. You saw what would happen if you cut off the supply. You're afraid of a backlash. That's why you have Jurassic Park out here around your house. Wherever this house is. But why not just put a bunch of land mines out there instead of making Frankenvines down in your lab?"

"Land mines are a deterrent but once they know they are there, the military has ways of disabling them. The world you saw today is one that looks natural and safe. But for those that are intent on doing harm to me or Jane or even you now, they will learn that they have made a horrible assumption. And they can't destroy this place, a thousand acres here in southwest Virginia, because if they do, they know they truly would be destroying the opportunity for cures to continue. And before you ask, the Komodo dragons have been altered so that they can live in this environment. I provide them artificial heat because they prefer a very warm climate, in excess of 90 degrees, so they usually don't leave that area but nature is never one hundred percent predictable."

"How did you know I was going to ask about the Komodos?"

"That was just a hunch knowing how inquisitive and how very intelligent you are. You saw a creature that you recognized and wondered how it could live here. I knew you would ask. I am not sure if you are aware of this, but your sister is very smart too. That was mostly hidden as she withdrew into her own world while she was growing up. But now it is flourishing. One of the things that would suggest to me that you are not aliens is that your intelligence comes to both of you very naturally. Your parents were extremely intelligent."

Yeah. You should've seen my father play Jeopardy. And now that you mention it, I guess you're right about my mom too. After all, she kept us all alive until, well, until it was time.

"How do you know that?"

"I performed an autopsy on them before they were buried. Both your parents had more than usual convolutions in the frontal lobes, much more. That formation in their brains indicated an above-average ability to think and solve problems; in fact, to even see problems differently from others."

"Good to know. But they didn't have blood like us, did they?"

"No, they did not. That is a unique genetic anomaly."

"Or an alien quality, but I won't continue to dwell on that. I would like to know where they are buried though. Do you know?"

"Yes. They are buried here on the property. Why?"

My father's image appeared next to Dr. Po. I smiled as I listened to him.

Tell him why, boy. Tell him you plan to be some ghoulish grave robber. Tell the midget that. Tell him something that reminds him how different you are.

"I'd like to go by there. Pay my respects to my mother and piss on my father's grave."

"The manganese level in your blood prompts the aggressive action you suggest regarding your father. But if you wish to do what you want, I would not stop it. The graves are in the field of the flowerballs. I would not advise going in there without the Symbion cord implant, though."

See there you go, you little shit. You'll have to go under the knife of a puppet to get to me. You didn't want to do that, boy. I heard you say so to him and I know you're thinking it now. You want to read that manual first and find out about the puppet's new little snowflake he created. You even wanted to watch the surgery first. But now you got to let Dr. Pinocchio, cut your strings if you want to find me. So, it appears you are fucked again.

"When can we schedule my operation, Dr. Po?"

"As soon as possible. We can do it tonight as a matter of fact. I would like to wait at least eight hours since you have eaten, but the procedure doesn't take long. And the operation won't get rid of your hallucinations. We will need to reduce the level of arsenic, lead, and thallium in your body to do that. And to be honest with you, lowering those levels along with lowering your manganese will help moderate your aggressive nature, which is something we should consider doing."

I don't know what he thinks I see, but he knows I see something. I just hope he can't see your ugly ass.

"I don't want any of that done, Doc. I know you must have seen something in my brain waves; something that lets you know I'm seeing things at times, but that's okay. I can handle it. I don't want anything changed. You just said my sister needed purpose and focus, well, what you may refer to as hallucinations, provides that same purpose and focus for me. So please don't take that away from me. Right now, I need it to be able to process everything, and whatever I am seeing helps me to do that. Promise me you won't do anything to affect my body chemistry."

"I can promise you that we will not do anything for the moment."

Good. As long as I can still see Jack if and when he comes back, then I can put up with your ugly ass and foul mouth. Oh, wait a minute, there's a hole there. In your mouth and throat. Amazing you can still talk.

Fuck you.

That's the spirit. Funny, huh? Seeing how you are some sort of fucked up spirit?

"Doc. I just thought of something, if you took back the Symbion supply from the medical community, what happened to all the children that got cancer? Children that you could have cured. Isn't there a way that you can do something that still helps them?"

"I have done that, John. I said I stopped the supply when I found out what was happening but I do continue to supply all those doctors I do trust, only in a much more controlled manner. Pediatric oncologists, as well as other oncologists and doctors, continue to receive access to the Symbion molecule and I have not seen any mutations yet in any children. Perhaps it may not ever happen but I continue to monitor all of that with my very close colleagues."

"And those with sickle cell? Those continue to get cured too?"

"Yes, John. And other cures will continue to happen as I find ways to eliminate the mutations from occurring. One is too many."

Hell, he's not perfect. But he's honest. He's trying to do all the right things. I see why my sister trusts him so much.

"Thanks. That means a lot to me."

Before I could ask any more questions, my sister came into the solarium with a plasma knife hanging on her belt like an actor in a science fiction movie getting ready to step foot onto a planet with hostile alien beings.

"Looks like a Narcoleptan from what ADAM is telling me. It's in Jonesborough, Tennessee. I can get there in several hours if I leave right now."

I was right. She is stepping out of the spaceship onto a hostile planet.

"I'm going with you."

"You can't go with her, John. You will be at too much risk without the implant. And you being at risk, places your sister at risk."

"How about just giving me a booster shot of Symbion? That should help, right? And you saw what I did with the Vahemic. I can handle myself if you give me one of those knives."

"Yes, it will help but you would still be at risk. Their fangs and claws are very poisonous. And they are much stronger and more aggressive than the Vahemics."

"Jane told me how dangerous they were. But, Doc, not until a few moments ago when we were talking, did I even think I wanted to do this. But I can't let anything happen to her. Not when I am here now and can help her. These monsters were human at one time and I struggled with the idea of even being sent out to kill them. Even though I may wrestle at first with the idea of taking the energy from other living things in order to help myself, I can understand the need to do it. And I have a feeling that one of those thallium, lead, arsenic, or manganese spikes in my blood will allow me to survive. Granted, I know I can't have the surgery right now, but if you want me to do any of this, you're going to let me go with my sister."

"The poison in their fangs and claws is very powerful and I am not sure even a Symbion booster shot as you called it, will be enough to protect you, should they tear open your skin, much less remove a limb. I am afraid you would die if that happened."

"How old are those trees you're working on, Doc?"

"Some are over five hundred years old."

"They live a long time and I'm sure you are one of the reasons they do. You care for them and make sure they have everything they need to survive. You did that for my sister and you saved me and I know you will do everything possible to allow me to live a long time. But I don't have time to wait to be pruned and watered. I just need a shot because right now I will do whatever has to be done in order to make sure my sister has everything she needs to survive."

"Jane, will you go get the truck ready?" Dr. Po said as he hit a button on his chair that moved him down to the floor. "I will need to get some Symbion to give your brother."

Jane looked at me and smiled. "See you in a few minutes!" she said as she went running from the solarium.

"Thank you, Doc."

"Thank me when you return."

"I will. But I have one more question before I go. Jane says I keep bringing back memories that she had forgotten when we are together. So far, they have all been pleasant memories, but can I also bring back other memories – other bad ones that she has appeared to have buried?"

"It is possible."

"You are monitoring her brain, aren't you?"

"Yes, I am. She has a neuronal mesh that links her to Marie. I also want to place one in you when you have the operation for the Symbion cord."

"I thought so. And I will agree to that as long as you don't adjust my blood levels unless I say it is necessary. Agreed?"

Yes, I see it now, Marie. John sees more than one person in his mind. That is why he doesn't want the hallucinations to go away. There is another person who helps him understand. One bad, one good. Just like when he was growing up. I should have seen that.

"Agreed, John."

"Will you let me know if my sister starts having hallucinations? Or whatever lets you know she is reliving or seeing something she shouldn't ever have to see again?"

Dr. Po nodded his head yes.

"Thanks, Doc. Hey, do you think we can ever live to be five hundred years old?"

"No, I do not think we can."

"They did in the Bible."

"I am not God, John."

"You don't have to be, Doc. God works through you. If he wants it to happen, I think you would be the person he helps find the way to do it."

Dr. Po didn't say anything but I could tell he was appreciative of my comment. In fact, I think it embarrassed him.

"This way, John. But when you confront the Narcoleptan, be very careful. As I said, I am not sure the additional Symbion can save you should you become seriously injured."

"Define serious."

"Dismembered limb. Disemboweled."

"Shit, that is serious. But hell, I've been shot in the head and had a severed spinal cord. Even been declared dead a time or two. What's a severed arm or guts hanging out of my body going to do to me?"

I could tell Dr. Po thought I might be hallucinating, so I just smiled.

"I was dead for a long time, Doc. Long before the policemen shot me. I just wouldn't admit it until now. Don't worry, I'll be okay."

Chapter 14
Symbiotic Relationship

After I got the Symbion booster, I followed Dr. Po to where Jane was waiting for me. She was standing next to a large Ford F-650 truck.

Odd. I thought there'd be some explosion in my head or an electrical shock to my body from the shot. Wait a minute. Now I feel something. Whoa! Like a surge of adrenalin. Yep. I'm awake now.

"Holy Shit! That's the biggest truck I've ever seen!"

Okay. Take it down a notch, Curly. Dr. Po is going to wonder if giving you that shot was a good idea or not.

"Yeah. The damn thing is awesome. I think it would drive straight up the side of a wall. And I know it would go through a wall. Been through several of them."

"Now, Jane. We have talked about that before. Don't worry, John. Though the truck can switch to a manual system when necessary, Marie would not allow it to go up the side of a wall. And your sister is right. It will go through concrete walls without an issue, but trying to go through solid steel would present a bit of a problem."

Jane shrugged her shoulders and smiled.

"You said that it can change to a manual system when necessary; so, are you controlling everything from here?"

"Yes. Marie controls the onboard computer system. And I have redesigned the motor as well as some other items in the truck to ensure safety and provide a defense and assault capability. The horsepower has also been adjusted and transformed into a fully electric system with self-charging batteries that will last seventeen years."

"Shit. Does anyone else have this technology?"

"No. I am working through some trust issues with regard to that."

"You sure we aren't related, Doc?"

"In some ways, we are indeed. Jane, do you have the LBEs with you? Along with a plasma knife for John?"

"Got them, Doc."

I saw Dr. Po look at my sister in a strange way when she said that and I laughed. "She's never called you Doc, has she?"

Dr. Po smiled. "No, not until today. But I must admit, I don't dislike it. We will be monitoring both of you from here," he said as he handed us what looked like contact lenses. I watched my sister put hers in, so I did the same without even asking. I knew Dr. Po would tell me what they were before I even asked and he did.

"Those contacts will protect your eyes from the Narcoleptan's poison. We will also be able to see through your eyes with them. Jane's neuronal mesh allows us to keep an eye on her brain waves but until you have that, John, I cannot monitor your brain activity and spikes as closely as I would like. I will be closely checking your brain and body metabolism as best I can via the truck and the clothes you are wearing. Both are Symbion sensitive. John, listen to your body. Not only will the sweat alert you to the presence of the Narcoleptan, but it will also tell you when your strength is waning. Since you do not have the cord device that will allow you to reconvert, you will need to get back to the truck, should you feel that happen. The truck will protect you from anything."

"What do you mean my sweat will tell me my strength is waning? Won't I just feel tired? I know my sister mentioned our sweat tingling earlier, but I didn't know we had magic sweat."

"You are more attuned to your body's metabolism with the Symbion circulating through your system. I'm sure you felt the surge of energy in your body when you got the shot. Now, you will start to sense your body is dying when your strength is dissipating."

"Dying?"

"Yes, but you won't actually be dying, just weakening at an accelerated pace. Therefore, I am giving Jane an additional Symbion shot for you, just in case."

"All-righty then. And you said this truck will protect us from anything?"

"Yes, it would remain intact even in an F-5 tornado. You may regurgitate on yourself numerous times as you spin around, but you will be safe."

"Don't puke going around in circles, Doc. Ask Jane. I could stay on the Tilt-a-Whirl all day."

As soon as I said "Tilt-a-Whirl," I saw my sister smile. *She's remembering more and more.*

"Jane, you can tell John more about the defense and survival-enhanced features of the truck as you travel. I should see you back here in about six hours. Bring back as much of the being as possible. Also, John, there are tasers in the truck and you should take several with you if and/or when you ever leave the truck. It will give you an energy boost if you use it on yourself, but you will still need to get back into the truck as soon as possible. You will not be in a state to defend yourself against a Narcoleptan if you are going through a reconversion phase. This being is not like the Vahemic that you so easily dispatched. As impressive as that was, I am afraid you would have been dead if that was a Narcoleptan. They are much more powerful and very unpredictable."

I nodded my head and heard my sister say, "Yes sir, he knows all that. I think we're good to go now. I'll make sure everything is okay. I promise."

My sister walked over and hugged Dr. Po. I could tell she had never done that either as I watched him standing there awkwardly, wondering what he was supposed to do before she released him from her embrace and walked to the truck. I started to laugh but I stopped and lowered my head so it wouldn't look like I was staring at him or making fun of his discomfort.

I then remembered how his life started. Even though the woman who saved him probably loved him dearly, I knew in that one moment, he still felt and remembered the alienation that my sister and I had experienced every day. Our mother loved us profoundly but she could only do so much. Just like his. He was right. We were alike in many ways.

I turned toward Dr. Po as I got to the truck. "One question before we take off. You mentioned LBEs. What are those?"

"I knew that question was coming. They are Light Bullet Emitters - Positron emitting devices."

"I'll be damned. Devices, hell. Those are weapons. They're laser beams, aren't they? I knew you had to have some sort of laser beam."

"No, they are not laser beams. They emit positrons. Positively charged electrons that destroy negatively charged electrons when they encounter them. Continuous bombardment on a human at a high enough level would put a hole through their body. When the Narcoleptans are hit by these positrons, they feel as if their body has been assaulted with a flaming red iron. This is a high-intensity positron device, but I could not make it any stronger or it would not be mobile enough to use. Therefore, one light bullet will not annihilate the mutated beings it encounters, but multiple light bullets at the same entity will accomplish that desired outcome."

"Does anyone else have these?"

"Large ones, yes. Used for medical purposes but not ones of this size that are designed to kill rather than heal their target."

"Oh, hell yes!"

"I would temper your enthusiasm a bit, John. If the LBE energy source malfunctions, the explosion would kill you and anything within a mile radius."

"So, you're telling me the gun just won't jam or stop working because the power source is low? Because it's really a miniature nuclear reactor and if it explodes it will kill everything around us?"

"I am sure they will function as designed. I've only had two malfunctions and I have corrected those problems. But you should know the benefits as well as the hazards of the weapons you are using."

"Well, I guess I won't feel anything when a malfunction occurs, will I?"

"For a millisecond you would feel your body coming apart like a billion grains of sand being thrown about by a hurricane but after that, no, nothing at all."

"You should make that into a Haiku or something. Very inspirational. So will these light bullets kill the Narcoleptan?"

"Yes, provided the being stood there and allowed you to shoot it numerous times. But it will not do that. The first time they are hit, they become angry but also more cautious. Like I said earlier, it makes them feel as if a part of their body is on fire. Several shots in the same area will make them feel like someone pulled their arm off. If you are able to hit them in the same general area at least three times, that part of their body will disintegrate.

"But they move so fast, hitting them three times in the same part of the body is almost impossible, plus, as I am sure Jane told you, they have a chameleon-like ability and will disappear when threatened. If injured, they will decide to either attack or retreat. Jane has found that she has only been able to kill them with the light bullets once. The abdomen of the being she shot three times disappeared and then the remaining parts fell to the ground like broken limbs from a tree. The other two times, she hit the creature with several shots, and then was required to use the plasma knife to kill them. The injuries she incurred were healed with her implant. In your case, all you can do is hope you are not bitten or ripped open with their talons. The suit you are wearing will help. Your body chemistry will help. The booster shot will help. But you will still be in significant danger and at risk of death if you are injured by them."

"Yeah, I get it, Doc." *I know you're trying to get a point across but I spent my entire youth growing up in the kind of world you are warning me about. If you're slow, you feel the blow. Lived with that rhyme in my head for a very long time.*

I stepped up into the truck and heard Jane call out some numbers. The truck engaged and began moving out of the tunnel. When I turned to look back at Dr. Po, he was gone.

"For someone with such short legs, he sure can move pretty damn fast."

"The legs are primarily robotic limbs at this point. He performed surgery on himself when he realized he had an advanced form of degenerative bone disease. His arms are the same way. I think he plans to operate on his spine when he's sure the robotic surgical process he's developing will be successful."

Hell. He is a damn cyborg.

"Shit. Why not just put his head and body into a robot big enough to crush things? You know, Klaatu barada nikto, Gort."

"Don't tell me. I know that phrase. You used to say it all the time. It was one of your favorite movies. Wait a minute - don't tell me. I'll get it."

Please don't access the wrong part of your brain, Jane. The one where you have placed things and forgotten about them. Shit, I need to be more careful with what I say.

"'The Day the Earth Stood Still.' The robot was Gort. You loved that movie."

"Yes, I did." *After I saw that movie, I wanted the ability to make the world stop like Klaatu. Or destroy things like Gort. Almost every day... but we can't discuss that. In fact, we need to change the topic.*

"Those numbers you said earlier. Location by satellite?"

"Yes. We just sit back and enjoy the ride."

"So, according to the doc, you've killed three of these Narcoleptans and one just blew up?"

"Yeah, that was cool. But one of them bit me pretty badly on my shoulder. I cut his mouth off before he could do that again or disappear. Like the good doctor said, if I hadn't had my implant that day, I may not have made it. They are very aggressive, John. It seems like something happened to their brains with the Symbion molecule that caused everything to go haywire. They don't kill humans or animals because they need to do so in order to live, like the Vahemic. And even though Dr. Po hasn't said so, I think they kill just because they enjoy it."

Fuck. Danger, Will Robinson. Danger. Change the topic.

"Got it. Now, tell me about this truck."

"I will, but first tell me what you and Dr. Po were talking about when I went to the armory. You were talking about me, weren't you?"

"Nailed it. You're not really one of Po's computers, are you?"

"Ummm, maybe."

More sarcasm. Good.

"I was telling him how impressed I was with the woman I saw and I thanked him for helping you and bringing me back to be here with you."

"That's a good start, but that's not all you talked about."

Shit. She might really be one of his computers.

"I also asked about the Symbion distribution and he told me how he is still taking care of children so that they don't get cancer or sickle cell and that he is still making sure sick adults are being treated by some doctors that he trusts. That made me feel good. And then I told him I struggled...*No, don't go there. Don't say anything about killing humans becoming monsters…* uh, that I struggled with taking energy from other live beings in order to survive."

"And?"

"And that I have come to terms with it. That I understood the need to do it. I understood I needed to do it in order to be here with you."

"Good. What were those spikes he was referring to?"

"Oh, just something with my blood chemistry. Causing some abnormal brain wave spikes. He just plans to watch it when he puts in that neuronal mesh that you already have."

And as soon as I said that I saw him. Sitting right there between us. Smiling. If you could call it a smile considering he really only had one lip, a few teeth, a big hole in his mouth and throat, and two black caves for eyes. And though I knew he was smiling, I understood he wasn't here to wish us both good luck.

Shit. Get the fuck out of this truck.

You should be glad I'm here. Your damn sister can't drive.

You are fucking pathetic. She isn't driving. The computer is driving. For someone who Dr. Po thinks was smart, you're pretty fucking stupid. May have something to do with the worms eating away all of your brain.

Yeah, well wait until one of those things you're chasing gets hold of your ass. You'll hope you still have a brain.

How the hell have you seen them? You're in my mind, not hers. They buried your ass a long time ago. You know, sometime after she dropped those hot charcoals in your mouth and eyes. God, I love saying that.

She says she doesn't see me, but I'm still there in her mind, I promise you. I'm pretty sure she will see me someday. Like you. You're just able to do it because, like I said a thousand times, you are different.

Believe me, when I get back, I'm going to make sure no one sees you ever again. Including me.

Won't happen. You can try, but won't happen. Hell, you aren't that stupid to believe I'm just going to go away.

"Is everything okay, John?" I heard Marie ask. I knew why she was asking. Somehow even without the neuronal mesh the truck was picking up some strong brain activity.

"Yes. Everything is fine."

I then heard Dr. Po's voice. "Are you sure, John?"

He knows too. Of course, he does. If Marie knows, he knows.

"Yeah. I'm okay."

"I understand, John."

Yep. You understand.

"So - you going to tell me about this truck or not?" I asked my sister.

"Well, it has 1500 horsepower. The headlight beams can actually blind people if we turn them all the way up. Probably could light up a small town with them. It is waterproof and tornado-proof and the tires cannot be punctured."

"I suppose when you come to a lake you just drive across it like a boat?"

"Not exactly, though it will float and keep us alive. But once it encounters a total water environment, it closes itself off and we can engage some flotation devices beneath the truck. Sort of like a heavy-duty motorized raft at that point. The water can impact the batteries and some of the oxygen generators and the carbon dioxide distribution system of the truck if it doesn't shut itself off to excessive penetration. There's enough food in the back of the truck for us to survive up to a month if we had to stay in this truck that long."

"By food, you mean some of those protein concoctions you've been drinking?"

"Yes. You'll like them."

I just smiled and nodded and then remembered how Dr. Po made me think I had a cheeseburger and strawberry milkshake in the hospital. He said, "You can make the body believe it is tasting what it desires." So maybe, she's right.

"So, if we come across an alien invasion, we could wait it out, huh?"

"For a short period. Dr. Po tries to anticipate worst-case scenarios and I'm sure he would get to us within a month some way or another."

"Yeah, it was pretty obvious that the good doctor tries to anticipate worst-case scenarios when you gave me a tour of his place."

"He's worried about being attacked by people who don't understand what he's trying to do. He has helped the world so much already. He wants so badly to eliminate the destructive part of the healing process. I'm sure he'll figure it out. He just needs time to do so."

"What happens to people that wander onto the property, or say the Komodo gets out of the property and hurts someone? A fence wouldn't keep the copperbrown from getting out either."

"Marie manages that. There is a fence but it's a lot like the plasma doors. They are opened and closed by Marie to allow the mice, deer, and rabbits or the bees and butterflies and birds to come in, and she closes it should one of Dr. Po's hybrids try to wander out. Somehow the insects and birds are immune to the poppy pollen and, like the mice, also immune to the flowerballs. The larger animals seem to instinctively know what to stay away from. Dr. Po has told me more than once that even though man tries to control nature, and to some extent he can, with dams, solar panels and the like, he usually ends up realizing he has been trying to lasso the wind."

"Dr. Po is a very smart man."

All of a sudden, the hair on my arms was standing straight up and my skin was tingling. The computer grid on the truck said we were still fifteen minutes away from our target area but I knew something wasn't right. I could hear something else breathing just as if it was running along right beside us. I could even feel the anger in its body and its desire to kill us. I looked out the window and though I couldn't see anything I knew it was there. I was sure of it.

"Can you show me how to shoot one of these LBEs?"

"Sure. Just make sure you aim at a rock or the ground. It will still create damage to whatever it hits, but who cares about a hole in a rock or the ground?"

Jane retrieved one of the LBEs and began to open her window when I grabbed her arm and yelled, "No!"

Jane gave me a strange look, but I could see she almost immediately knew why I wanted the LBE. "How did you feel that before me?"

"I don't know but show me how to use the damn gun!"

Jane quickly showed me what needed to be done and informed me of the five-second delay that occurred once you pressed the power button. I pushed it and the electric window switch at the same time and as the window opened, I aimed toward nothing. Nothing I could physically see but at the same time, I sensed it was there. I knew at once I had hit the being. I smelled something strange just outside the window and fired again.

I hit the electric window switch but the window would not close all the way, leaving about a one-inch gap. And though Jane didn't see it, there was a faint outline of a talon and I heard something scream that made me think of Mrs. Cunningham. Not the Mrs. Cunningham on the porch that night, but a Mrs. Cunningham that was having the skin peeled off her back.

And then it was gone. There in my lap was a large brownish-black and red talon. I closed the window and stared at Jane who was staring back at me and the thing that was in my lap.

"Don't touch it. That's a Narcoleptan claw. Front one, I believe. Let me put it away. Any poison on it will not affect me. Open up the glove compartment and pull out that thing that looks like a miniature can of deodorant and spray the area where the talon was. Anything lingering there that can cause you harm will be dead in seconds after you spray it."

I followed her orders and watched her retrieve a metal canister and drop the talon into it.

"What is happening?" Marie asked.

"John shot a Narcoleptan. He somehow sensed it before I even knew it was there. I have its talon in a canister."

"I felt the Narcoleptan's presence. It was running alongside the truck. I could hear it breathing. I could even feel its anger. Its desire to kill us."

"Amazing," was all I heard Dr. Po say. I wanted to laugh but my body was so amped up that I didn't even want to smile because I knew I would look like Dr. Frankenstein's face when he yelled, "It's alive!" and I didn't want him to see that. But I knew what he was thinking now. He was worried about me going on this trip and getting killed and now that I had done something he hadn't expected, everything had been changed back into the context of some science experiment.

"ETA one minute," Marie announced and Jane looked at me and grabbed the other LBE. She handed me several Tasers and a plasma knife and one minute later the truck came to a stop.

The screen changed to some sort of infrared heat-seeking picture and I watched as a line went around a series of circles that had numbers associated with them. The circles indicated distance in kilometers and I mumbled, "Shit. We aren't in the damn European union over here, are we? Did something happen that converted the world to the metric system while I was in a fucking coma? Why don't those circles indicate feet? I don't want to have to calcu..." but I couldn't finish my rant before Marie interjected.

"Distance indicator changed," and the meters became feet on the screen. The display indicated that there was nothing out there but I knew it was wrong. I could feel their presence.

"Hold on," I said as I grabbed Jane before she opened the door. "Don't go out there yet."

"Nothing is around us, John. The screen doesn't show anything and I don't feel anything. I'll be fine. You can wait here if you want. It shouldn't take me long especially since you've already wounded it."

"Jane. Don't go out there. Believe me. There's more than one."

Jane looked at me like I was crazy and Dr. Po's voice came into the truck telling Jane to get the medical kit from the back and retrieve the Symbion booster for me. I wasn't sure what was happening but I could still sense the presence of more than one being and then it happened. I heard the voice; the raspy voice that reminded me of my father but I knew it was not him.

The voice was saying to stand back. That he wanted one to go toward the truck and for the others to stand back. To wait until we got out and then they would attack. That he wanted to take our heads off and bring them to the puppet. To show him the heads of something that was inferior to him. To show him there was more than just two.

"Dr. Po, I believe we may be in trouble here. Your sensors don't show it, but there's more than one Narcoleptan here. Don't ask me how I know but I do. They want us to get out and then they will attack us. Watch the screen. One will show up in just a second. It's a trick. A trick to convince us that's the one we came after."

The screen lit up with a presence moving toward us. Jane looked at me and I knew she could feel it now too, though she still didn't understand what was going on. But Dr. Po listened. As I thought and hoped, in that moment he became that doctor that I knew he would be. He understood.

"Jane, do not open the door. Marie is placing the truck into lockdown. Take your hands away from the door and inject your brother with the Symbion. We will coordinate everything from this point forward. Be ready for visible identification."

With the second injection of Symbion, my body felt like a pinball machine going off and if I had the neuronal mesh in my brain, it would be lighting up Po's machines with a new high score. I could tell at that point that there were seven of the beings out there watching us and I knew one of them was the leader – the one with the raspy voice. He was coordinating everything.

The shadow on the screen came closer and closer and we watched as it leaped onto the truck. It was as if we had been hit by a lightning bolt and now the being was visible, unmoving on the hood of the truck. I told Jane to roll down her window and we aimed at the head and both shot, watching the small projectiles of light enter the being's head at the exact same time, in the exact same place causing it to explode. Without us doing anything, the windows were then re-engaged and locked.

After the being's head exploded, I heard the voice again. It told the others to leave. It said that they would come back another time. And then they all ran away; all except one. One that was told to follow us. And though Jane couldn't see it, I saw it in my mind and rolled down my window and shot. It ran toward the truck and I shot it again. It jumped up into the air and landed on the other side of the truck.

I opened the door and Jane screamed for me to get back in. It materialized as I jumped out and vaulted over the truck toward me. I shot it again, the hole opening up in its chest as it fell to the ground next to me. I pulled out the plasma knife and cut off its head before it could move and then looked all around me.

The one that I knew was the leader was still there, watching me from a distance. I could see it was smiling as it bared its teeth. It even seemed to be laughing before it disappeared. I then saw another image, that of a man in a hospital. A man I didn't know. The doctor was telling him he had pancreatic cancer but they had a new treatment that should cure him. The man stared up at me from the hospital bed, and then he was gone.

I announced to Jane that they were gone now and she agreed that she felt nothing either. She told me to get in the truck while she cut up the dead being with the plasma knife and put the parts into transport containers. When she got back inside, she instructed Marie to disinfect everything and I felt and saw a fine mist in the air. It was gone almost as soon as I felt it though, and Jane told Marie to "get us home."

"Are you going to tell me what just happened?" she asked.

"I saw the beings. In my mind. I can't tell you how but I did."

"Maybe it has to do with those spikes you and Dr. Po have been talking about."

"Yeah, maybe, sis. Maybe."

"I'm sure he'll discuss that with you once we get back. But if anyone listening wants my opinion, I hope it's a permanent aspect once you have the cord and neuronal mesh implant. Then every time we go out, you'll see them and we'll shoot them and kill them before they know what happened. That's a win-win-win if you ask me."

It's something, sis. It certainly is something.

"Yeah. I suppose we will talk. And by the way, your description of the Narcoleptan. It's a good one."

Except there is another. Another fangry and angry thing with a mind of the other. Not an other that's dear, but an other I fear. Yes, sister. Dr. Po and I need to talk. And if you want to be there, Dr. Seuss, I'm cool with that.

Jane and I didn't talk about anything else on the return trip and even when we got to the compound, I told Dr. Po I was tired and wanted to rest. He didn't argue the point. I knew why. Even without the scientific evidence, he knew my brain had a lot of spikes earlier and I needed to rest. Neither he nor I was sure what had happened but it appeared that I was connected to those creatures somehow. Perhaps it was the level of thallium or the lead or the arsenic or the manganese or the Symbion interacting with one or all of those elements. I didn't know and I didn't care. Not tonight at least.

I found my way out to the flowerball field that night and just as I expected, I was not impacted at all by the poison due to the Symbion that still flowed through my body. And just as I predicted, the specter of the old man that looked like a grainy image on a black and white TV with bad reception was there. Taunting me. And because the asshole was standing there, I knew exactly where to dig.

Considering all that had occurred that day, I slept very peacefully until sometime in the middle of the night when I got up to go to the bathroom. I sprinkled some grayish-white powder into the toilet before I sat down and I smiled when I heard Emily tell me that there was an excess of calcium and phosphorus in my stool.

"It's not excessive, Emily. I suspect it will be very normal from this point forward." I grinned and continued to relieve myself of a lot of pent-up hostility that I wasn't aware existed in my colon.

Chapter 15
When the nightmare awakens you

When I awoke the next morning, Dr. Po was sitting by me in his antimicrobial metal chair looking out the windows. These windows were clear and I could see through them into the gardens.

"You been sitting there long?"

"No, not long. Emily said you would be waking up in the next ten to fifteen minutes and I came up here and waited."

"Man, it's creepy that you and the brainy bunch know that much about me and my body just because I'm in some sort of special bed and Emily is analyzing my sleep and my oxygen and carbon dioxide levels to make sure I don't have sleep apnea. Which, by the way, I know I don't snore. I've always slept with one eye open in a figurative sense. Survival mode, I suppose."

"Excellent scientific and psychological assessment. She is indeed doing all of those things and yes, I suppose it is kind of creepy as you say. But in time I believe you will overcome that feeling, just as you have overcome every other obstacle you have encountered in your life. Now, if you will allow me to skip the usual morning pleasantries, tell me exactly what you saw out there."

Dr. Po's chair turned around silently and he looked at me through his red glasses that made him appear every part the cyborg, now that I knew his arms and legs were mechanical to some degree.

"I saw the Narcoleptan running along beside the truck. Then I heard one of them speaking in a raspy voice to the others. Setting up a trap. This wasn't just some crazed monster out there trying to kill someone or something. This was an organized group. In fact, I could tell that there were seven of them and they had someone calling all the shots. A head narc telling them what to do and I could hear it communicating to the others. It told them it wanted to bring our heads back to you and show you there was more than just two."

"More than just two?"

"Yeah. I saw that damn monster smiling at me like the pictures of the wolf in a Little Red Riding Hood picture, and then it disappeared. The next thing I saw was an image of a man lying in a hospital bed. Staring at me. I heard the doctor say he had pancreatic cancer but there was a new treatment that could cure him. The man with the cancer; something tells me he was the leader and the one who was talking to me. I have no idea how but I'm sure of it. There is something different about him. I could feel it because I had seen that cold stare many times in my life. This person possesses a knowledge of something else though. And he wants to show you how strong he is and what his abilities are. He was laughing at me and you and my sister. This being was evil, Doc, and trust me, I know something about evil."

"That is impossible. The mutations created by the Symbion molecule and the process to cure pancreatic cancer do not create a being like that. Much less one that can organize them into a group like a pack of wolves. There is nothing in science that would explain that type of behavior or genesis."

"Funny you should mention Genesis. Maybe you're looking for answers in science when the answers lie elsewhere."

"What does that mean?"

"Shit, Doc. For as long as there has been man, there has been good and evil. There were monsters on this planet long before you exposed some of them to the Molecular Transition Science. You didn't know. No one would know. They don't come to the doctor telling them they are evil. They just say they have cancer. And I doubt you ask, do you? Have you added some other questions to the medical history profile that aren't usually asked? Like, do you smoke or drink, and oh by the way, do you worship Satan?

"I doubt it. To you or any of the other doctors, they were and are just cancer patients that need to be cured. Only this one wasn't just cured. It developed into something else that neither you nor anyone else would have ever dreamed of."

"There are events that occur that go beyond the explanation of science. Though when you ask most scientists, they won't acknowledge it. So, I suppose what you are saying is possible."

"You know it's possible. Hell, you didn't even know about the converter gene until you were operating on us according to what Jane told me. And now, you can't explain what happened to me last night. I saw and heard them when Jane couldn't. And because of that, I was able to kill them and save us and come back here and let you know. That war or invasion you're worried about is coming and it's worse than the corporate or government healthcare bureaucrats or Vahemics that you thought might be driven to come here. What is amassing outside of the gate is a lot worse."

Dr. Po didn't move or respond. I could tell his neurons were probably exploding like fireworks as he sat and weighed what I had just said. And for now, that was all I could hope for. I knew if he didn't consider what I was saying had merit, we were doomed.

"Do you know why I wear these red glasses, John?"

"I thought it might have something to do with your eyes being sensitive to light or something."

"In a roundabout way, you are correct. The glasses emit ultraviolet rays and kill bacteria and viruses that are in the environment around us all the time. They also allow me to see."

I watched as he removed the glasses and when he did, I saw empty sockets where his eyes should have been.

"The electronic system I developed retracts into the back of my eye when I remove my glasses, and an invisible plasma shield is placed over my eye orbits to protect all the equipment that is attached to my optic nerve and the glasses. I realized I was going blind years ago and if I didn't do something to fix the problem, I would lose my sight. I show you this to let you know, probably in a more ostentatious manner than usual, that I am not blind to what you are saying.

"I have been aware for a long time that you are hypersensitive to the Symbion molecule. Giving you the booster shot yesterday was a calculated risk, but one I was willing to take. I know placing the implant in you could possibly create a world in your mind that might overtake your senses and create something that neither you nor I would be able to tolerate. I now also know, that by not placing the implant in you, I am not sure we will have a chance to survive."

I watched him put his glasses back on, and then I couldn't see him anymore. All I could see was my father sitting in that chair berating me. Telling me over and over again, "You're different." And then I remembered what Emily said when I was on the toilet and I yelled in my mind, *"You're damn right I'm different, and it's fucking time to embrace it!"*

"I am different, Doc. Different from my sister. When the big bad wolf saw what we could do to two of them, it was afraid. For just a second, I could tell it was afraid and it knew it needed to leave or risk dying. But then it wanted to show me it wasn't scared and that's when it bared its teeth and smiled. That was an evil smile. Now I'm sure you can't change my body chemistry and I think you see that too. You need my body chemistry to react differently with the implant. Just as you know it will.

"My sister doesn't know this but what I saw last night, I've seen before. In my dreams when I was a child. I just attributed the nightmare to the movies and the world I was living in. Vivid dreams of monsters weren't anything abnormal for me. I swear, Doc, I've seen this nightmare before. And you may not believe it, but I think I was meant to see it. To be here now. To help you. There's a reason I have a connection with this abomination. Perhaps in some way I always have."

"Emily, prepare John for surgery this morning. When you shower this morning, John, Emily will make sure you are prepped for surgery. I will wait here while you get ready and escort you down to the surgical suite. After the surgery, you can eat."

I started for the bathroom and then stopped. "What would you do if you found out Jane or I was more like my father? Cruel, sadistic, evil."

"I would let you die."

"How did you know we weren't like that?"

"Because I saw what happened to your mother. I knew neither one of you killed her."

"But you saw what we did to our father."

"I did."

"And that didn't worry you? Doesn't that in itself suggest some sort of psychopathology?"

"Psychopathology? I am afraid you heard that word too often as a child. No, I don't think it suggests that at all. I think it suggests an extreme will to survive that most people don't have. As I have told you before, I know what kind of home you and your sister lived in."

"But what if after you saved us, we became more like our father than you expected?"

"Then as I stated earlier, I would let you die."

"How?"

"You are not superhuman, John. A gun, poison, light bullets. They will all kill you. It just may take longer due to your enhanced genetics and the medical phenomenon that permeates the cells of your body."

"And once I have the implant?"

"It would take even longer. But as you noted in my garden and during the short time you have been with me, I not only have the ability to create that which heals man, but also that which will destroy man. But what does this 'What if?' discussion accomplish? What is it that you really want to say or ask?"

"I just wonder about free will a lot. The free will we have that allows us to do good and to do evil. It sounds like an easy enough concept to grasp but I find it very difficult to do so."

"Yes, I realize that happens with you. I have seen the medical manifestations of it within your brain."

"Perhaps there shouldn't be free will, Doc. Have you even considered that?"

"As a matter of fact, I have. But I realized some time ago, I am not God. Just because we could make a very predictable inference at the time of creation of the genetic predisposition to evil, doesn't mean it will occur."

"I bet with you controlling the dice, it would still be a better world than it is now."

"Man without free will, John, is not man. It is not something that this world will ever encounter. If you are a religious person, you have a vision of what the end looks like. If you are not a religious person, you just know you live and then you die."

"What are you, Doc?"

"I am of the opinion that there is the possibility of a better world now and a better one in the future."

"Because of what you can do?"

"Because of what I cannot do."

I nodded my head and realized that I was in the presence of one of the smartest men in the world. And though it helped to hear what he said, I also realized that the Haunted House ride that Jane and I were now on would be more like a roller coaster in a thunderstorm. I had thought I would enjoy going on that ride with my sister every day but I knew from this point forward, it would also create a world full of trepidation and uncertainty. This ride would be truly scary every time we paid for a ticket and put the broken safety belt across our legs. And then I heard Jack.

"You never know how much you really believe anything until its truth or falsehood becomes a matter of life or death to you. It is easy to say you believe a rope to be strong and sound as long as you are merely using it to cord a box. But suppose you had to hang by that rope over a precipice. Wouldn't you then first discover how much you really trusted it?"

Yeah. I suppose I would, Jack. I suppose I would.

Chapter 16
The cord

Emily told me to close my eyes as she sprayed my body with a different kind of mist and I could even smell it this time. It reminded me of the Emergency Rooms that my mother took me to at least a dozen times.

"You may open your eyes now, John," Emily instructed and when she did, I saw Jack sitting on the toilet smoking a pipe.

"Check this out, Jack," I said as Emily bathed me in warm ultraviolet rays that I knew were destroying the billions of bacteria on my skin to minimize infection after surgery. "Pretty cool, huh? The light - it's killing bacteria on my skin."

"Yes. I know."

"Why are you here now?"

"I'm not sure. These interactions are dependent on you, not me."

"The rope. What you said about the rope. You were referring to the surgical implant that Dr. Po is about to put in me, weren't you? What you tell me now doesn't seem to be as much of a riddle as it once was."

"Yes, I was referring to that. I believe you can see with much more clarity than I ever did at your age."

"But the device, it will connect me to my past. I know it will. Dr. Po is aware that it will too. And that scares me. I think it may even scare him a bit. I was full of anger and resented authority and that hasn't changed. I do really respect and like Dr. Po, but what if this implant only makes those bad feelings worse?"

"The fact that you are asking that question should be proof to yourself that you will not allow that to happen. Our past just provides us with a basis for how people see us. It does not define who we are unless we continue to dwell on it our entire lives. And in doing so, realize we have accomplished nothing in the end. It is the present and future actions we take that will define who we are."

"I want to help my sister, protect her. I want to help Dr. Po and do the right thing. But how will I know what the right thing is?"

"Have you read those books I gave you?"

"No."

"They will provide the framework from which you gain awareness. But that awareness will be of little value if you are not able to utilize it in a way that is realized when you unite your brain with your heart."

"That's very poetic. Poetic and wise. But you've always been that."

"I believe those that read my poetry would suggest otherwise."

"Funny, Jack. But it still bothers me that I've seen this being before that tried to kill my sister and me the other night. I saw it in my dreams when I was a child. It seems like fate has brought me to this moment in time."

"You struggle as I did with understanding the serpentine nature of life. You forget what we have talked about so often, the free will that man possesses. Fate is not a cruel or forgiving mistress that dictates what will happen to you. You decide what will happen to you. Remember, all those that are in Hell are there because they chose to be there. All those that aspire to do something greater have that ability."

"Are you saying that I am being given the ability to do something great? That Dr. Po's implant will give me that ability?"

"I don't know what you are being given, John. I only know you have free will to do with it what you so desire."

"Did I tell you that I read your books about Narnia when I was a child?"

"No, but I assumed as much. I believe that readers of the books saw more within the words than I ever considered."

"Then why didn't you tell them otherwise?"

"First of all, it's not for me to do so. And if they saw God in those pages, so be it. God uses us in different ways, so if the stories led some to God, then I'm happy that they did."

"Do you think grinding up my father's bones and shitting on them will make him go away?"

"I have to admit, John, in all my life, I was never provided the opportunity to answer such a question. I am not a psychiatrist but I suppose that in some way, that type of psychological release would be viewed as having a benefit by some. For me, I do not see the need to harbor that much anger for someone who is already dead."

"You did not see what he did to me or my sister or my mother."

"I did not and I am not judging you. I am merely trying to answer a question that was posed to me."

"You are now prepped for surgery. Please place the robe around your body and your feet inside the foot covers that are now available to you in the open cabinet."

I followed Marie's directions and looked back at Jack who was still sitting there smoking his pipe. "Will I see you later?"

"Again, that is dependent on you, but if I was a betting man, I would think that you and I shall converse again at some point."

"Does it mean I'm crazy talking to someone who is dead?"

"I suppose that all depends on that person's actions once he has held those conversations."

I laughed and said, "See you later, Jack," as I opened the bathroom door. Though it felt like I had been in there for twenty minutes, it had only been four.

"Follow me," Dr. Po said as he walked out of the room and turned left instead of right.

I had never seen anything but a large window there, but as were most things in this building, what I was looking at was not what was really there. The window dissolved as Dr. Po instructed Marie to open the surgical elevator. He said nothing else to Marie as if there was only one destination for the elevator in which we were on. When the doors opened, I saw someone else I recognized. The nurse from the hospital – Sam.

She was even prettier than I remembered. That red hair and her green eyes. Like two olives that had been plucked from a jar with some sort of black pimento that Dr. Po created in the center of them. How come I had never noticed those before?

"You remember your nurse, Samantha, don't you?"

"Yep."

"I have asked her to come help me here for a little while. She will be assisting me with your surgery and then will be helping with some other medical trials I am about to begin."

"Hello, John."

I smiled at the sound of her voice. I didn't realize how much I had missed it until I heard it.

"You're not going to remove my eyes during surgery, are you?"

She laughed and Dr. Po looked at me strangely.

"It's a joke. Something she said to me at the hospital. When she convinced someone, probably you, to remove my restraints. She asked me if I was going to gouge out her eyes in order to get out of the room. You know, via the retinal scan."

"That person she convinced was indeed me. Samantha is a very good nurse. Exceptional really and I trust her medical opinion. She was correct when she said you would not be a threat to the staff or her. Although the others on staff didn't believe it, so she ended up being the only nurse to assist me with you until you left the hospital."

"Well, thank you, Sam."

I didn't even feel the elevator moving but within a moment, the doors opened.

"No problem. Now, follow me and get on this table. You're going to get some medicine that will make you feel very relaxed. You will probably go to sleep but you won't need to be intubated. The surgery should take a couple of hours. Are you ready?" Sam asked.

"Yeah," I said as I held out my arm. "Hook me up. Send me into dreamland."

After she started the IV, I saw Dr. Po standing next to her. "Same ladder contraption, Doc?"

"No, John. This one is kept in the surgical suite. Don't worry. I have done this surgery one other time."

"Shit. Dr. Po - making a joke." I laughed before their faces disappeared. I thought I heard Dr. Po talking about The Who and I wondered why he would be talking about a rock band. And then I heard him saying someone from the Who would be flying in to meet with them later in the afternoon. I wondered if Dr. Po had any elephants on the property and I laughed. Of course, he did. I was sure that Horton was out there and he would hear that plane as it flew over.

I then heard Sam say something about the surgery being over and I opened my eyes. She was right there, smiling down at me. I wanted to ask her if her eyes had ever been in a martini before, when I saw Dr. Po rising up beside her. He was checking something on my abdomen.

"How do you feel, John?"

"I feel great. Am I wired for sound now? I want to make a good impression on The Who when they get here. When is the concert?"

Sam laughed and Dr. Po just looked at me with his red eyes.

"Amazing. Simply amazing. The neuronal mesh is embedded and functioning and the device I implanted in you not even twenty minutes ago seems to be almost completely assimilated into your body. In fact, it appears functional now. Shall we try it, John?"

"Why are you asking me?"

"It's your body."

I wasn't sure if it was the drugs or what but that question from the doctor confused me for a moment. And then I realized, it wasn't the drugs. It was respect. Respect from a doctor asking me for my opinion regarding something he had done for me. No one in the white coats had ever done that before. I shook my head yes and saw Dr. Po acknowledge my comment before he turned toward Sam.

"Bring over that cage, please."

"Cage? Doc, what do you have in a cage? Are you sure about that? I don't know what's in there, but if it's in a cage it must be an animal of some kind, which is sort of freaking me out."

"I anticipated you would have that type of response. That is why you will not see what is in this cage, but I can tell you that the animal is anesthetized and was killing deer on the property. It is a large carnivore. It was also wounded and would have had to be killed eventually as it only knows one thing to do once wounded, and that is do anything it needs to in order to survive. So, the threat to everything within the compound was heightened and needed to be addressed. This is a humane way of doing so."

I nodded and watched as Dr. Po took the skin-like vacuum-shaped hose attached to my body and moved it toward the cage that I could not see. It seemed as if my body had a hundred fingers as I felt the hair of the animal and then had a weird sensation as if I became a part of the animal itself. I could feel its abdomen going up and down as it breathed and then my entire body felt like it was a leg that had fallen asleep and was now beginning to regain blood flow. Thousands of pins and needle-like sensations traveled along every inch of my body and then it all stopped. For just a second, I was at the top of the roller coaster, staring down at the hundred-foot drop. And then the coaster went flying down the rails and I could feel the energy and speed of every car racing through my body. It only lasted fifteen or twenty seconds before the coaster made all the twists and turns and came to the end of the ride. I was excited and energized as I imagined myself stepping off the ride and then I looked up at Dr. Po and Sam.

"Amazing," Dr. Po repeated quietly as I watched the hose that now looked more like a cord, retract into my body with some help from his hands.

"It is already sealing up the surgical site. Amazing. Simply Amazing. Much faster effect with you than with your sister. How are you feeling?"

"Like the adrenaline rush from riding a very fast roller coaster," and then I looked down at the cage. "Somewhat sad too. Please, tell me what it was."

"It was a mountain lion. They don't often get onto the grounds, but this was not the first time it has occurred. A large stag wounded it before it died."

"Can't control nature, can we, Doc?"

"No, we cannot. And even though you say you feel pumped and energized, you need to rest for the remainder of the day. Considering how things are progressing though, I would imagine the surgical site would be one hundred percent healed by tomorrow. Amazing isn't it, Samantha?"

"Yes, very much so," Sam replied as she smiled at me. And I wasn't sure if it was the roller coaster ride or just the way she looked at me, but I sensed she was talking about something more than the surgery.

"Okay. I get it. Do as the doctor orders." *Damn. What the hell did I just say? Never said that before. You are getting to me, Doc.* "By the way, where's my sister?"

"She is outside on the grounds. She told me to let her know when the surgery was complete and then she would come stay with you. She was going out to the waterfall. She likes spending time out there and thinking."

"Doc. I really feel good. You said everything looked really good. I think the word you used was amazing. Since everything is 'amazing' as you say, would it be okay if Sam walked me outside? With this device inside of me now, I shouldn't be bothered too much by your dandymines and witch's blooms."

"I'm sorry, John, but Samantha needs to help me in here. We need to get this area cleaned up and prepared for some visitors."

"The band?"

"Yes, John, the band," Dr. Po replied and for just a moment, I thought I saw him smile. "But you do make a good point. With your implant in place, and the surgical site almost healed, your assumption that you should be safe is probably a correct one. But, please go directly to the waterfall, retrieve your sister, and then come straight back to the house and rest."

Again, the little man in the white coat surprised me. *Amazing* I thought and smiled.

"Are you going to help me get dressed, Sam?"

"I will get you some clothes if that's what you mean."

"Yep. That's what I meant." Sam handed me the clothes and showed me to the elevator that led to the tunnel exit. Just before I got on, I asked her if she could have dinner with me later that evening.

"I'm afraid I won't be able to do that. I'm meeting with the band, you know."

"Okay, okay. I know it's not really the band. So, 'Who' is it?"

"Funny. The WHO in this case refers to the World Health Organization. Some members are coming by to discuss some disease situations in Africa to see if Dr. Po can help."

"Can he?"

"If anyone can, it will be him."

"Yeah. That's what I think, too," I said as I got on the elevator.

As the doors closed, I heard her say she would see me after dinner, and though I wanted to stop the doors from closing I couldn't. But it didn't matter. I would get a chance to see her later and I knew my intuition was right. She wasn't just referring to the surgical site when she replied to Dr. Po's question. She liked me. I suddenly realized I had never had a girlfriend and I was going to be twenty-one years old next year. *Damn. That's messed up. I wonder how old she is. She's a nurse so she's older than me, that's for sure.*

As good-looking as she is, she's probably had lots of boyfriends. Probably doctor boyfriends. Why would she be interested in me? I never even graduated from high school. And she knows everything about me. She's seen everything on me. Shit. I'm not sure this was a good idea I thought. When I looked up, I realized I had walked by the death bush and was heading into the woods, and then I stopped.

It felt like something had reached up out of the ground and grabbed my ankles and I couldn't move. I saw the chalk-like beings chasing the deer. There were three of them and as I stood there like a statue, one of them saw me and stopped following the deer. It stared at me, raised its nose in the air, and let out a scream like one of those howler monkeys.

I watched as my sister ran by it not caring that it had stopped running. She was laughing as she passed it chasing after the other two.

"Stupid fucks!" she yelled out. "Always looking for an easy meal. Well, this deer will be your downfall. I saw you looking at it, just outside the gate, but you didn't see me, did you? Too damn bad for your fucked up milky-white asses."

Just as she ran by the one staring at me, it jumped toward me like nothing I had ever seen before. I looked around for something to use as a weapon but there wasn't anything. "Shit!" I yelled, as the damn thing leaped into the air and seemed to be flying toward me in slow motion. I dove to the ground and tried to get under it but as I did, its claws tore into my back and I screamed.

My back was on fire. I suddenly felt the being jump onto my back and take a huge bite out of my shoulder with two layers of teeth that felt like saw blades. I yelled again before I heard Jane shout, "Get down!" I pushed my head into the dirt, as the being tried to scream before it became silent and the weight was violently removed from my back.

"John, he took a chunk out of your shoulder. Put your cord into the ground now. Never mind, I'll do it," she said as she lifted up my shirt and touched the implant. I could feel those hundreds of fingers reaching out and touching hers as it got closer to the ground. As soon as it connected with the dirt, it felt as if each one of those fingers was a root that began digging into the soil. As they did, I felt the pins and needles awakening again, only this time it was much more limited. Jane could tell that as she began to speak to me.

"You weren't supposed to be out here. You're supposed to be inside. I'm going to need to get that deer. Stay here," she said as I moved my head and looked up to see her running away. My shoulder and back felt like they had burst into flames now, and what energy I got from the cord that was buried into the ground was like raindrops falling onto flames. Comforting when they hit my back, but unable to extinguish the fire.

I tried to sit up and though it felt like hell to move, I managed to push myself up from the ground. I moved but the cord remained in place as if it knew it needed to stay where it was or I would die. I watched as she decapitated both of the dying Vahemics that had brought down the deer and then saw her pick up the deer and run toward me. When she laid the injured deer next to me, she placed my cord into it, and I immediately felt the flames extinguished from my back and shoulder.

I looked at the dead deer and I began to understand something that I knew I wasn't going to share with Dr. Po. My sister had purposely opened the gate in order to allow those Vahemics to come onto the grounds. She had lured them in with the deer. It was reckless behavior.

And as I was carried and half-dragged toward the house, I immediately realized that I didn't need to tell him anything. I was certain he already knew about my sister's uncontrolled behavior. Marie would have seen it and notified him. So, I then asked myself if he had put a kill switch in the cord. If he knew anything about free will, he'd be stupid not to I reasoned. And as soon as I thought that, I knew the answer to the question that I had just posed.

Psychopathology. He said neither of us suffered from it. But the good doctor always plans for the "what if."

I would have said the same thing when asked that question, Doc. Because in the end, it really doesn't matter, does it? You know what to do.

Chapter 17
Band-Aid

Before we even got back to the house, Dr. Po was asking both of us what had happened to me. I didn't bother to ask how he knew. I'm sure that the neuronal mesh was showing all sorts of spikes as well as informing Marie of other chemical markers that indicated my body was stressed.

"Just nature, Doc. Had a little run-in with nature."

"Vahemics," my sister added. "His back was ripped open and his shoulder had a chunk of it taken out."

"Jane, bring him right to the surgery suite. Samantha, prep the OR. Don't worry John, you will be fine."

Funny, as soon as he told me not to be worried, I began to worry. I know he told me I wasn't Superman, but I think subconsciously I thought I had been given some sort of invincible power with the cord implant. I was flying too close to the sun, I suppose. Wings melted and it hurt like a son of a bitch to have those wings burned off my back.

Before we went into the OR suite, my sister and I were sprayed with a mist and hit with a round of dark purple lights that flashed on and off for about ten seconds. I heard Marie say, "external organisms eradicated," and the circular glass door opened. Sam was waiting for us on the other side of the door and she told Jane to lay me on my stomach on the table.

"Sure. Take good care of him. I'd hate to lose him when I just got him back."

What the hell? My sister is worried now too. Damn. This must be some serious shit.

"Jane, will you bring the Vahemic's body into the lab? Place it in the storage chamber. I will examine it later."

"There's more than one, Dr. Po. There are three."

"Three? How many attacked your brother?"

"Just one. I killed the other two. Well, I killed all three of them but not until one of them got to him. They were chasing a deer. I think they're getting bolder and maybe a bit careless."

"Yes, perhaps. We will talk later, Jane."

"See you later, big brother," she said and was gone before I could reply.

Sam was applying some liquid to my shirt and not only was it making my back and shoulder feel better, but it was also dissolving my clothes. "Damn that feels good."

"Yes, it should. It's a numbing solution, antiseptic, and solvent that dissolves the material in some of Dr. Po's clothing. Once I have this applied to your back and shoulder, I'll be starting an IV and giving you an anesthetic. The cuts on your back and shoulder will require surgery. In fact, that cut on your shoulder reminds me of the one your sister had. Same exact place, only this is much deeper."

As the needle entered my arm, I saw Dr. Po at the front of the table and he was looking at me at face level.

"John, as I have said before, the chemical composition in your body will help tremendously with the poison that the Vahemic has injected in you with its claws and teeth. But I am very worried about the extent of the cut on your shoulder. It took away some of your bone, so the poison entered your bone marrow. I will give you a very high dose of antibiotics and a booster of Symbion, but we will need to use your cord again."

"Yeah. I had a feeling you were going to say that."

"Don't worry. You will be unaware of the animal but to be honest with you, it is not a wounded animal. It is one of many that I keep here for my research."

"Just make sure it's not a dog or cat. No dogs or cats, Dr. Po, please."

"It isn't and I understand."

"See you after the surgery, John," Sam said and I wasn't sure if it was her voice or the drugs but her words seemed so warm and caring.

Seconds later, I lost sight of them though I did hear Dr. Po tell Sam to retrieve the swine. And even though I felt the mind-numbing effects of the anesthetic, I still felt the shot of Symbion when it entered my body and my cord being activated and the hundred finger sensation again as it attached itself to the pig's body.

The pigskin felt very much like the skin of a human. I could feel its heart beating and I could hear it grunting as its breathing grew labored. I knew I was killing it, but I also knew it was necessary if I was going to live. The pins and needles feeling returned to my body and just like before, I went over the hill on the roller coaster and as the sensation left, I could feel my wounds healing. It was as if I was looking at my cells through a microscope, opening up other cells, and seeing parts of them light up, and this process repeated over and over a hundred times a second.

The electricity in my body shut down momentarily before I sensed my cord reattached to another pig. This time I wanted to object, but I couldn't. I could see my cells beginning to light up again as if I was looking at a brilliant nighttime sky. I saw shooting stars, and with each one of them, I felt my body growing stronger.

Eventually, the sky began to darken, and I heard myself yelling, "Wake up!" I opened my eyes but did not see Dr. Po or Sam. As I looked around the room, I saw that I was in our old house sitting in front of our television watching cartoons. Elmer Fudd was chasing Bugs Bunny and then he stopped. He turned toward the television screen and started talking to me. He said he didn't appreciate me killing Porky and Petunia and pointed his shotgun at the TV. The gun exploded and the glass shattered as the pieces of the television screen flew into my face and body.

I ran into the kitchen to clean my wounds and saw my father on the kitchen floor with the top of his head gone and the shovel lying next to his body. I turned to look for my sister because I knew what was coming next, but I didn't see her. Then I heard my father speaking to me.

She's outside heating up some charcoal. She'll be back in a minute. And you will try and drop some of those burning charcoals in my mouth and eyes but this time I'm ready for you.

"What do you mean?" I said as I turned around and fell back, but the kitchen countertop stopped me from falling all the way to the floor.

You should know better than to fuck with the big bad wolf. Don't you learn anything from that cartoon shit you watch all the time?

Then I knew. My father, the dreams I had, the Narcoleptan that talked to me. I was able to connect to that being because of my shit-ass father.

Hell, I had lived with a Narcoleptan for my entire life but he just never changed his appearance. And as soon as I realized that, the son of a bitch started to change. His eyes began dripping blood and looked like little pieces of peppermint candy. His face reformed into a muzzle and twelve long fangs. His entire body was full of hair and the claws on his feet and hands looked like supersized versions of my father's handheld garden rake. And there it was. The picture I had drawn with a crayon and given to Dr. Banks, who said I had an overactive imagination and wanted to talk about being a fish. Shit.

Want to try and drop some of those charcoals in me now? Tell the puppet, I'm coming for him and his little dog too.

Little dog? This isn't 'The Wizard of Oz,' you dumb shit.

How do you know what it is and what it isn't? You're being operated on. Under anesthesia and the magic little potion that the puppet invented. I was your father for a moment and then the big bad wolf. Seems to me, this place could be whatever the hell you or I wanted it to be.

Well, you fucked that up, you son of a bitch. It will never be what you want it to be. I control this. A good friend told me that. So, fuck off. I'm going to look forward to killing you again, whatever the hell you call yourself now, and I may grind your bones up and put them with my father every morning.

What you do to your father makes me laugh. You won't be able to do that to me. We will kill you and everyone in the house that Po built. And the only reason I am telling you this, is because you are right. You and I are connected. Too bad you have to die. But I know you. I can feel you. When I kill your sister, you won't be happy and that will make me have to kill you. So sad, but I don't think we would have ever gotten along. You are too different. Ohhhh, I felt the anger as soon as I said that. You are so predictable but I so love the anger. Damn. I think they are finished with your surgery. Those Vahemics are not to be messed with when they are hungry. See you later, John Deaux.

And just like he said, I woke up as if from a long nap, and there was Sam looking down at me. I was in another room. Not my room but some sort of room like the one I was in at the hospital. *Was I really ever at the hospital?* Everything seemed very familiar but I was confused.

"Am I back in the hospital at UT?"

"No, John. You are in a recovery suite here at Dr. Po's. It's much like an intensive care room in the hospital. I can see why you think so. And before you ask, the surgery went very well. I know you get tired of hearing Dr. Po say this but the way your body reacts to the Symbion and now with the cord implant providing you energy, it's really quite remarkable how you've started to heal."

"Sort of like Superman, huh?"

"Not at all like Superman. The Vahemic's teeth would have broken off if they tried to bite his body and their claws would not have opened up your back like a tree that a grizzly has used to mark his territory."

She put you in your place. Wasn't that the stupid kind of thinking that got you into this mess? Dumbass. Wise up.

"Is the doctor around, Sam? I have something interesting to discuss with him. Things that I saw and felt while I was having surgery."

"I'm afraid he won't see you until later this evening. He's with 'the band,'" she said as she winked. "But there is someone else that would like to see you."

I didn't even see her standing on the other side of the room until then. And my sister noticed the lack of attention.

"You do remember me, don't you? Your sister? The one that saved your life?"

"Damn it, Jane...I..," and then I stopped. I was going to chastise her for what she had done but I knew this wasn't the time. I wasn't sure if there would ever be a right time but I knew it wasn't now.

"You were saying 'Damn it...' what?"

"I was saying damn it, of course, I remember you. Your name is Maria Von Trapp."

She laughed. "Yes, that's right." She came over and took my hand. "Sam, if you want to take a break, I'll stay here with him."

"Can I get something to eat?" I asked.

"Yes, I'll go get your cheeseburger and strawberry milkshake and be back in a few minutes," Sam promised.

She remembers.

I started to ask Jane why she did it and then I stopped as I remembered about Marie and Dr. Po. They could probably hear us and I didn't want that. I couldn't ask her about it until we were outside, but that wasn't going to work either. Dr. Po and Marie can hear whatever they want to hear now. And then just like before, my brain told me all this debate was unnecessary. *He knows already. I just need to talk about everything with him. Make sure we're on the same page. Test him one final time.*

Sam returned with my food and while I ate, I asked a lot of questions. I wanted to know more about her. And if Jane had heard all this before, she didn't seem to mind. Sam told us why she had become a nurse. How her mother was a nurse and her father was a doctor but her parents didn't push her into the profession. It felt like she just had a calling for it. She said she truly liked helping people.

Where the hell were you when I was growing up? Apparently, I missed all the 'medicine is my calling' class individuals in my many encounters with the healthcare profession. I only met the 'who's next' shift.

She said that she met Dr. Po at UT Medical Center when he treated both her parents who were heavy smokers and both had lung cancer. He cured them and she had them for another two years before they died in a diving accident off the Gold Coast of Australia.

"Jesus Christ! What kind of diving accident?" I asked.

"They were attacked by white sharks and their bodies were torn in half."

"Holy fucking shit. I tried to tell everyone about those damn sharks and...ah, hell." I didn't need to continue. Both she and my sister were laughing so hard they were crying.

"Funny. Sick man in bed. Critical care patient. Where does it say in the nursing manual, 'fuck with the patient?' I bet it doesn't say that anywhere."

"Your blood pressure spiked for just a second and now it is more normal than it has been since you came out of surgery. Jane told me to say that and she was right. She knew it would help you in your recovery. I wouldn't be surprised if Dr. Po didn't move you back to your room later this evening. Speaking of which, Jane, can you stay with him? Dr. Po told me that if John continued to improve, to come up and meet with the people from Africa."

"Yeah, no problem. I'll be here. Fun getting back on the Scrambler, wasn't it, bro?"

I had to admit she was right. Next to the Haunted House ride, the Scrambler was our favorite. Our mother never went on it. She didn't like it because she said it made her dizzy, but my sister and I loved it. Just missing those cars as they flung you around and around. Laughing as the cars came close to hitting each other.

Damn. Another epiphany. Getting flung around without getting hurt. Now I can see why we liked that ride so much. Hell, I should go into psychotherapy.

"Remember when those guys had their arms almost torn off trying to shake hands as they went by each other?"

"They didn't follow the rules. Keep your hands and arms inside the ride at all times," I replied and we both laughed.

Then we looked at each other for what seemed like ten minutes as we both tried to think of something else to say. She had told me she didn't want to be reminded of the past and that was all we had together until just days ago. And now we were both in some sort of science fiction movie acting out roles we weren't familiar with yet.

"So, what have you been doing the last two and a half years?"

"Well, once I was able and Dr. Po let me, I visited you every day. Then I usually had a cooking class or learned how to make quilts. Learned how to do pottery too. And after that, I learned how to kill things. I really am better at the last one. I liked that class the best."

"Yes, I can tell. But later when I'm out of this bed, can you show me how to turn a pot?"

"Turn it into what?"

We laughed again and I knew as Marie was monitoring me, she could see that my sister's presence was a very effective healing tool. From that point forward, we had no trouble with conversation as I listened to all the ways she had trained and learned how to deal with the mutations that now threatened society. An hour later, Dr. Po walked into the room.

"It seems like you are doing very well, John. Let me check your back and shoulder for a moment and then we can talk."

Dr. Po raised up on his moveable chair and I turned over to accommodate his request. I winced but the pain now was a tenth of what it was prior to surgery.

"Yes. Very, very good. I would say in three days, you will only have some faint scarring on your back. Your shoulder will take a little longer and I may recommend another boost from your cord implant but we will just monitor that and then decide."

"Thanks, Doc."

Dr. Po sat at bed level to my left and smiled as he looked at Jane. "So, you said there were three Vahemics?"

"Yes. They were chasing a deer. Don't you think Marie should have caught that?"

"Probably, Jane. Probably. I will have to examine that later. Would you mind if I talked with your brother alone for just a little while? I want to ask him about several things that occurred the other night with the Narcoleptans. Perhaps you can find Sam and assist her?"

"Sure. See you later, brother. And you too, Doc."

As soon as she left the room, Dr. Po began. "Your sister let the Vahemics into the compound. Marie saw it and informed me. I didn't think she would do that with you around, but I am sure she never imagined you coming out to see her. That was a very costly error on my part and I hope you can forgive me."

No sense in backing away from the subject now. "Have you told her about a kill switch in the cord?"

"No, because it would not matter."

Damn. Just like I thought. And hoped. He is an honest, decent man. A damn smart doctor and a caring and good man.

"How does it work?"

"It releases a poison into your body. You just go to sleep and your organs stop working. It is painless and works in less than a minute."

"I understand why, Doc, and I appreciate you being honest with me. In fact, I'm glad it's there."

"Thank you, John. Now, regarding that man you saw in the hospital bed; Marie and I have done a great deal of research and have discovered his identity. His name was Vincent Merkel. He had pancreatic cancer and he was, as you suggested, one who pursued mysticism in his life."

"Mysticism? I think you're being kind in using that word. I think it was more like he worshipped the devil or some shit like that."

"Yes, you are correct. As I said before, I knew you would be hyper-sensitive to the Symbion, but I didn't think of this type of event occurring. The connection between the two of you does not conform to scientific principles."

"Doc, I realized something as you were operating on me. I've grown up with Vincent Merkel my whole life. He had a different name and even though he may not have had any satanic symbols around the house, he was just as evil. Look at my records and see if you have anything from my therapist meetings with a Dr. Banks. There's a crayon picture I drew of him. Well, him as a Narcoleptan or my father as the wolfman. Either way you interpreted it you would be right. Dr. Banks, of course, said it was just my overactive imagination and something I saw at the fair, but he was a dumbass. It was my father and now it's this Vincent Merkel. While I was having the surgery, he was talking to me in a nightmare vision of some kind. I'm convinced it's because of my father that I can communicate with him somehow. He claimed that he and I were connected and he once again said he plans to kill us all."

"It is all so unscientific, but I cannot find another explanation of what is occurring with you and this man. There is more too, John. Mr. Merkel was a postman also at one time in his life. Strange coincidence, isn't it?"

"You and I both know it isn't a coincidence and you and I both know he's no longer a man."

"But there is no such thing as psychic ability. I have researched it at length and though there are some unexplained predicted events, there is nothing to suggest it was anything but luck or the ability to take much better educated guesses based upon what was known."

"There wasn't a cure for cancer until you came up with the Symbion molecule and then grew the Dahliarium in your lab. And the cord implant and the Molecular Transition Dynamics science. None of that existed before you. You said the other scientists didn't believe you. Why should we not believe this is indeed happening? How many of those other scientists have encountered a Vahemic or Narcoleptan and lived to discuss it?"

Yes, Marie, I know what John is saying is true. It is impossible to dismiss this connection he says they have. How else could he have seen them or known what they were thinking? But how did the pancreatic cancer treatment transform the patient into a Narcoleptan? That is a scientific anomaly that I cannot explain. Unless. Unless his reference to "more than two" meant he also possesses the converter gene? Is he telling us he also had the converter gene and that the Symbion treatment of his pancreas created the beast he is now? This is a converter gene mutation? Is that possible, Marie? We can't afford to be wrong. Not now.

"Dr. Po? Are you okay?"

"Sorry. I was just thinking about everything that you have been telling me."

Yeah. There is a lot there to take in, isn't there?

"John, as you know, the World Health Organization came here today. They asked for my help with an Ebola outbreak in Uganda. I have been working on a serum that is composed of genetic components of Dahliarium, manipulated by Symbion into creating hybrid human helper T-cells and killer T-cells. The Dahliarium and Symbion make the helper T-cell one hundred times more effective in seeking out the infecting virus and activating the Killer T-cells that release the perforin and cytotoxins at ten times their normal rate."

Though I was trying to follow what Dr. Po was saying he realized I was struggling to understand.

"I am sorry. At times, I sometimes forget my audience and understand I mean nothing derogatory by that comment. The T-cells are white cells within the body that fight infection. The perforin punctures the cell wall and allows the cytotoxins to enter the cell and kill the virus. It has worked here in the lab setting but I have not tried it outside of the lab."

There was a strange look on Dr. Po's face that I had never seen before and for a moment, I didn't know what it was. And then I understood what his facial expression was telling me because I had seen it in my own a thousand times. Doubt.

"It doesn't always work, does it?"

"No. There is a ten percent probability that this will not work."

"And when you say, not work, you mean they could be given this vaccine and still die?"

"Yes."

"But isn't there a good chance they will die anyway? And isn't a ninety percent chance of being cured much better than a hundred percent chance of dying?"

"Your optimism is infectious. And fortunately, the death rate is not one hundred percent. It is closer to ninety percent once infected, but still, what you are saying has merit."

I laughed. Even when making a joke, Dr. Po couldn't stop being a scientist. But that's what made his attempt at humor so funny. And eventually, my laughing made him smile. But only for a moment as he looked at me with a different level of concern.

"There is something else, John. I am afraid of a mutation occurring. There is always a chance of a mutation and we have no idea what that would look like or how dangerous it could become."

"What do the folks in WHO-ville say?"

"Whoville? Do you mean the scientists from the World Health Organization?"

"Yeah. You need to read some more Dr. Seuss, Dr. Po. Believe me, it will help."

"Perhaps I should. But for now, all I can tell you is that I fear those scientists. They were fine with the level of mutations from the cancer cures. They didn't care that I could not quantify nor confirm that there would be possible mutations with this cure. I find that very disconcerting. If they were to gain control of the science I have created, I am afraid the cures could become worse than the disease."

"Again, I doubt if any of them have faced a Vahemic or Narcoleptan, have they?"

"No. So far, they have allowed me to try and control this issue and they have promised to keep it hidden from the world. But I am not sure how much longer they can keep that position."

"I'm afraid we should fear something much worse, Doc. Something that wishes to do us harm now."

"Yes, I know that now. I am sure you will let me know if you have any other interactions with him, won't you?"

"You'll probably know it when I do. You have my entire body wired for sound with that neuronal mesh, don't you?"

"Yes, I suppose you could say that. Does that bother you?"

"At first, the thought of it did. But now, I'm glad you're there. I trust you and I have never been able to say that to very many people. Especially in your line of work."

Dr. Po smiled.

"I have given the Ebola medicine to Samantha and asked her to go to Uganda and test its effectiveness on a much wider scale; to see if she can more or less quell this outbreak. She will be at risk of catching Ebola, but it's a low risk. She knows how to interact with those types of patients, but I would like for someone to accompany her and protect her. I..."

"Don't need to say another word, Doc. I am willing to go and help."

"You cannot go, John. It would be too dangerous. You have wounds that aren't fully healed, and even though your chemical composition will in all likelihood prevent the Ebola virus from surviving, and you would be in a biohazard suit, it is still very risky. Unfortunately, I am afraid your sister would not be as focused as she needs to be in this type of situation, so I am very reluctant to ask her to accompany Samantha on this journey."

"Can we not delay her trip until I am well?"

"The longer we delay, the more people will die."

"Got any more pigs, Doc?"

"Yes, John, I do."

"Don't you think you should hook me up?"

"Yes, John, I believe I should."

Chapter 18
Vanilla

Dr. Po attached my cord to several more pigs and the reaction I experienced was even more intense than the previous procedures. The roller coaster height increased a few hundred feet and the ride lasted much longer. The energy spread across my body as if every cell was being hit by an electric current, torn apart, and then reformed to heal the damaged areas.

Dr. Po asked if I was up to walking and I told him no, but I did feel like running. And he, of course, replied, "Amazing," and told me to get dressed. Once dressed, we walked to another room that I had never seen. It looked like a combination library and sports bar. The walls were lined with books and there were spaces to just sit and read, and also tables with laptops where you could relax while exploring the internet.

The bar was semi-circle-shaped with six stools positioned around it. In the middle of the bar were two robot-type objects with mechanical arms. On the top of their metal shoulders was a computer screen with the face of a woman on it, smiling at us. Behind the bar, a waterfall appeared to be only a few feet away from the glass. The sound of the water rushing downward all around the bar could be heard as you approached it.

"The windows work like giant binoculars," Dr. Po explained as he sat on a bar stool which lifted him to a comfortable position at the bar surface. I didn't see him enable a switch to make that happen. He could see the confused look on my face and responded.

"The stools evaluate your weight and the sensors on the bar evaluate your height. The bar stool moves up as soon as you sit on it to a comfortable position for your body. When you want to move it down, you just need to tell the lovely bartender to lower the seat. The waterfall you are looking at is actually several miles away but I liked the effect of being able to sit here and feel like it was really close. I developed and placed special microphones at the waterfall that enhance the sensation of it being just outside the glass."

Amazing, I thought and laughed to myself. "I really like this room, Doc. Never been in a real bar before. Been in lots of libraries but not ones that look like this."

"Marie, would you make John a strawberry milkshake and, for me, a gin and tonic?"

"Certainly, Doctor."

All of a sudden, I understood that woman on the monitor screen was an image of his mother at some time in her life. I liked that about Dr. Po. He enjoyed having things around him that reminded him of his mother, just like I would have if I had anything. I watched as the robotic arms made the requested drinks and then I remembered the Dahliarium and how it was named.

"Dr. Po?"

"Yes."

"Why did you name the Dahliarium after the woman who discarded you like a piece of trash?"

"'If one by one we counted people out for the least sin, it wouldn't take us long to get so we had no one to live with. For to be social is to be forgiving.' Those are not my words. They are the words of Robert Frost and they always resonated with me. Are you familiar with his work?"

"Yes, I've always liked his poetry but never heard those particular words. They're very beautiful."

He forgives that which many could not. I sure as shit couldn't. He cared about not being able to save Billy. He protects my sister even from herself.

And before either one of us could say anything else, Sam and Jane came into the room but as far as I was concerned, nothing else needed to be said. I understood why now and I was humbled by the shadow of a two-and-one-half foot giant.

"So, how do you feel?" my sister asked as she sat down beside me.

When I told her, "Good," I did my best spy impression of trying to notice Sam without her knowing I was watching her, as she sat down next to Dr. Po.

"Yeah, I feel even better than good. Dare I say, 'amazing?' But I'm not the expert. What do you think, Doc?"

Dr. Po nodded his head as he sipped his drink. "Everything is going better than expected. Your brother responds extremely well to the Symbion therapy. I will want to look at his wounds later this evening but for now, his assessment is correct."

"Marie, I'd like a Budweiser and I think Sam would like a Heineken. Right, Sam?" my sister asked.

I had never seen my sister drink a beer and it surprised me for a moment but then I realized she would be twenty later this year. Considering what she had been doing for over two years, drinking a beer seemed appropriate. Hell, considering what she had experienced her entire life, she probably deserved as many as she wanted.

"Hey, Doc, is it too soon for me to have a beer too?"

"I wouldn't recommend it, considering you just had surgery and anesthesia."

"Yeah, I understand."

Sam grinned as she looked at my sister and then at me. Her eyes locked into mine for a moment and I wondered if I would have a chance to be with her alone later today. Then I remembered she did tell me that she would see me after dinner tonight. But now that all this had happened about going to Africa, I wasn't sure when she or I would eat. In fact, I wasn't even sure what time it was.

"What time is it, by the way?"

"It is 7:16 p.m., John."

"I believe that means it's dinner time. Can I get something to eat in here?"

"You should probably have a liquid dinner tonight considering you just came out of surgery. One of my high carbohydrate, protein formulas that..." and then he stopped. I could tell he realized the person he was suggesting this liquid dinner to was not like the other patients he had taken care of in the past. Solid food was not going to be an issue for me. In fact, I suspected he even doubted a beer would be detrimental to me but he didn't say it.

"Actually, John, order anything you would like. Am I to assume it will be a cheeseburger again?"

"Not tired of them yet. Marie, a cheeseburger and some chili cheese fries, if you wouldn't mind."

"Not at all, John. It will be ready in about ten minutes."

Marie gave my sister and Sam their beers and I held up my milkshake and said, "Cheers," and everyone including Dr. Po repeated the word and took a drink.

"Jane, I am sending Samantha to Africa tomorrow to help with an Ebola outbreak there. I am hoping your brother will be well enough to accompany her. I would prefer him to go because he is not strong enough to take care of our household yet, should anything require mediation. They should be back in less than a week."

Hell yes, Doc. Damn good way of not telling the exact truth.

My sister agreed without even being aware of what Dr. Po was doing. He had just told her that he didn't think she would be able to safely assist Sam in Africa, but all she heard was that she was stronger than me and needed to stay around here. He really did understand her. I was becoming a firm believer that he understood her better than she understood herself.

"Now, while you three continue to get acquainted, I am going to go over there and read some books that John recommended a little while ago. He suggested some stories that were written by a medical colleague that he thought I would find interesting."

Funny, Doc. Dr. Seuss. I got it.

Sam looked at me and finished her beer before she told us she needed to leave to prepare for the trip.

"If I'm going with you tomorrow, don't you think you should bring me up to speed on everything I need to know? I've never been in a biohazard suit, you know. Never been around Ebola patients either. Not sure what I'm going to see over there."

"First of all, you need to be cleared by Dr. Po, but yes, once I'm finished getting things ready for the trip, I'll come back here. After you've finished your dinner, you should go over there and begin researching everything you can find on Ebola and Uganda. They have had outbreaks there before. You don't need a password to get on the computer. They all have retina detection sensors on them that allow you access. See you later, Jane."

I watched Sam leave and then looked over at my sister who was grinning at me. She ordered another beer and then nudged me with her arm.

"I think my brother has his first girlfriend. And just so you know, I approve."

"She's not my girlfriend," I retorted defensively like I had been taunted by a school kid on the playground. And before I added anything else to the rebuttal, I realized it wasn't necessary. Jane and I weren't children anymore. Yes, I was naïve with regard to women, but I didn't need to be goaded into an argument. No, I didn't need to justify my actions now. I should just use this as an opportunity to get closer to my sister.

"I wish she was my girlfriend. I like her. I like her a lot."

"Yes, I like her a lot too."

"So, you know her pretty well?"

"She assisted Dr. Po with my cord. And it was true what she said about her parents. I met them when Dr. Po helped cure them. They are fine now from what I know. They both really did have lung cancer but they were never attacked by sharks. That was funny though, don't you think?'

"Hilarious." *Actually, it was funny now that I know it wasn't true.*

"And Dr. Po also helped Sam with her cancer."

"Her cancer?"

"Yes, she had brain cancer. But she's cured now."

Even though I heard Jane say she was cured, all I could think of was brain cancer and the Narcoleptan mutation. My sister could see that in my eyes.

"Eat your cheeseburger. She's fine. Dr. Po did her surgery and treatment over a year ago. If anything was going to happen, it would have already. Your girlfriend is fine."

Jane began eating my chili cheese fries but I didn't care about them anymore. I didn't really want them now. Sam's cancer and that crayon picture I made for Dr. Banks were like a faulty neon sign crackling on and off in my head. I didn't even hear my sister talking until I heard her say the word Vahemic.

"Huh? What did you just say about the Vahemics?"

"I said I let them in. I know you heard me tell Dr. Po that somehow Marie let them get in, but I let them in. I've done it before. It allows me to train and get better at killing them. I just didn't think you would be there and I'm sorry about that."

For a second, I thought about telling her that Dr. Po already knew but then I realized that would be a mistake. Their relationship was what it needed to be for now, and I appreciated her telling me the truth.

"I wish you were going to Africa instead of me. I remember how you and mom looked at all those travel magazines when we went to the library."

Though I knew it couldn't happen, I sincerely wished it could happen for her. She would love seeing Africa, even though the sick village would not be anything anyone should see. I didn't think the reference to mom and the travel magazines would trigger a painful memory either.

"You're right. We did do that a lot, didn't we? I loved looking at those magazines with her," she said as she looked off into the distance for a moment.

"But that's okay, John. Like Dr. Po said, you probably aren't ready to be here by yourself. And I've done a lot of traveling, more than I ever thought I would. I've been to a lot of the states and even some parts of Canada. You'd like Canada. At least where I was in British Columbia. In Vancouver. Dr. Po took me on a floatplane trip into the wilderness. We stayed in a beautiful resort and even went salmon fishing, if you can believe it. I think some of the salmon were bigger than him, but we had a blast."

"Dr. Po - fishing? Are you kidding?"

"No, I'm not. He's been very good to me. Really good. I would do anything for him."

"I can see that. And you appear to be very happy."

"I am, John. With you here now, I don't think it could get any better. Be careful over there in Africa, big brother. Do whatever Sam tells you to do."

"You need to be careful too, Jane. I know how skillful and confident you are in yourself now, but you need to be more cautious. You have a lot you need to show me, remember?"

"I remember. Now finish your dinner and then do some of that reading your girlfriend suggested. I'll see you later."

I hugged Jane before she left, and after eating I opened up the computer. I read several chapters of Po's Molecular Transitions Dynamics book and then began researching the Ebola virus. Dr. Po was still reading in a corner of the room, and I thought I heard him laugh a couple of times before I nodded off. When I woke up, he was gone and standing over me was Sam.

"What time is it?"

"10:30. How much reading did you get done?" she asked as she sat down next to me.

I smelled something different about her. She had on perfume. She had never worn perfume around me before and it smelled like vanilla. Not overwhelming vanilla but just enough to let you know it was there. I thought about how nice she smelled and I realized I was just staring at her, when my brain yelled out to me that she had asked a question and I needed to respond.

"Uh, sorry. I read a couple of chapters of Po's Molecular Transition Dynamics book and several articles about Ebola and the outbreaks in Africa and how there's not a cure for it yet."

"First of all, I'm very impressed you got through two chapters of Dr. Po's book on molecular science. I'll be even more impressed if you tell me you understood it."

"Yeah. I understood most of it, though the carbon allotropes and strontium isotope fusion with the amino and carboxyl groups of the amino acids utilized to discover the Symbion molecule is still swirling around in my head. Not sure I have that all clear in my mind yet regarding the structure but I think he purposefully left some of the key reactions and components out of this part of the discussion. Pretty advanced stuff but the pictures were real pretty."

"Funny."

"Seriously. He does have some very intricate diagrams in there. Yes, I was being a little sarcastic, but the diagrams were very helpful. It is fascinating science. I would have read more, but I knew I needed to learn about the Ebola virus and where we're going. Is the Ebola really as bad as described? It's a horrible way to die. I hope Dr. Po's cure works."

"Unfortunately, it is just as bad as described. But I've seen what Dr. Po can do and I'm confident that what he has developed will stop many from dying."

I nodded in agreement and started to ask her about the mutations that concerned Dr. Po but there was something in her eyes, those olive eyes; that suggested it wasn't necessary. At least I thought they were telling me it wasn't necessary. It may have been that I just became hypnotized by them.

Hey, Dr. Lector. Still interested in putting those little olives in a pimento loaf or something? Get a grip, man.

"Did you read about the Hazmat suit you'll be wearing? Are you okay with that? It can feel claustrophobic for some people."

"Uhh...what?"

"The Hazmat suit? Claustrophobia? Are you okay? You seem a little distracted."

"Yeah. Sorry. I was just thinking about something else. I'll be fine with the suit. I read all about it and I'm not claustrophobic. At least I don't think I am."

"Good. Do you have any questions for me?"

Neon lights exploded in my mind when she said that. "Yes, I do, if you don't mind sitting here and answering several hundred of them."

Damn. Several hundred questions. Kind of creepy don't you think?

"Several hundred? Hold on," she said as she got up and got a glass of wine for herself and a glass of water for me.

Okay. Okay. Not creepy. In fact, she made a joke about it. Sort of.

"You need to stay hydrated, so drink this water and ask away."

She doesn't seem concerned. Ok, definitely not creepy. So far, so good.

"Jane said your parents had lung cancer, but they're okay now?"

"Yes, they're fine. Cured. You didn't think that was mean of us, did you? It did make you relax once you realized we were pranking you."

"Yes. I'm fine with it. Cool. All copacetic. No proble-mo."

Shit dumbass. I'm fine with it was sufficient. Are you going to pee on yourself next?

"But she also told me that you had brain cancer and Dr. Po treated you. Are you okay now?"

"Yes, except on the full moons. Then I get a real antsy feeling."

Shit....hold on, genius. She's just messing with you.

"For someone that likes to 'give it' to people you seem to have a hard time understanding when people are giving it right back to you. I'm just kidding. I'm good. Cured. Are you okay?"

I shook my head no. And then I heard my brain yelling at me again. *Be honest with her, you idiot. She likes you. She put on perfume for a reason.*

"Actually Sam, I've never really had a relationship with a girl; I mean a woman; I mean, hell I don't know what to say; a member of the opposite sex - besides my sister and my mom. And I'm not suggesting this is a relationship or anything, but I haven't you know, well, I haven't really sat down and talked to someone like you before. So, I'm a little nervous."

"A woman. You've never talked to a woman before?"

"No, not like you."

"What do you mean like me?"

"Someone who is as beautiful and smart and nice as you are and has probably been on all sorts of dates with lots of smart doctors and other interesting men like that."

"I have had two boyfriends in my entire life. One I left and one left me. For another man."

"Are you shitting me?" I asked as gulped some water.

"You can't control nature, John."

The water spouted out of my nose like a whale's blowhole and landed on us both. She just wiped herself off with a napkin and then started laughing. When she laughed, I laughed and took another drink.

"Don't do that in the Hazmat suit, okay?"

I almost repeated my whale impression, but I was able to swallow the water before that happened, and I laughed even harder.

Where were you, Sam? Where were you when I was younger? Whoa, hold on there, Lone Ranger. Not a good idea seeing how the earlier version of you probably wouldn't have been very appealing. Accept the fact she is here now. Talking with you.

"Do you mind if I ask you about my sister? Do you think she's okay?"

Really smooth transition there. Shit.

"Yes, I do. But don't mistake her enthusiasm for life today to be a reflection of her detachment from the past. Yes, Dr. Po has taught her that the past doesn't define her. It was just a moment in time that allowed her to find relevance here in the present, but I think she harbors some unresolved anger at times. She tries to hide it but I see it. Dr. Po sees it. And if you are as smart as I think you are, you have seen it. "

Sounds like Jack talking to me. Only this version is so much better looking. Damn. For once, someone is talking about anger issues and not referring to me.

"Do you know I can remember everything from the time I was born? I can remember the doctor taking me from my mother. I remember my body feeling energized like they had plugged my umbilical cord into an electrical socket and as I watched them cut it, it seemed like I shocked the doctor that was holding me. Kind of weird considering what has happened, don't you think?"

"Actually, I'm not surprised you sensed that or that you remember it. I knew you were different the first day I took care of you."

Different. Yeah, I heard the word but it didn't bother me. In fact, I liked the fact that she said it. I even liked the way she said it.

"Do you think Marie and Emily are watching us?"

"Most definitely. That neuronal mesh in your brain monitors you twenty-four seven."

"Well, I wonder what this will do to the sensors," I said as I leaned over and kissed her. She took my face in her hands and held it as we kissed.

"I thought you hadn't been with a woman before?"

I smiled and thought about how wonderful vanilla smelled and tasted.

Chapter 19
Three old friends

"Wow," was the first word that came so eloquently out of my mouth. I couldn't believe I said that and I know my face turned beet red but Sam knew exactly what to do to make me feel better about my unschooled verbal comment.

"Wow is right," she replied and kissed me again.

"You know I'm betting Marie may be seeing some large spikes in my brain waves right now."

"Large, huh?"

"Well…"

"You need to get some rest, John Deaux. If Dr. Po clears you, we'll be leaving at 7 in the morning on a private plane to Africa. It's about a ten-hour flight and there is a seven-hour time difference. It's 11 p.m. here and 6 a.m. there. So, it's not an easy trip on our bodies. Well, mine at least. Not sure about yours."

"Can you look at my back and shoulder and see what you think?"

"That's very unique sex talk. Very original."

"No, I…"

"Turn around. I'm kidding. You've got to get better at seeing the sarcasm."

First a discussion about anger issues that aren't related to me. Now my inability to see her sarcasm. Yep. She's got you all messed up.

Sam retrieved some gloves from behind the bar and then pulled up my shirt. She didn't have to remove any bandages, because there weren't any. The wounds were covered with a clear, antibacterial spray.

"Dr. Po is so skillful. His antibacterial liquid wrap has exceptional healing qualities but, even so, the wounds on your back are essentially non-existent. Your shoulder wound is still faintly visible but considering there was bone damage, it looks remarkable. I think you'll be cleared to go. And with a little more rest tonight and then more sleep on the plane, perhaps with another shot of Symbion and some more wrap, you should be in good shape."

She put the gloves away and then grabbed my hand and pulled me up out of the chair, close to her. "Is that a large EEG spike or are you just glad to see me?"

This time I got it. My brain waves and other parts of my body were under control. At least for the moment.

"I need to get some rest. My nurse said so. But I'm not sure I know how to get back to my room. In fact, I am sure I don't know how. You'll have to take me, you know."

"Yes, I know. Come on, Mr. Deaux."

When she stood in front of the bedroom door with me, she put her hand on my cheek and kissed me softly. "You are aware, that all you had to do was ask Emily or Marie for assistance and they would have led you back to your room?"

I just smiled.

"Shit. The student becomes the teacher, huh? Well, I'll just have to keep my eyes on you. See you in the morning."

I didn't move as I watched her leave and though she didn't turn around, she knew I was watching her walk away. As soon as she entered her room, I went inside mine and allowed Emily to check my body while I was in the bathroom. She suggested I drink another glass of water before I went to bed. I did as she asked and got in bed and as I closed my eyes, I saw Sam's face.

I found myself looking up at the ceiling of darkness because I couldn't sleep. I kept thinking about Africa and about Sam. It wasn't long before I heard the door handle turn and I pulled my head up on the pillow so I could see better. The light from the hall cut through the room like a knife removing a sliver of darkness and I could see someone coming through the door.

It was Sam. I was excited and nervous and felt like I was getting on the Scrambler ride for the very first time. I knew she wasn't there just to check my wounds again. As she came through the door, every detail of her body was as clear as if I had developed night vision.

"Can't sleep, John?"

"No."

"Maybe I can help you relax," she said as she turned on a light next to the bed. "Since you told me you've never been with a woman, I thought you might like to see a woman undress."

I tried to reply but all that came out of my mouth was a garbled mess that sounded like I was gasping for my last breath. She started unbuttoning her pajama top and I could see her very healthy-sized breasts in a black bra.

"Is that EEG spike getting large again?"

I'm surprised she had to ask considering the tent that I had made with the sheets but I swallowed and was able to utter something more understandable, even though the "yes" still had a little more hiss to it than it should. She reached back and unclasped her bra and her large breasts were there with her nipples staring at me, and me staring at them. Like her eyes, they were hypnotic. It was then I noticed something a little strange. There was hair on her chest.

I closed my eyes and opened them again and saw even more hair on her chest. I began to wonder if this was some sort of defect that she was hiding or some side effect of the treatment that Dr. Po had given her. The hair on her chest was becoming thicker and her face began to change too. Her mouth started to enlarge and move outward as it formed a muzzle like a wolf. Teeth started to emerge from the muzzle and drool dripped from each one of them.

"Dr. Po isn't aware that I have become a Narcoleptan but I knew you would suspect it, John. It would just be a matter of time before you realized it and then you would figure out that I had been communicating with Vincent. I'm not sure how you intercepted his thoughts but it doesn't matter. You won't be intercepting anymore," she said as she lunged toward me. Her body fell on mine and those teeth began tearing away my skin.

I screamed and the lights came on and I heard Emily asking me what was wrong.

I looked down at the several pillows on top of my body and it appeared that I was strangling one of them.

"I'm fine, Emily. Nightmare. That's all."

"Yes. It appears so based on your body chemistry and brain waves. I have spoken with Marie and Dr. Po and they suggest you take one of the small pills that I am illuminating now on your bedside table with a large glass of water. If your body temperature spikes, Dr. Po will be coming in to assess."

I once again complied with Emily's directions and this time as I closed my eyes, I made myself think about Jane and me and my mother at the fair. I dreamed we were having fun for the longest time and did not wake again until heard Emily in my brain telling me it was time to get up. When I opened my eyes, Dr. Po was sitting there.

"Not unexpected," I said as I sat up and smiled at him.

"What was the nightmare about, John? It is important that I know. Did Mr. Merkel contact you again?"

Well, this was going to be a little awkward. How do I reply to this?

"No, I didn't hear anything from him, but I did dream about a Narcoleptan attacking me."

"Was it in Africa? I ask that only because I have done more research into the supernatural phenomenon that you suggest exists. I wonder if this is some kind of vision."

Damn. He's going to have Marie reading Tarot cards in just a little bit.

"No, it was here. I think I just substituted the Vahemic attack for a Narcoleptan. You know your brain does funny shit like that."

"Yes. Dreams present one image that, when analyzed, actually denotes something else. Let me look at your back and shoulder, please."

He accepted that like I knew what the hell I was talking about. Damn.

I removed my shirt and I could see him in the mirror using some sort of device that looked like a magnifying glass as he looked at my back and shoulder.

"What is that thing?"

"A magnifying glass."

Shit. Maybe you are ready for your Ph.D. oral exams now.

"I have modified it though. It sees through the epidermis and calculates the number of bacteria in the area that I am looking at and can identify any indication of infection. Your back is fully healed and your shoulder is 99.3% healed. I think a shot of Symbion before you leave should be all that you need."

"That's what Sam said last night."

"That is not surprising. Like I said, she is a very good nurse. I trust her judgment. But before you clean up and prepare to leave, I do want to talk to you for a moment. You make me question myself as I have never done before. I allowed you to go with your sister to hunt those Narcoleptans when I knew you could have been killed. That is very unlike me but if I had not done that, Jane may have been seriously wounded, perhaps even killed.

"We would not have known about Vincent Merkel either if you had not gone on that trip, so I realize letting you go was the right thing, even though from a medical position, it was wrong. I also let you go outside after the implant surgery, because I miscalculated Jane's behavior, and that time you were injured. But again, I learned something from that decision. Your body is even more remarkable than that of your sister. Your healing ability surpasses hers and I would not have known that otherwise, even though there were many instances when I suspected it.

"I am reluctant to believe in kismet or karma, and certainly not the supernatural, but there is something else going on with you and me and the world around us, that I cannot explain. I only hope I am not putting you in another situation where you and I learn that I failed to do the right thing as your doctor and you suffer irreparable harm."

Damn. I've never had a doctor show so much care for me or speak to me as a real person. No wonder my sister seems to love him and why Sam has so much respect for him. I'm becoming pretty attached to the man, too.

"I know you're worried about new and different mutations, but I'm not worried at all about what you've developed, Doc. I'm sure you'll be helping people that need your help, just as I know you'll always continue to do. And I will promise you that Sam and I will be safe. Along with the pilot and whoever else you have going with us."

"There is no one else. Marie will fly the plane. It will just be you and Samantha."

I should have known.

"Regardless, we're good. Doc."

"Thank you, John. I appreciate your trust in me."

"No problem, but along with that trust, can I take two LBEs with me?"

Dr. Po smiled and nodded his head.

 "Then, Doc, you have nothing to worry about."

"I am afraid that is not something I am capable of doing."

"Read some more of those books I suggested," I said as I went into the bathroom and closed the door.

"I read every one of his books yesterday," Dr. Po said in a whisper that only he could hear. "He was a tremendous visionary. More than people give him credit for. I only hope our world does not become a demented mockery of the ones he created for us to enjoy." Dr. Po left the room and went to check that Sam had everything they needed.

After I cleaned up, Emily directed me to the first floor. She had several nutrient bars and a thick drink waiting for me in a small eating space behind one of the four doors located in the central seating area. Jane was also there waiting for me.

"Good morning, big brother. Ready to save the world?"

I wasn't sure what to say so I just nodded and smiled.

 "Man, looks like you need some energy. You need some of these high protein, high fat, energy shakes that Dr. Po created. They'll get you going. I like the vanilla and chocolate ones the best but I told Emily you preferred strawberry. And those energy bars he makes are damn good too."

I bit into one of the bars and tasted the thick drink and my sister was right. They were both very good. "I don't guess I can get cheeseburgers in Africa, can I?"

"Who knows? McDonald's is everywhere. I looked at the map with Dr. Po last night. Pretty damn isolated where you're going, but if there isn't a McDonald's, I bet there's a Hardee's. Remember how it seemed no matter where we went, there may not have been anything for miles around, but somehow there would always be a Hardee's?"

The memory made us both laugh.

She remembered something from the past but it wasn't traumatizing. It seems as long as I'm associated with it, she represses the rest. How long will that happen though?

"Well, if there is one there, I'll take a picture of it with my cheeseburger."

Before I could finish my breakfast bars and drink, Sam joined us with Dr. Po. She was carrying a small case which she set on the table and opened to reveal a fancy-looking hypodermic. Must be the Symbion that Dr. Po referred to earlier.

"Arm or butt?" she asked.

Jane laughed as I rolled up my sleeve and Sam gave me the shot. Dr. Po came over and engaged the metal chair that raised him to the height of my shoulder. Without asking, he lifted up my shirt and pulled out the magnifying glass to examine my back and shoulder. My sister was mouthing a word that made me laugh. I laughed even more when I heard Dr. Po say the exact word she had indicated he would say, just seconds earlier.

"Amazing. Within seconds, the Symbion appears to have closed the shoulder wound completely. Simply amazing."

"Is that the only shot I need to get? Don't I need a bunch of immunization shots or something?"

"If not for your unique body metabolism, yes, you would be getting immunization for various diseases prevalent over there, but they will not survive inside your body," Dr. Po replied.

"Okay, next question, how long do you think we'll be there?"

"I think you should be back within seven days if everything goes as planned."

I didn't want to ask him what would happen if things didn't go as planned. I knew he had already worried about that and had probably already discussed several contingency plans with Sam.

"If you have any more questions, Samantha, or Marie, or I can help you with them. We will be in constant communication with one another. Samantha, will you take John down to the transport now?"

I wasn't sure if he didn't know what to say or was unable to say goodbye or good luck, but as quickly as he said that, Dr. Po left the room. Jane grabbed me by the arm and told me to follow her and she led me down to the truck. She hugged both me and Sam and then we left.

"This doesn't become a plane, does it? If it does, my sister failed to mention it."

"No, of course not. We just need it to get to the plane."

"Yeah. That makes sense. How long a drive is it?"

"Not long, about an hour."

"Okay."

I wasn't sure what else to say beyond that. Every time I looked at her, all I could see were her olive eyes, and this time they weren't just on her face. They were also on the nipples of her breasts staring at me. So, I sat there telling myself what I was thinking was normal, not fucked up at all, and hoping that wasn't what serial killers said just before they really 'nutted up.' Sam was checking things in various bags so I just hoped she would continue to do that for most of the trip. But after about ten minutes of silence, I realized I was wrong in that assumption.

"Why are you so quiet? Are you worried about the trip?"

"No. Not really. Dr. Po said he packed some LBEs, so with those and with you leading the way, and Marie and him essentially with us, I'm sure we'll be fine."

"There's something else you aren't telling me."

Shit. Talk about psychic ability. Here you go, Doc. You had one working with you all this time and didn't even know it.

"I had a nightmare last night. It involved you. I'm not going to go into the details but you turned into a monster."

"Oh really? Was I naked?"

"Where in that sentence did you hear naked? I said you were a monster."

"When you said you weren't going to go into the details, that's where it says I was naked."

Son of a bitch.

"Here," she said as she turned on her computer and then handed it to me. "Click that icon that says JD."

Oh shit. If these are naked pictures of her, Dr. Po may cancel the trip because all my physical monitors are going to really go off the chart.

When I clicked on the icon, a "Three Stooges" short started playing and I looked at her and smiled.

"Jane told me this would help you relax on the trip."

"I think I am falling in love with you."

"Yep, that's what most men say when I prepare 'Three Stooges' videos for them to watch."

I sat back and fell into another world as I watched the video until we got to the plane. Another world that I remembered and which brought me a great deal of joy. When we loaded everything on the plane, Sam gave me a strawberry protein shake, an energy bar, and a pill. She said the pill would help me relax. She was right. I don't know how many "Stooges" shorts I watched before I fell asleep.

That period of sleep on the plane was probably the best sleep I had ever experienced in my entire life. I dreamed I was at the fair with Larry, Curly and Moe, my mother and sister, and Billy. My sister even enjoyed the Stooges as we walked around the carnival playing games and they made all of it more fun. We even saw Dr. Seuss doing a book reading and we stopped to listen for a long time, not caring that we were the oldest children there sitting on the ground looking up at him. And when we got up to go on the Haunted House ride, Sam was there waiting for us. I asked my mother and sister if I could ride it with her, and they both said yes. I could tell by the look on Sam's face that she understood I really was falling in love with her. And she took me by my hand and smiled as she sat down beside me and the doors of the ride opened.

Chapter 20
Lost Jewels

When I woke up, the plane had landed. The seat I was in moved from a reclining position to upright as if it knew I was awake and needed to sit up. A door was open on the plane and I could see Sam outside loading containers onto a metal device with metal arms and large wheels. It was dark outside but the lights on the plane lit up the area around us for at least several hundred feet. I began to notice the sounds of the jungle that up until now I had only heard on National Geographic shows.

How does Horton sleep with all this noise? I don't know, Dr. Seuss, but I think we're going to find out.

"Good morning, Mr. Deaux. You slept very well. You had many REM cycles for extended periods. Your blood pressure and pulse were so low that I was beginning to be concerned, but Dr. Po said everything was normal. You were just in a very deep sleep. So even though it's a little after 2 a.m. here, we have a lot of work to do. It's about a five-mile hike through the bush to get to the village. Once we get everything loaded, we need to get moving. The tribal chieftain and shaman of the village are expecting us at sunrise."

"What is that thing you're loading stuff on?"

"What does it look like?"

"A wagon with metal arms."

"Good - I can check that off. Patient is awake and aware," Sam said with a sarcastic grin which I acknowledged with one of my own. "That is exactly what it is. A battery-charged wagon similar to what they used on the moon, only this one is much faster and can carry more weight. It could even carry both of us if necessary."

"Got it. But before I help with the loading, can you show me where the LBEs are? There are a lot of noises out there in the dark that I'd like to be prepared for should one of those noises decide that we smell good enough to eat."

Sam walked to the door of the plane and I moved aside as she showed me the LBEs. I picked one up and adjusted the shoulder strap so that it would hang behind me.

"Get that case and the other one too, please," Sam said as she pointed to a couple of metal containers. "Just so you know, it's when you don't hear the noises that you should be worried."

"Again. Got it," I said as I placed the containers on the wagon. "By the way when do we eat?"

"Four more containers, then we make some shakes and get several bars and some nuts your sister said you liked. We eat, and then we start out."

"You brought cashews?"

"Yes, cashews are a good source of energy and fat, with the fat being the good kind of fat. I bought several pounds for the village chieftain and shaman. You never go to these remote places without a gift, even if you are here trying to save the village from becoming something the elders decide to burn into oblivion."

"'The Three Stooges' and cashews. Did I tell you I was falling in love with you?"

"Yes, you have said that already. Tell me again when we are headed back home but for now, let's concentrate on what we came to do."

She thinks I'm not focused because I said that. That's not good. Just calm down and don't think of anything weird like breasts with eyes. There you go. Breasts with eyes. Yeah, that will help. Wait, she said to burn the village into oblivion, didn't she?

"They would do that? Burn down the village?"

"Yes, if we don't stop the outbreak and save those infected, that's exactly what they will do. And those that are infected, though still alive, will be burned. And we won't be able to stop it. The only thing we could do at that point would be to give the infected ones enough narcotics to kill them before they were burned."

"Are you prepared for that?"

"Yes, unfortunately, I am. Are you?"

"I wasn't but I will be. I promise I will be."

I understand why you're saying that. Even though you know the man is a genius, you still have some doubts about whether the vaccine will work, don't you? It will work, Sam. But there is no need to debate that with her. You know she is hoping it will. She is just prepared like you need to be.

It was a little after 3 a.m. when we began our walk to the village. The wagon lights lit up our path and had been programmed by Sam just before we left. Though the ground in this part of Uganda wasn't that rough, the wagon moved over any obstacles in its way, unless the obstacle was bigger than it was. Then it just moved around the obstruction, lighting the way for us to follow.

We had walked for about two hours and it was still very dark when I felt the sweat on my arms begin to tingle as if I had found a source of static electricity. Though I looked around, I couldn't see anything and that's when I heard it. The silence. The animal noises had stopped. I grabbed Sam and pushed her to the ground as two lionesses bounded toward us. I hit both of them in the head with the LBE and watched as their heads exploded. "Damn!" I yelled at the effect that the positrons had on non-mutated beings.

Sam pushed a button and at once, the wagon stopped and began scanning the area all around us with the light. The scan discovered another lioness on the ground looking at us, but when the light hit her, she ran off.

"It's a shame such beautiful animals had to die," Sam said. "But there was not an option. You did the right thing. Your sweat is a remarkable tool."

I looked at her and though I wasn't sure I liked being called a tool, I knew she meant nothing by it. And then I heard it.

To them, we are just another antelope. I suppose you could call us a Humalope walking the trail with vials of hope. And there he was. My old friend, the good doctor in the back of my mind, helping me feel more at ease; comforting me like he always did.

But even after being calmed somewhat by the rhyme, I was still asking myself, *did you see what those positrons did to those damn lions? Shit.*

These damn weapons are lethal, and I felt a lot more confident as we walked along in the dark. And then something struck me as odd.

"Considering how Dr. Po thinks of everything, why didn't he just put some sensors on the wagon that would warn us of an impending attack?"

"He did. I inactivated them. The sensors were programmed to shoot LBEs at anything within twenty feet of us. He knew that could be an issue in Africa but he didn't feel comfortable without having them. He told me about the override but cautioned me about using it. I'm sorry, John, I should have told you when we first started out. I was relying upon your body to alert us should anything become an issue. I didn't want a curious animal to get killed when it didn't have to, but now I know I shouldn't have taken that risk. Will you forgive me?"

"Sam, you know I have a lot of respect for you, but that decision sounds a little...uh...."

"Crazy?"

"Yeah. It does."

"I can't help it. I love animals. I don't want to see any of them die."

"How about the human animals? Shouldn't we be included in that list?"

"Of course, we are. I'm sorry. I'll turn it back on."

I remembered my sister telling me how our bodies wouldn't alert us to the copperbrowns because she said they would be tingling all the time. Why did my body alert us to the lions? They weren't mutations. They were just animals. And Sam would have known that about my sister and the copperbrowns. What did she know about me that made her think differently? Upon hearing the word at the end of the question, I knew the answer. She and Dr. Po talked. She knows my body chemistry is different. I then remembered something from Jack's writing. "Only a real risk tests the reality of a belief." Damn, she believes in me just as much as Dr. Po. Hell more. She could have died.

"How much further do we have to go?"

"About another hour and a half. Look off into the distance. The blackness that surrounds us is beginning to fade just the slightest. Within the next hour, the sun will start to rise. I really don't think the major predators will be active for very much longer.

"You stay right beside me and have the LBE out and ready to use and I'll agree to keep the alarm off on the wagon. But on the way back, we have it on. I know what you mean when you say Dr. Po was worried about not knowing. But he was more worried about what could happen when we administered the cure than with the animals that we might encounter even if it was at night."

"I understand what you're saying. He warned me about the mutation effect. He was afraid of that and I agree with you. On the way back, we'll keep it on. Thank you for being understanding," I replied.

She leaned over and kissed me on the cheek. If she only knew what power she had over me with that tender kiss. She could have told me right then and there that I needed to wade through a large watering hole with a crocodile in it just so the wagon wouldn't be destroyed, and I would have done exactly what she said. After a few seconds, I realized how stupid it was to think like that.

Shit. I'm not going in the water unless the wagon goes first and its sensors are activated. And Sam and I would be in that damn wagon. And then I realized something very important. Probably something Dr. Po already knew. My sense of survival exceeded any other desires I may have. No matter how strong those desires were or were becoming. I was sure he could see that even now in the biological markers in my body or brain that he was certainly monitoring.

The rest of our walk to the village was uneventful. The sun began to rise and like a defective solar oven, it started to bake the already overcooked landscape. Eventually, we saw several people standing on a dirt trail that led into the village. Sam waved to them and the large black man that appeared to be wearing a necklace of straw and feathers waved back to her.

"John, the man waving to me is the village chieftain. The woman next to him is the tribal shaman. She has painted her face white and that is not a good sign."

"What do you mean not a good sign?"

"It means she believes that the spirits of the land are revolting and will soon take over the village. She paints her face white so that they will recognize her as one familiar with the spirit world and will listen to her."

"So, you're telling me she's dressed up to look like a ghost?"

Sam nodded her head. "Let me do all the talking okay? This could be a very tense moment."

"Not a problem, bwana Sam."

Sam stopped a few feet away from the chief, took the bags of cashews, and told me to wait by the cart. She walked up to the chief, bowed, and offered him the nuts. I saw him smile and nod to her. But the woman that Sam referred to as the shaman did not look at her. She stared at me and she sure as hell wasn't smiling. She looked like she had been constipated for a very long time and was pretty pissed about it. She started pointing at me and then said something to Sam that I'm sure wasn't a Ugandan "welcome" in any language. I had seen that look before. The look of distrust was apparently the same regardless of where you were.

Sam looked back at me and said something to the shaman using a lot of hand gestures. The shaman glared at me and spit at the ground. The chief waved his hand in front of the shaman and she stood there for a moment before she turned and walked away. Sam came back to the wagon and pressed her finger on the bio-sensor activation. As the cart began moving forward, we walked beside it.

"What did the shaman say?"

"She said you smelled funny."

"Funny?"

"Well, I'm not that sure about the word she used. It was either funny or different, or perhaps even foul."

Oh, I knew what the word was. It was different. Yeah, that's what a tribal doctor said about me, halfway around the world. At least the doctors over in the US didn't spit at me. Yeah, I could tell me and her were probably not going to get along.

"I shouldn't be alone with her, should I?"

"No. You stay with me at all times. Got it?"

"Got it."

The chieftain led us to the back of the village where there were three large huts. Men with long spears blocked the entry to each door. I didn't need Sam to translate what the chieftain was telling her. Those homes were where the Ebola patients were housed.

"Time to get in the suits. It's going to be hot as hell in there. We'll need to hydrate before going in and we should only be in there for twenty-minute periods at most. I'm hoping that will give us time to see everyone in the hut. We will come out, change our suits, re-hydrate, and then repeat the process in the next hut. You okay with that?"

"I'm very okay with that. The sooner we get out of here the better. That shaman woman makes me feel very strange. I don't think she is helping the people here. In fact, I think she is killing the people somehow without the chieftain knowing it."

"How do you know that?"

"I sense it."

"Shit, John. I can't tell the chieftain that. I'm not sure what would happen but until I can show him we can do some good for his people, he will believe that shaman over us."

"Can you give me a shot of Symbion? I have a feeling that something bad is coming our way."

We turned around when we heard the villagers cry out. The shaman was walking toward them with a large basket in her hand. The chieftain motioned for Sam to come toward him as he held the shaman from advancing with a motion of his other hand.

Sam shook her head several times but the chieftain didn't seem to care what she said. After talking to him, she walked back and looked at me.

"The shaman wants to test you. She says you have demon blood in your body and she wants to prove that to everyone."

"With her little friend in the basket, I suppose?"

"Yes."

"There's a snake in there, isn't there?"

"Yes. According to the chieftain and the shaman, the demon can hold the snake and not get bitten. The non-demon will be bitten."

"Shit, is this Salem? If I drown, I'm not a witch. If I don't drown, then I'm a witch and you burn me at the stake. Well, Mrs. Evangeline Shaman there doesn't understand just how different I am. Tell the chieftain that I'll take the test, but only if the shaman will take the test too."

"John..."

"Tell him. She'll agree, knowing that I will go first. She doesn't think I'll survive."

"I don't know what's in there and you may not survive."

"Sam, you trusted my body earlier. Don't doubt it now."

Sam nodded and walked back to the chieftain. I watched his facial expression and knew he was agreeing to my terms. He said something to the shaman and she nodded her head in agreement.

I knew it.

The people from the village gathered around us, keeping a safe distance away. They knew that the wicked witch's little basket wasn't holding Toto. It held something pretty nasty. She put the basket on the ground and stood back as I looked around for a minute before I bent down and removed the lid. The agitated snake almost bit me in the face, but I caught it with my hand before it could strike, even though it was like catching a large limb of a tree that was about to hit you in the head.

"That's a Gaboon Viper, John," Sam yelled out. "It deposits more poison with its bite than any other snake in the world. Be careful."

I wanted to say that we left careful on the plane but I wasn't able to say anything. I was focused on the six feet of muscular lead pipe I was trying to hold. I gripped the enormous brown and tan snake for a moment and then extended my left arm. It sank its very long fangs deep into my forearm. "Fuck!" I yelled and dropped the snake to the ground. It sensed all the people around it and remained motionless except for its tongue, which moved constantly in and out of its mouth.

Damn, those were long fangs. I was afraid they would come out the other side of my arm. I already felt the poison spreading through my body and I began to feel dizzy. My arm hurt like someone had driven nails into the bones and I dropped to my knees. I bent over so I could lift my shirt up, just enough so that my cord could enter the ground without being seen, and hoped. My hopes were answered because even in the sunbaked ground, the life teeming just below the surface was abundant and I could feel myself fighting off the poison. Within a minute, I stood up and smiled. The village people yelled and began chanting and though I didn't know if it was for me or for the shaman, I didn't really care. The look on the shaman's face told me all I wanted to know.

But what I took for a frightened look on her face, I soon realized wasn't that at all. She was just pissed off that that damn thing had stuck those two-inch fangs into my arm and I wasn't dead. Maybe she thought I was a real demon and the snake wouldn't bite me. But now that I had been bitten and survived, she knew what she had to do. She walked over and picked up the snake and when it bit her, she just smiled at me.

She's probably immune to the damn thing. That bitch. I knew then she had taken some sort of anti-venom. But it didn't matter. At least now, she couldn't call me a demon anymore.

"How are you?" Sam asked as I walked back to her.

"I'm fine, but I don't trust that sham bitch. She's an evil witch and is killing people. Maybe not with that snake but with something, I can promise you."

"Okay, well you need to rest a minute, get hydrated, and let me give you a shot of Symbion. It will help clear that poison out of you."

"You mean that shot I asked for a little while ago, just before you told me to be careful."

"Yeah, that one. This one has to go in your ass, by the way. Can't use the arm because of the snakebite."

"Nice try, Nurse Ratched, but I can detect your sarcasm now. You won't be able to get that by me anymore."

Sam elbowed me and I smiled. I could tell she thought I was smiling because of her and to some degree I was. But I was mostly smiling because I learned something very important that day. It was a "Eureka" moment for me. I now knew the entire world was different. Before now, I had always referenced the world according to me; in particular how everyone in 'the world' viewed me as different.

But my world was only so big. A particle of sand in comparative terms to the real world. Africa showed me that. In this remote region, these people were confronted with a deadly virus. To them, it was a monster and in reality, it was a monster, but not one of dreams or nightmares. It was a virus with definitive chemical and genetic characteristics. Science had identified it, but over here, in this particular village, superstition and tribal custom defined it in another way.

Some people may call that ignorance but it wasn't. It was just the way they had learned to live and survive in a very harsh environment, where the chieftain and shaman, right or wrong, provided the framework for the world they lived in. This world in which I found myself was very different from the one I came from, but in some respects, it was the same. Though my world was much more modern and advanced, it didn't matter. Evil and disease existed in this one, just like the one in which I lived.

No wonder Dr. Po prepared for the worst. He defined the worst in scientific terms, but until now, I had seen it in its much more basic form. The worst for me was just called evil - human and mutation. But now I knew the worst had other names; Ebola or whatever it was they called the virus and whatever it was they called that shaman bitch. Regardless, I knew as soon as I got that shot of Symbion from Sam, Jules would be lost forever.

Chapter 21
Black Death

Sam gave me the shot and my whole body immediately regenerated. Along with that energy came an increased awareness of the evil that permeated this village. Out of the corner of my eye, I saw the shaman watching us from a distance. I turned and looked at her and she did not move away. She stood there defiantly. My body felt as if it was being pulled toward hers on a conveyor belt until I was right in front of her, staring back into her eyes.

It was then that I heard the cries of family members outside a hut and I rushed toward them. Inside the hut, the shaman was opening up another straw basket, and instead of the brown and tan snake falling from it, a long slender black snake crawled out onto the patient on the cot. The snake bit that person and moved on to another at the shaman's coaching and bit that one too. Within minutes, both of those people were dead. The snake slithered out beneath a crack at the bottom of the hut and was gone. The witch then looked at me and said something in her language that I knew was an insult of some kind.

I looked at Sam and asked her what "pum bav ooo" meant.

"Mpumbavu? It means fool. Why?"

"Because that witch over there called me that."

"When? I didn't hear her say that."

"I was in her mind. Or she was in mine. It doesn't matter who was in whose but I saw her. I saw her killing those with the Ebola. She dropped a long black snake onto them and it was following her orders as it bit people and then slithered away."

"Here, drink a lot of this. And eat this too. Let me check your…"

"You don't need to check anything, Sam. I'm not shitting you. I don't know why the Symbion is doing this to me but it is. I told Dr. Po about it.

I saw the Narcoleptans before they attacked me or Jane. I saw the man who was directing them. He reached out to me. Talked to me. He is a fucked up evil son of a bitch and believe me, I am very familiar with those kinds of people.

"Damn. That's why there's the connection. I told Dr. Po I had a connection with the Narcoleptan because of my relationship with my father but it's more than that. I grew up in a world so full of evil that the Symbion was like a switch that was waiting for the right links to be made so my mind could see beyond just what my eyes saw, just as my body tells me of things before you or I can even detect it. The Symbion and the chemical composition of my blood now make those connections.

"You know about the sensitivity of the sweat on our skin. Well, it's more than that with me. My experience with my father and the Symbion's interaction with my chemical 'imbalances' as you once referred to them have extended the capacity of my mind. You can't stand there and say you don't think that's possible. You trusted your life with my ability to feel danger before it killed us. Well, now you need to trust me when I tell you about what my mind can see. Before that bitch over there ends up killing us all."

Sam didn't say a word. She didn't need to. She simply conveyed her unspoken trust with her olive eyes that looked deep into mine. The trusting look hardened into one of determination and she began preparing us for entry into the quarantined areas.

"Here, hydrate. We'll be going into the part where the people are less sick first. The band, as you called them, made sure that the chieftain separated the ill based upon the time they became sick. Dr. Po believed that if the cure was going to work, we would need to give it to those who had the best chance of getting well, meaning the ones that have been sick the shortest time."

Makes sense. Dr. Po is always thinking.

I drank the bottle that Sam gave me and got another one before I started putting on the hazmat suit. Sam was geared up and began hydrating as she watched me dress. Once we had everything on except the hoods, she removed what looked like several fancy toolboxes from the cart.

"These are cooled transport mechanisms for the serum. They are keyed to open with my left finger only. I will open them once we are in the hut, put on my other glove, and then leave the box in there when we're finished. It's too dangerous to remove the boxes or my gloves once we are inside and I've started to administer the serum. There could be infected blood on the container and or my gloves, undetected by us. Dr. Po has made sure that whatever serum is left or whatever is on the box, will be destroyed within one hour of me opening it.

"I will ask you to give me a syringe for each patient and I'll inject each one. You'll place the used syringe in this biohazard bag and I'll double bag it after we're finished, along with our suits. Don't worry, there are no needles on the syringes. The device is one that Dr. Po developed. The end of the syringe is like the outer texture of a strawberry; rough to the touch. Once it is activated it moves forward and scrapes the skin, releasing the serum, and then it retracts and is covered with an antiviral and antibacterial shield that envelops the 'strawberry.' In fact, he allowed me to name this when he had the syringe patented, just prior to distribution to the medical community. I called them strawberry shots."

I just smiled and let her continue.

"After we have taken care of each patient, you and I will go to the entrance to the hut and begin to remove our suits. I'll do one step and then you'll mirror what I just did. Once we have our suits off and placed in the double bags, I will spray us both with an antiviral mist that's in a container attached to my belt. It will cover us entirely in seconds and will destroy anything viral on our bodies. Follow my instructions without fail, John. A misstep could cost you or me our life. Do you understand?"

I wanted to say, "I'm not worried about the Ebola. I think you forget how my blood doesn't really allow for shit like that to grow. I'm more worried about what the wicked witch of East Africa has waiting for us in there." But I didn't. I just shook my head, letting her know I heard her and understood what she was saying. But that wasn't enough for Sam. Not this time.

"John, I really need..."

"It's okay, Sam. I understand what you're saying and I'll be fine. You know I'm probably even better prepared to go in there than you, but I'll do as you tell me. There is one thing though. We aren't going in there without the LBEs. Whether you wear one or I wear them both, we are going in there with both of them. And you are going to set this cart up in defense mode or whatever it is you need to do so that no one fucks with it."

"The LBEs look like weapons. I'm not sure we should get them out right now."

"The LBEs are weapons and it doesn't matter what you think. We are doing it. Give them to me. They won't say anything. Remember, I'm not a demon anymore. I am just your assistant and/or bodyguard. Just spray the LBEs when you spray us as we leave the hut. Trust me. Everything will be fine."

Plus, I don't give a shit if they think they're weapons. I want them to think that. I want that witch and whoever else she has influenced to know we are armed and they need to be scared of us.

Sam handed me the LBEs and I put the straps over my neck so that a weapon was on each side of my hip. She activated the cart and then said something to the chieftain that made him realize it would be very bad if anyone was to touch it. He called for four large men with spears to come over to him. He told them something and then each of them followed Sam as she posted them as sentries around the cart.

We placed the hoods over our heads and started into the first quarantined hut.

"What did you tell the chieftain?"

"That the cart had guns on it like the soldiers carry and would kill anyone that disturbed it."

"Good."

There was very little light in the first tent. Eleven people were inside and about half of them were lying down, while the other half sat on the sides of the cots, looking at us. Sam started saying something to them that I'm sure was part "don't be scared by the way we look" and "we have medicine for you" but that didn't stop them from looking like they were waiting for the devil. Their eyes kept darting around in hopes they could somehow find a way to escape the hidden monster that pursued them.

Though I didn't know what she said, I saw a young boy raise his hand and Sam motioned for him to come forward. She spoke to him and he smiled and pointed at us and she said something else and he laughed.

"This is a very brave little boy," she told me as she opened her box and cracked open what looked like two flares. They didn't burn or emit any smoke or smell, but they did light up the area where we all stood. They were like spotlights that only illuminated us by someone holding them from somewhere on a balcony that didn't exist.

Dang cool flares, Doc. You knew about the dark huts, didn't you? Damn, of course, you did.

Sam placed a red biohazard bag next to the box. She told me to put the syringes in there after she used them and then asked me for the first one. She spoke to the boy again and he held out his arm. She inoculated him with the syringe and handed it back to me. I knew she asked him if it hurt because he smiled and shook his head no. As soon as everyone heard the question and saw the response from the little boy, the others in the tent started lining up for their shot.

The last two people in that tent were having trouble getting out of bed and Sam told me to get the bag and bring two of the syringes with us as we walked over to them. She administered the shots to them in their beds and though I didn't understand what they said, I knew what it meant as they managed a very weak smile. Sam took the bag of used syringes and tied it up with tape that was attached to the side before she placed it in another biohazard bag and tied it as well.

She then removed two one-quart containers from the box, along with some small, round, flat plastic discs that stretched into what looked like the plastic dispensers on the tops of cough medicine bottles, and some protein bars. She passed out the bars to the people in the tent, telling them it was food that would help them get better. Then she poured one ounce of fluid up to a dark blue line inside the cough medicine top-shaped cups, demonstrating to all of them how much they needed for each dose, and told them again how that fluid would help them get better. They all smiled and said the same word. It sounded like "ah-san-te san ya." Sam replied by saying "care-e-boo" and though I didn't speak the language, I knew I had just heard words that meant "Thank you" and "You're welcome."

Sam closed the box and touched a button on the container to lock it. I heard a click and what sounded like the activation of an ultraviolet light and understood that the destruction of the box contents had been initiated. She brought me over to the front of the tent and opened another large biohazard bag and showed me how to disrobe. Once the biohazard suits were off, she sprayed us, the box, and the bags with the antiviral mist that she spoke of earlier. She picked up the bags and we walked back to the cart.

After disengaging the weapons on the wagon, she pushed another button and a robotic arm placed a large bright yellow container on the ground and opened it. The bags went into the container and the robotic arm closed it. A spray was emitted which I knew would kill any germs it touched and the robotic arm held the container shut with its clamp-like metal hand. Sam handed me another bottle to drink and another protein bar.

"I know you may not feel thirsty or hungry but you need to drink and eat before we go into the next tent. We lost a lot of fluid in there even though you may not feel like we did."

I did as I was told and looked around for the shaman but she was gone. "How do you think things went?"

"It went well, John. Very well. You did good. We'll know in twenty-four hours if it's going to save them. I think they have a very good chance, considering their state of disease and knowing what Dr. Po is capable of creating and manufacturing. What did you think?"

"It was good. I felt comfortable. I didn't see anything that caused me concern, except for now."

"What do you mean?"

"The shaman is gone. I don't like that."

"The chieftain probably told her that she didn't need to be around here now. You have those LBEs strapped to your body. I don't think you should be worried."

"It's when you don't hear the noises that you should be worried. Someone really smart just told me that earlier today. Helped save our lives. When you don't see that shaman, you should be worried."

"I understand, John. Finish your drink and the protein bar and we'll gear up and go to the next tent."

The difference between the next tent and the first one was like walking from an ER waiting room into a crash site where the bodies lay on the side of the road, provided the crash site was at a sewage plant. No one was sitting up on the side of their bed in this hut. They were lying on their cots and all you could smell was vomit and diarrhea. The stench was sickening but I remembered Sam telling me not to get sick in the suit, so I closed my eyes for a few seconds and concentrated on not doing so. Within a minute I could smell the faint scent of roses and I smiled as I realized how strong my mind was becoming. When I opened my eyes, I saw the air purifiers that Sam had put on the ground in front of the door and on the other side of the hut.

"Dr. Po thought the smell might be quite bad when we encountered those where the disease had progressed significantly. These air purifiers have the slightest scent of roses and also permeate the air with antibacterial and antiviral agents. Makes a world of difference, doesn't it?"

I nodded my head as I thought about how my magnificent mind's ability might need some additional refinement.

Dumbass.

I counted fourteen in this tent as Sam told them who we were and what we would be doing. She didn't ask for volunteers this time; she just got the materials ready and we started going from bed to bed. Some of the sick were strong enough to acknowledge us and say thank you but others were not even awake. Sam sprayed those patients with a canister that was in her pocket and she didn't have to tell me what she was doing. I knew she was trying to kill the bacteria in the fecal matter and vomit that surrounded them.

"Ebola is our main concern, but we have to try and hope that we can destroy anything that may cause a secondary infection due to their already weakened immune system. I knew this would be an issue, as did Dr. Po, and I only hope we aren't too late. I'm afraid of what we'll see in the last tent."

I agreed with her. But for an entirely different reason.

We returned to the cart and as we drank and ate once again, Sam warned me of what we could see in the third tent. I didn't interrupt her or ask any questions because I wasn't afraid or concerned about what she was saying. I was more concerned about the fact that the shaman was still nowhere to be seen. I just told her I was ready when she was, so we suited up and headed toward the last tent.

The smell emanating from that tent was overwhelming before we even reached it. Sam told me to wait outside for a moment but I said I wouldn't do that. We were going in there together or not at all. She didn't argue. Just before we entered, I looked up and saw the signs of death flying in a circle above us. I looked around one more time for the shaman but she wasn't present.

Just her fucking flying monkeys, I thought as I followed Sam inside.

She set out the scent devices and just like Po, she anticipated the need for more than two this time. I counted six people in the beds and though I looked closely at each of them as Sam prepared everything, I saw none of them moving. Two of them didn't even seem to be breathing but that didn't surprise me. Sam sprayed each person after inoculating them, and we moved on to the fifth person; a collection of stained rags covered the emaciated body. I handed Sam the syringe and then I touched her shoulder as I saw the rags move. Though we both knew the virus-filled blood and diarrhea were deadly, at that moment, they were less frightening than what stared at us from beneath one of the torn sheets.

Sam whispered, "Black death," as the snake flicked its tongue once. As it did, I shot its head with an LBE, but not before it had pricked Sam on the hand. She dropped the syringe and I pulled her away from the cot. What remained of the black snake continued to sway from side to side for a few moments longer, dead, but with undead fragments of muscles.

Another large black snaked move from beneath the legs of the person in the adjacent cot, and as if it knew its partner had been killed, it flicked its tongue once at us and slithered away into a small dirt hole that had been dug out under the back wall of the hut. As soon as it disappeared, we heard someone scream but that was not one of our main concerns at the moment. I told Sam that both of the people in the cots were already dead, but she wouldn't listen to me and continued to inoculate them. I could tell the pain in her hand was intense as she dropped the last syringe onto the ground.

"My hand is useless now, John. You'll have to get everything ready before we can leave. Don't worry, I have about twenty minutes before I won't be able to talk. Take your time and we'll be back to the cart in enough time for you to give me the anti-venom that Dr. Po prepared just in case."

I had to help Sam take her biohazard suit off and once that was done, we were ready to leave. I carried her back to the cart and held her finger up to the biosensor that deactivated the cart's weapon system.

"The Black Mamba anti-venom. It's labeled. Inject the syringe into my neck. Into the carotid artery. Do it quickly. Find the pulse in my neck and inject it there."

I hesitated for a moment and I saw her starting to struggle to breathe. I found the faint pulse in her neck and hit the injector button on the side of the syringe. When I pulled the syringe back, I thought there would be blood spurting out from the long needle piercing her artery but then I remembered - the strawberry syringe. The shot just left a small pink indentation on her neck and I could see it taking effect as soon as it entered her bloodstream.

Her breathing was returning to normal and she looked up at me and smiled.

"Damn hand feels like someone hit it with a sledgehammer, but I can tell my body is recovering. The pain will be minimal in another twenty minutes."

"Don't tell me, Dr. Po enhanced the anti-venom serum to be even faster acting and it has other properties like reducing pain and infection from other creepy crawlies."

"It does. You did great in there by the way. You shot a damn snake with an LBE. How did you do that?"

"Water guns at the fair. I was pretty damn good. And you do remember me telling you about the black snake and the shaman? That vision or premonition that I had. You do remember that, right?"

Before Sam could answer, we heard the screaming again and we turned around to see the shaman crawling on her hands and knees out into the middle of the village. Then as if a giant hand reached down from the sky and squeezed her abdomen, shit and vomit exited her body simultaneously in a violent manner as she fell to the ground.

"I suppose she's the one that screamed," I said sarcastically but what Sam said next stopped me cold.

"John, she has Ebola. And she was bitten by the Mamba. We've got to inoculate her before she infects other people. But before we do that, I will need the Ebola serum too. That snake. The snake bit the Ebola patient and then it bit me."

Chapter 22
African Ghosts

"Steady me, John," Sam said as she walked toward the crowd beginning to gather around the shaman's body. She shouted out to them and whatever she said made them stop. The chieftain came over to Sam and I imagine she told him that the shaman had the disease because he had the large men with spears make everyone move farther away from the body.

"And tell me again why we need to inoculate her? Why not let that piece of shit, who is now covered in shit, just die?"

"First of all, I will need the Ebola serum. I'm feeling fine now from the snake bite. Well, I'm at least able to walk on my own. When I go back to the cart, I'll get the other box of vaccines and inoculate myself. We need to try and save her so she doesn't spread the disease. Plus, if we save her, we may change the way she thinks about things. She may even become more helpful for the village."

That's not going to happen. I grew up with this shaman, only I called her a postman.

I heard Dr. Po talking to me. It was like he was in my mind and then I remembered the neuronal mesh.

"John, are you okay? Your blood pressure is very high. Has something happened to you or Samantha?"

"Sam was bitten by a black mamba and the shaman of the village was also bitten by a black mamba and she is infected with Ebola. Oh, and the black mamba that bit Sam killed one of the patients with Ebola. Other than that, everything is going great."

"Samantha's vital signs are elevated but nothing that I would call serious. She has been given the anti-venom and the Ebola serum?"

"The anti-venom but not the Ebola vaccine. Why aren't you in her head like mine? You have that ability, don't you?"

"The ability, yes. The permission, no."

Why the hell does that not surprise me?

"Hold on. She just gave herself the vaccine. We're going over to the shaman and try to help her into one of the huts. I guess we'll be putting on one of those spacesuits again. Though I don't necessarily agree with trying to save her."

"Samantha thinks otherwise, doesn't she?"

"Yes, but I just want to go on record that I think it's a bad idea."

Sam placed what looked like a very small hearing aid in her ear and began talking to Dr. Po.

Why didn't you do that earlier? Well, I guess it could have come out in the Ebola hut and that wouldn't have been good. I get it.

"Dr. Po, we inoculated thirty-one villagers and are going to try to take care of the shaman. They were in various stages of the disease. I think at least twenty of them are strong enough to allow the serum a chance to kill the virus. Though I provided vaccinations to all, I'm pretty sure two of them were already dead. I didn't have time to check any vital signs. We just went in and did what we needed to do and left. Then the black mamba encounter. So, as John said, we're getting ready to try and help the shaman but she looks bad. I would guess, at least ten days into the viral process by her appearance. I don't know how I didn't notice that when we met."

"I do. Evil masks a lot of things," I explained.

"You do realize what you will need to do now, Samantha? We prepared for it. Everyone will need vaccinations."

"Yes, I'm aware. Once we move the shaman into the tent, I'll discuss that with the chieftain. I see no reason to isolate the rest of the village though. Just tell them to keep to themselves for at least forty-eight hours, don't you think?"

"Yes, in complete agreement. Sorry for the problems you encountered. Let me know if you need anything or have any other issues that we didn't anticipate."

"We will."

"John, I am just talking to you now. Samantha cannot hear me. I heard what you said about the evil masking the virus's presence. I no longer dismiss the observations that you possess as irrational. Samantha may be less inclined to believe you so you will need to act as you believe is in the best interest of all involved. Do not allow her empathy to become a compassionate death for either of you. I trust you."

One of the smartest men on the planet just told me he trusted me. Trusted what I did or thought. God, I hope that isn't some sign of the apocalypse.

Just then that I saw a man wearing a pith helmet and smoking a pipe. He had on a khaki jacket over a white collared shirt, khaki pants, and old brown shoes, and was standing there looking down at the shaman. He turned and walked toward me and I recognized him at once. It was Jack.

"You're here too?"

"I suppose I am or I wouldn't be talking to you."

"Why now?"

"You know that answer, John, I don't. Our conversations originate from you, not me."

"Trust. I'm struggling with hearing that word from a man that I highly respect. It's thrown me for a loop I suppose."

"Turning on the light, where there was once only darkness, can have that effect. It takes a while getting used to, but to be honest with you, I believe it took me a lifetime to get accustomed to the transient nature of the changes that occurred over time."

"Does that mean I've changed?"

"Of course, you have, John, both physically and mentally."

"It's the mental part I worry about."

"I saw nothing in my life that demonstrated to me that anything we do, will eradicate suffering. If a thing is free to be good, it is also free to be bad. And free will is what has made evil possible. Why then did God give them free will? Because free will, though it makes evil possible, is also the only thing that makes possible any love or goodness or joy worth having."

"Yes, you told me that before."

"It bears repeating."

"Why? I understand what you're saying about free will. I get that now. Unless you're trying to tell me something else."

"I am not trying to tell you anything. As you know, these conversations initiate from you, not me."

"You're speaking in circles now. I don't like it when you do that."

"I never intend to, but that's how our thinking works sometimes. It goes backward and forward and around our brain as if there was some well-worn path in there that we travel over and over, most times not even aware we are on it. But sometimes as we walk along it, we see something new that we hadn't noticed before, only to realize later it had been there for a very long time and overlooked. New or overlooked, it always reveals something important to us."

"I don't understand what you're saying."

"Irony is often difficult to see."

"Irony"

"Yes, indeed. Much more subtle than sarcasm of which you are most competent, but very seldom as biting or as harsh as the words that arise from a cynic. There is humor and empathy in irony, and on the rare occasion, a harsh truth."

"You are frustrating me right now, Jack."

"I'm afraid I frustrate many people. Yet, here you are, halfway around the world on what is known as the dark continent, scorched by an intense light."

I then heard Dr. Po interjecting. "John, are you okay? Your EEG waves are spiking."

And just like that, Jack was gone.

"Yeah, uh, I will be, Doc. I was just thinking about something for a moment, but I'm okay. In fact, I'm good. But I need to go now because Sam is looking at me funny. She thinks I zoned out for a moment, but I was just looking around us to make sure everything was okay, like you asked. And from what I can tell, it appears to be so for the moment. I will make sure we stay safe. We're going to suit up now. Talk to you later."

And thank you.

"What were you looking for?" asked Sam.

"Whether or not I have the ability to help the shaman. What do you need to discuss with the chieftain? And what was that about 48 hours?"

"John, Dr. Po and I realized that we may have to inoculate the entire village. The fact that the shaman has been infected and has probably been in contact with most everyone, in one way or another, indicates we need to do that now. We came prepared for that, but it will take us a while to do it and we're going to need the cooperation of the chieftain. He may say no, wanting to wait and see what happens to those that we have already helped, but I'm hoping he will be more open to the idea."

"Why not tell him that a chieftain of a dead village is not much of a chieftain anymore?"

"Well, I suppose I could take that approach, but I'm not sure that's the right thing to do right now. When we get to the shaman, we'll take her into the third tent with the other very sick ones. I'll spray her body and the area around her with the antiviral mist which will destroy anything on it. Don't worry about stepping in shit or vomit. We won't be able to avoid it but don't worry. Everything that is in it will be dead."

"That makes it all so much better."

"If it makes you feel better, bring a plasma knife with you."

"Yea, I thought I might do that this time."

Sam sprayed the area around the shaman and her entire body before she let me come close. I could feel how hot her body was through my gloves when I picked her up. I knew the sun was hot but this wasn't all due to the sun. I just laid her on the ground inside the tent. Sam had said there was no need to disturb the other bodies on the cots.

Smart, I thought. And even though I looked for something to jump out at us, I saw nothing moving at all within that tent.

Sam gave the shaman the Ebola vaccine and then started to pull out the Mamba anti-venom when I stopped her hand. "Do you feel how hot she is?"

"Yes, she's burning up with fever. I don't need to check it. Look at her eyes. They're dripping blood. I'm afraid the Ebola vaccine will be too late to save her."

"Sam, I suspect what we're looking at is just an early glimpse into what walks around in Hell. How long before someone dies from a black mamba bite without anti-venom?"

"Probably within six hours, but in her weakened condition it could be much faster."

"The anti-venom won't help her, Sam. We need to leave."

I heard something behind me and pulled out the plasma knife and watched as the arc lit up the room. All I saw was one of the men closest to us sitting on the edge of his bed and looking at us.

"That man looked like he was barely alive an hour ago," Sam whispered.

The man smiled at us and then uttered, "Ma-u-tee-in-a-coo- ja."

Sam quickly stuck the syringe in the ground next to the shaman's body and emptied its contents into the dirt.

"What did he say?"

"He said, 'Mauti inakuja.' It means death is coming. Let's get out of here now."

I helped Sam wrap up the biohazardous material and we left in a hurry. Even though she sprayed us with the bug-killing film in the tent, she sprayed us again once we got back to the wagon. She handed me another drink as she took one for herself and walked over to the chieftain.

She talked to him while pointing to the huts and to the other villagers as she explained what she needed to do but he shook his head no several times. He also pointed toward the huts and then at me and I saw Sam nod before returning.

"You don't need to tell me, Sam. I know what he said. He's a coward."

"Not a coward. Just a tired, old man who's willing to die. The shaman was his sister. His wives and children have already died. He only allowed us to come because of that little boy. The little boy that we met in the first tent, the one who volunteered first, was his grandson. He was hoping we could save him."

"Shit."

"Yeah. Shit."

"So, what do we do now?"

"We wait. We wait and see whether the chorus of ghosts become so loud that they are only silenced by the end of a spear or by the sound of a grandson's laughter."

Chapter 23
Ashes

"How many people have died in this village?"

Sam took a drink and pushed some buttons on the cart that activated the robotic arms into the air, lowering the back door. A soft humming noise came from the arms as the back half of the cart became immersed in shade.

"How the hell is that possible?"

"There are mechanisms in the ends of the arms which emit a series of sound waves that deflect the sunlight."

"We couldn't just put up a large umbrella of some kind?"

"We have that as a backup should these devices fail."

Of course, we do.

As we sat down, I could see the concern on her face for the first time since we left.

"A little over 200 have died by now, I would imagine. It was close to that number when the scientists came to see Dr. Po."

"Dr. Po was looking for an environment where he could test the serum, wasn't he?"

"Yes."

"You told him we should inoculate the entire village from the very beginning, didn't you?"

"Yes."

"But he didn't want to do that because he was afraid there would be some sort of unpredicted outcome."

"Concerned, yes. But it didn't matter. The chieftain wasn't going to allow it anyway. I wasn't even going to ask until the shaman got sick and then I thought he might relent, but...well, you know the answer."

I took a drink and looked around the village. It seemed deserted.

"You know, not all the side effects from the cures resulted in something inhuman being created. There was some blindness, some minor paralysis, and even some deaths. And though those side effects were only one-tenth of one percent, Dr. Po felt as if he had failed each time. He wouldn't admit it to anyone, but I could tell that it bothered him immensely. And then when the horrible mutations began to manifest, he was shaken to the core of his soul. That's when I saw fear in that man's face for the very first time."

"But I thought that was due to the doctors failing to follow the protocols?"

"For the most part, yes. But there were a few that were unexplainable. As a result of that, he became very guarded about the use of what I consider the greatest medical discovery in the world."

"I've never met a doctor who cared that much about anything."

"Neither have I. Hundreds of thousands of people have been cured because of him. Free of disease and now able to spend precious time with their children and grandchildren, able to see a graduation or a marriage that they would have never seen, or able to go to a place in the world that they had never been before.

"And the children, the children who would have had their lives cut short, can live life as if nothing ever happened to them."

"You convinced him to do that, didn't you? To always make sure the children continue to get the Symbion."

"No. That was all Dr. Po."

I should have known that. He remembers the suffering of a child. That's something you never forget.

"But now I'm worried, John. Worried that he will allow the monsters to control his actions. I felt like the clouds were clearing somewhat when he found your sister and trained her and saw how she could help him. But then you came along, and I could see his confidence growing with each day your health improved. He knows you're special. Even more so than your sister. I know what he sees in you because I see it too. It's hope."

I sat silently for a moment and tried to grasp what Sam was saying. She took my hand and I turned to look at her. Her dark green eyes glistened as I gently wiped away the shimmering effects of her eyes from her cheeks.

Sam leaned her head on my shoulder and we sat quietly watching the day transition into evening. The chieftain came over to us, and said something to Sam and she smiled and nodded. He laughed and then looked at me and held out his hand. I took it and he gripped it tightly as he swung it up and down two times and then let it go as he grinned and walked away.

"The chieftain likes you."

"Because he shook my hand?"

"Yes. That's a very big deal especially since his sister told him that you were a nyeupe pepo."

"What the hell is that?"

"A nyeupe pepo is a white demon."

"You should have told him what I think of his sister."

"I didn't have to. He saw you carry her into the tent."

Yeah. I may regret that. Damn witch.

"What else did he say?"

"He wants us to come eat with him tonight."

"He wants to eat dinner with a white demon?"

"He knows a white demon wouldn't try and help his people. He doesn't believe everything his sister tells him."

"Oh damn. Please tell me you said no."

"Don't worry. I declined in a most gracious way saying that you were on a restricted diet because you've had severe stomach cramping since you got here that gave you a great deal of gas."

"A simple no thank you wasn't sufficient?"

"A simple no thank you would not have been sufficient. They were preparing goat and roasted grasshoppers; a very special meal."

Sam laughed, but I was perfectly fine letting the chieftain think I had gas. Better to be thought full of gas than eating goat and grasshoppers.

"You just treated people with one of the deadliest viruses in the world, stuck your hand into a basket that you knew contained something deadly, and killed a black mamba without blinking. And you look more relieved now because you don't have to eat goat and grasshoppers."

"Point?"

"I would kiss you but I don't think that is wise considering everything we did today."

"I'm not sick. Can't get sick. Dr. Po told me that so there," I said as I stuck out my tongue. "I may fart a lot tonight but I'm not sick."

Sam laughed and blew a kiss to me.

"I have some more of those rose-scented aerosols, so I'm not worried. Let's get the wagon ready for tonight. We can open up the rear side compartments and there are some air mattresses that will inflate once we remove some of the equipment. They're actually pretty comfortable. They fill up with an 80% helium and air mixture. And I have some protein bars that taste a lot like cheeseburgers. We can even make some strawberry milkshakes with some cold water and ice cream paste that Dr. Po developed."

"Jane said she doubted that I'd be able to get a cheeseburger or milkshake over here. And even though Hardee's are everywhere, as we walked to the village today, I figured that the liability insurance an owner would need to keep the business operating here was just a tad too much. I didn't know we were going to bring one with us."

Sam smiled as she moved some of the supplies around and prepared our "Hardee's" dinner. It probably tasted as good as any I had ever had. We sat for about an hour after eating, not saying much, just listening to the sounds of the world around us and looking at a sky full of stars. I had never seen so many stars in the night sky before. And then I remembered something I had read in one of those travel magazines that my mother and sister were always looking at. I recalled picking one up because there was a story about the sky and how your view of the sky was determined by how far north or south you are of the equator. Though the earth around here looked barren and very inhospitable, the people around here could take refuge in a night sky like this. Every night.

Sam reported to Dr. Po that we had eaten and everything was quiet for the moment so we were retiring for the evening. It was about 10 p.m. our time, and Dr. Po said to make sure that we took every precaution. Sam assured him we would and said she would let him know about the patients just as soon as she had new information.

Sam turned on the spotlights around the cart and we got out for a minute while she prepared our sleeping quarters. Black plates spread out over the wheels and up along the sides of the cart.

"Those are polyhexafluoroethylene plates. Similar to Teflon, but Dr. Po lowered the coefficient of friction even more. Nothing can crawl up those sides."

She deployed the beds which filled up within seconds and turned off the equipment that was responsible for the sound waves. A thin mesh metal screen extended from somewhere at the front of the wagon until it covered the entire thing. Then we both got inside and with the touch of another button, a similar black shield stretched from the ground up to the screen on the back of the cart.

"No insects can get through that screen but because we still need to be concerned about bacteria and viruses, I'm going to release another antiviral mist. I won't activate the LBEs but I do have some lasers that are calibrated to engage if the motion detectors sense anything with a certain size and form coming toward us. We're safe here. I know you won't sleep without an LBE next to you and with your plasma knife, but I promise you we are safe."

"So, if I understand you correctly, those lasers will zap a scorpion or spider if they get close enough to our cart, but not a human or a dog?"

"Yes, small snakes too, and the larger ones can't crawl up the sides of the cart."

"Great. I hope I hear the lasers going off all night. I love the sound of a bug zapper. My neighbor, Mrs. Cunningham, had one on her back porch. I could sit there all night listening to the bugs get zapped. I bet those lasers sound even cooler when they hit some of those big exoskeletons on the bugs around here."

Sam rolled her eyes and shook her head. "Go to sleep, John."

"Yeah, I will. Just need to hear some zaps first."

"Don't worry, you will. Some of the scorpions can get quite large here. Five or six inches."

"Hell yeah. Zap 'em, Sam."

"Good night, John."

"Good night, Sam."

I continued to look at the night sky until I heard it. Two lasers went off simultaneously and it must have been some big scorpion because it sounded like a half dozen eggs had been cracked open. I smiled and closed my eyes and listened to a few more things get zapped before I fell asleep.

I was tired and though I didn't want to remember the day that we had experienced, I relived every moment of it. I saw the snakes and the sick people and then I saw her. The shaman was staring at me and I could hear her talking. At first, I couldn't understand what she was saying but then I recognized the voice. It wasn't her voice. It was the one that now haunted me. Merkel.

It's these quiet times that allow us to connect really well. We can sense each other's presence in these moments, much more so than when our brains are filled with other concerns. You seemed to have convinced the puppet that there are more truths in this world than those that can be defined by scientific properties and processes. Why he doubts that is odd, considering that he has changed science as everyone once defined it. Puzzling, isn't it?

I will kill you one day.

It will take more than a shovel, John. Yes, I know a lot about you and your sister now. I'm planning on visiting her and the puppet, maybe before you return.

"John! It's Dr. Po. Wake up! You are beginning to have a seizure."

You don't want to wake up yet, John. You know you and your sister aren't the only ones that are special. We all have special clothes. We're all connected. The ones I wear allow me to disappear when I want to. You can't do that, can you?

"John, this is Dr. Po! Open your eyes! Now! Wake up!"

My sister will kill you if you confront her.

I don't think so. But time will tell. You should wake up now though. She is looking for you.

I opened my eyes and heard a familiar scream. It sounded like those damn monkeys. The ones that hated being inside the cage and threw turds at you. And as if on cue, I heard and felt a large thud against the Teflon-like shields and then an even more disturbing sound. The shields were being ripped open and I saw a large tear down the middle of them as if they were sheets being torn apart by a cat. A very large cat.

Sam woke up and before she could ask me what was happening, something jumped onto the metal screen above us and the screen barrier began to sag. That's when we both saw her. Her face looked like burning charcoals that were no longer black but were now white-hot. With each second that passed, some of the white ashes blew away, revealing more burning embers. Except they weren't burning embers. They were tissue and muscle fragments from huge blood vessels pulsating up the side of her neck and face.

She screamed again and spit at us through the mesh. The spit hit my hand and it burned like acid. Sam saw the ulcer it was creating and handed me some glasses as she rolled toward me. I put them on, just as the thing bent down and tore away part of the screen. It reached in with large talons and just missed cutting open Sam's back. I tried to get the LBE but Sam was laying on it, so I pushed her away as another talon came sweeping down, missing her by a fraction of an inch as it punctured the air mattress I was laying on. My back hit the bottom of the cart but it didn't worry me, because behind that claw, was the being's head.

The eyes burned red within the ash-like face that continued to change as the skin blew away from it, revealing more muscle and bone. I was able to grab one of the LBEs as she pushed her head toward me. I shoved the end of it into her mouth full of several rows of sharp, jagged teeth and fired.

The light bullet went through her head. I could see the stars in the sky from the hole that was created, but the being still wasn't dead. She swiped at me again and this time the claws knocked the LBE out of my hand and almost took my hand with it. My hand was hanging limply, halfway detached from my wrist, when Sam sliced the monster's claws off with a plasma knife. The creature screamed and raised up her head and then leaped from the mesh. Just as she did, Sam hit a switch. Grotesque screams filled the air for a few more seconds before the LBEs that Sam activated on the cart destroyed it.

Sam put the plasma knife down and sprayed my hand with an anti-bacterial mist and wrapped it with some transparent bandages They felt soothing and immobilized it so that no further damage could occur.

"Don't move your hand or do anything to aggravate the injury. I need to find something else to bind the radial artery that has been severed and then we'll need to do some surgery as soon as we talk to Dr. Po and he can determine the damage to your hand."

"Whatever. But before you do that, I want to see that damn thing."

"That's not safe. There may be others."

"I'll take an LBE with me. I want to make sure that bitch is dead."

Sam didn't argue. She lowered what remained of the back shield and positioned the high-intensity spotlights toward the village. The shaman that had become the Vahemic-like mutation was dead. Its head was reduced to fragments and its body was now depleted of blood and oxygen. There was even a dead mamba, cut up in multiple pieces as if it had been prepared by a sushi chef.

Good riddance, you fuckers. Your damn snake poisoned the helpless and you poisoned the living. You both got what you deserved.

Chapter 24
White cloud

The crowd gathered around the dead shaman but neither they nor the chieftain recognized what was lying there on the ground. Sam shouted something that must have been about staying away because the chieftain again positioned some large men with spears around the dead being. He approached the cart and she yelled once more to him and waved her hand back and forth. The chieftain and his bodyguards stopped but continued to watch, not sure what to do or what had exactly happened.

I returned to the cart and Sam took off the bandage and sprayed something else on my radial artery which was no longer spewing blood but was still leaking like a busted pipe. The substance had a musty metallic smell.

"Doing some soldering?"

"It's a combination of Bacillus anthracis and zinc metalloprotease and Symbion. It activates your prothrombin and Factor X directly. In simple terms, it forms a clot but doesn't damage the vessel as cauterization would do. It allows us to be able to use the vessel later if the damage isn't too extensive."

Forming a clot was an understatement. Before she had even finished spraying it around the artery, the bleeding had stopped.

"Bacillus anthracis. Isn't that anthrax?"

"A type of it, but this is a non-virulent variant." She got Dr. Po on the computer and began telling him about my injury. She raised my hand carefully in front of the camera so that he could see it.

"What do you think, Doc?"

He ignored my question and talked to Sam.

"You placed the clotting component on the radial artery?"

"Yes."

"You will need to stitch a svs into place next to the artery. And then give him a booster shot of Symbion and engage his cord. Quickly, Samantha. Within the next ten minutes would be optimal."

"Yes, sir," she said as she pulled out a small piece of pale red tubing from a clear package and began stitching it into place as she asked me to hold up my hand.

"What did this, John?" Dr. Po asked me as Sam worked.

"The shaman became some sort of Vahemic-like mutation."

"Have you seen anything else like it from the others who were treated?"

"No. Not at all. What is this svs you're talking about, Dr. Po?"

"Symbion vessel sheath. Your radial artery has been severed and is no longer functioning the way it should. Samantha sealed it off so you wouldn't bleed to death. Your hand will need to regenerate a new vessel. It's not uncommon for your body to do that. It's called angiogenesis. That's how tumors grow, but we are certainly not trying to grow a tumor. Your body does it naturally too. We are just going to help it along a bit. The sheath she is stitching into your body is made up of your own muscle and endothelial cells that I have maintained in the lab. It is a mesh material held together by the Symbion molecules."

"I'm finished, Dr. Po."

"Very good, Samantha. Tell the village chieftain you need to see his cattle. I am sure he has some. Probably Ankole cattle. They are quite large and will be sufficient for what John needs right now. You know what to say."

"What about the Ebola, Dr. Po?"

"The Symbion shot and John's blood along with the regenerative aspect of his cord should prevent the virus from being able to take hold anywhere in his body. I am sure of it."

Sam helped me stand up. Before we walked away from the cart, she re-engaged the lasers and I took a couple of LBEs and placed them around her neck and mine. She said a lot of words that I didn't understand to the chieftain but I knew what we were going to do and what she was probably saying. I was going to have to place my cord onto some live cows.

The chieftain nodded his head and told the guards to stay with the dead shaman and then assigned several more men to guard the path to the cart. He led us to his lodge and showed Sam his own cattle pen. As we walked toward them, the chieftain returned to his home.

"What did you tell him?"

"I said we needed cattle blood to heal the infection in your hand."

"I suppose anywhere else that would have sounded strange. But just another day here, huh?"

Sam didn't respond to the attempted humor but I couldn't blame her. I didn't find it that funny either. I watched her inject something into the neck of one of the large steers which caused it to immediately fall to the ground.

"It's not dead, John. It's anesthetized. You need to place your cord on it now."

I bent down on one knee and placed my hand on the animal that laid there. Its chest was moving up and down and its heart was beating in a slowed but rhythmic manner. "I'm sorry," I whispered and turned my head away after I placed the cord on the animal's chest. I felt like I had plugged myself into an electrical outlet. I could even feel the electrical impulses traveling directly into my hand as if they knew that is where they were supposed to go. Within a minute the animal was dead and Sam called me over to another one.

Shit, I thought, but I knew that there wasn't an option. I knelt down beside the next animal and repeated the process. I now understood how drug addicts became addicted to stimulants that they injected into their bodies because my entire body was buzzing. I thought I could actually see blood vessels growing out from my arm into my hand. It reminded me of something I had seen on "Nat Geo" once where they showed time-lapsed photographic images of mold spreading out over some dead carcass. It was hypnotic and sickening at the same time because I knew the genesis of that activity.

"Another one, John. Come over here now."

I looked at her and shook my head, but instead of anesthetizing the animal, she had cut its throat. The blood was leaving its body, flowing onto the ground. I knew why she did that. She understood I wouldn't kill another animal willingly so she did it for me. I could do nothing except what she said and I placed the cord on its chest. I watched as it took its last breath and then looked up at Sam. Though my entire body was alive with activity, my vision of Sam was distorted by the tears that in my eyes.

"It's all necessary, John. Don't forget that. Don't ever forget that."

I heard the words and even though they didn't mean that much to me at the moment, it was impossible for me to remain despondent. The top of my head felt like it was expanding in order to make room for my brain. Every cell in my body radiated energy that seemed to cause all of them to jump around like I was internally popping some kind of popcorn. All the endoplasmic reticulum, Golgi bodies, and mitochondria, I suppose, were electrified and regenerating the damaged cells in my body and providing me more strength than I had ever experienced.

And though all this was happening to my body, my mind was not confused or clouded in any way. In fact, I was more focused and alert and aware of everything around me than I had ever been. I could see the cells illuminated in my body; glowing like bioluminescent beings in the dark depths of the ocean. It seemed like I had night vision goggles on when I looked out into the darkness. I could identify thermal images of animals in the dark all around us, knowing that they smelled the blood and death that rose into the air and wailed to them like a siren.

"We need to get back to the cart. But first, Sam, you need to tell the chieftain that the cattle are dead and that there are many animals out there in the darkness that are attracted to the death. He should burn the cows. I have probably infected them in some way and neither they nor the animals should eat those dead cattle."

When Sam left the chieftain's lodge, she looked at me and I could tell she didn't have an answer to the question on her face.

"What is it?"

"The chieftain asked if they would be safe after they burned the cows. I didn't know what to tell him."

"We came here to save them, right?"

"Yes, of course we did."

"We don't know what's going to happen with the others. The only way we can protect them tonight is to have them come and stay out by the cart. Can you adjust the LBEs so that they will cover the villagers if they lay down next to it?"

"I think so."

"Then tell him to bring his village people to the cart and camp there next to us under the light. Tell them there will be weapons on the cart that will destroy anything that comes toward them. Turn on the LBEs and lasers and adjust them to the perimeter of the camp and then add ten feet. I'll also walk among them through the night with the LBE. I won't allow anything to hurt them."

Sam followed my instructions and after we got back to the cart, she sprayed the area where the parts of the shaman lay with an anti-viral mist that covered the bloody ground like a translucent blanket. The chieftain and villagers soon arrived and Sam showed them where to set up camp and explained about the weapons and that I would be walking among them through the night making sure nothing hurt them. The old man looked at me and smiled.

"Nay u pay pon, nay u pay key fo," he said as he placed his arm on my shoulder and sat down next to the cart.

"I got the first part. What was the second thing he said?"

"He said the white demon was now 'nyeupe kifo' - white death."

"That's better than black death, don't you think?"

Sam nodded and smiled as she looked down at the chieftain and said something else. The old man grinned and stood up. Sam helped him step up into the cart and told him to lay down on the air mattress. When he did, he began to laugh.

"Nay u pay key fo hu ponda wing u yea u pay."

Sam smiled and nodded again. "He said 'nyeupe kifo hupanda wingu jeupe.' The white death rides on a white cloud."

"Damn. Sounds like he just called me John Wayne or John Wick, doesn't it?"

"Yeah, maybe. But all I heard was John Deaux."

"Riding a white cloud though, right?"

"Yes. Riding a white cloud."

Chapter 25
A different kind of medicine

It was noon on Sunday when Dr. Po found Jane sitting at the library bar, eating a dish of ice cream while looking out at the waterfall. She acknowledged his presence with a pat on the stool next to her and a smile. He accommodated her request and as he sat down, the stool elevated to a position at the bar that was calibrated for him to be comfortable.

"Ice cream is a wonderful medicine. I don't think doctors realize just how important a tool it is in their 'medical bag.' Of course, back before the medical community knew better, it was used as a reward for a child that had just undergone a tonsillectomy. Now the anesthesiologists and surgeons tell the parents that it's best to avoid ice cream or any dairy products after surgery due to the risk of nausea or vomiting."

"I still have my tonsils."

"Yes, you do, Jane. I doubt you ever even had a cold growing up, much less a throat infection, did you?"

"No, John and I were never sick like that."

"What are you eating?"

"A caramel and chocolate fudge sundae with roasted pecans and lots of whip cream and of course a cherry on top. Actually, five cherries, if I'm being honest."

"Sounds delicious. Marie, could I have one of those too? But in addition to pecans, I would like some pistachios, some peanuts, and some cashews. And I want five cherries too."

"Good thing you don't have a nut allergy, Dr. Po."

"I used to, but I like nuts so I found a way to suppress my body's immune system from having a reaction when I want to eat them. I just take this little pill and I am good. And by the way, I never agreed with the medical community about not giving ice cream to children after having any type of surgery, especially tonsillectomies. There were ways to prevent the nausea."

"I always liked that about you. You try to think of ways to make the patient feel normal when they are going through something scary and very abnormal. I know you did a lot for the cancer patients to make sure they had something they could eat that tasted good and didn't make them sick while helping them heal. You've done so much for those that have been hurt in one way or another. You don't get the credit or recognition you deserve. And I know that doesn't matter to you, the recognition and stuff, but you still need to hear it, if only from me."

"Thank you, Jane. It means more coming from you than you can imagine."

"It's strange how we came to be together, isn't it?"

"Why do you say that?"

"I mean considering who I was, which was essentially a nobody, just a poor little girl growing up in a bad home. I didn't have any ailments that would have led me to you, yet here we are."

The robotic Marie placed the sundae in front of Dr. Po and handed him a spoon with her metallic fingers. "Is there anything else I can get for you?"

"No, thank you, Marie. This looks amazing."

Jane laughed at his comment and Dr. Po looked at her questioningly.

"You say it a lot you know - the word 'amazing.' That's what I was laughing at."

"Do I? Hmmm..." Dr Po mused as he took a bite of his sundae. "Yes, I suppose I do. I have reason to. I have seen a lot of amazing things in my life and continue to each day that I live."

"You create 'amazing' every day you live, Doc. It's just...uhhh. It's just nothing really."

"You and your brother are amazing. You do know that, don't you?"

"Yes, I do now. Have you heard from them, by the way?"

What do I tell her, Marie? I've never lied to her. Yes, I've omitted some details at one time or another but only for her benefit. But I've never lied to her. Yes. You are right. We won't start now.

"Yes, I did, earlier today. One of the sicker patients transformed into some sort of Vahemic mutation but John destroyed it. I haven't seen any evidence of it yet so I'm not sure if it's what we are used to seeing or something completely different. John did suffer an injury to his hand but I am sure he will be okay. I saw the wound and Samantha did a great job caring for it. The last message I received was that John was doing well and that they were still there, observing and waiting to see if the vaccine will heal the patients."

"John will be okay. He's very strong."

"He is indeed, as are you."

Jane looked off at the waterfall. "You never did respond to that comment I made earlier. About how strange it was for us coming together as we did."

"Somehow it just happened, Jane. I liked the analogy you used of the missionaries you read about in Operation Auca with the Huaorani tribe in Ecuador. You came into my life when I needed you."

"Yeah, I know I said that but I think about all that stuff and wonder sometimes how it all happened. Things just don't happen by chance. And those missionaries helped those savages stop killing people by converting them to Christianity. I stop the savages from killing people by converting them into bits and pieces. Not quite the same, is it?"

Dr. Po considered what Jane was asking him. He knew it was time to discuss something with her that he had avoided for some time now.

"You enjoy killing the mutations, don't you, Jane?"

She did not try to deflect the truth or avoid answering the question. She simply said, "Yes."

"Does it help you in some way?"

"Actually, it helps me remember. It helps me remember each time I went down into that basement with my father. My father, the man who was supposed to protect his little girl, did things to her that no one should ever have to endure. These mutations that stalk this world, will never be able to hurt me more than what I experienced in that darkness. Each one I kill is one less time that I have to think about that part of my life "

"Jane, you do not have to explain anymore."

Her eyes looked right through him as she continued. "No, I want to tell you. I know you think I put all that behind me and I even told my brother the same thing, but that's not entirely true. We've never talked about the details but I want to tell you what he did to me. He took me down into that basement forty-seven times. Forty-seven times he did things to me that no child should ever have done to them. I got to a point where I left my body when it was happening. I watched what he did to me from outside myself and I said I would find a way to end it all one day.

"Luckily, my brother did that for me. But not before that bastard killed our mother. John and I have never talked about any of this but I know he wondered, as I did, how our mother could allow that to happen. The abuse to her, John, me. I don't have the answer to that, and I don't expect you to give me one, but I have forgiven her. She did try. I loved her because she did try.

"But that number, forty-seven, is burned into the back of my brain as if it were tattooed there. I figure once I kill three times that many mutations, I will no longer carry the burden he placed upon my soul, provided there is still one there, or if there was ever one there. Anyway, there is some sort of internal calendar somewhere in my mind and body and I place a mark on it each time I kill one of those monsters. 91 to go, Doc. 91 to go.

"I'm sorry I lied to you about the Vahemics the other day. They didn't just follow the deer onto the grounds. I lured them in. I suppose we would have gotten around to this discussion eventually because I suspected you always knew."

"Yes, I suppose we would have."

"But understand, Doc, I'm not just killing these things for me, but also for my mother and my brother and for any other person out there that could be harmed. No one should be harmed by a monster. Once all the monsters are gone, then I won't have to hurt anymore. And if they're gone before I get to 91, I'm good with that. No one should be harmed by any monsters, should they?"

"No, they should not, Jane."

"Do you think the monsters will go away once I've killed them all? I mean from inside me? The memories?"

"I am not sure. I am sorry but I just do not know."

"Yeah, I didn't think you would, but I knew you would tell me the truth. You always tell me the truth when I ask a question. I appreciate that about you. But I have to believe that the monsters will go away. I'm not afraid of dying and I'll do whatever you tell me to do to help make the world a safer place. I consider myself very fortunate to have that opportunity. To be able to sit here with someone who truly cares about me and look and hear that beautiful waterfall that is miles away but looks close enough to touch. So, if you say I came into your life when you needed me, that's fine with me. You came into my life when I needed you too, so everything is cool."

"Cool."

"Did you just say 'cool'?"

"Appropriate, yes?"

"Yeah, very," she laughed before asking, "Dr. Po?"

"Yes, Jane."

"Can monsters be forgiven?"

Dr. Po paused. He wasn't sure what to say as he thought back to his childhood. Molecules didn't just bump into one another and make him or Jane or cancer or the mutations. He was horribly deformed and given up for death but had been saved. And he had saved hundreds of thousands because of that act of kindness. And that act of kindness wasn't just random. It couldn't be. It was purposeful. He was sure of it now. The gifts that he possessed weren't random either. Granted, he had to search for them and work at refining them, but he had been blessed with a mind and skill set that very few others attained over multiple lifetimes.

But knowing that, did that mean that monsters could be forgiven as Jane asked? Does one act of unending kindness mean that others have the ability to change, even if they commit horrible crimes or murder? He looked at Jane and thought about John trying to save people in Africa. He remembered what the good doctor that John told him to read said: "Life's too short to wake up with regrets. So, love the people who treat you right, forgive the ones who don't, and believe that everything happens for a reason." He had his answer.

"Yes, Jane. I believe some do."

"That means that some don't, right?"

"I suppose you could frame it in that manner."

"I prefer thinking that they don't. Is that wrong?"

"Again, Jane, I am sorry but I am just not sure."

"Because I like killing the mutations; that's why you sent John to Africa instead of me, isn't it?"

"It is not the only reason. His blood components are different from yours. I deemed he would be at less risk for the Ebola virus."

What I just said was true about John's metabolic system being stronger, but it bothers me that she believes that 'monsters' do not deserve forgiveness. Her anger issues may exceed John's but she has been very good at repressing them. I certainly don't know the answer to her question, but I know now is not the time to discuss the kill switch with her. We will do that at a later date.

"Dr. Po, there is a call coming in from Samantha from Africa. Would you like for me to put her on the screen?"

"Yes, Marie, please do," he said as he took another bite of his sundae.

"Hello, Dr. Po. Are you eating ice cream?" Sam asked with a surprised look.

"Yes. Jane was enjoying a sundae, so I decided to join her."

"Jane," I said as I came onto the screen, "how are you?"

"The question is, how are you, John? And how are the patients?"

"I'm fine. Very good as a matter of fact. The regeneration and healing of my hand is amazing," I said with a laugh.

I could see Jane glancing at Dr. Po and him smiling. A real smile that filled up his face.

"I told Dr. Po that he said amazing a lot. He gets the joke, John."

"Roger that. But let me give you back to Sam and some friends. You'll soon understand why the word I used was very appropriate."

"I'm going to get out of the camera shot and let you see the chieftain, Akida, and his grandson, Zuberi. I'll interpret for them," explained Sam.

The old man and the young boy stood in front of the camera and the old man began to talk, followed by Sam.

"The voices of the dead are silent now. My sister is a shadow in the dark, never to be seen again. All I hear is the sound of my grandson. His laughter is like the sun; it brings life back into our village. Thank you, Doctor Po."

The little boy standing in front of his grandfather was grinning and Sam let him speak. "Tuku visuri na asante kwa Sam na John. Roho inayotembea kati yeto imeondoka."

"He said, 'Thanks to Sam and John, the ghost that walks among us is gone.' You did it, Dr. Po! Almost all of the sick are recovering. All except four that were severely ill. They died, but I think they were already very close to death before I administered the vaccine. The rest are well. No side effects. You did it. You found a cure!"

Chapter 26
Less monsters

Dr. Po simply deflected the compliment as he spoke. "Sam. Before you start back to the plane, I need you to get a sample of skin and blood from the Vahemic. And John, can you hold your hand up to the camera?"

Sam looked as shocked as I was when we heard Dr. Po refer to her as Sam and not Samantha. But I guess when Zuberi called her Sam, that meant that was going to be her name from now on.

Good call, Dr. Po.

I held up my hand and when I saw the light intensify, I knew somehow Dr. Po was looking at my hand with that special magnifying glass.

"The angiogenesis is occurring more rapidly than I anticipated. What should be a large wound, considering the extent of the injury, is just a large scar at this point. How does your hand feel, John?"

"It feels weird in a way. It's as if I can feel the blood flowing into and out of my hand with each heartbeat. In fact, though this may sound weird, I think it's getting stronger."

"I would say amazing but as you know, your sister has told me that I say that too much. So, I am looking for alternatives. How does awesome sound?"

"Very un-Po like."

"Yes, I am leaning toward agreement with you on that matter. But your hand is doing very well. Sam, would you give John another shot of Symbion tomorrow when you leave? I am assuming you are not going to go back to the plane tonight in the dark."

"Yes, we will stay in the village tonight."

The little boy came back on the screen and tugged on Sam's arm. He said, "Kaa na kula nasi," several times and Sam nodded her head yes.

"It appears that you are being asked to dinner if I interpret that young man's words and expression correctly."

"Your interpretive skills are correct, Dr. Po."

"Good. It will give you more time to oversee the disposal of the infected bodies. I'd also like for you to get some blood from those four that died. Did the Vahemic destroy the food and liquid supplements we had planned to leave with the village?"

"No, all that is intact. The only things destroyed were the mesh curtain and the rear polyhexafluoroethylene plates. But we will just spray ourselves really well with the bug repellent and keep the lasers on tonight and I think we'll be fine."

"Yes, I think you will. We should see you around one or two tomorrow then. Be careful and good work, Sam. Very good work."

"Thank you, Dr. Po. We'll see you tomorrow."

"Hey, what about me?"

I saw that I made Dr. Po smile again and I even detected a hint of a laugh.

"You didn't let me finish. Good work, John. See you tomorrow too," and with that, the connection was ended.

As soon as the screen went dark, I turned to Sam.

"I am not eating grasshoppers tonight."

"Don't worry about it. I'll remind Akida of your stomach issues. Just have some of the nutrient bars and some of the liquid supplements. Everything will be fine. But before we have dinner, I need to get some samples and spray the dead bodies before I tell them to burn them."

"Okay. I'm coming with you."

Sam started to object but when she saw me place the LBE over my shoulder, she knew it would be a waste of time. Plus, I could tell she really knew it was probably a good idea if I was watching over her. After all, we were still in a very dangerous area at night and she was still dealing with Ebola victims.

"We'll need to suit up again."

"Yeah, no problem. I'm ready."

Sam told Akida what they needed to do before they could cremate their family members and gave directions for using the anti-viral and anti-bacterial sprays in the future. She also told him they needed to burn all the huts where the sick had been housed. She then showed him and Zuberi how to use the disinfectant canisters to cover the ground, once the huts were gone.

At dinner that night, the village laughed and celebrated the return of their loved ones. While they ate, with his grandfather's permission, Sam taught Zuberi how to use the dietary and liquid supplements after they left. He thanked her, and after dinner Zuberi and his grandfather walked us back to the cart.

When we got there, the chief asked Sam, "Ingekuwaje roho nyeupe ililala kiwa wingu lake jeupe?" and she laughed. She pointed at me and said, "Roho nyeupe hulala juu ya kivuli chake vile vile." Both Akida and Zuberi nodded their heads and bowed toward me before they turned around and left.

"I'm not sure what you said, but I've got to admit, I kind of liked the bowing. You said something cool. I know it. John Wick cool, didn't you?"

"Yeah, I think so. They asked me how the white ghost would sleep without his white cloud and I said that the white ghost sleeps on his own shadow just as well."

"Wow. Cool as shit. I'd prefer some pillows though. Do we have any pillows?"

Sam laughed. "Do you think we came here without several of everything?" At the touch of a button the side panel where the first air cushion had emerged, brought forth another one and I grinned.

"Damn. I love that little genius."

"Me too." We got into the cart and she reengaged the broken rear shields as much as possible, turned on the defense mechanisms, and we both went to sleep. I heard no zapping before I dozed off and when I awoke, Sam was already up and preparing the cart for the journey back to the plane.

"What time is it?"

"About 6:30. Let me look at your hand. Damn. Dr. Po was right. It now appears that you have three very large vessels supplying blood flow to your hand. The severed radial artery has reopened and restored itself. Beside it is the svs that I put in and your ulnar artery is working just as well. The angiogenesis that has occurred in a little over twenty-four hours with the Symbion and your cord regeneration is remarkable. The wound is almost healed. I bet by the time we get back, no one will even be able to tell your hand was hanging from your wrist. I wouldn't be surprised if your hand wasn't stronger and had an even greater sense of touch."

"I have to admit, it does feel really good."

Sam gave me the Symbion shot and before we finished loading up the cart, the entire village came over to see us off. The sick patients, arm in arm with their family members, bowed their heads and thanked us. Healthy members of the village also came up to us and did the same. After they had all expressed their sincere thanks, Akida and Zuberi came forward.

"Zuberi niongee," Akida said and moved to the side as his grandson stood in front of him.

"Ah tanka twos an Goad baless you boat."

One might say his English was imperfect that day, but they would have been wrong. Those words would stay with me for a very long time. I saw Sam's tears as she leaned down and hugged Zuberi and shook hands with his grandfather. I held out my hand and Zuberi grabbed it and shook it twice, as his grandfather had taught him. I smiled as I bowed my head to the one I was sure would become the new leader of the tribe. When the chief placed his hand on my shoulder, I did the same with him and he grinned.

As we walked back toward the plane, Zuberi and several other children accompanied us for about half a mile until they stopped and yelled at us as they waved goodbye. We waved back at them and Zuberi bowed once more before he said something to the children and they turned back toward the village.

Though we both felt good about what we accomplished, after about a mile, I reverted back into soldier mode.

"Have you got the LBEs engaged on the cart?"

"No, but I will turn them on if you think it's necessary."

"Sam, you know it's necessary. We agreed. We don't know what will happen and though everything seems good from the Ebola cure, I don't think we should take any chances. Something still doesn't feel right to me."

Sam nodded and turned them on.

"Thank you."

"No problem. I understand and I agree with you. You have reason to be concerned.

"What did you say, Sam?"

"I said I understand and agree with you."

"No, after that."

"I didn't say anything else."

Shit.

What's wrong, John? I was just reaching out to you. To remind you of our special bond. I don't want you to forget that.

Keep talking, asshole. And don't worry - I don't forget anything. You should know that about me by now.

How many more miles before you reach the plane? About three, isn't it? I would be careful. What looks like a herd of antelope might be more than just a herd of antelope. Hope you have a safe trip home, John.

I scanned the area as soon as the voice of Merkel went away but I didn't see anything that caused concern. There were a few giraffes in the distance and some baboons up in the shade of the trees but that was all. As we walked, I debated whether I should tell Sam about my conversation with Merkel but decided she needed to know.

"Sam, I need to tell you something. He's reaching out to me again. The Narcoleptan that I told you I have a connection to. He spoke to me the other night before that evil bitch attacked us. And he just did it again. Warning us. I was aware of him, and the others like him, the first time I went out with Jane. Now, I think he's bringing them together – the Narcoleptans and the Vahemics. I'm positive he had something to do with that bitch attacking us."

"John, it scares me to think these beings are being driven by something other than the will to survive. You're telling me that there are other motives; an evil force directing them?"

"Yes, that is exactly what I am saying."

A herd of gazelle ran by us several hundred yards away. The sweat on my body felt as if fifty car batteries had been hooked up to my legs and were generating a current into my skin. The annoying but characteristic chatter of hyenas encircled us and I told Sam to stop the cart and get inside.

There were eleven hyenas watching us as they cackled and moved around in circles. They had moved closer since running the gazelles away and now ran toward us for ten yards or so and then stopped as they seemed to talk among themselves in a whining and growling way.

That's odd. How do they know they are out of the range of the LBEs?

I could sense something else was out there with them. I couldn't see it, but when several of the animals moved, I noticed how they altered their movement as if something propelled them out of the way. They then rushed the cart and the LBEs engaged and began to kill all that approached. But I also saw a shadow moving among them. I didn't wait to decide if it came from the collection of hyenas running toward us, so I aimed the LBE and shot. The positron hit nothing but a tree several hundred yards away.

"What are you doing, John? I can't stand to watch this," she said as she turned off the LBEs.

I didn't have time to yell, "No!" because I suddenly caught a glimpse of the shadow leaping toward us. I shot again and this time the howl of the camouflaged being let me know the LBE hit it.

"Shit!" Sam screamed. The creature came into view on the other side of the cart. It was looking at us with blood dripping from its eyes and missing an arm, but it was far from dead as it leaped toward Sam. I jumped in front of her and the claws ripped down the front of my body. It burned like I had been immersed in acid. Even though I aimed at its head, the positron bullet went through its neck. When I saw its head hanging onto its body by only clumps of matted hair, I realized that disintegration of its neck was probably the best thing I could have done. I shot once more at its head and the pieces of it pelted me like smelly chunks of bloody gravel. Each one that hit my body burned.

"Don't fucking move!" Sam yelled at me as I leaned against the cart. I looked down at my chest and I thought I could see broken parts of my ribs and my heart beating. *That's not possible,* I said to myself, and then Sam's face began to blur. I thought I heard her scream, "Fuck!" before I heard nothing else.

I was in the dark again. A place I had been many times before. I was on the carnival ride, but this time I was alone. The ride had broken down again and it felt hot. "This ride is experiencing a momentary loss in power. As soon as we can restore the power, we will turn on the fans."

Shit, I'm not sitting here while they try and get that generator running. It may take hours I said to myself but I couldn't get out of the seat. I tried to unbuckle the seat belt, but it felt wet and it hurt when I touched it. In fact, it hurt like hell and I leaned back in the chair and groaned. I then saw the tattered wolfman's eyes light up and begin talking to me.

You may not make it out of here this time, John. That's a nasty cut on your chest. Is that your heart I see?

I looked down at my chest and I saw what the wolfman was talking about and realized he was right.

Here, let me pull it out of your body and end this, it growled and when it did, I pulled the arms off the fucking stupid machine. I felt the shock from the wires that sparked and watched the red eyes of the dilapidated monster fade to black.

One less of them, I thought as I sat back and tried to breathe. It was becoming very difficult to do, so I just closed my eyes and concentrated on getting as much of the stale air in my lungs as possible. *Boy, it'd be fucked up to die on this damn ride* I thought and wondered why my sister and mother weren't there with me.

Chapter 27
Plain view

A dim light came on some time later. I wasn't sure if it was minutes or hours but I felt the power restored to the fans and air returning to the tunnel. The ride started back up but my car seemed to be stuck on the track. I heard them say, "Never leave the car if the ride stops," but I didn't particularly give a shit. I was getting off and finding out what was wrong.

As I examined the tracks, I could see that one of the links on the chain was unattached. When I tried to reconnect the coupling, the damn electricity took hold of my hands as if I had put them in a vise, and I couldn't pull them away. For a moment I thought my hands were burning, but even in the dim light, I could see they weren't blistered; they were not even red. My entire body was coming alive like I was the tattered and broken wolfman machine being restored to its original form. Eventually, the electrical charge stopped and I pulled my hands from the track. I sat back down in the car and closed my eyes. A cool breeze blew on my face and I heard someone talking to me. It wasn't the idiot that usually ran the ride. No. It was someone I knew. My sister's voice. And she was reading to me.

"This is the story of the great war that Rikki-tikki-tavi fought single-handed, through the bathrooms of the big bungalow in Segowlee cantonment. Darzee, the Tailorbird, helped him, and Chuchundra, the musk-rat, who never comes out into the middle of the floor, but always creeps round by the wall, gave him advice, but Rikki-tikki did the real fighting."

Rikki-tikki-tavi. I read that to her so many times. She's never read it to me before now. This is nice. It reminds me of the moments when we had fun growing up. Times that we stole away from the monster.

"He had forgotten the egg. It still lay on the veranda, and Nagaina came nearer and nearer to it, till at last, while Rikki-tikki was drawing breath, she caught it in her mouth, turned to the veranda steps, and flew like an arrow down the path, with Rikki-tikki behind her. When the cobra runs for her life, she goes like a whip-lash, flicked across a horse's neck....

"Then he jumped. The head was lying a little clear of the water jar, under the curve of it; and, as his teeth met, Rikki braced his back against the bulge of the red earthenware to hold down the head....

"As he held, he closed his jaws tighter and tighter, for he made sure he would be banged to death, and, for the honor of his family, he preferred to be found with his teeth locked....

"Singer and tailor am I - Doubled the joys that I know- Proud of my lilt to the sky, Proud of the house that I sew - Over and under, so weave I my music, so weave I the house that I sew. Sing to your fledglings again, Mother, oh lift up your head! Evil that plagued us is slain, Death in the garden lies dead. Terror that hid in the roses is impotent - flung on the dung-hill and dead! Who has delivered us, who? Tell me his nest and his name. Rikki, the valiant, the true, Tikki, with eyeballs of flame, Rikki-tikki-tikki, the ivory fanged, the hunter with eyeballs of flame.....

"Rikki-tikki had a right to be proud of himself. But he did not grow too proud, and he kept that garden as a mongoose should keep it, with tooth and jump and spring and bite, till never a cobra dared show its head inside the walls."

"His blood pressure is dropping, Dr. Po!"

"Administer two shots of Symbion. John! Listen to me! Wake up, John!"

I sensed the familiar substance going through my body. Once again, I asked myself if this was how an addict felt when he shoots heroin into his veins. No, it can't be. The effect those drugs have on the human body work through receptors in the brain that produce euphoria and control pain. Don't you remember? Symbion affects every cell in your body. It forms unique bonds and makes each cell into a hyperactive engine, which performs in its own unique manner, controlled by the cellular modifications that only exist in a statistically incomprehensible small number of individuals. I believe that number is 2.61 x 10 to the negative tenth power, or 2.

Wait a minute. Is that me explaining things to myself? Or is that Dr. Po explaining things to me? Sounds more like him. He's trying to get my attention. He's yelling at me. What's going on?

I opened my eyes and saw Sam looking down at me. She was standing next to a monitor with Dr. Po's face on it.

"Hey, what's up, Doc, as my friend Bugs would say? What are you doing? Are we back home yet?"

"John, in just a few moments, my face is going to go away and what you will see on the monitor, will be your blood cells. Sam is preparing to insert the intravascular microscope into your femoral artery. I need you to concentrate on those cells you see. I will explain to you what you are seeing, but you need to focus on them and as we look at them together, I will describe for you what their function is. Concentrate on them and their function. That's all I need you to do right now, but it's very important that you do that. Do you understand?"

"Sure. I understand. Sort of an advanced cell biology course, huh?"

"Very advanced. Bring the cells into focus please, Sam."

I think, Marie, if I explain to him the function of each cell, his mental will to endure should enhance his body's innate ability to survive. We have already attached all the pigs we had to his cord and given him all the Symbion that was available, but the damage that the Narcoleptan has inflicted on him places him in a critical condition and they are still two hours away from home.

Sam has cleaned out the wounds and applied the antibacterial-viral wrap but that is all she can do. Five of his ribs were broken and pulled from his body, exposing and damaging one of his lungs and nicking a very small piece of his heart. Sam stopped the bleeding in his heart and lung with the bacillus-zinc-Symbion clotting material and inserted a chest tube, allowing him to regain lung function, but it's his gut that worries me the most. His abdomen was ripped open and some of his small bowel is now outside of his body. It was lacerated and Sam could do nothing besides clean it, stop the bleeding, and try and keep it from getting infected and contaminating the rest of his body. Poison from all the wounds is circulating through his system and I am certain the only reason John is alive now is because of his cord regenerative ability, the extra doses of Symbion, and his high levels of iron, selenium, and manganese.

But now, his blood pressure is dropping. Despite all of his healing ability and the unique properties he possesses, his body is succumbing to the poison and infectious release of bacteria from his small bowel. I need his mind to help fight the battle. With the chemo, radiation, and cancer all working to drain their bodies of life, I've seen the minds of my cancer patients overcome all of the pain, lethargy, and even depression that the disease and cure was inflicting upon them. Before I had Symbion, that was their last defense.

If John is going to survive the plane flight, I need him to use his mind now to fight his injuries. His will to survive and endure years of pain and abuse, along with his high intelligence, should enable his brain to boost the natural healing properties of his body. It just has to. If it doesn't, I am afraid he will die.

"John, look at your red cells now," Dr. Po was saying. "See those red blood cells there? They are normal. They have a donut shape to them, but look at those other ones. They are spiked and some of them even have a sickle shape to them. That is the poison from the Narcoleptan affecting their shape and if they do not maintain their normal shape, they cannot function as they should."

"My friend Billy had sickle cell disease, Doc. I saw those cells in a book once when I went to the library to research his disease."

"Yes, John. But look at these cells too. They are lymphocytes and those there; those are granulocytes, in various stages of development."

"What do you mean?"

"I mean your bone marrow is generating as many cells as it can right now. It is trying to fight the Narcoleptan poison that is shutting down your body and the potentially lethal endotoxins being released by the bacteria that are now circulating in your bloodstream.

"Sam has given you several infusions of your own blood, but I do not believe your bone marrow is currently able to keep up with what is necessary to combat the poison attacking your body. I need you to look at some cells that I am going to show you on the other monitor, while you still focus on the cells that you see via the intravascular microscope.

"We are going to focus on the hematopoietic stem cell and the lymphoid progenitor cell. This cell is the lymphoid progenitor cell and creates killer cells, T lymphocytes, and B lymphocytes. Look at them,

John, and focus on them. This cell here, the hematopoietic stem cell, creates a multipotential stem cell which in turn creates a myeloid progenitor cell which makes those granulocytes you see circulating in your body, as well as your red blood cells. Look, there go several eosinophils. There is a basophil and monocyte and several more lymphocytes. All of those cells engulfed in a sea of red blood cells.

"The average body makes one hundred billion types of these cells each day. I need you to focus on all these cells that are created in your bone marrow, and use your mind now to push your bone marrow to make more. You have the ability to do that, John. Not only is your body metabolism unique, but your mind also shares that uncommon trait. You can create more cells when you need to. The Symbion in your system will help you do that. There are over 7 billion people in the world, John, and you are one of only two who are able to do that."

"2.61 x 10 to the negative tenth power."

"Yes, John, that is correct. That is how unique you are. Concentrate on making those progenitor and stem cells and then the cells that you see circulating in your bloodstream. Do not focus on anything else but that. It is very important."

I could tell by the way Dr. Po said "important" that he was very worried. I then heard another Doctor talking to me and I smiled as I looked into my body.

"This," cried the Mayor, "is your town's darkest hour!
The time for all Whos who have blood that is red
To come to the aid of their country!" he said.
"We've GOT to make noises in greater amounts!
So, open your mouth, lad, For every voice counts!"

I hear you, Doctor S. - the Whos needed to tell Horton they were there! I need to tell the poison that I'm here, don't I? I felt myself looking into my own body and I could see my bones and then inside of the bone. I saw the soft sponge-like tissue in the center of the bone. Some of it was red and some of it was yellow and I understood it was the red part I needed to focus on. I saw those cells on the monitor, only this time they were in my head and I tried to see them in my bone as if I was there, making them with a microscopic tool of some kind that I knew Dr. Po must have invented. And I didn't stop. I didn't stop doing that until I felt something in my body making me tired and I closed my eyes.

Sam looked over at Dr. Po in the operating room as they were preparing for John's surgery.

"I've never seen anything like it. The white cells and red cells were pouring into his bloodstream as if he had set up some sort of cloning factory in his bones. How did you know he would be able to do that?"

"I did not know for sure. I only thought it was a possibility. Amazing, isn't it?"

Sam smiled at the sound of that word. She hoped she never stopped hearing it. "If only the person who coined the term 'mind over matter' had been there. He would have seen what it truly meant."

"That was Sir Charles Lyell, Sam. In 1863, in 'The Geological Evidence of the Antiquity of Man.' He was referring to the evolutionary growth of the mind of animals and man through time."

"Well, I would call this evolutionary, wouldn't you? I think it would have blown Sir Charles' mind."

"Interesting choice of words, but I believe it would have certainly expanded his thought process. Okay, Sam, we will start with the small bowel repair, then proceed to the lungs and heart. After that is done, I will do the bone grafts. We will wait to apply the skin grafts later; after the surgery and after we have engaged his cord at least four times. And if that goes as I think it will, we will do something else for him. I have an idea that arose from your trip to Africa. I think we can do something that may make him even more unique."

Chapter 28
Statistically the same

It took five and a half hours to complete the bowel repair and as they prepared for the lung and heart surgery, Sam paused for a moment and closed her eyes. Dr. Po heard her sigh as if she was trying to find the energy to continue.

"Sam, I don't know what I was thinking. You have had minimal rest since you got back. The bowel repair took longer than I expected. I will do the heart and lung repair and the bone grafts with Marie and Emily's assistance. You need to rest. Go talk to Jane and let her know how things are progressing. And then sleep. I will come and update you later. I will have Emily give you a mild sedative to allow your mind to rest. You have done more than ten nurses and several physicians could have accomplished. You have been extraordinary and you saved John's life."

Sam started to object and tell Dr. Po that she felt responsible for John's injuries, but she didn't. She simply nodded and left the OR suite. She found Jane in the library in one of the large recliners reading travel magazines. As soon as Jane saw Sam walk into the room, she jumped up to hug her.

"How...?"

"He's doing very well, considering the extent of his injuries. Let me get some tea and I'll come sit down and tell you everything."

While Sam waited for her tea, the events of the last week replayed in her mind. She saw people cured who would have died. She saw a village come back to life. The smile of Zuberi would stay in her mind for the rest of her life and give her great comfort. But she almost died twice, saw a new kind of mutation, and performed the most sophisticated surgical interventions she had ever done to save a friend's life. She saw a hand regenerate another blood vessel when it should have been amputated, and she saw a mind will itself to manufacture more blood cells. She had been there to witness what those in her profession would deem impossible. And yet she was consumed with guilt and wondered what she should tell Jane about what happened. If not for John, she was sure she would have been killed; many would have been killed. She didn't know what lay ahead of her but she was scared about John's recovery and concerned about everyone's future.

"Like I said, he's doing really well," Sam said a bit hesitantly as she sat down next to Jane and sipped her tea. "He had some very serious injuries. His hand was almost torn from his body but the repair…it was…well, it was unbelievable really. He now has three major vessels supplying blood to his hand."

"Wow. He'll be able to crush beer cans with it now, won't he?"

Sam managed a weak smile.

"I'm not sure what he'll be able to do but his hand will indeed be different. Stronger certainly, but probably even more than that."

"I know. Just nervous talk. I'm worried and you sound very tired. Are you just tired or are you worried too?"

"Both. The Vahemic damage was easily repaired. But the Narcoleptan tore open his chest and abdomen. John certainly saved my life but um…uh…"

You can't tell her. Not now.

"But, uh, he sustained serious damage to his ribs, lungs, heart, and intestines. Five ribs were broken, his lung was punctured and his heart was nicked. But I think the greatest concerns are the infections from his small bowel and the poison of the Narcoleptan. Dr. Po has repaired the bowel and they are working on everything else right now."

Jane's face turned the color of aspirin and Sam took her hand.

"Jane. Your brother is not like other people. You know that. The bowel repair went extremely well and his body has done some extraordinary things so far to fight off the infection and poison."

"Dr. Po told me his blood components were different from mine. He thought he would be able to withstand the virus better than me."

Sam nodded. "He's fighting, Jane. Dr. Po, Marie, and Emily will do an excellent job repairing his heart and lung and ribs, and as you know, he has your brother's skin and bone on hand for grafts and such. He sent me out of the OR to get some rest but I know they won't stop until everything is fixed."

"His cord. That will help him recover, won't it?"

"Yes, of course. I hope you don't mind but I'm feeling very tired now. Dr. Po had Emily put a sedative in my tea. I need to go lie down for a while."

"Why don't you just lay down on the sofa over there? I'd like to stay here with you. It makes me feel like I'm doing something. Being here, sort of watching over you."

Sam nodded and laid down on the couch. She was asleep within a minute. Jane whispered in her ear, "Thank you," and went back to her chair and opened another travel magazine.

John. Can you hear me, John?

I hear you, asshole. What the hell do you want?

You do realize where you are, don't you?

When I heard Merkel's question, I realized I, in fact, did not know. The last thing I remembered was Dr. Po talking to me from a monitor and telling me to concentrate on making blood cells. But I wasn't going to let Merkel know that I wasn't aware of what was happening. I knew that wouldn't be wise.

Make him tell you. He wants to taunt you. He will tell you sooner or later. He likes to think he is smarter than everyone else. You know this asshole better than he thinks.

What the hell do you want?

Do you think the little puppet would place an electric cord into my body? That I could use to help me heal? I'm not sure you would have made it back here from Africa and I'm not sure you'll even make it off the OR table without your little special adapter.

Dr. Po is operating on me. Okay. Just keep quiet. Let him go on. You know he wants to talk.

I believe it would work as well with me as with you. Perhaps even better. After all, I can make myself invisible. And I have much more strength and mental capacity than you. I hope you don't die. I want to make sure you're awake and aware of everything I do to destroy those that matter to you.

Fuck you, asshole. Don't you have anything better to do than brag about useless shit to me? You're one major giant turd. Grew up with one similar in size. You're not telling me anything of value. You're just a disgusting and annoyingly chatty cockroach.

I'll do more than annoy you. I will make you wish you weren't born. You, your sister, and the little puppet. I am evolving. My faith ensures that I will change. I'll never be gone from your head, John. Not until I'm holding it in my hand.

Watch out for the shovels, shit head. Sometimes they come flying out from nowhere.

As the familiar electrical currents surged through my body, Merkel's voice disappeared. I wanted to wake up but I couldn't. All I could do was lay there and feel the currents ripple up and down through my body. They felt good and I knew my body was healing.

We have been in the OR suite with John now for almost twenty hours. I've taken a few moments to rest here and there but, thank God, I do not need much sleep. And who would want to sleep when you are doing what we are doing? This is invigorating. The Symbion and John's cord regenerative properties have allowed us to make repairs to his heart and lungs as if we were simply removing a gall bladder.

We have reinforced his left and right coronary arteries and his inferior and superior vena cava with a Symbion vascular sheath. In this case, they will be acting more like stents as opposed to another vessel, providing additional strength for what I've placed in his legs. The Symbion vascular sheaths next to his femoral artery and veins in both legs that I attached to smaller vessels should grow from the nicks I made in his femoral artery and vein, which we stopped from profuse bleeding using the Bacillus anthracis-zinc metalloprotease-Symbion compound. If the angiogenesis occurs in his legs, as it did in his hand, the vascular nature and strength of his legs will be improved. If it does not work, I will need to perform additional surgery but I believe it is worth the risk.

"Marie? Emily? All that is left are the bone grafts for John's ribs. Can you two handle that? I will just supervise and rest my body a bit more. I believe I have tried to convince myself that I am stronger than I am."

"Of course, Dr. Po," Marie responded and they proceeded to complete the grafts.

"Nice job, Marie. Good, Emily. Yes, that's right. Excellent. Those will heal very well I believe. Marie, now spray a layer of antibacterial mist over the surgical sites. Excellent. Emily, will you please move John's table into the recovery and engage the ultraviolet lights? I will go let the young ladies know of our progress. Thank you both."

Dr. Po found Sam and Jane in the library. Sam was still asleep on the couch but woke up when she heard them talking. Dr. Po was sitting next to the couch on his collapsible stool and drinking a frozen concoction.

"Are you ready for me, Dr. Po? Whatever you gave me really knocked me out. I must have been very tired but I feel great now. How is John? What do we need to do next?"

"John is doing very well. All of the surgery is complete and his vital signs are excellent. He is resting now in the recovery area. Emily is watching over him."

"How long have I been asleep?"

"Eleven hours and three minutes."

"Why didn't you wake me, Jane?"

"You needed to sleep. You were snoring. I mean really snoring. Plus, Dr. Po let me know what was going on from Emily throughout the surgery and told me to leave you alone."

"What are you drinking, Dr. Po? It looks like a daiquiri."

"You were always very observant, Sam. I like the taste of rum and fruit. I find it very relaxing and stimulating at the same time. This is a frozen concoction of mango and lime and rum from the Cayman Islands. It is really quite good. Would you like one?"

"Don't we need to check on John?"

"Not for another eight hours. He will be assessed at that time and then we will decide what we need to do next. Emily has everything under control. I am going to have another daiquiri and go out and enjoy the waterfall. I may even have a cheeseburger. Would you and Jane like to accompany me?"

Sam looked somewhat confused and pulled her head back slightly. She had never seen the doctor look so relaxed. Especially considering the surgery he had just performed and the fact that he had been working for an entire day non-stop. It didn't seem possible.

Of course, it doesn't. That's why it is, she said to herself. *Things must have gone really well.*

"Well, I'll have a daiquiri or two or three or four and a cheeseburger too. How about it, Sam?" Jane asked as she got up.

"Sure. That does sound good," Sam agreed.

Perhaps it will make my mind stop running around in circles about what to say to both of you.

"Excellent," Dr. Po replied as his chair folded up and they walked toward the elevator to go outside.

After enjoying their food and drinks, Dr. Po announced he would meet both of them in the OR/Recovery suite in six hours. He was going to get some rest, but first he was going to review the analysis of the blood that Sam had brought back from Africa.

I awoke in the recovery room and saw the familiar faces looking down at me. At least, I thought I was awake. The ultraviolet lights made everyone look a little odd and blurry, so I wasn't sure if I was dreaming or not.

"How are you, big brother?"

"I'm not sure. You guys look a little weird. I'm not sure if I'm dreaming or not. But I guess I could be asking you that in a dream, so I'm not sure that question has any value. But if I was dreaming, I wouldn't ask myself that question, so I must not be dreaming. Unless that's what I would say in a dream."

"John, the medicine you have taken is still making you a little confused. But you are not dreaming. You are doing well. The medication you have been given makes the ultraviolet lights that saturate this room affect your vision a bit and makes us look 'weird' as you say. You have been in the OR and recovery area for a little over a day and a half now. But we've surgically repaired everything and it all looks good. There is no sign of infection or any effect from the poison at this moment. Your vital signs are in excellent order," Dr. Po explained.

"Your blood pressure is a little high, but that's to be expected," Sam added.

"Actually, Sam, I think that will be John's normal pressure from this point moving forward."

"But it's 145 over 100. That's hypertensive range."

"Look at those ultrasound images of his legs and his heart," Dr. Po instructed. He activated several of the robotic arms and pointed to the pictures that were displayed on a monitor.

"Oh, my God," Sam whispered as she put her hand up to her mouth.

"'Oh, my God,' is not a good thing to hear when you first wake up from surgery. Just so Sam doesn't get worried and completely understands everything she is looking at on the monitor, maybe you should explain things to her, Dr. Po."

"Yeah," Sam said as she smiled. "So, I completely understand."

"John's heart appears enlarged and it is, but it is still normal. The main arterial and venous vessels: the aorta, pulmonary artery, and coronary artery, as well as the inferior and superior vena cava, which take blood to and from your heart, have been strengthened with Symbion vascular stents so that they can handle the additional blood flood flow created by your legs.

"Due to the amount of Symbion that is now in your body and from the regenerative nature of your cord, along with the Symbion heart muscle cells that I injected into your heart, your heart has grown in size, but it is not weakened by that growth. It is, in fact, stronger and provides more capacity for the increased vascularization of your body.

"The angiogenesis that I witnessed in your hand as a result of your injury in Africa, prompted me to evaluate whether that same process could be duplicated with your legs. So, I re-created that injury to your femoral arteries and veins, and surgically implanted Symbion vessel sheaths next to those injuries. If you look at the monitor, you can see that John now has two functioning femoral arteries and veins in each leg, thus the increased blood pressure, and thus the increased need to strengthen his heart vessels and tissue.

"Oh, and lest we forget, the bone marrow that you stimulated while in Africa, continues to produce cells at a higher-than-normal level. Not to the extent that it was at that time, but still more than usual. Hence with more blood cells, you need greater capacity. I will need to continue to watch this closely over time, especially regarding your spleen, liver, and kidneys, but for now, everything seems to be functioning better than expected. It appears the Symbion has improved their function as well. It's really quite impressive."

"Just so Sam understands all of this, Doc, exactly what does all that mean?"

"It means, John, that you should have greater strength in your legs, greater stamina, and an even greater ability to ward off infection, should you sustain an injury. That's the good news. It also means that you will bleed out much quicker than a normal person, should you sustain an injury, especially if you injure your leg in any serious way. Because of that risk, you will need to be prepared for that in the future, but that shouldn't be a problem. I think I can make the Bacillus anthracis, the zinc metalloprotease, and the Symbion compound in a more compact fashion that you can easily carry with you. Perhaps it might even become a part of your clothes. Still trying to put form to thought on that. But anyway, if you keep improving tomorrow, we will place the skin grafts onto your body and continue to allow your body to fully heal."

I could see the fluorescent light from Mrs. Cunningham's bug zapper flickering on and off in his head as I remembered. "I saw the cells in my bone marrow. I could see them in my mind, as you were talking to me. You and my other doctor friend."

"What other doctor friend?" Dr. Po asked.

Before I could answer, Jane interjected. "Seuss. Dr. Seuss. He helps him all the time."

I smiled at my sister as she placed her hand on my shoulder.

"You read to me, didn't you? You read 'Rikki Tikki Tavi' to me."

She nodded yes.

"He talked to me too."

"Who?" Dr. Po asked.

"Merkel. He was there with me in Africa. He was here too, during the surgery."

"Who's Merkel?" Jane seemed very confused as I knew she would be. But it was time she learned about him.

"He's the Narcoleptan leader. The one who was there the first time you and I went out. He was why I knew those creatures were there, setting a trap. He has a link to me and I can talk to him through our minds. He told me how he plans to kill you and Dr. Po. He said he is evolving and getting stronger every day. He brags about how he is invisible and how much stronger he is, but he wishes he had a cord. He knows about it and wondered if you could give him one, Dr. Po.

"He reached out to me in Africa too. Just before the Vahemic and the Narcoleptan attacked. I know this sounds crazy but he is controlling all of these attacks somehow. Dr. Po, what I said the other day...when we talked about pure evil. The mutations, these monsters...they aren't due to the cure. Not entirely. I believe the cure only initiates the transformation. The evil nature of the person completes the metamorphosis and he is controlling it all."

"Like a butterfly," my sister said rather thoughtlessly.

"Well, yes, if that butterfly turned into a fucking dragon. Dr. Po, I realize it's hard to accept this, but I also know you see that something else is going on too."

"Interesting."

"Interesting?"

"Yes, the blood that Jane brought back from Africa. The shaman's blood; the Vahemic. The blood is no different from the other Ebola victims except for an excess of monoamine oxidase."

"What is that?" John asked.

"It is an enzyme – a catabolic enzyme of norepinephrine and serotonin. There is a theory that suggests it plays some role in the emotional and social behavior of people as they mature."

Marie, why didn't we see that before now?

"Merkel told me how you changed the biochemistry world, Doc, and yet could not understand why you scoffed at the existence of the psychic world. He also said he had noticed how I was beginning to change your viewpoint. He seemed to look forward to that somehow. But this enzyme. Perhaps, this is the organic link to what I have been telling you about.

"While we were in Africa, Sam told me that there were very few problems with the cures at the beginning but then the mutations started happening and how much that affected you. You believed you were responsible. But you weren't. I am sure it's Merkel and that enzyme that exists in people. Higher levels of it in some people caused them to respond differently to the cures and to mutate into something evil. But that evil was always there. The Symbion and the enzyme just combined in a way that brought out their true nature and Merkel is controlling all of this. You've got to see that now."

Everyone was looking at me and I could see that they were trying to process what they just heard. And then I remembered something else Merkel had said. As I uttered the words, it made me even more concerned. "He said he was like us - me and Jane. He said we wear the same clothes."

"Oh, my God."

Everyone turned toward Sam. "The same clothes. He was showing you how clever he was. Jeans. He was telling you that he has the same gene as you and your sister. He has the converter gene."

"Yep. Just blew up the lottery, didn't we? Now it's three in seven billion."

Chapter 29
Februus

The look on Po's face told me this wasn't the first time he had considered the possibility of another person having the converter gene. And then it hit me. Merkel, the pancreatic cancer patient. If he had the converter gene in his pancreas, I assumed Dr. Po had postulated as to whether the Symbion treatment for his pancreatic cancer created his mutated state. But he wouldn't suggest it because he wasn't sure. His statistical mind would not allow it. Dr. Po didn't live in a world of conjecture, must less a world of supernatural mysticism.

I also understood something about my sister and myself for the first time. We were mutations too. We didn't look like monsters. Nothing that resembled the creative makeup of horror movies or the disfigured beings that now existed but, nonetheless, we were mutations with the potential to be just as savage as anything in the movies or just as dangerous as the creatures that haunted the world today. But if the converter gene linked me to Merkel, why didn't it link to my sister? Or did it?

I had seen Jane's destructive nature. Dr. Po had seen it too. It didn't surprise me that she was the first one to break the silence as the rest of us tried to understand the significance of everything that had been said. She wasn't concerned with the significance. She just wanted to know what kind of monster she needed to deal with now.

"So, this Merkel dude is a Narcoleptan and talks to John in his mind. And he has the same kind of gene we do that gives us the ability to use the cord device. He doesn't have a cord, but he wants one. So what? He's a Narcoleptan that talks to my brother and according to John, has some sort of power over the other Narcs and Vemes. Good. Tell him to come on and bring his friends and we'll zap his ass and the rest of those evil shits into oblivion and be done with it all. Or even better yet, figure out a way for me to talk to him. I'll get him here. I don't know why I couldn't talk to him, do you?"

"I don't know, Jane. I think I'm connected to Merkel because of the nature of my blood. The Symbion reacts with it in a unique way. I'm sure it was that reaction and my relationship with our father that allowed me to see evil within my mind. I think it was all the anger that I've carried around with me then and now. That was never clearer than when I was over in Africa and I was injected with Symbion. I was immediately transported into the evil mind of the shaman and could see that she was killing her own people and how she wanted to kill me and Sam. Now it all comes together with the knowledge of this converter gene. All the puzzle pieces are in place and the picture is complete."

Perhaps there is a part of your brain that won't allow it, Jane. A protective strategy you developed over time to block out that type of evil. You probably can communicate with him but I'm not sure that's a good idea now. No, I just need to keep him talking to me. And he will, considering that he thinks it annoys me. I'm very familiar with that type of arrogance.

"Let him keep talking to me, Jane. He doesn't need to mess with your mind. I can do what you suggested and we can, as you say, zap his ass to hell."

"It is something that we need to continue to investigate. It's a powerful theory, John. And an interesting interpretation, Sam, but none of this can be proven right now. I can't dismiss the fact that John says that he has these premonitions or thoughts that warn of impending danger because each time that danger has proven to actually be present. What John is suggesting is something I have already thought of, considering how his body is changing with the Symbion. It certainly affects his brain very differently. I have seen the scientific evidence of that. And I agree with him. Let John continue to reach out to him, not you, Jane. It will be a better control mechanism for us all."

Dr. Po understands. He sees the unpredictability of my sister and I bet he's wondering the same thing. Why can't she already communicate with him?

"I can see them in the dark too."

"You can see what in the dark, John?"

"In Africa, after my hand was injured and my cord was connected to the cattle. I could see the animals, the predators out in the dark. I could see a thermal image of their bodies approaching the village, attracted by the scent of death."

"I've never been able to do that," Jane said as she slowly looked at me and then at Dr. Po.

She sounded jealous. But she had never been jealous of me. Ever. Something is happening with her. What she said about the change occurring in people; dismissing their evil nature as a cause for their transformation by comparing it to something as simple as a caterpillar changing into a butterfly is reflective of something else. That was an odd analogy, considering everything she's seen and endured. It's as if she is disconnected from reality again. Is this the young girl becoming a Von Trapp for a moment or does it mask something much more dangerous? She said that old world was gone. Forgotten. But now, I'm not so sure.

"If the cord regeneration created thermal imaging capability, then that leads me to believe that the other phenomenon that you say occurs, is something within your own body's changing nature."

"Why can't I do that, Dr. Po? And those vessels that you put in John's legs and the bigger heart? Shouldn't I have those too? Don't you think that would help me eliminate the dangers we're facing?"

Dr. Po paused before he responded. I knew why but I could see that my sister didn't. At least, I hoped she didn't.

"Yes, Jane. That does seem like something we should explore. When I am sure your brother is healed, we will examine the angiogenesis capability of your vascular system. With regard to everything else that has been discussed, I will need time to investigate and examine the concepts. For now, I would like for us all to leave and allow John some more time to recover."

"I don't want to lay here all night and think about everything, Doc. And I don't want to be sedated just so I can rest. You say everything looks good, so why can't you go ahead and do today what you planned for tomorrow? Let's get on with the skin grafts. I'm mentally ready. I think I'm physically ready too."

I knew he couldn't come up with a reason not to do what I suggested. But he still looked at Sam for reassurance. She sensed that and replied. "I agree with John. Why wait?"

"Alright, then. Why wait, indeed? Emily; please move John's bed to the operating suite. Sam, would you please get the OR ready for the skin grafts? And would you please help Jane prepare for the OR? I think she would want to be there to see everything."

I saw Jane smile. Dr. Po understood. He feared the same thing I did and wanted to quiet the noise within her. He had been doing that for a long time. The knowledge of that gave me great comfort. I was sure we would discuss all of this after the surgery.

I received several doses of Symbion before I was administered the anesthesia and the surgery began. This time as I drifted off into the darkness, I was prepared. I didn't tell anyone else but I knew if Merkel could connect with me, I could also find him. So, in my Symbion dream world, I went looking for him. I soon found myself in a house looking down at a man who was kneeling in front of an odd-looking totem pole. The faces on the totem were all different and appeared to have been carved by someone who was definitely a horror fan.

The man had his back to me and I wondered who it could be. I sensed it was Merkel but he was no longer a man. He had been changed. Who was this? And just as I asked that question, the man turned around. He was smiling as he pulled the knife across his neck and laughed as the blood spurted out. But instead of dying, his body began to change. I saw the familiar plague-filled eyes and the blood dripping from them. And then the Narcoleptan was standing right in front of me.

He said nothing and his body began to change again. The familiar pale, ashen body of a Vahemic was being formed. The blue lips and mouth full of sharp teeth smiled at me. And then it was gone. But I still heard the voice. The voice of the arrogant asshole I was seeking.

I thought I annoyed you. Yet here you come looking for me. I am honored. But what you see, or in this particular moment, don't see, is the continued evolution that I am undergoing, John. I don't just exist as one of the mutations you're familiar with; I am all of them. I can become either one of the beautiful creations at any time. My time here in this world has been rewarded.

Don't worry, you don't have to respond. I didn't tell you this before, but I killed many people when I was only a human. I suppose some people may describe me as a serial killer but I was more than that. I was just practicing my religious freedom and making the world a better place. Purifying it for the time that is approaching. The time when I will become a more vibrant version of what my God wants me to be.

I am no longer the person known as Vincent Merkel. I am Februus. Februus, the purifier. I am fulfilling my destiny, John. I sought out my destiny while you stumbled into yours. I altered the protocols after I saw what could happen when you did. The change in me enhanced my God-given talents and enabled me to develop quite a following. But you were lucky. You and your sister had a good teacher growing up, one that allowed me to connect with you. I know your sister would like to talk with me but for some reason she resists. I think once I have the cord placed in my body, I'll be able to communicate with her too. But wait, what am I saying? Once I have the cord, she'll be dead. And you will be dead and then the little puppet will be dead. He is dying. Did you know that? I don't think he can prolong his life too much longer. I just hope I get to him before he dies. I need his help. Will you tell him I'll be there just as soon as I can?

John, you aren't saying anything. Are you speechless? It is stunning, isn't it? Witnessing greatness and being in the presence of a deity?

All I could think of was my father glaring at me and saying, "Asshole!" before I took the top of his head off with a shovel.

You're right, Merkel. I am amazed. I wasn't aware that piles of shit could talk that much but I suppose since you are so full of shit you needed to find additional ways to defecate. So, I guess what you're doing now could be called oral defecation. Yeah, I like that description, don't you? Boy, these are special times. I suppose anything is possible. By the way, you stink. I don't know, but sort of smells like I stepped in a humongous pile of dog shit. Ever consider taking a shower once in a while? Ah, forget I said that. I doubt you would ever be able to wash that stench off of you. I mean shit stinks. It just does. I'll see you later, Merkel. And if you haven't figured it out already - I came here and found you. You might want to remember that, you dumbass.

I heard what sounded like a hundred monkeys screaming as I opened my eyes and found myself in the recovery room with Dr. Po.

"Skin grafts are in place and everything looks very good, John. Your organs are functioning well. No sign of any infection. Your hypersensitivity to Symbion and your regenerative powers are beyond anything I could have envisioned. A few more days in this sterile environment and a couple of additional cord connections, and I think you may be able to get out of here and eat a real cheeseburger. We will just have to be careful not to stress your small bowel any more than we need to while it continues to heal."

I was about to tell him about Merkel when he began to talk about Jane.

"John, your sister worries me. You and I have talked about this before but I wasn't aware of how much her past still haunts her. When you were in Africa, she spoke to me about the pain she endured as a result of your father. She remembers each of the unspeakable acts done to her. She hasn't forgotten any of it or repressed it as she has told us. She believes that killing these beings that harm others is a way for her to find solace. That she will somehow be freed of the memories that haunt her. She actually looks forward to killing them because each one of them brings her one step closer to being free, at least in her mind."

Oh, dear God. My poor sister. She couldn't forget. I wanted to believe her but it wasn't possible for her to forget. Now the butterfly statement makes sense. She can remember. She has always remembered.

"I am reluctant to give her any more power at this time, because I am not sure she will ever be free. I am afraid that her past is all-consuming. And I am not sure how I will be able to tell her that. I am hoping you will be able to help me. I don't think she will do anything to harm us or anyone that she loves or respects, but she knows she has been reckless. She admitted it. She will listen to you, John. You will need to help her as we find a way to destroy what, as you say, 'evil' created."

"Dr. Po, there was something I didn't tell you about Merkel when I was in Africa. He told me he was invisible. That didn't make sense to me since he was a Narcoleptan and they are basically invisible anyway. But I reached out to him during this last surgery. And now I understand what he meant by that. He can change. He can become a Narcoleptan or a Vahemic. He can change into them at will. And something else he said to me confirms that he is controlling all of this because he said he made the mutations by altering the protocols. And I am positive he altered his own protocol to become a Narcoleptan. I bet if you find the records, you will see that he had some sort of brain treatment."

"Yes, you are right, John. It is impossible to dismiss your connection anymore. The epilepsy protocols were altered when he had them. The hospital records indicate that. He is a brilliant man; very capable of understanding the science I developed and he has an extremely high level of monoamine oxidase. The fact that he would make these mutations is extremely troubling. It is terrifying. And it appears he is evolving too, just like you, because he also possesses the converter gene."

I knew he would figure it out.

"I'll help you with my sister, Doc. I understand what you're saying. I was concerned earlier when she said something that I found odd. It reminded me of the time when she was a young girl and how she was capable of disassociating from the evil world she encountered with my father. I believed her when she said that old world was gone, but now we both know that's not true. It tears at my very being and I'll do everything I can to help her."

"Thank you, John. I will let you rest now. Just tell Emily if you need anything, other than solid food. Though I think a milkshake would be okay. I will be back in to check on you in a few hours."

His chair moved him toward the floor and then I saw him walk away. I wanted to say something to comfort him but I didn't know what that would be. As soon as he was gone, I thought of what I should have said. I should have told him that I hoped he knew he was actually a giant among all the other men I have ever met.

"Yes, I think he would have liked that very much, John." Jack walked in and sat down beside my bed. "The scientific knowledge that man possesses is remarkable. I am amazed at his accomplishments."

"Jack. What are you doing here?"

"You know the answer to that question, yet you continue to ask it."

"You're here because I wanted you here."

"Yes."

"To tell me what?"

"I'm not sure."

"I am confronted by evil, Jack. I can't escape it."

"All that live are confronted by evil."

"This one thinks he is a god. And he may have powers similar to one."

"The descent to hell is easy and those who begin by worshipping power, soon worship evil."

"I'm not sure I'm strong enough to destroy it. And it wants to destroy me. My sister. My friends. Just when I'm learning how much good there is around me."

"Badness cannot succeed even in being bad in the same way in which goodness is good. Goodness is, so to speak, itself; badness is only spoiled goodness. Evil is a parasite, not an original thing."

"You are sitting there like a teacher as if you're quoting lines from a book."

"Being called a teacher is indeed a compliment. I am assuming you meant it as one and did not intend to be curt or dismissive."

I just smiled and Jack continued. "John, you have the ability to do good. But you also have the ability to do evil. This person you are referring to has that same ability but it seems he has made his decision and he will regret it one day. Lost souls here on earth will be lost souls in Hell. Do not discount your ability to do what is right or to be something that can be filled with glory from your desire to confront this evil. His future is no more certain than yours is, nor does he control it any more than you do."

"You're saying that I can destroy him."

"I am saying that all things are possible."

"I think I will go and kill another parasite. I wish they didn't exist, but you would just tell me that they do, and as such, we need to deal with it. So, I guess I'll deal with it."

"Yes, I think you will."

Chapter 30
Dr. Po

I didn't see Jack leave. I closed my eyes as I felt the familiar caress of the sandman's potion flowing through my body. I think Emily was instructed to give me something with a little more pixie dust in it to control the activity in my brain because all I did for a long time was sleep. No dreams. No voices. Nothing but numbing calm against the storm that was on the horizon. Sometime later that night I opened my eyes and saw Dr. Po beside my bed. It reminded me of the very first time that I saw him and I smiled.

"Hello, John. You know I did some research on that Beaker fellow you kept calling me the night you came back into this world. I understand why you said that now. And please know I am not offended by it in any way. I know he was someone you found comforting as a child, and considering your state of mind at the time you said it, I take it as a compliment."

I nodded and smiled. "You really knocked me out. How long have I been asleep?"

"A little over twelve hours. It's 2 a.m. And yes, I did give you something stronger to help you sleep and to keep your brain quiet. You needed to rest. Your internal organs are all functioning exceptionally well. Your bone grafts are fused and only in a radiological manner, can you even detect that they exist. Your skin grafts look like they were attached months ago. Tomorrow, I mean later this morning, I will give you some solid food. Some eggs and oatmeal and if you would like, a milkshake of some kind."

"That sounds good. A strawberry milkshake would be great."

"Goodness - a strawberry milkshake? What a surprise."

Some more Po sarcasm. That's a good sign.

"Emily, will you prepare three scrambled eggs, a bowl of oatmeal, and a strawberry milkshake for John at 7 a.m.?"

"Yes, Dr. Po."

"So, I'm doing even better than you thought?"

"Yes, as you always seem to. I keep underestimating the effect that Symbion has on your body and the overall regenerative abilities it creates through the cord attachment as well as when it is administered to you directly. I am not sure I will ever be able to predict that because I think you will continue to change. What you are today, will not be what you are tomorrow. I didn't truly understand the cumulative impact that this molecule would have on your body."

"So, maybe I can get out of here tomorrow?"

"Yes, that is my hope as well."

"Have you had any warnings from ADAM?"

"No, we haven't. Not since you and Sam returned."

"Isn't that unusual?"

"No. it may seem like a long time to you because you have been in a constant battle since the time you came back to us, but it's only been three and a half days since you returned from Africa. Granted you were away for seven days, but we have gone several weeks without a warning in the past, so I am not inclined to believe something else is occurring."

"How did you know I was suggesting that?"

"John, I don't have to be a psychiatrist to understand what you are suggesting. You are worried about what Merkel may be planning. Why else would you ask about ADAM? Though I haven't figured out where he is getting the Symbion yet."

"Even though you control the distribution of it, you and I both know that if he needs it, he will find a way to get it. He's smart and very cunning. Did you know he was a serial killer? He told me that when I contacted him during surgery. I'm not sure how many he killed in his human form, but considering he was a postman and I grew up with the poster child for an evil postman, I suspect it was quite a few. I think that damn agency needs to do something about their interview process."

Dr. Po smiled.

"He also said he tried to reach out to my sister and she resists him. We all heard her tell us she can't talk to him but it bothers me that he said she resists him as if she knows he's there. I may be reading something into those words but I think there's something she isn't telling us."

"Interesting analysis, John. It is something we should indeed consider."

"He said something else. He said he has evolved into a God of sorts. He calls himself Februus, the purifier. Sounds like an ad for some detergent, doesn't it? Arrogant prick. But he really wants that surgery, Doc. He thinks that will be the game-changer for him and make him too powerful to destroy. Maybe that's what he thinks will ultimately make him that God. And though I won't let him sense it when I'm with him, I know he is a powerful and evil son of a bitch. But if he thinks he's going to come into this house and hurt my sister or Sam or you…"

I stopped in midsentence as I realized what I was saying. Merkel was not my father. Yet, he wanted to make me have that same feeling of hopelessness. But that wasn't going to happen. Not this time. Not ever again.

"Sorry, Doc. I was letting my anger get the best of me for just a moment."

"No need to apologize. I understand. If he had the cord surgery, he would become even more dangerous, but I will ensure that never happens."

"There's something else, too. Something that I don't want to believe but I have to ask. He said you were dying. That you didn't have very much longer. Is that true?"

"I have a Grade 3 Ependymoma that originated in the spine. It is very rare. Surgery would be the best option, but based on my MRI that would not be suitable in my case. Over time, yes, it will kill me."

"What about Symbion treatment? You developed a cure; why aren't you treating yourself?"

"John, you can look at me and see my predisposition to genetic mutation. I fear what will happen should I inject my body with Symbion. I am not afraid of the other outcome from not injecting it."

"How long?"

"I would estimate less than a year."

"How much less than a year?"

"Less than 10 months I suspect."

I knew it was exactly 10 months when he said that. Dr. Po didn't suspect anything. He knew.

"Damn. How does that asshole know about your illness?"

"I don't know the answer to that."

It's the evolution of his body and mind like Dr. Po said. But if his mind and body can evolve, mine will continue to do so too. I'll make sure of that.

"Is there anything else you can do?"

"There are many things I can do. I am not ignoring myself, John. Understand that. But I need you to be well. I brought you into this battle if you recall. You and your sister. I hope you both can forgive me for that."

"Dr. Po, you saved us. You need not worry about asking for forgiveness. None is required."

"I am not sure if that is correct. You and your sister were a scientific endeavor at first. But then when she was healed and I saw what she could do, I used her to help correct what I thought were my failings. I still am not sure they are not. And then there was you.

"I had never seen another person like you from a medical perspective. Above and beyond your sister. And I knew that there might be even more significant problems with you from a mental aspect should I push you into the same world as your sister, but I did so anyway. I believed you were capable of even more. So again, I am not sure I should not ask for your forgiveness."

I realized it would be senseless to argue with him. The man was a genius and had saved hundreds of thousands of lives. Including me and Jane. But there he was asking me for forgiveness. I suddenly saw my mother's face, like she was a shadow emanating from Dr. Po's body. There one moment only to disappear the next, because his arm moved an inch. And then I knew what I needed to do.

"I forgive you, Dr. Po."

"Thank you. That means a great deal to me to hear that."

Yeah, for several others too, I think.

"Can you check the blood from the other mutations to see if the monoamine oxidase is present at high levels?"

"From the patients that received chemotherapy before the Symbion, probably all of them. From those that only received radiation therapy, probably most of them, but not all. I have already initiated that study. I have been in discussion with many colleagues and they are beginning that analysis. I have helped them modify their testing equipment where necessary, but most of them had the capability and the knowledge of what I was asking them to do. I suspect that I will have the answers back later this evening."

"You will share the results with me and tell me later what you're doing for yourself?"

"Yes, John, I will."

"Dr. Po?"

"Yes?"

"You know, I have never known you as anyone other than Dr. Po. What is your full name?"

"It is Edmundo Auguste Alejandro Po. A bit pretentious, don't you think?"

"No, not at all."

It seems appropriate.

"Nice to meet you Edmundo Auguste Alejandro Po. My name's John Deaux. That's with an e-a-u-x, not o-e."

The giant of a man smiled.

Chapter 31
National Pastime

Later that afternoon Dr. Po came in with Sam.

"I thought you might like to see someone besides me," Dr. Po said as he activated a robotic arm that moved down over my body and began to project images up onto a monitor.

"Sam, will you perform an examination of the surgery sites while I look at his body in a more cellular manner?"

"Of course."

"How do you feel?"

"I feel good. Ready to get out of bed. My legs, hand, hell my entire body, just feels different."

Different, good. Mom, are you listening?

"Yes, I would imagine it does. Your skin grafts look wonderful. Very little evidence of surgery. Let me turn on the ultrasound for a minute. Your small bowel looks very good, heart and lungs look great. Vital signs are the new norm. Everything is very, very good. What do you think, Doctor?" Sam asked.

"I concur and I see nothing to suggest you should not get out and start walking a little bit. See how things feel. Perhaps you and Sam can walk out to the waterfall. That would be a good exercise for you, there and back."

"Won't she be in danger with all the puffdragons and copperpots that you've got growing and crawling around out there?"

"She is familiar with everything out there and has the appropriate attire necessary to be safe."

"Yeah. You're not going to believe this, but Dr. Po made me a Symbion perfume that I wear so that the plants next to the house will let me out. And I know what to stay away from. We'll be fine. It's a beautiful day."

Symbion perfume. Of course, he did.

"Your clothes are in the bathroom. Don't stay long. Just walk to the waterfall and back. And then come meet with me and Jane in the solarium. I will be monitoring your vital signs but I don't think this will be a repeat of the last time you went for a walk after surgery. Nothing will attack you. Emily has already examined the area and it is clear. See you in an hour or so."

We walked out the back door and just as Sam said, the death bush moved away from her as we stepped onto the grass.

"See, you aren't the only one with special chemical components."

"Well, technically I am. You're just wearing perfume."

She elbowed me and laughed. She put her arm through mine as we walked and I couldn't remember the last time I had felt this good. This was Haunted House at the fair good.

"Were you ever scared? When we were in Africa?" I asked.

"Of course, I was. I was scared to death when you were attacked that second time. I thought I was going to lose you. And this has been haunting me since then. I have to apologize. When I turned off those LBEs…I…"

"Stop. It's okay. No worries. You saved my life. You saved a village."

"John, you saved your life, my life, and the lives of the villagers. I just did what I was trained to do. I kept you alive, but you did the saving part. It was you and Dr. Po. I was just an extra set of helping hands."

"Very special hands and I couldn't have done what you did. I would've just had a showdown with that evil witch of east Africa."

"Well, thanks for the kind words. Don't you think the sun feels wonderful?"

"Yes, the sun feels great, but you feel even better." *And smell just like vanilla. I didn't know how much I liked vanilla until I met you, Sam.*

She stopped and pulled me closer to her. She pressed her body against mine and pulled my head down ever so softly and kissed me.

"I believe the blood flow to all of your lower extremities is working extremely well, John. I can't imagine how you are going to be able to walk like that. Your pants seem awfully tight right now."

"What do you suggest we do?"

"You could lay down on the ground right here and watch me undress."

"Is that safe?"

"Marie, will you put up a small perimeter around John and me while we sit down and rest a minute? We found a nice spot to look at the waterfall."

"Certainly. Perimeter established."

I lay down on the grass and watched as Sam took off her top. This time when I saw her breasts, there was no hair growing on them. She took off her pants too and then laid down next to me and placed my hand on one of her breasts.

Shit. Second base. Oh shit, second base, I thought, but unfortunately, I was thinking out loud.

"Yes, John. Second base. Do you know how to massage second base? Here let me show you."

She placed my hand on her breast and moved it around in a rhythmic manner. All I could think of as she did that was marshmallows. A large bag of marshmallows that I was checking for freshness. I closed my eyes and thought *Whoa – this is crazy* but again I was not saying it only in my mind.

"You want to stop? Are you okay? Is there something wrong?"

"No, I'm sorry. I...uh...it feels amazing."

"Yes, it does feel amazing," she sighed as she kissed me again and gripped my crotch.

"Your vascular system is working very hard. Hmmm...I think I need for you to try out third base," she whispered as she moved my hand down into her panties. "Move your hand around," she said as she unzipped my pants. "Whoa!"

"What? I'm sorry... uh..."

"It's okay. Really. Just a bit softer. You're not rubbing out a stain...just touch me gently and then move your fingers around the outside of my...yep, found it...that's it...softly," she moaned as she grabbed hold of me and began moving her hand up and down.

"Shit, oh shit, I'm going to..."

"Hey...no problem...it's okay, really. This was your first time. I knew that. I fully expected...Damn!" she said as she saw that I was still ready for fourth base even though there had been a sacrifice pop-up.

She climbed on top of me and I felt like we were ready to ride on the Scrambler. I was wrong. It was a thousand times better than the Scrambler and I didn't want to get off. Neither did she. I wasn't sure when we stopped but when we did, neither of us could talk. In fact, I was thinking how glad I was that Dr. Po had reinforced my heart vessels because I thought my heart might explode.

"Is it like this every time?"

"Uh, no," Sam said as she ruffled my hair.

"Shit. I was hoping it was."

She laughed. "What I meant to say was, no it's not like that with others. I have a feeling that it would be like that or even better each time we did it."

"Oh. Should we do it again?"

"Oh, yeah."

"When?"

"Why not now?" Within minutes we were back on the Scrambler, and then the roller coaster, the Haunted House ride, the Ferris wheel, and the bumper car rides several times. As she lay beside me afterward, I looked up at the sky and felt like I was on the merry-go-round, watching the birds flying in a circle above us.

It's funny how they look like a merry-go-round. Flying around like that. Wait a minute. That's not a merry-go-round.

"Fuck."

"Yes. That was indeed one hell of a fuck."

"No – look! Up in the sky. The birds, something is wrong."

Sam looked up and saw the familiar outstretched black wings floating in the air in a circular routine. I had seen them hundreds of times living out in the country. I had also learned early on in my life that roadkill didn't disappear by accident.

"Probably a dead squirrel or rabbit that went somewhere it shouldn't have."

"Let's go look. Just to make sure, okay?"

We got dressed and headed toward the black circle. We approached the edge of the tall bank that looked across at the waterfall and saw the decaying remains of an opossum.

"They try and kill the copperbrowns, but they aren't very successful. Nature has not kept up with Dr. Po's evolutionary influence."

"Damn. You know, I never liked opossums. But when I learned they ate a lot of insects and killed poisonous snakes, I changed my opinion of them. They are ugly little animals though, aren't they?"

"Depends on whether you're an opossum or not."

I laughed at Sam's reply and for whatever reason picked up a large rock. It was about the size of my hand.

"How far is it over to the waterfall?"

"About 300 yards. You can't reach it with..."

She didn't finish the sentence before I threw the rock. We both watched it disappear behind the cascade of water.

"That shouldn't be possible."

"I could always throw a baseball pretty good when I was younger. My hand feels ten times stronger. And my legs. Time me," I said as I took off running toward the house. I ran there and back and though I was a little out of breath, I felt good.

"That can't be right."

"What?"

"You just ran a mile, a hilly trail of a mile in 3 minutes. Do you know what that means?"

"I could win at the Olympics."

"Damn, John. Seriously. You are some sort of ...."

"Mutation? Defect?"

"No...no..."

"It's okay. I'm okay with that label if you want to use it. I've always been different. I just didn't understand how different until now. But you must promise me something. Don't tell Jane yet. I need to discuss something with Dr. Po first. Promise?"

"Promise. I understand."

"Good. Shall we head back?"

"Unless..."

"Oh, I agree. Tell Marie to put that perimeter back up."

"How was the outing?" Dr. Po asked as we walked into the solarium. Jane was sitting with him drinking a milkshake concoction of some kind.

"It was amazing."

Jane laughed and winked at Sam.

"Are you sure you are okay? Your blood pressure and brain waves spiked several times during your walk."

I could see that my sister wanted to suggest the reason for the biological changes, but she politely said nothing.

"Yeah. I got a little out of breath when we got close to the waterfall. But I'm fine. My hand feels really good and my legs do too. In fact, I wanted to talk to you about an idea I had."

"What is it?"

"When Jane and I were younger, we played Frisbee a lot. I was really good at it."

"Yeah, I remember that. You were like a ninja with the darn thing. Knock cans off fences, put them through gaps in tree limbs. You were really good."

"So, I was wondering, could you make some sort of plasma knife device...something circular that I could activate, and then toss it, and once I throw it, the plasma source is energized so that it cuts through anything it hits?"

"Interesting. I think that is very possible. I can certainly look into it. I have had a similar idea for a while now. You just gave it form. Is that all?"

"Yeah, I think so. For now. "

"Good. Well, I have some information for all of you. I got the results of the blood work on the mutations. The monoamine oxidase enzyme was elevated in every case. It's no coincidence. You were right, John. Somehow the Symbion acts like a catalyst and prompts their change."

"Evil is a parasite, not an original thing."

"Profound statement, John. Very profound and apparently very applicable."

"Those are not my words. They're Jack's. I mean C.S. Lewis. He said that long ago. He is...I mean, was a very interesting man."

"I have read some of his work. Apparently not enough. Intriguing. By the way, I think I will have that clothing ready for you later this afternoon. It has a clotting substance embedded in the fibers of the material. I would like for you to come by my lab later and try it on."

"Sure. Maybe after we get something to eat. Sam, are you hungry?"

"Starved."

"I see where I stand now on the hierarchy," Jane declared.

"Oh, I'm sorry, Jane. I saw you with the protein shake and I just figured...never mind. Will you have something to eat with us?"

"Yes, I would love to."

"Dr. Po, I failed to ask you too. Would you care to join us?"

"No, I will be in my lab. Come down after you eat."

"Okay. See you in about an hour."

And then we'll talk some more. About the legs and my hand and my sister. And the opossum. Simple killed by the un-simple. For some reason, I was meant to see that today. I know I have kidded you about reading tarot cards, Dr. Po, but this opossum's death has meaning for all of us.

"Yes. And by the way, I am working on something else for you and Jane. I want to try something with you both. I think I can accelerate your immunity to the Narcoleptan and Vahemic poison."

"You mean, they couldn't hurt us?" my sister asked. I could tell she realized how naïve her question was as soon as she asked it. Both those beings had talons and teeth like saws and metal earth-moving equipment.

"No, they could still hurt you but you wouldn't die from the poison. Or be as affected. It would require less energy on your part to accelerate your healing."

"Cool."

"Yes, I think that would be very cool," Dr. Po answered as he left the room.

More sarcasm and now the use of "cool" in a sentence. Admit it. You're rubbing off on the man. Hopefully, not in a bad way.

I smiled as I thought about him and the two women who had their arms locked in mine as we walked to the bar to get something to eat. We all smiled a lot that night and it felt good to do so.

Chapter 32
Decisions

After eating, my sister and Sam both said they wanted to freshen up which I was pretty sure meant they needed to go sit on the toilet, so I said I'd meet them down in the lab. When the elevator door opened, Jack was there waiting for me.

"Dr. Po's lab?"

"Yeah. How did you know where I was going, Jack?"

"Your conscious and subconscious intermingle quite frequently now. I'm not a medical person so I can't say for sure. But you wanted me here with you on your way to the lab."

"The dead opossum, killed by a genetic mutation. A simple creature killed by a genetically enhanced creature. Doesn't that say something to you?"

"Yes, the world has changed."

"Is that it?"

"It's changed a lot."

"Jack..."

"Change comes about in waves, John. Think about it. An agrarian society turned into an industrialized society that changed into a world of technology that is now measured in nanoseconds. Nanoseconds. Who would have thought that a real word, twenty years ago? Communication that took months, and then days, changed to minutes with the worldwide ability of phones and satellites in the heavens. Computers now link up the world and in fact, create new worlds. A cure for a disease that seemed incurable. The waves just hit the shore a lot more frequently and faster than they used to."

"Yeah, I can see that. So, what am I supposed to do?"

"John, you continue to doubt yourself. Why? You mentioned to Dr. Po about evil being a parasite. You and I talked about that not long ago. People have free will to do evil and to do good. The person that haunts you, and this world, turned toward evil because that was his choice. He will regret it. Murderers do not reign in Hell. There is only one ruler there and he is a jealous and cruel tyrant."

"It scares me. More so for my sister and Sam and Dr. Po. What if I can't save them? My sister has grown up with monsters and they still haunt her and consume her life. But Sam and Dr. Po are seeing them for essentially the first time."

"If you cannot save them, you cannot save them. You are not God any more than this person who refers to himself as Februus is a God. No one's salvation exists in this world. You are beginning to learn that. I believe you're just scared and there's nothing wrong with that. A brave man that is not scared is a fool. You are not a fool, John."

The elevator doors opened. I walked out and looked back at Jack who had not left the elevator.

"Don't you want to see the lab?"

"Perhaps another time. I'm sure you'll tell me about it," he said as the elevator doors closed.

I walked into the laboratory and Dr. Po called out my name without even turning his head.

"John, come over here and look down into this enclosure. The two pigs. Look at them."

I walked over and looked down. Two pigs were eating a trough full of fruit and vegetables. I wasn't sure what I was looking at besides pigs. "What am I supposed to be seeing here, Doc?"

"The pigs were injected with an anti-serum that I made from your blood. And then one of them was injected with Vahemic poison while the other was injected with Narcoleptan poison. I estimated the poison dose on what one would expect from one swipe of their talons. Look at them. They are unaffected when they should be dead."

"And so...?"

"It means what I suspected was true, though I didn't say it in Jane's presence. You have already developed an immunity to the poisons. I suspect you are almost completely immune to Vahemic poison and close to being immune to Narcoleptan poison. How do you think we should use that information for your sister?"

"She should be given the serum. It's just that simple."

Dr. Po seemed surprised by my response but didn't hesitate in replying. "I agree. I will start that immediately."

He's still concerned about making a stronger monster. But my sister will not become a monster. I'll make sure that doesn't happen.

"Come try on the clothes and then we will test them."

"Before we do that, Doc, I need to tell you something that happened on the walk. There were some things I could do that you should know about. I threw a rock, from the bank of this side of the waterfall all the way through the waterfall. At least a two-pound rock. And I ran from the waterfall to the house and back in three minutes. "

"For the first time in a while, with regard to you, I can say that doesn't surprise me. I knew your capability and strength would be enhanced by those surgical modifications. You should know, that they will continue to develop. At some point, their ability to enhance your strength will cease but for now, you are still on the upward curve."

In another world or time, I would have been jumping up and down thinking I was becoming some sort of superhero, but all I could think about when Dr. Po said that was - would that be enough? Would that be enough to destroy Merkel?

"There was something else that bothered me. I saw a dead opossum. Killed by a copperbrown."

"I'm afraid that does happen, John. The opossums are not able to withstand the copperbrown's venom." Dr. Po answered and then paused for a moment. "My goodness," he sighed.

"Something that should have been so simple for me to understand and it escaped my awareness. People say I am a very intelligent man, John, but in many ways, I believe you are much smarter than me. I've produced a world within a world. One that was driven by my desire to be alone and unhindered by the monsters I created within humanity, only to be oblivious to the monsters I have created in nature.

"I am afraid I have suffered from the same arrogance that plagued you when you were younger and now confronts you today. This is a perverse offense on a grand scale and I can only hope I can undo this injustice and be forgiven for my hubris."

"Dr. Po, the enzyme...you didn't create the monsters. They were created by...."

"Yes, they were created by the cures. The cures that I developed."

"You couldn't have known about Merkel and what he would do once he learned of the science, and the alteration of protocols. It wasn't your fault. He was making followers."

"There were problems even before Merkel. And I was here, in my lab, focusing on finding a way to undo the issues that occurred. Then I found you and your sister and I knew I had an opportunity to correct the problem that I created, or at least helped create. I understand what you are saying but I should have known to check for that enzyme. Making me aware of what I have done to nature, illustrates that to me now. I have failed a thousand times a thousand."

"You're wrong, Dr. Po. You have succeeded a hundred thousand times a hundred thousand times. Evil corrupted the good you did. A wise doctor once told me he wasn't God and didn't pretend to be one. You don't know what you don't know and there was no way to predict what Merkel would do. None."

"I think that will be a debate I have with myself for the remainder of my life."

"Dr. Po?"

"Yes, Marie."

"ADAM has informed me that there is a significant amount of activity within the area around Asheville. Several families have been killed in a town called Clyde, North Carolina."

"Asheville? Clyde? I don't recall releasing any Symbion to any facilities in that area. Ask SAM for confirmation. "

"SAM has confirmed what you stated. None."

"It's Merkel, Doc. Can you inject me with some of the Narcoleptan poison and a couple of booster shots of Symbion? I'll reach out to him. I'm sure I can find him before he finds me. Let me try."

Dr. Po led me into one of his labs that had a large chair and a machine that looked like a square octopus, except there no sucker devices on the arms. Instead, there was a round shower head on the end of each of the arms, and each shower head appeared to have a surface of tiny pins.

"I will do it under one condition. I will monitor all parts of your brain, including the top part of your spinal cord through this modified EEG equipment."

"Those look like pretty sharp pins on the end of those arms."

"They are sharp pins on the ends of those arms."

I am a genius, you know. Shit.

"Your brain will feel no pain, John."

"What about my head and neck?"

"That will be painful, I'm afraid. Normally I would administer an anesthetic but in this particular scenario, I do not think that would be wise."

Fuck it. "Okay, let's wire me up for sound, Doc."

I could feel the poison entering my body and then the Symbion electrical charges just as soon as the thousands of pins entered my skull and neck. It was like someone was trying to peel off the top of my head. I wasn't sure if I screamed or not, because it felt like I did but I didn't hear anything. It was just dark and I was very hot, as if I had been buried alive.

Just the thought of being in a coffin made me start hitting my hands on what I thought would be the lid but I felt nothing solid. There was only stale black air, and even though it was air, I could still feel it as my fists pushed outward. I remembered this feeling now. It was as if I was sitting in the broken-down Haunted House ride during a very hot fall day waiting for it to start moving again. And then I saw them. I couldn't count them all but there were Vahemics everywhere moving through the mountainside and then one stopped and pointed. It was pointing at me and when it screamed like a monkey, I heard Merkel's voice.

Come join us here in North Carolina. The campgrounds are beautiful. I am sure Asheville will be beautiful. We need to pick something up at the SECU cancer center. Then I think we will explore more of North Carolina. Maybe I can get that surgery I need. We will see.

The monkey screamed and when I opened my eyes, I realized the monkey that was screaming was me.

"You made contact with him, John. Your EEG waves were untraceable. There was something going on in your brain that I have never seen before. I am hooking your cord to a small bovine. Your pain will be gone in a minute.”

Dr. Po was right. The instant the cord was attached to the animal, my pain disappeared.

“SAM is wrong. Merkel was a Vahemic and said he was going to the SECU cancer center. He is going after Symbion.”

“Marie, tell SAM to evaluate distributions to other parts of North Carolina.”

“Confirmed. 1000 cc’s to the Linebarger Comprehensive Cancer Center at UNC in Chapel Hill, exactly one month ago.”

“Marie, is there a pediatric cancer unit at SECU in Asheville?”

“Yes.”

“You have discovered another failing of mine, John. I have not been tracking the sharing of Symbion between pediatric cancer centers. I now realize I should have been.”

“Jane and I need to go there. There was a whole gang of Vahemics with him. A lot of people are going to die if we don’t get there.”

“Did you see any Narcoleptans?”

“No, but they were probably hidden in the forest. I wasn’t there long. Where ever there was. He has an army with him. He’s going there and then he’s coming here. But I know Jane and I can stop them before they get here.”

“There is no time to evaluate if the clothes work or if there are any anti-venom reactions from Jane’s body. I am concerned about transfusion associated graft vs host disease when I give your sister this anti-serum made from your blood. The risk is low but it could also be very destructive to her body’s organs.”

“Well, we can’t wait around, Doc. But don’t worry. I am sure she will be okay and we’ll be very careful when we get to Clyde. We’ll take as many LBEs and plasma knives as we can carry. And I promise you, nothing will happen to either of us.”

“I do have something else for you though. Let me show you where your clothes are and I will be right back.”

I had just changed into the new clothes when Dr. Po came back with three circular discs that resembled metal Frisbees.

“Shit! How could you have done this so fast?”

"Like I said, I had been thinking of something similar. I already had the plasma generator developed. I just needed a housing and trigger mechanism. The circular form and the trigger in the middle was the perfect idea. They aren't quite ready but they will be soon. I just wanted you to see how well your idea worked."

"Thanks. I can't wait to try them out when we get back. And by the way, the clothes feel perfect."

"The clotting mechanism will activate as soon as there is a tear. I am also going to give you some more of this anti-clotting agent in syringes, should you need it. Be careful, John."

"Before I go, Doc, I want you to hear this from me, face to face. I am doing what I was always meant to do. I know that now. It just took me a while to understand it all. What looked like a bad decision at the time, turned into the best decision that I ever made. And that is not subject to debate."

Chapter 33
Clyde

I was waiting at the truck for Jane as she entered the garage. Sam and Dr. Po were walking with her.

"I almost forgot, John, here are your contacts. They will protect your eyes from the poison," Dr. Po said as he handed them to me.

"Guess what, John? I now have thermal vision like you, and I should be immune to the poison now thanks to my big brother!"

Dr. Po gave her Symbion shots and the anti-serum. And no adverse effect - no graft vs. host reaction. Thank you, Dr. Po. She will be fine. I promise you.

"Remember, Marie will control the truck and she and I will be in constant contact with you the entire time you are gone. Be careful and do not take any unnecessary risks. I am certain this man has set a trap for you."

"Don't worry, Doc. He doesn't know what badasses me and my brother are now."

"Yes. Nevertheless, be careful and allow the truck to help you. It has equipment that can be quite useful in this type of situation. Stay close by it. The sensors on it will help protect you."

I understood what he was saying even if Jane didn't.

Don't stray from the truck. It makes sense. Use the truck as protection and a weapon.

Sam hugged Jane and kissed me on the cheek. Though I wanted to kiss her and take her in my arms, her body language and face suggested she wanted nothing else to be revealed regarding our relationship.

"It's a two-hour and forty-two-minute drive to Clyde. Remember, you have access to Marie and I at any time. See you later tonight when you return."

Jane hopped in the truck like she was going on a camping trip and I climbed in the other side. When the door closed, the truck engaged and we were headed out of the tunnel. Even though Jane had already given me a brief summary of the truck's capability, I began posing different scenarios to Marie about its defense mechanisms and she explained things to me.

"If the truck becomes engaged with predators, simply say, "Amp," and the truck will become electrified with ten thousand milliamps of current. 100 milliamps are considered a lethal dose to a human. Ten thousand milliamps should kill any creature that is on the truck. Be aware though, that once you engage that function it will place a substantial drain on the batteries. Though the truck will still be able to function in every other manner, another deployment of that capacity will require thirty minutes before the batteries are sufficiently recharged.

"The headlights will light up an entire city block. The windows and the truck itself cannot be breached. It is capable of withstanding an F5 tornado. It is waterproof and has now been equipped to sustain you with water and food for three months. The seats will recline to become a bed. The tires are puncture-proof, but should they get ripped off the wheel, the metal wheel can be driven for an infinite number of miles. The metal will not overheat, but the ride may be a little less comfortable."

"Any LBEs on the truck?"

"No. But there are outlets on the front, sides, and rear of the truck that can ionize argon gas to three thousand degrees."

"Like a plasma knife?"

"Essentially, yes, but they are not actually a knife even though the arc that is generated is three by five feet in diameter and will incinerate anything that comes within its presence. They are initiated by pressing the buttons labeled as such on the dashboard of the truck. They can also be employed by stating the word, 'Bond.'"

"Bond?"

"Yes, that was your sister's idea. Dr. Po agreed. It is distinctly different from 'Amp.'"

Jane shrugged and said, "Bond. James Bond," and laughed. I shook my head and laughed too. I realized that Dr. Po had accepted all these names that my sister came up with because he knew it allowed the unfamiliar, the unbelievable, to conform to her reality. A world of monsters that a fragile mind made less monstrous just by a name.

"Anything else?"

"There is a total destruct device on the truck that will destroy two city blocks. That cannot be activated by either you or your sister. It can only be initiated by Dr. Po."

"I've never been to Clyde, North Carolina before, but if that total destruct package was put into use there, I'm thinking that you might be wiping Clyde clear off the map."

"If you were in the town proper, the answer is yes. But Clyde is very rural, so depending on where you are, the destructive nature of the truck explosion has various models regarding the amount of life that would be annihilated."

"So why in the hell is he there?"

"Who is he?"

"Merkel."

"I am unable to answer that."

"Sorry, Marie. I was just thinking out loud."

"There are numerous camping and hiking areas around Clyde. Does that help answer your question?"

"Yes, Marie. Thank you. The son of a bitch is killing people in an anonymous way. Showing us how strong and deceptive he is. Destroy lots of campers and no one would know about it for a day or two. Murder committed out in the open, but still unseen."

"Are there any other questions?"

"None for the moment, Marie."

We drove for ten silent minutes before my sister broke the nervous stillness that encircled both of us. "Are you really that worried about this nutcase Merkel?"

"Yes, I am."

"More so than when we were growing up? We couldn't protect ourselves then and we survived. We can protect ourselves now. We can do a lot more now to those that want to hurt us or others."

She certainly remembers. Maybe she thinks Dr. Po told me everything or she just isn't aware of what she's saying. Either way, it doesn't really matter now.

"Yes, it worries me even more so now than when we were growing up."

"Shit, John. You've got damn superpower now! So do I. We can kick his ass and his little misfit army all the way from Clyde to California. Don't you remember that night? That night when the police tried to take you away? I wouldn't let them. And I won't let this asshole take you away either. We'll be okay. We'll destroy his ass forever tonight. I will enjoy putting my plasma knife into his eyes."

Plasma knife. Charcoal embers. They are the same. The same way to make another monster pay for his actions. Yes, she remembers. Everything.

"We need to be more careful this time, Jane. I'm connected to him. I understand what he wants to do, so you've got to listen to me, okay?"

"No problem. I've got your back."

"I know you do. Doesn't this truck have a stereo? Surely, it has some killer stereo."

"Oh, hell yes. Marie, play Jane's mix."

The sounds of "Gimme Shelter" by the Rolling Stones blasted from all around the cab. *Yeah, sounds appropriate,* I said to myself. I closed my eyes and the seat reclined, sensing my slightest body movement, and listened to a Rolling Stones concert all the way to Clyde.

"Arrived at destination," Marie announced and we suddenly became very alert as the truck came to a stop in the middle of downtown Clyde. It was dusk and we were in front of a Subway with a couple of cars in the parking lot. As we checked the truck's monitors, all we saw were a few vacant buildings, a closed realty office, and a closed local arts and craft store. That was it. There was nothing else open or moving around except in the Subway.

"You want a foot-long cold cut combo or a turkey and roast beef with cheddar?" Jane asked as she looked over at me.

"Funny."

"I'm not kidding you. I'm hungry and I'm going to get something to eat. You see any reason why I shouldn't?"

I started to say something but then I realized, her lack of fear was just how her body was wired now. It was a coping mechanism and a survival mentality that I could not and should not change. All I needed to do was try and steer it in the right direction.

"Cold cut combo, with lettuce and tomato, spicy mustard, green peppers, and a large Dr. Pepper. But before you go out there... Marie, will you evaluate the area for any activity? Anything within a 5-mile radius."

"One-quarter of a mile from you, at a gas station, are several cars and four humans. There are also two homes a half-mile from it, with eight humans, four dogs, and twenty-one goats. Nothing else detected."

"See you in a minute." Jane hopped out of the truck and entered the Subway. I got out too with an LBE and kept my head on a swivel as I stood guard. Ten minutes later, Jane came out and we got back in the truck. She handed me my sandwich and drink.

"I love Subway," Jane sighed as she began eating what she always ordered - a meatball marinara with extra provolone and Swiss cheese. "It was always a treat going there when we were little."

"Yeah, it was."

Well, she remembers the good times too, so that's something positive.

"Marie. Move out of town and take us to the closest campground."

"That would be the Lake Junaluska Campground, 6.8 miles from here."

"Yes, that's perfect. Proceed."

Though I wasn't really hungry, I ate my sandwich and tried to imagine what Merkel was planning. He was here. He wanted me here. Was this where he thought he could kill my sister? I thought about injecting myself with Symbion but I decided to wait until we got to the campground before doing anything. If there was nothing there, I would inject myself and then I would go find him. I looked at Jane who was enjoying her sandwich, seemingly oblivious as to what we would soon encounter.

Even though she was a much bigger and stronger version of herself, I still saw my little sister; but now she wasn't looking over her shoulder or wondering what would happen when we got back home from the Subway. No, this time she was unafraid of the monsters that awaited us and I was going to make sure she stayed that way for as long as I was alive.

The campground was off North Carolina state highway 74 on a long circular road called Camp Adventure Drive that turned into a gravel road about a mile from the entrance. The entrance to the park was blocked by a barrier gate that was activated by a person in the booth at the far left of the entrance. We pulled up to the gate and waited for a minute but nothing happened.

I said, "Amp," just as the reason the gate hadn't opened jumped onto the truck. We heard the howler monkey scream of the Vahemic as the electricity jolted its body and watched the chalk-like creature fall onto the hood, unmoving. I didn't need Marie to tell us what was going on in the campground. Jane and I could see the thermal images of people being chased by demonic creatures. The red outline of the normal-looking bodies changed as the silhouette lost segments that provided its form.

"Looks like a fucking arcade game," Jane observed. I couldn't dispute what she was saying but I couldn't ignore how unemotional she was about what we were seeing. I couldn't ignore it, but I didn't dwell on it either. That would have been foolish. We needed to kill as many of these things as quickly as possible and I needed the person next to me to be trying to set a new record on the arcade game we were getting ready to play.

"Move forward Marie, and 'Bond,'" I instructed. The truck broke through the gate and the plasma arcs were activated around it. Jane laughed as three of the beings lost their legs when they tried to approach us, only to lose their arms or heads as they tried to claw themselves up onto the truck.

"Man, there's a bunch of them out there, John. We can't stay in this truck. They're killing everyone in the campground."

"Yeah, I know. But we need to stay together, Jane. You and me, moving forward together. You watch my back and I watch yours."

"Yeah, just like before, right, brother?"

"Yeah, just like before." I told Marie to stop and we jumped from the truck. Jane shot an LBE at a Vahemic that flew out of a tree over my head, blowing a hole through its body. It fell down beside the truck and again I yelled out, "Bond!" The plasma arc came on and sliced through its shoulders, removing them from the body. I shot an LBE into its head which disintegrated into what looked like hundreds of tiny little flakes of white paint.

We moved through the campground more or less ignored as the Vahemics were more concerned with what was running away from them as opposed to what was stalking them. We watched them throw body parts out of the trailers like they were thieves discarding items of little value. As they emerged from the trailers, Jane and I would hit them simultaneously with our LBEs, blowing off entire sections of their bodies. If their head wasn't destroyed by our first shot, one of us would ensure it soon became chalk ash with more precise positrons entering its body.

This carnage went on for hours. We tried to save the people in the campground, but we could not, no matter how hard we tried. There was no way to keep track of how many Vahemics we killed but it must have been over fifty. We were covered in mostly human blood because of the depleted blood volume of the hungry Vahemics, but neither of us had even received a scratch. Finally, there was just silence. We scanned the area but the only thing we saw moving were some of the upper parts of a few Vahemics which still had functioning heads, crawling around and trying to figure out a way to live a little longer. Jane and I made sure each one we saw didn't live any longer than it took us to find it.

The entire area reminded me of a scene from the history books about the Civil War. Still photographs of the battle's aftermath taken by Matthew Brady, Alexander Gardner, George Barnard, or Timothy O'Sullivan. Funny, how their names popped into my mind as I saw their black and white images fading in and out of what I was looking at now. They couldn't take live-action shots back in those days, only stills. And like the Civil War photographs taken then, body parts were strewn all over the ground; only with what I saw now, there were disturbing colors. Fragments of bodies and gaping holes, which looked like they had been removed or created by cannon shot, lay all around us, albeit in ash-white bodies that weren't human; but still, those pictures were vivid too. My sister put her arm around my shoulder as we walked back to the truck.

"I had your back the entire time, brother."

"Yes, I know you did."

"I counted fifty-five, I think. Kind of hard at times because some of the bodies didn't have heads. How many did you think we killed?"

She wasn't concerned at all with the hundred or more family members that were killed. She only wanted to know about the monsters.

Like Dr. Po said, salvation in numbers. I wanted to cry but I couldn't. Not now.

"Yeah, that sounds like the right number."

"Good. And I got at least half of them. So, I'm closer. Getting a lot closer."

I couldn't tell whether she didn't realize what she was saying or she didn't care what she was saying. Again, either way, it didn't matter. I knew she was looking at some score on an arcade game and was pleased with it. It was a strange feeling to be standing beside her among all that carnage and to be thinking about a game, but our lives had always been intertwined with arcade games and fairs. Those memories would never leave us and though we were looking at the very same thing, I knew we both now saw something completely different.

One of us played the game thinking it would provide them salvation. One of us played the game because he had to remove the dark from the world in which he now lived. One was still trying to claw herself out of the dark. The other one hoped he could find the good that would help them both walk out into the light.

Unfortunately, neither one of us would find what we were seeking in Clyde. And I wondered why Clyde had misled us? Whoever Clyde was, I was sure he didn't mean to. He was just fooled like the both of us standing there. Clyde was just naïve. Naïve and full of death.

Chapter 34
Who?

Blood and poison covered our bodies as we approached the truck. I was sure Dr. Po had prepared for that, even knowing we were both now most likely fully immune to the Vahemic's poison. I stopped Jane as we got closer but apparently, she was thinking the same thing.

"I got this. Marie. Engage decontamination protocol," Jane called out.

She led me to the front of the truck and the lights became vibrant shades of purple that I had also seen in Dr. Po's OR suite and recovery area.

"Please turn around," Marie said and we followed her instructions. "Again," she said, and a minute later repeated the same thing before we heard, "Disinfection complete."

"Marie, Dr. Po," I started with my report. "We met with an army of Vahemics at the Lake Junaluska Campground, about seven miles outside of Clyde. There were over fifty and though we have destroyed all of them, they killed all of the people that were here. I now know Merkel wanted us here as a distraction so he could get to the SECU cancer center, but there's nothing else we could have done. He knew we would come here to try and save the campers but that allowed him easy access to the cancer center. Have you checked to see if anything has happened there?"

"Yes. I have been in contact with them since you departed. Nothing has happened there and their entire quantity of Symbion is intact."

"Damn. Something isn't right."

"John, perhaps your brain is acting in a manner that cannot be anticipated. It is possible that auditory and visual hallucinations could be occurring along with your intact visionary contacts. Your EEG was unlike any I have seen when you last reached out to him and you did have numerous seizure-like activities before the tracings became unreadable."

"I suppose that's possible, but it hasn't happened before. Every other time, the message, the vision, the conversation that I remember; all of it, has been right."

"Yes, that is true, but as we discussed, I am unable to predict the cumulative effect that Symbion has had on your body and though most of it has been positive, perhaps this is a negative effect that is another unexpected and at present, unexplained event."

What he was saying could be true, but I also sensed that something else was going on. I couldn't explain it but I had a sickening feeling. Like watching my sister go down into the basement with my father. Even though I had already killed so many terrible things this evening, that image of my sister made me want to kill something else.

"I think I should take a large dose of Symbion and try and reach out to him again."

"John, that could be extremely dangerous. The outcome cannot be predicted."

When Dr. Po said the outcome could not be predicted, I knew he was implying that the outcome might be fatal, but I didn't care. I couldn't watch my sister go down in that basement again and I was going to stop it from happening. And in order to do that, I needed to see Merkel.

"I understand, but I'm going to do it."

"John, before you do that, I want you and Jane to get away from your current location. I need you to park the truck in the middle of the campsite, take all the supplies you need, and begin hiking back toward home. It is almost midnight now. Marie will direct you and I will dispatch another truck to pick you up. The scientific and medical worlds, as well as the federal and local governance, are aware of the mutations that were created, but society as a whole is limited in its awareness.

"I am afraid if other campers happened upon the scene that you described, it would incite a panic in the community, and eventually the world, that would not be easily overcome. It would be the outbreak of communal terror that I have been fearful of for a very long time."

Jane went calmly to the back of the truck. She was just doing what she had been told, perhaps aware, and certainly uncaring as to what Dr. Po truly meant. I had to admit, I didn't need to ask what he planned to do. I just needed to understand how it would happen.

"What happens after we park the truck and leave?"

"Once I make some changes to the onboard computer, a positron reactor will be created in the mechanical and battery components of the engine. It will implode and destroy the campground. It will look like a meteorite hit that area. And though these types of celestial occurrences are rare, the world accepts that they do happen. As such, the destructive nature of that event and the subsequent loss of life will be more easily accepted by society as a whole. I have deep regret that I am required to do this. I am afraid that it will be something that will never be far from my thoughts."

"How far do we need to be away before that happens?"

"I would like for you to be ten miles away."

I knew I could easily do that in about an hour with the strength that I had now in my legs, but I didn't know if my sister could keep up with me.

"I think Jane needs a shot of Symbion. With that, I'm pretty sure, we can be ten miles away within an hour. I'll wait to take the extra doses of Symbion that I'll need to reach out to him until the truck picks us up."

"Acceptable, John. The truck should be there by 3:30 a.m."

"Is Sam there, Dr. Po?"

"She is. She has been monitoring the entire conversation."

"Hey, John. I'm so sorry for what you and Jane had to do. I cannot imagine."

"Sam...I just wanted to tell you...that...uh...uh...would you please make sure that you and Dr. Po are safe until we return? I'm not sure where Merkel is right now but he's coming your way. I really think this was just a reason to get me and Jane away from the house. I want to make sure I'm there to greet him when he arrives."

"Yes. Dr. Po and I will be very safe. You and Jane be careful. I love you, John."

Damn. She said it. She actually said it. Do I say it back now?

"Hey, what about me?"

"I love you too, Jane. Watch over your brother for me, will you?"

"Yes, I will."

Later. I'll tell her later.

"See you around 6," I said as we disconnected and I began putting together my backpack.

I made sure that I had the Symbion doses and the additional clotting material that Dr. Po had placed on the truck for me. Jane and I each had an LBE and several plasma knives. I drove the truck to the middle of the campground and then walked back to Jane and gave her a shot.

"Think you can keep up with me?"

"Yeah, I suppose I have to. Sam wants me to protect you. I think she said she loved you or some crazy shit like that."

"Some crazy shit like that. Come on," I said as I started jogging out onto the gravel.

We were exactly ten miles away when we heard the explosion and turned around to see the sky light up. Marie told us to continue on about another mile and wait by the side of the road and that the truck would be there in another hour and a half. I don't know if Marie had intended it, but exactly one more mile placed us by a roadside picnic area. We sat down, took off our backpacks, and began eating and replenishing our fluids.

"I don't know how Dr. Po makes these liquids that look like dirty water and these dog biscuits taste so good, but hell, I could eat and drink this stuff all the time."

"You do eat and drink this stuff all the time."

Jane smiled at my comment, but even in the darkness, she could see the look of worry on my face.

"John, it will be okay. We did everything we could to save those families, but we just couldn't. Now we need to sit here and rest up. Be ready for when this Merkel douchebag pays us a visit. And we will be ready! And we'll destroy the abusive bastard. This time we'll use a plasma knife shovel."

Her memories blended with reality and I was sure now that it was intentional. She knew Dr. Po had told me and she was fine with that, as was I. We would kill that asshole but we needed to rest now. The truck arrived at exactly 3:30 a.m. just as Dr. Po had said. We stowed our backpacks in the back, keeping our LBEs and plasma knives with us as we got in the cab. When the truck started moving, I told Jane that I was going to inject myself with several doses of Symbion and that she should call Dr. Po if anything strange started to happen with me.

"Define strange."

"I stop breathing or something like that."

"Stop breathing for how long?"

Before I could reply, she began to laugh. "Go ahead, Memento. Dream away. I'll be here."

Memento. The guy at the fair who claimed he could read people's minds. I had forgotten all about him. We only saw him once but we both knew he couldn't read people's minds. He said stupid shit like, "I see an animal in your life," and the person would cry out, "Yes!" in an amazed voice. Hell, most of the people there had a pet and if they didn't, most of them would have seen some sort of animal off in the woods or on the road while they drove to the fair. Dead or alive. He just said stuff that he knew he could manipulate in some way to make them think he could see into the future. Funny how she thought of that right then.

I smiled at her and gave myself the Symbion, then notified Marie and Dr. Po that I had done so and closed my eyes. I drifted off into a world that the familiar molecule could now create for me and I found myself at the fair in Memento's tent. Only this time, Merkel was lying on a table in front of him and Memento was telling him that he was cured. He sprung up from the table and all the people in the tent began to clap. Everyone except me.

The next thing I knew, I was standing outside a hospital and Merkel was there wearing Memento's cape and hat with a strange look in his eyes as if he was beckoning someone in a trance to come toward him. When they got close enough, he pulled out a knife and slashed their throat. I yelled and heard my sister call out my name. I couldn't see her but felt a familiar electrical charge being administered to my body and I began to calm my breathing and relax.

I was then back at the fair, and I saw Merkel, again dressed up like Memento standing outside his wagon. Every so often, he'd pick someone out of the crowd and tell them to come inside. The person he had chosen would then come back out looking like the tattered wolfman or the vampire with the missing fang on the Haunted House ride and all the people would "ooh and ahh" and clap just before the wolfman or vampire ran up to them and ripped open their stomachs. When the people looked down at their insides that were dropping onto the ground, they laughed until they fell over dead.

I wanted to run away but I bumped into a mailman who yelled at me to watch where I was going. He handed some mail to Memento. I then started to think Dr. Po was right. I was beginning to hallucinate. Everything in my past was becoming mixed up in my mind and I couldn't concentrate anymore. But then I heard Merkel's voice.

It was coming from the guy that ran the game where you paid a nickel to toss wooden rings onto milk bottles.

Hey, John. Come on over and take a shot. Three bottles and you get a free converter gene. The odds of getting three in a row are three in seven billion, but that's nothing for you.

And then I saw the mailman again and he was telling me to watch where I was going, and I shook my head and ran away. I ran until I saw my sister waving at me in front of the Haunted House ride. I went over to her and we got on the ride.

Halfway through the ride, it stopped. Merkel's voice announced, *'We are having mechanical difficulty, please wait.'* A pale, thin man with slicked back hair came in to fix the ride and he said, "It's not a coincidence." The words floated in the air around our heads and reeked of alcohol. I recognized him. It was the postman who had delivered the mail to Memento and he smiled as he spoke again.

There's a lot more but I'm not sure if you want to hear it or not. It's quite amazing.

That word. Amazing. He's trying to talk to me like Po. I felt my pressure spiking. Another electrical charge surged through my body and the pain in my head stopped and I was calm again. My body and mind were in control but I was still very pissed.

Go ahead, shit head. I'm listening.

And there I was. Sitting in a chair on Memento's stage and the crowd was laughing at me as he made me move my arms and legs up and down like I was hypnotized. And he began talking.

As I've always said, John, we have a lot in common. My father was abusive too. An abusive drunk, but he only hit me. Hit me a lot and eventually, I came to like it. In fact, I wanted to be like him. I helped him kill my mother and then I helped him change. You met him earlier in North Carolina, but I don't think you even knew who he was. He was very pale and probably just another pile of arms and legs to you. You would say evil corrupts good, but I think Symbion just makes evil better. I know, I know; we may just have to agree to disagree on that point.

And though I didn't understand about the monoamine oxidase until later, I could always tell a sociopath or, if I got lucky, a psychopath, a mile away. That's why I waited in the parking lot of the cancer center. Like you told the good doctor, they didn't ask if you had a religious preference on their questionnaire when they were treating you. All I had to do was alter the treatments for those people that preferred to worship something or someone other than God and then I could produce all of those wonderful creatures.

Funny thing was, I didn't change until much later after the treatment had been altered for me. I was simply cured for a while. But I knew something was different when I killed that person in the parking lot of the hospital. I seemed to be drawn to that place and it felt so different. I knew I had been changed and how to fulfill my destiny. Though it was a place of science, I knew it would eventually become a holy temple.

What do you mean altered for you?

I mean if someone doesn't follow the protocols, and if you have the right chemical in your blood, then you are going to change. Change in a way that has become quite a troublesome point of reference for the good doctor. He didn't know though. He still doesn't, but I want to make sure you know.

And if you see your sister here at the fair again, you should ask her a question. Ask her who made who. She'll know what I'm talking about. I am really looking forward to that surgery and you won't believe how my chameleon-like abilities will continue to evolve. Now move your legs and arms at the same time and jump off the stage onto your head.

When I jumped off the stage, everything went black. I stared into the darkness until someone opened the tent and a multicolored light hit my face. I heard laughter and ran out of the tent and found myself in a strange colorful world. A world of odd-looking people and talking plants and animals. But I recognized this world and I wasn't afraid.

I heard someone call out my name and he was waving his trunk at me. It was Horton. And standing next to him was Sally O' Malley. She waved at me too and came running toward me, telling me she never thought I would get there but that I needed to be very careful about talking to the Whos.

Why?

'**Because they will kill you**!' she exclaimed as her head changed into that of a Narcoleptan. She tried to bite me and I screamed, "*NO!*" until I felt the electrical impulses that quieted me and I opened my eyes. Jane was removing my cord from her abdomen and she smiled at me.

"What time is it?"

"5:55 a.m. We're almost home. Why?"

"Dr. Po, are you there?"

"Yes, John."

"Are you doing anything with the WHO this morning?"

"Yes. Dr. Ubeme from Kampala is coming here with several of his colleagues to get the Ebola cure serum. Sam is meeting with them now. They just arrived."

"A Doctor U bay may? No! Dr. Po - that's Merkel! He's changed. He can change his appearance. He may look like a Ugandan, but he isn't. That name. Can't you see? It's 'Obey me'. It's him, telling us once again how smart he is. Don't let him in! Whatever you do, don't let him in!"

"I am afraid that has already happened."

Chapter 35
Unpredictable discord

"Hello, Dr. Ubeme. I am Sam."

"Shutting down perimeter," Sam heard Marie say and she stood back. Dr. Ubeme grabbed her as the door shut behind them.

"Actually, you can call me Februus and though I am not sure, oh yes, I see them here, several of my colleagues were able to get in too before that computer voice said they were shutting down the perimeter. But I doubt you can see them as they have changed. They're in camouflage mode now.

"You look stunned, Sam. I am Vincent Merkel. Perhaps John hasn't told you that I have changed into a God-like being. My real name is Februus. I know how all you mortal beings love seeing miracles, so watch this."

The black doctor changed into a Vahemic and then into a Narcoleptan and then back into the black doctor before finally changing back into his original human form.

"Amazing, isn't it? What do you think, Dr. Po? I know you're watching us from somewhere. How do we get into this place? I bet there are all sorts of little mousetraps around here so we'll have to be very careful. But you will make sure of that, won't you Sam?"

"What is going on, Dr. Po?" I asked.

"Merkel is with Sam. They are in the front courtyard but not in the house. The house and the perimeter have been locked down but Merkel and several others, probably Narcoleptans, got in."

"Shit. Don't do anything until we get there. We're almost there. Don't let him in the house! We will save Sam. Just give us a minute."

I could tell that Jane was worried and I couldn't have her worried right now. I needed her to be angry. I might regret what I said later but I didn't care. Not now while Sam's life was in danger.

"That asshole is going to try and take Sam down into the basement and do things to her. You're not going to let him do that, are you?"

I then saw the person that I needed to see. The one that looked like she had blood dripping from her eyes. The one that wanted to kill anything that got in her way.

"I will kill that mother fucker. And carve his eyes out and make him eat them."

Yep. I'll pay for this later but I don't care right now.

We drove into the underground garage where Dr. Po was waiting for us in an electric chair of some kind and we followed him into his laboratory. We could see Merkel holding Sam on the monitors.

"There are two other Narcoleptans out there with him in the gardens. Marie has the thermal images of them. Marie has also located one hundred and five other Narcoleptans around the perimeter of the building."

"This ought to do it," my sister said as the grin on her face made you think of Halloween images, not family. Neither Dr. Po nor I said anything. We both understood what she was thinking.

We heard Merkel's voice. "So, hello? Hello there in the beautiful building! By the way, these gardens are quite spectacular. I must have a tour of them after the operation. Sam, what's the name of that voice that spoke to us earlier? I'm sure that Dr. Po has named it."

Sam remained motionless and silent.

"Oh, come now, Sam, I'm not going to hurt you unless Dr. Po doesn't let us in the building. I suspect John is back from his little trip to North Carolina by now. John, you wouldn't want to see me hurt this pretty young woman, would you? I have a feeling you like her."

"This Vincent Merkel is an abhorrent accumulation of nucleic acid and protein," Dr. Po almost spit on the monitor.

That made me want to laugh and it cleared my mind and helped me focus.

"Tell Sam to bring them around to the back. To the death bush entrance. Then have Marie open up the plasma perimeter out by the waterfall trail. Keep it open until all the Narcoleptans are in that area. That is where we will kill every damn last one of them."

"Hello, Vincent. This is Dr. Po. The computer voice you are referring to is called Marie. Sam, will you take Vincent and his colleagues, through the garden to the waterfall trail? This will give you a chance to enjoy some of the gardens before your surgery, Vincent. But do not stray from the path that Sam takes you on, and do nothing to harm her. If either of those things occurs, you will die before you ever get that surgery you so desire."

"Excellent, Dr. Po. Lead on, Sam. And please explain to us what we're looking at as we go. Don't leave anything out. I'm sure it's fascinating!"

"Okay, Jane, we need to load up and get ready."

"I know there isn't a lot of time but I need to give you and Jane something, John."

We followed Dr. Po into another lab where they were laying on the table. Three metal Frisbees.

"They work now, John. But only if you or Jane trigger them. Touch your finger to the middle of the device and throw it. Within five seconds, the argon gas will be ignited, creating an arc around the entire device. It will stay on for thirty seconds and disengage. If anyone or anything else touches it, it will explode, destroying anything within ten feet of it."

"I can't wait to see these things remove some of their limbs and heads. That will be fun, won't it, John?"

I nodded but saw that Dr. Po had something else to show us. He led us over to another table. What appeared to be two machine guns were laying on it.

"I've been working on something else for some time now. I have created Symbion-carbon bullets for these devices. These solid bullets will transform into a gaseous form as soon as they hit anything with a temperature above 90 degrees. Within that gas is a very toxic substance, consisting of Mycobacterium bovis and avium, along with Yersinia pestis, and several enteroviruses that cause hoof and mouth disease. Highly contagious and very deadly. The bullet will kill any living thing it penetrates within 60 seconds. And I do mean it will kill anything. Beast and/or man.

"I could not find a way to load these into the LBEs so you will have to use this new weapon to shoot them. I needed a way to keep the bullets cooled. Both of these guns will hold twenty of these bullets at 60 degrees until you deploy them. I am sorry I didn't make more. I am afraid, once again, I did not anticipate correctly."

"Don't worry, Dr. Po. This will get 40 of them. With the LBEs and the metal Frisbees, I am just sorry there aren't more of them here to kill. Vincent will wish he was never born."

As Jane looked at the weapons, her eyes were wide open like she was a child again remembering the time she got a tricycle for Christmas. It was a used tricycle that mother had painted red but it didn't matter. My sister rode that tricycle from morning until night that day even though it was below freezing outside. I can remember my mother making me go out and get her every hour or so and bring her inside to warm up so she didn't get frostbite. Funny, how that thought jumped into my mind at that very moment.

Yeah, I hear you, mom. I will protect her from the bites today.

"These gardens are absolutely vibrant. What are those orange and yellow flowers? Are those poppies?"

"Yes, they are. They're quite fragrant too."

Vincent walked over to smell them, but as he did, he caught Sam out of the corner of his eye, getting ready to run.

"Hmm. Steve. Can you come here a moment?"

A Narcoleptan appeared and snarled at Sam who almost fell backward when she felt the hot breath on her face. Then she laughed.

"What are you laughing at?"

"Steve? Really? Is I-gor with you too?"

"No. Her name is Jennifer. And she would love to snap your body in two, but we can wait to do that later. Those flowers," Merkel pointed at. "What do you smell?"

The Narcoleptan inhaled the poppy pollen. it shook its head and its whole body shuddered. Within a minute it was dead.

"This utopian garden appears somewhat dystopian," Vincent commented. "What is in that pollen?"

"Stonefish venom."

"Goodness. The flowers around here will kill you, won't they?"

"If you're lucky."

"Yes. Well, let's say we end this garden tour and get to the waterfall trail. Okay? Did you hear that, Dr. Po? We're coming around to the waterfall trail as you asked us to do."

"They are within ten feet of the entrance," Marie informed us. Jane and I picked up the guns and placed the shoulder straps around our necks. Dr. Po handed me a backpack to carry the metal Frisbees and then we checked back on the monitors. We watched Vincent looking for a camera while holding Sam and then saw his hand change into a Nacrcoleptan claw.

"Open the door, old Dr. Poor, said Barnacle Bill the sailor. Open the door, or I'll cut the whore..."

He didn't finish his sentence. Sam broke free of his grasp, ran, and jumped into the death bush. The two-inch fire thorns penetrated her body like a hundred darts and she died within seconds from the sea snake venom.

We all just stared at the monitor in shock and disbelief. My sister tried to say something but was unable. Dr. Po was visibly shaken and fell to the floor. I helped him up but could say nothing either as my mind and body went completely numb. Seconds later, I gathered my wits and told Marie to open the waterfall plasma perimeter door. This was not the time to think about what had just happened.

"Perimeter door opened," Vincent heard the computer voice state but he misunderstood what Marie meant. Nevertheless, he ordered the other Narcoleptan into the death bush and smiled as it moved away from it due to the Symbion in its body. He jumped back though when he saw the Narcoleptan's head explode as three LBEs hit it simultaneously. When it died, the death bush closed around it.

The other Narcoleptans poured through the opening in the perimeter and I ordered Marie to close it when all of them were inside. Within several minutes, we all heard her say, "Perimeter closed," and I could tell Vincent realized the trap had been set. He transformed into a Narcoleptan before he disappeared.

"He's gone. He's not even on the thermal imaging screen," Jane said.

"It doesn't matter. Dr. Po, are there any cattle being held on the property?"

"Yes. We have pigs and cows on the science farm."

"Can you release them onto the waterfall trail?"

"Yes, but they…"

"Do it. Do it now! Jane, we need to get down to the entrance."

Dr. Po watched us leave without saying anything else. Jane and I waited at the plasma door until we heard the cries of the animals mixed with the screams of the Narcoleptans, and then we burst out onto the trail. The animals created confusion and cover for us, as the Narcoleptans chased the animals and neglected to see what was stalking them. They didn't see the metal discs coming that sailed through their bodies, removing heads and arms. Jane shot the entire load of twenty microbial bullets into twenty different beings within one minute and then started shooting at every other Narcoleptan she could find. The LBE created holes in their bodies and if they paused for a moment to wonder where it came from, they were dead.

I moved through the animals and the Narcoleptans, cutting both with my plasma knife, uncaring if it was a cow or pig or a being that Merkel had created. I shot the microbial bullets at beings that thought they were hidden in the forest because they were invisible, only to realize the only thing invisible was the microbial and viral dust that was killing them. The flowerballs distracted them and as the spores outlined their bodies, I shot the microbial bullets until the icy chamber was empty, and then ran up to one of the dying Narcoleptans and shoved the gun down its gasping throat.

My arm was punctured by its fangs and I quickly yanked it from the beast's mouth. The clotting ability of my clothes stopped the bleeding, making me, in effect, immune to their poison. I ran as hard as I could to retrieve the metal Frisbees and knocked two Narcoleptans to the ground and then blew their heads off with the LBE. I reactivated the Frisbees and threw them, cutting through the heads of three more of the vicious creatures.

Merkel could not believe the destruction he was witnessing at the hands of the two humans who were slaughtering all of his inhuman and powerful beasts. They were no longer the apex predators. He darted toward the waterfall and eyed the bottom of it, unsure if he could escape by jumping in, when one of the metal saucers abruptly cut through his legs, causing him to drop to the ground. He became visible just in time to see Jane standing over him. He reached up to tear away her abdomen as he felt the 3000 degrees of the plasma knife take away his sight and the top of his head.

Chapter 36
The Cures

I saw my sister kill Merkel but I had no chance to pause and enjoy the scene that reminded me of the last night at our home. I turned around and found that I was at the fair again. But this time, all of the rides seemed to be moving in slow motion. Entities that shouldn't be on the rides were trying to get off, but they were moving too slowly. Their malformed arms and legs waved at me, so I cut them away and they fell to the ground. The carnival lights blinded them as I detached parts of their grotesque heads or jaws. Sometimes their heads exploded and for a brief moment, I saw the skin pull away from their faces like cotton candy, only for the wind to blow it away with a gust. It didn't smell like cotton candy though. It smelled rotten and it made me angry.

I ran through the Haunted House ride and when I saw the dysfunctional and tattered monsters, I didn't laugh or smile as before. I simply made sure they would never move again as I cut away anything that moved. When I came out of the ride, more of the deformed beings appeared in the distance but vanished as I approached them. It was as if they had been hit by lightning and I was knocked back to the ground for a moment. Something slashed my leg and without thinking I brought the glowing ember I held in my hand down across whatever had cut me and felt it slice through something large. It too smelled rotten and made me even angrier.

My leg was bleeding profusely one minute and became a pinprick trickle the next. Jane yelled at me to move and I rolled over just as the glowing disc flew across me and cut through several of the large beasts. For the next ten minutes, my sister and I moved through the crowd of misshapen beings like an intestinal virus on board a cruise ship. The creatures flailed away at the air as if they were too sick to stand up when the real reason their arms were thrashing was that they were no longer attached to anything that would have given them any control.

I was cut a few more times and though the suit stopped most of the bleeding, the last cut across my stomach continued to bleed. I had to pull out one of the clotting syringes and inject it into my stomach. I paused when I heard Jane call out, "What's wrong, puddy tat? Did you lose your claws?" She threw the metal Frisbee which did exactly as she asked sarcastically seconds earlier.

My momentary lapse in attention allowed me to witness a tattered wolfman jump onto my sister's back and bite into her shoulder. I heard her yell and fall to the ground before I threw my knife at it. The knife went through its mouth just before it bit her again. My sister laughed as the being's head fell by her side. She looked over at me, raised her fist in victory, and then fell down beside it.

I jumped up and ran to her, shooting anything that was in front of me. In fact, I killed every moving thing around me, shooting the light bullets into creatures that even appeared normal to me for a moment before the bullets made them explode. I cut away beings that clawed at my feet and shot large jaws that were still moving as I tried to reach my sister. And just before I cut through the last creature that touched my leg, I stopped. I examined the bloody white ugly face and I saw its eyes staring into the distance, unmoving. The opossum snarled when I nudged it and it scurried away as I looked up and around me and realized everything else was dead.

I knelt by my sister and propped her up against a tree. I took her cord and connected it to the bark.

"That won't be enough to save you but it will give me a chance to get you back to the house."

Jane smiled and I watched as she removed the cord from the tree.

"There were enough today, John."

I couldn't say anything and my eyes became so cloudy I could see nothing until I wiped them clear.

"You know, don't you?" she asked

"Yes, I know."

"They were all evil, John. I made sure of that. I was there that day when they were treating Merkel and I felt like I was in his presence again. I read his chart and I knew it was him. When he came for the epilepsy treatment, I made sure the protocol was altered. I wanted to burn his brain into his skull but it didn't happen. The hospital just hid the records, afraid they would be sued. He survived and then he just made more and more of them. I didn't mean for that to happen. I never wanted to hurt you. When I saw your face after Sam died, I was afraid. I was afraid of where you might go again.

"I killed him today for you, John. This time I was killing him for you. Did you see me kill him?"

"Yes. You did as much as you could today to protect me."

"Will you forgive me, John?"

I could hear Jack as if he was standing behind me, whispering into my ear. "Everyone thinks forgiveness is a lovely idea until he has something to forgive."

"Yes, Emily, I forgive you."

I thought my sister would never regain her humanity but I was wrong. At the very end, she looked up into my eyes and told me she could not kill herself. She was afraid that she would never see our mother or me again if she did that.

"I'm afraid, John. But don't let Dr. Po activate the button."

That was the first time I ever heard my sister admit she was afraid and it was the first time I saw terror on her face. I asked Marie to play "Do-Re-Mi" from "The Sound of Music" and I saw a smile cross her face at the sound of the familiar song. She died after saying, "Mi, a name I call myself."

I wiped the tears off her face that were falling from my cheeks and I lifted her head and kissed her on the forehead.

"I love you, Emily. I will always love you. I'll see you again. You and me and Mom will go to the fair and spend the whole day there. Eating everything we want and riding the Scrambler and the Haunted House ride over and over. I hope you can forgive me too."

I laid her softly on the ground and then walked over and pulled Sam from the firethorns. I held her in my arms until it became dark and then light again and when it did, I saw Dr. Po standing next to me.

"I am sorry, Jules. I never saw the connection. I never…"

Before I could reply, I heard Jack, whispering to me again. "You have not chosen one another, but I have chosen you for one another." And I knew what I was hearing referred to everyone that was important in my life.

"Stop, Dr. Po. You have nothing to apologize for. You saved humanity. You saved my sister and she was finally able to vanquish all the demons that haunted her. You gave me the chance to see that. You provided the opportunity for me to love her again and to love a very caring and beautiful woman. I have you to thank for all of that."

"Pain is inescapable within life. It creates doubt and sometimes undermines the believer's faith. It gives atheism a crutch to lean upon. It supplies those that subscribe to evil, fuel for their fire. But without evil or pain, there is no God or goodness. Life is indeed a difficult road to navigate and the knowledge that wisdom provides us is at times nothing more than a reason for us to lash out at the heavens. For some, they yell and don't wait for an answer. For others, they hear a voice that comforts them."

I had heard those words before; from Jack, only this time they came from Dr. Po. The small man who stood taller than any person I have ever known.

"I read some more C.S. Lewis last night. Brilliant man."

Yes, he was. Like another one I know.

"John, I have been thinking about the Grade 3 Ependymoma; the cancer that I have. I have been thinking about a new molecule. A bi-Symbion molecule consisting of a chromium-iron bridge that might be very effective with neural progenitor cells. And if that is the case, then perhaps with the neurons, astrocytes, and oligodendrocytes, I might be able to develop a cure."

I looked at my friend and smiled.

"But I would need your help. And if it works for me, I would like to try it with you. You have a very high IQ and a remarkable brain and with the Symbion in your body, I'm thinking it might have a very beneficial effect."

'You saying you want to make me smarter?"

That's what a remarkable brain says, I suppose. Shit.

"I want someone to carry on the work, Jules. I cannot think of anyone better than you."

"Yeah, okay. But it's John, not Jules. Had a lot of ribbing when I was younger, family jewels and that sort of thing."

Dr. Po nodded his head. He understood.

I gently laid Sam onto the ground and looked up again at the small man that towered over me. He was made as God intended Man to be. Good. Honest. Generous. Fallible. Brave.

Jack told me once that God became man so that men could become sons of God. Dr. Edmundo Auguste Alejandro Po was that. Most people who knew him or had met him in person would probably never see that. But that was because they only saw the many physical imperfections that he possessed. Even those who were aware of his profound scientific knowledge would think him strange and misguided at times. They would never suspect how much he struggled with his genius. And they would also never truly know how much he did to help the world.

But in an imperfect world, full of imperfect men, the one I was looking at and could call a friend, was as close to perfection as could be achieved and still be called a man. And if I was being honest, even though he had a flawed misconception of the world and failed to see that evil corrupted good when given the opportunity, I believe he truly understood now what that "parasite" looked like.

The next day, after some stitching up, Dr. Po and I had a private ceremony for Jane and Sam and we sprinkled their ashes beside the waterfall. Dr. Po released a group of butterflies along with the ashes and it was as if they had been trained by him. They seemed to carry the ashes on their wings as they flew toward the water. Okay, maybe it was really only one or two butterflies and Dr. Po didn't release them but I'm going to remember it as if he did.

Over time, as I thought about my sister, and even myself, I realized that the past doesn't define you unless you allow it. The memories of your past don't ever go away. They remain with you in some sort of file cabinet in your brain. Protected by a door that you purposefully access at times, but one that can also be opened for you without you even being aware, until you start seeing the data within the file revealed.

Sometimes the memories are in black and white but other times they are as colorful as a spring day in the south. Regardless, you would remember. And then you would laugh or cry or remember when you rode the Scrambler or the Haunted House ride, or the scariest roller coaster you had ever been on. And just like then, the adrenalin would make its presence known, providing you a thrill once again.

Sometimes that memory hurt, but the pain somehow brought you closer to the person who caused it, so that it would always be remembered. Jack taught me that. Those moments that exist in our past become moments that exist in the present because we want them there. Those are the ones that help define you. Those are the ones that become part of your molecular being and help form the way you act or react to the world around you.

My memories of my sister and mother and Sam never dimmed. They just got brighter with time. They provided me light when I needed it and comfort when I felt alone. I had learned that life-altering disease was non-discriminatory and was not affected by whether you believed in God or not. It just happened, but it happened less and less because of what Dr. Po helped create. Cures continued; and that neural progenitor cell hypothesis he spoke about earlier - you know, the one with the bi-Symbion chromium-iron bridge? Well, that cured Alzheimer's and Parkinson's disease.

Jack tried to teach me that total enlightenment could only be achieved when one could find the ability to forgive what is truly evil. On that particular point, I told him that we would have to agree to disagree for the time being. He said that he understood. And considering that there were still monsters showing up in the world, I guess he could understand my reluctance to buy into that concept completely.

Monsters are always going to exist but that no longer bothers me. I realized that you just live your life and if they get in your way, you just kick their ass. I now look forward to each day that I'm alive. I mean, what's more fun than watching people get better from new cures and watching evil sons of bitches heads explode? That never gets old.

"Continued accumulation of phosphorus and calcium in your fecal matter. Suggest immediate modification of diet."

"Sorry, Emily. I'm sure what you say is true, but don't worry. I'm working on it."

Addendum

My goal with this book was not to diminish the terrible pain that cancer and other serious diseases bring upon us. Actually, it was the exact opposite. It was my desire to show through the pages of this book that there are always new cures, always new miracles happening and always hope. I know there are people working in a lab somewhere, unknown except for the technicians and scientists who work alongside them, or perhaps by a few of their peers, occupied with a tireless and fervent desire to find new cures and new ways to combat cancer and other diseases.

I anticipate that you will find this book interesting, not only for the subject matter but for the story that I tried to create in the realm of science fiction. It was my first attempt at that genre and it was very difficult for me as I know with science fiction, some sort of science within the framework is necessary for it to work. I believe I developed that world and I think the characters will capture your attention because when it comes right down to it, regardless of the genre, you still have to tell a story with characters that people find interesting and in a manner that the reader finds entertaining.

The other important aspect of this book that I pray I made visible to everyone as they read it, was that even though positive life-changing events occur every day, you cannot escape the fact that evil exists in the world. If given a chance, evil will corrupt science, corrupt man, and try to strangle hope out of anyone's conversation. But it cannot win. Miracles will continue to happen every day. It just requires us to look for them and never give up.

Unfortunately, everyone is touched by cancer at some time in their lives, whether it be through a loved one, a friend, or perhaps even themselves. My mother and father both died of cancer. My brother died of cancer. My wife, sisters, brother-in-law, father-in-law, and cousins are all cancer survivors and I have even had several encounters with skin cancer, albeit and thankfully, the least invasive type.

As such, half of all profits from this book will be distributed to agencies that provide help to patients and caregivers with their cancer battles. I hope one day money will no longer be needed by anyone with that diagnosis. I am optimistic that in the future that condition will no longer be considered anything worse than being diagnosed with a cold.

This book also involved another serious subject - domestic violence and abuse. Cognizant of those situations from my forty years of work in healthcare, I always tried to help those that I could. I will continue to do so with financial support to organizations that provide a safe haven and help to those who endure that horror.

Acknowledgments for quotes, character, and title references:

Page 1 - "The Collected Letters of C.S. Lewis" - Published by Harper San Francisco, 2005.

Pages 68, 70, 299 - "The Problem of Pain" – C.S. Lewis, 1940.

Pages 68, 136 - "A Grief Observed" – C.S. Lewis, 1961.

Pages 69, 87, 199, 253, 264 - "Mere Christianity" – C.S. Lewis, 1952.

Pages 70, 138 - "The Great Divorce" – C.S. Lewis, 1945.

Page 253 - "The Allegory of Love" – C. S. Lewis, 1936.

Page 234 - "Horton Hears a Who" – Theodore Seuss Geisel, 1954.

Pages 230-31 - "Rikki-Tikki-Tavi" from "The Jungle Book" – Rudyard Kipling, 1894.

"The Three Stooges" – Columbia Pictures, 1934-1946.

"The Sound of Music" – Screenplay written by Ernest Lehman, based on the memoir "The Story of the Trapp Family Singers" by Maria Von Trapp; directed by Robert Wise, 1965.